ERAGON

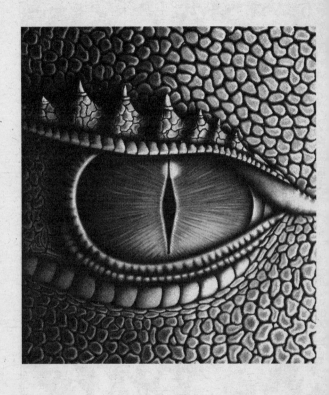

ERAGON

INHERITANCE

BOOK ONE

Christopher Paolini

Published by Laurel-Leaf
an imprint of Random House Children's Books
a division of Random House, Inc.
New York

Originally published in different form by Paolini International LLC in 2002.
This edition was originally published in slightly different form in hardcover
in 2003 and subsequently in paperback in 2005 by Alfred A. Knopf
Books for Young Readers, an imprint of Random House Children's Books,
a division of Random House, Inc., New York. This edition published by
arrangement with Alfred A. Knopf Books for Young Readers.

www.randomhouse.com/teens

Educators and librarians, for a variety of teaching tools,
visit us at www.randomhouse.com/teachers
RL: 7.0

ISBN: 978-0-440-24073-0

June 2007

Printed in the United States of America

10 9 8 7 6 5 4 3 2 1

This book is dedicated to my mom,
for showing me the magic in the world;
to my dad, for revealing the man behind the curtain.
And also to my sister, Angela, for helping when I'm "blue."

CONTENTS

Prologue: Shade of Fear...1

Discovery 8

Palancar Valley 12

Dragon Tales 27

Fate's Gift 51

Awakening..55

Tea for Two..68

A Name of Power..82

A Miller-to-Be 87

Strangers in Carvahall..91

Flight of Destiny 102

The Doom of Innocence...109

Deathwatch 119

The Madness of Life 132

A Rider's Blade 134

Saddlemaking 157

Therinsford...162

Thunder Roar and Lightning Crackle 180

Revelation at Yazuac 189

Admonishments 198

Magic Is the Simplest Thing 209

Daret 222

Through a Dragon's Eye 235

A Song for the Road 247

A Taste of Teirm 252

An Old Friend 260

The Witch and the Werecat 289

Of Reading and Plots 306

Thieves in the Castle 310

A Costly Mistake 322

Vision of Perfection 341

Master of the Blade 350

The Mire of Dras-Leona 359

Trail of Oil 365

Worshipers of Helgrind 372

The Ra'zac's Revenge 385

Murtagh 389

Legacy of a Rider 397

Diamond Tomb 404

Capture at Gil'ead 415

Du Sundavar Freohr 428

Fighting Shadows 438

A Warrior and a Healer 452

Water from Sand 463

The Ramr River 474

The Hadarac Desert 484

A Path Revealed 493

A Clash of Wills 507

Flight Through the Valley 517

The Horns of a Dilemma 539

Hunting for Answers 553

The Glory of Tronjheim 574

Ajihad 588

Bless the Child, Argetlam 615

Mandrake Root and Newt's Tongue 634

Hall of the Mountain King 643

Arya's Test 664

The Shadows Lengthen 684

Battle Under Farthen Dûr 702

The Mourning Sage 722

Pronunciation Guide and Glossary 732

Acknowledgments 739

A Special Preview of *Eldest* 743

PROLOGUE: SHADE OF FEAR

Wind howled through the night, carrying a scent that would change the world. A tall Shade lifted his head and sniffed the air. He looked human except for his crimson hair and maroon eyes.

He blinked in surprise. The message had been correct: they were here. Or was it a trap? He weighed the odds, then said icily, "Spread out; hide behind trees and bushes. Stop whoever is coming . . . or die."

Around him shuffled twelve Urgals with short swords and round iron shields painted with black symbols. They resembled men with bowed legs and thick, brutish arms made for crushing. A pair of twisted horns grew above their small ears. The monsters hurried into the brush, grunting as they hid. Soon the rustling quieted and the forest was silent again.

The Shade peered around a thick tree and looked up the trail. It was too dark for any human to see, but for him the faint moonlight was like sunshine streaming between the trees; every detail was clear and sharp to his searching gaze. He remained unnaturally quiet, a long pale sword in his hand. A wire-thin scratch curved down the blade. The weapon was thin enough to slip between a pair of ribs, yet stout enough to hack through the hardest armor.

The Urgals could not see as well as the Shade; they groped like blind beggars, fumbling with their weapons. An owl screeched, cutting through the silence. No one relaxed until the bird flew past. Then the monsters shivered in the cold night; one snapped a twig with his heavy boot. The Shade hissed in anger, and the Urgals shrank back, motionless. He suppressed his distaste—they smelled like fetid meat—and turned away. They were tools, nothing more.

The Shade forced back his impatience as the minutes became hours. The scent must have wafted far ahead of its owners. He did not let the Urgals get up or warm themselves. He denied himself those luxuries, too, and stayed behind the tree, watching the trail. Another gust of wind rushed through the forest. The smell was stronger this time. Excited, he lifted a thin lip in a snarl.

"Get ready," he whispered, his whole body vibrating. The tip of his sword moved in small circles. It had taken many plots and much pain to bring himself to this moment. It would not do to lose control now.

Eyes brightened under the Urgals' thick brows, and the creatures gripped their weapons tighter. Ahead of them, the Shade heard a clink as something hard struck a loose stone. Faint smudges emerged from the darkness and advanced down the trail.

Three white horses with riders cantered toward the ambush, their heads held high and proud, their coats rippling in the moonlight like liquid silver.

On the first horse was an elf with pointed ears and elegantly slanted eyebrows. His build was slim but strong, like a rapier. A powerful bow was slung on his back. A sword pressed against his side opposite a quiver of arrows fletched with swan feathers.

The last rider had the same fair face and angled features as the other. He carried a long spear in his right hand and a white dagger at his belt. A helm of extraordinary craftsmanship, wrought with amber and gold, rested on his head.

Between these two rode a raven-haired elven lady, who surveyed her surroundings with poise. Framed by long black locks, her deep eyes shone with a driving force. Her clothes were unadorned, yet her beauty was undiminished. At her side was a sword, and on her back a long bow with a quiver.

She carried in her lap a pouch that she frequently looked at, as if to reassure herself that it was still there.

One of the elves spoke quietly, but the Shade could not hear what was said. The lady answered with obvious authority, and her guards switched places. The one wearing the helm took the lead, shifting his spear to a readier grip. They passed the Shade's hiding place and the first few Urgals without suspicion.

The Shade was already savoring his victory when the wind changed direction and swept toward the elves, heavy with the Urgals' stench. The horses snorted with alarm and tossed their heads. The riders stiffened, eyes flashing from side to side, then wheeled their mounts around and galloped away.

The lady's horse surged forward, leaving her guards far behind. Forsaking their hiding, the Urgals stood and released a stream of black arrows. The Shade jumped out from behind the tree, raised his right hand, and shouted, "Garjzla!"

A red bolt flashed from his palm toward the elven lady, illuminating the trees with a bloody light. It struck her steed, and the horse toppled with a high-pitched squeal, plowing into the ground chest-first. She leapt off the animal with inhuman speed, landed lightly, then glanced back for her guards.

The Urgals' deadly arrows quickly brought

down the two elves. They fell from the noble horses, blood pooling in the dirt. As the Urgals rushed to the slain elves, the Shade screamed, "After her! She is the one I want!" The monsters grunted and rushed down the trail.

A cry tore from the elf's lips as she saw her dead companions. She took a step toward them, then cursed her enemies and bounded into the forest.

While the Urgals crashed through the trees, the Shade climbed a piece of granite that jutted above them. From his perch he could see all of the surrounding forest. He raised his hand and uttered, "Istalrí boetk!" and a quarter-mile section of the forest exploded into flames. Grimly he burned one section after another until there was a ring of fire, a half-league across, around the ambush site. The flames looked like a molten crown resting on the forest. Satisfied, he watched the ring carefully, in case it should falter.

The band of fire thickened, contracting the area the Urgals had to search. Suddenly, the Shade heard shouts and a coarse scream. Through the trees he saw three of his charges fall in a pile, mortally wounded. He caught a glimpse of the elf running from the remaining Urgals.

She fled toward the craggy piece of granite at a tremendous speed. The Shade examined the ground twenty feet below, then jumped and landed nimbly in front of her. She skidded around and sped back to the trail. Black Urgal blood dripped from her sword, staining the pouch in her hand.

The horned monsters came out of the forest and hemmed her in, blocking the only escape routes. Her head whipped around as she tried to find a way out. Seeing none, she drew herself up with regal disdain. The Shade approached her with a raised hand, allowing himself to enjoy her helplessness.

"Get her."

As the Urgals surged forward, the elf pulled open the pouch, reached into it, and then let it drop to the ground. In her hands was a large sapphire stone that reflected the angry light of the fires. She raised it over her head, lips forming frantic words. Desperate, the Shade barked, "Garjzla!"

A ball of red flame sprang from his hand and flew toward the elf, fast as an arrow. But he was too late. A flash of emerald light briefly illuminated the forest, and the stone vanished. Then the red fire smote her and she collapsed.

The Shade howled in rage and stalked forward, flinging his sword at a tree. It passed halfway through the trunk, where it stuck, quivering. He shot nine bolts of energy from his palm—which killed the Urgals instantly—then ripped his sword free and strode to the elf.

Prophecies of revenge, spoken in a wretched

language only he knew, rolled from his tongue. He clenched his thin hands and glared at the sky. The cold stars stared back, unwinking, other-worldly watchers. Disgust curled his lip before he turned back to the unconscious elf.

Her beauty, which would have entranced any mortal man, held no charm for him. He confirmed that the stone was gone, then retrieved his horse from its hiding place among the trees. After tying the elf onto the saddle, he mounted the charger and made his way out of the woods.

He quenched the fires in his path but left the rest to burn.

DISCOVERY

Eragon knelt in a bed of trampled reed grass and scanned the tracks with a practiced eye. The prints told him that the deer had been in the meadow only a half-hour before. Soon they would bed down. His target, a small doe with a pronounced limp in her left forefoot, was still with the herd. He was amazed she had made it so far without a wolf or bear catching her.

The sky was clear and dark, and a slight breeze stirred the air. A silvery cloud drifted over the mountains that surrounded him, its edges glowing with ruddy light cast from the harvest moon cradled between two peaks. Streams flowed down the mountains from stolid glaciers and glistening snowpacks. A brooding mist crept along the valley's floor, almost thick enough to obscure his feet.

Eragon was fifteen, less than a year from manhood. Dark eyebrows rested above his intense brown eyes. His clothes were worn from work. A hunting knife with a bone handle was sheathed at his belt, and a buckskin tube protected his yew bow from the mist. He carried a wood-frame pack.

The deer had led him deep into the Spine, a range of untamed mountains that extended up and down the land of Alagaësia. Strange tales and men often came from those mountains, usually boding ill. Despite that, Eragon did not fear the Spine—he was the only hunter near Carvahall who dared track game deep into its craggy recesses.

It was the third night of the hunt, and his food was half gone. If he did not fell the doe, he would be forced to return home empty-handed. His family needed the meat for the rapidly approaching winter and could not afford to buy it in Carvahall.

Eragon stood with quiet assurance in the dusky moonlight, then strode into the forest toward a glen where he was sure the deer would rest. The trees blocked the sky from view and cast feathery shadows on the ground. He looked at the tracks only occasionally; he knew the way.

At the glen, he strung his bow with a sure touch, then drew three arrows and nocked one, holding the others in his left hand. The moonlight revealed twenty or so motionless lumps where the deer lay in the grass. The doe he

wanted was at the edge of the herd, her left fore-
leg stretched out awkwardly.

Eragon slowly crept closer, keeping the bow
ready. All his work of the past three days had led
to this moment. He took a last steadying breath
and—an explosion shattered the night.

The herd bolted. Eragon lunged forward, racing through the grass as a fiery wind surged past
his cheek. He slid to a stop and loosed an arrow
at the bounding doe. It missed by a finger's
breadth and hissed into darkness. He cursed and
spun around, instinctively nocking another arrow.

Behind him, where the deer had been, smoldered a large circle of grass and trees. Many of the
pines stood bare of their needles. The grass outside the charring was flattened. A wisp of smoke
curled in the air, carrying a burnt smell. In the
center of the blast radius lay a polished blue
stone. Mist snaked across the scorched area and
swirled insubstantial tendrils over the stone.

Eragon watched for danger for several long
minutes, but the only thing that moved was the
mist. Cautiously, he released the tension from his
bow and moved forward. Moonlight cast him in
pale shadow as he stopped before the stone. He
nudged it with an arrow, then jumped back.
Nothing happened, so he warily picked it up.

Nature had never polished a stone as smooth
as this one. Its flawless surface was dark blue, ex-

10

cept for thin veins of white that spiderwebbed across it. The stone was cool and frictionless under his fingers, like hardened silk. Oval and about a foot long, it weighed several pounds, though it felt lighter than it should have.

Eragon found the stone both beautiful and frightening. *Where did it come from? Does it have a purpose?* Then a more disturbing thought came to him: *Was it sent here by accident, or am I meant to have it?* If he had learned anything from the old stories, it was to treat magic, and those who used it, with great caution.

But what should I do with the stone? It would be tiresome to carry, and there was a chance it was dangerous. It might be better to leave it behind. A flicker of indecision ran through him, and he almost dropped it, but something stayed his hand. *At the very least, it might pay for some food,* he decided with a shrug, tucking the stone into his pack.

The glen was too exposed to make a safe camp, so he slipped back into the forest and spread his bedroll beneath the upturned roots of a fallen tree. After a cold dinner of bread and cheese, he wrapped himself in blankets and fell asleep, pondering what had occurred.

PALANCAR VALLEY

T he sun rose the next morning with a glorious conflagration of pink and yellow. The air was fresh, sweet, and very cold. Ice edged the streams, and small pools were completely frozen over. After a breakfast of porridge, Eragon returned to the glen and examined the charred area. The morning light revealed no new details, so he started for home.

The rough game trail was faintly worn and, in places, nonexistent. Because it had been forged by animals, it often backtracked and took long detours. Yet for all its flaws, it was still the fastest way out of the mountains.

The Spine was one of the only places that King Galbatorix could not call his own. Stories were still told about how half his army disappeared after marching into its ancient forest. A cloud of misfortune and bad luck seemed to hang over it. Though the trees grew tall and the sky shone brightly, few people could stay in the Spine for long without suffering an accident. Eragon was one of those few—not through any particular gift, it seemed to him, but because of persistent vigilance and sharp reflexes. He had hiked in the mountains for years, yet he was still wary of them. Every time he thought they had surrendered their secrets, something happened to upset his understanding of them—like the stone's appearance.

He kept up a brisk pace, and the leagues steadily disappeared. In late evening he arrived at the edge of a precipitous ravine. The Anora River rushed by far below, heading to Palancar Valley. Gorged with hundreds of tiny streams, the river was a brute force, battling against the rocks and boulders that barred its way. A low rumble filled the air.

He camped in a thicket near the ravine and watched the moonrise before going to bed.

It grew colder over the next day and a half. Eragon traveled quickly and saw little of the wary wildlife. A bit past noon, he heard the Igualda Falls blanketing everything with the dull sound of a thousand splashes. The trail led him onto a moist slate outcropping, which the river sped past, flinging itself into empty air and down mossy cliffs.

Before him lay Palancar Valley, exposed like an unrolled map. The base of the Igualda Falls, more than a half-mile below, was the northernmost point of the valley. A little ways from the falls was Carvahall, a cluster of brown buildings. White smoke rose from the chimneys, defiant of the wilderness around it. At this height, farms were small square patches no bigger than the end of his finger. The land around them was tan or sandy, where dead grass swayed in the wind. The Anora River wound from the falls toward Palancar's southern end, reflecting great strips of sunlight. Far in the distance it flowed past the village Therinsford and the lonely mountain Utgard. Beyond that, he knew only that it turned north and ran to the sea.

After a pause, Eragon left the outcropping and started down the trail, grimacing at the descent. When he arrived at the bottom, soft dusk was creeping over everything, blurring colors and shapes into gray masses. Carvahall's lights shimmered nearby in the twilight; the houses cast long shadows. Aside from Therinsford, Carvahall was the only village in Palancar Valley. The settlement was secluded and surrounded by harsh, beautiful land. Few traveled here except merchants and trappers.

The village was composed of stout log buildings with low roofs—some thatched, others shingled. Smoke billowed from the chimneys, giving the air a woody smell. The buildings had wide porches where people gathered to talk and conduct business. Occasionally a window brightened as a candle or lamp was lit. Eragon heard men talking loudly in the evening air while wives scurried to fetch their husbands, scolding them for being late.

Eragon wove his way between the houses to the butcher's shop, a broad, thick-beamed building. Overhead, the chimney belched black smoke.

He pushed the door open. The spacious room was warm and well lit by a fire snapping in a stone fireplace. A bare counter stretched across the far side of the room. The floor was strewn with loose straw. Everything was scrupulously clean, as if the owner spent his leisure time digging in obscure crannies for minuscule pieces of filth. Behind the counter stood the butcher Sloan. A small man, he wore a cotton shirt and a long, bloodstained smock. An impressive array of knives swung from his belt. He had a sallow, pockmarked face, and his black eyes were suspicious. He polished the counter with a ragged cloth.

Sloan's mouth twisted as Eragon entered. "Well, the mighty hunter joins the rest of us mortals. How many did you bag this time?"

"None," was Eragon's curt reply. He had never liked Sloan. The butcher always treated him with disdain, as if he were something unclean. A widower, Sloan seemed to care for only one person—his daughter, Katrina, on whom he doted.

"I'm amazed," said Sloan with affected astonishment. He turned his back on Eragon to scrape something off the wall. "And that's your reason for coming here?"

"Yes," admitted Eragon uncomfortably.

"If that's the case, let's see your money." Sloan tapped his fingers when Eragon shifted his feet and remained silent. "Come on—either you have it or you don't. Which is it?"

"I don't really have any money, but I do—"

"What, no money?" the butcher cut him off sharply. "And you expect to buy meat! Are the other merchants giving away their wares? Should I just hand you the goods without charge? Besides," he said abruptly, "it's late. Come back tomorrow with money. I'm closed for the day."

Eragon glared at him. "I can't wait until tomorrow, Sloan. It'll be worth your while, though; I found something to pay you with." He pulled out the stone with a flourish and set it gently on the scarred counter, where it gleamed with light from the dancing flames.

"Stole it is more likely," muttered Sloan, leaning forward with an interested expression.

Ignoring the comment, Eragon asked, "Will this be enough?"

Sloan picked up the stone and gauged its

weight speculatively. He ran his hands over its smoothness and inspected the white veins. With a calculating look, he set it down. "It's pretty, but how much is it worth?"

"I don't know," admitted Eragon, "but no one would have gone to the trouble of shaping it unless it had some value."

"Obviously," said Sloan with exaggerated patience. "But how much value? Since you don't know, I suggest that you find a trader who does, or take my offer of three crowns."

"That's a miser's bargain! It must be worth at least ten times that," protested Eragon. Three crowns would not even buy enough meat to last a week.

Sloan shrugged. "If you don't like my offer, wait until the traders arrive. Either way, I'm tired of this conversation."

The traders were a nomadic group of merchants and entertainers who visited Carvahall every spring and winter. They bought whatever excess the villagers and local farmers had managed to grow or make, and sold what they needed to live through another year: seeds, animals, fabric, and supplies like salt and sugar.

But Eragon did not want to wait until they arrived; it could be a while, and his family needed the meat now. "Fine, I accept," he snapped.

"Good, I'll get you the meat. Not that it matters, but where did you find this?"

"Two nights ago in the Spine—"

"Get out!" demanded Sloan, pushing the stone away. He stomped furiously to the end of the counter and started scrubbing old bloodstains off a knife.

"Why?" asked Eragon. He drew the stone closer, as if to protect it from Sloan's wrath.

"I won't deal with anything you bring back from those damned mountains! Take your sorcerer's stone elsewhere." Sloan's hand suddenly slipped and he cut a finger on the knife, but he seemed not to notice. He continued to scrub, staining the blade with fresh blood.

"You refuse to sell to me!"

"Yes! Unless you pay with coins," Sloan growled, and hefted the knife, sidling away. "Go, before I make you!"

The door behind them slammed open. Eragon whirled around, ready for more trouble. In stomped Horst, a hulking man. Sloan's daughter, Katrina—a tall girl of sixteen—trailed behind him with a determined expression. Eragon was surprised to see her; she usually absented herself from any arguments involving her father. Sloan glanced at them warily, then started to accuse Eragon. "He won't—"

"Quiet," announced Horst in a rumbling voice, cracking his knuckles at the same time. He was Carvahall's smith, as his thick neck and scarred leather apron attested. His powerful arms were bare to the elbow; a great expanse of hairy muscular chest was visible through the top of his shirt. A black beard, carelessly trimmed, roiled and knotted like his jaw muscles. "Sloan, what have you done now?"

"Nothing." He gave Eragon a murderous gaze, then spat, "This . . . *boy* came in here and started badgering me. I asked him to leave, but he won't budge. I even threatened him and he still ignored me!" Sloan seemed to shrink as he looked at Horst.

"Is this true?" demanded the smith.

"No!" replied Eragon. "I offered this stone as payment for some meat, and he accepted it. When I told him that I'd found it in the Spine, he refused to even touch it. What difference does it make where it came from?"

Horst looked at the stone curiously, then returned his attention to the butcher. "Why won't you trade with him, Sloan? I've no love for the Spine myself, but if it's a question of the stone's worth, I'll back it with my own money."

The question hung in the air for a moment. Then Sloan licked his lips and said, "This is my own store. I can do whatever I want."

Katrina stepped out from behind Horst and tossed back her auburn hair like a spray of molten copper. "Father, Eragon *is* willing to pay. Give him the meat, and then we can have supper."

Sloan's eyes narrowed dangerously. "Go back

to the house; this is none of your business. . . . I said *go!*" Katrina's face hardened, then she marched out of the room with a stiff back.

Eragon watched with disapproval but dared not interfere. Horst tugged at his beard before saying reproachfully, "Fine, you can deal with me. What were you going to get, Eragon?" His voice reverberated through the room.

"As much as I could."

Horst pulled out a purse and counted out a pile of coins. "Give me your best roasts and steaks. Make sure that it's enough to fill Eragon's pack." The butcher hesitated, his gaze darting between Horst and Eragon. "Not selling to me would be a very bad idea," stated Horst.

Glowering venomously, Sloan slipped into the back room. A frenzy of chopping, wrapping, and low cursing reached them. After several uncomfortable minutes, he returned with an armful of wrapped meat. His face was expressionless as he accepted Horst's money, then proceeded to clean his knife, pretending that they were not there.

Horst scooped up the meat and walked outside. Eragon hurried behind him, carrying his pack and the stone. The crisp night air rolled over their faces, refreshing after the stuffy shop.

"Thank you, Horst. Uncle Garrow will be pleased."

Horst laughed quietly. "Don't thank me. I've wanted to do that for a long time. Sloan's a vicious troublemaker; it does him good to be humbled. Katrina heard what was happening and ran to fetch me. Good thing I came—the two of you were almost at blows. Unfortunately, I doubt he'll serve you or any of your family the next time you go in there, even if you do have coins."

"Why did he explode like that? We've never been friendly, but he's always taken our money. And I've never seen him treat Katrina that way," said Eragon, opening the top of the pack.

Horst shrugged. "Ask your uncle. He knows more about it than I do."

Eragon stuffed the meat into his pack. "Well, now I have one more reason to hurry home . . . to solve this mystery. Here, this is rightfully yours." He proffered the stone.

21

Horst chuckled. "No, you keep your strange rock. As for payment, Albriech plans to leave for Feinster next spring. He wants to become a master smith, and I'm going to need an assistant. You can come and work off the debt on your spare days."

Eragon bowed slightly, delighted. Horst had two sons, Albriech and Baldor, both of whom worked in his forge. Taking one's place was a generous offer. "Again, thank you! I look forward to working with you." He was glad that there was a way for him to pay Horst. His uncle would never accept charity. Then Eragon remembered what his cousin had told him before he had left on the hunt. "Roran wanted me to give Katrina a message, but since I can't, can you get it to her?"

"Of course."

"He wants her to know that he'll come into town as soon as the merchants arrive and that he will see her then."

"That all?"

Eragon was slightly embarrassed. "No, he also wants her to know that she is the most beautiful girl he has ever seen and that he thinks of nothing else."

Horst's face broke into a broad grin, and he winked at Eragon. "Getting serious, isn't he?"

"Yes, sir," Eragon answered with a quick smile. "Could you also give her my thanks? It was nice of her to stand up to her father for me. I hope that she isn't punished because of it. Roran would be furious if I got her into trouble."

"I wouldn't worry about it. Sloan doesn't know that she called me, so I doubt he'll be too hard on her. Before you go, will you sup with us?"

"I'm sorry, but I can't. Garrow is expecting me," said Eragon, tying off the top of the pack. He hoisted it onto his back and started down the road, raising his hand in farewell.

The meat slowed him down, but he was eager to be home, and renewed vigor filled his steps. The village ended abruptly, and he left its warm lights behind. The pearlescent moon peeked over the mountains, bathing the land in a ghostly reflection of daylight. Everything looked bleached and flat.

Near the end of his journey, he turned off the road, which continued south. A simple path led straight through waist-high grass and up a knoll, almost hidden by the shadows of protective elm trees. He crested the hill and saw a gentle light shining from his home.

The house had a shingled roof and a brick chimney. Eaves hung over the whitewashed walls, shadowing the ground below. One side of the enclosed porch was filled with split wood, ready for the fire. A jumble of farm tools cluttered the other side.

The house had been abandoned for half a century when they moved in after Garrow's wife, Marian, died. It was ten miles from Carvahall, farther than anyone else's. People considered the distance dangerous because the family could not rely on help from the village in times of trouble, but Eragon's uncle would not listen.

A hundred feet from the house, in a dull-colored barn, lived two horses—Birka and Brugh—with chickens and a cow. Sometimes there was also a pig, but they had been unable to afford one this year. A wagon sat wedged between the stalls. On the edge of their fields, a thick line of trees traced along the Anora River.

He saw a light move behind a window as he wearily reached the porch. "Uncle, it's Eragon.

Let me in." A small shutter slid back for a second, then the door swung inward.

Garrow stood with his hand on the door. His worn clothes hung on him like rags on a stick frame. A lean, hungry face with intense eyes gazed out from under graying hair. He looked like a man who had been partly mummified before it was discovered that he was still alive. "Roran's sleeping," was his answer to Eragon's inquiring glance.

A lantern flickered on a wood table so old that the grain stood up in tiny ridges like a giant fingerprint. Near a woodstove were rows of cooking utensils tacked onto the wall with homemade nails. A second door opened to the rest of the house. The floor was made of boards polished smooth by years of tramping feet.

Eragon pulled off his pack and took out the meat. "What's this? Did you buy meat? Where did you get the money?" asked his uncle harshly as he saw the wrapped packages.

Eragon took a breath before answering. "No, Horst bought it for us."

"You let him pay for it? I told you before, I won't beg for our food. If we can't feed ourselves, we might as well move into town. Before you can turn around twice, they'll be sending us used clothes and asking if we'll be able to get through the winter." Garrow's face paled with anger.

"I didn't accept charity," snapped Eragon. "Horst agreed to let me work off the debt this spring. He needs someone to help him because Albriech is going away."

"And where will you get the time to work for him? Are you going to ignore all the things that need to be done here?" asked Garrow, forcing his voice down.

Eragon hung his bow and quiver on hooks beside the front door. "I don't know how I'll do it," he said irritably. "Besides, I found something that could be worth some money." He set the stone on the table.

Garrow bowed over it: the hungry look on his face became ravenous, and his fingers moved with a strange twitch. "You found this in the Spine?"

"Yes," said Eragon. He explained what had happened. "And to make matters worse, I lost my best arrow. I'll have to make more before long." They stared at the stone in the near darkness.

"How was the weather?" asked his uncle, lifting the stone. His hands tightened around it like he was afraid it would suddenly disappear.

"Cold," was Eragon's reply. "It didn't snow, but it froze each night."

Garrow looked worried by the news. "Tomorrow you'll have to help Roran finish harvesting the barley. If we can get the squash picked, too, the frost won't bother us." He passed the stone to Eragon. "Here, keep it. When the traders come, we'll find out what it's worth. Selling it is probably the best thing to do. The less we're involved with magic, the better. . . . Why did Horst pay for the meat?"

It took only a moment for Eragon to explain his argument with Sloan. "I just don't understand what angered him so."

Garrow shrugged. "Sloan's wife, Ismira, went over the Igualda Falls a year before you were brought here. He hasn't been near the Spine since, nor had anything to do with it. But that's no reason to refuse payment. I think he wanted to give you trouble."

Eragon swayed blearily and said, "It's good to be back." Garrow's eyes softened, and he nodded. Eragon stumbled to his room, pushed the stone under his bed, then fell onto the mattress. *Home.* For the first time since before the hunt, he relaxed completely as sleep overtook him.

DRAGON TALES

At dawn the sun's rays streamed through the window, warming Eragon's face. Rubbing his eyes, he sat up on the edge of the bed. The pine floor was cold under his feet. He stretched his sore legs and rubbed his back, yawning.

Beside the bed was a row of shelves covered with objects he had collected. There were twisted pieces of wood, odd bits of shells, rocks that had broken to reveal shiny interiors, and strips of dry grass tied into knots. His favorite item was a root so convoluted he never tired of looking at it. The rest of the room was bare, except for a small dresser and nightstand.

He pulled on his boots and stared at the floor, thinking. This was a special day. It was near this very hour, sixteen years ago, that his mother, Selena, had come home to Carvahall alone and pregnant. She had been gone for six years, living in the cities. When she returned, she wore expensive clothes, and her hair was bound by a net of pearls. She had sought out her brother, Garrow, and asked to stay with him until the baby arrived. Within five months her son was born. Everyone was shocked when Selena tearfully begged Garrow and Marian to raise him. When they asked why, she only wept and said, "I must." Her pleas had grown increasingly desperate until they finally agreed. She named him Eragon, then departed early the next morning and never returned.

Eragon still remembered how he had felt when Marian told him the story before she died. The realization that Garrow and Marian were not his real parents had disturbed him greatly. Things that had been permanent and unquestionable were suddenly thrown into doubt. Eventually he had learned to live with it, but he always had a nagging suspicion that he had not been good enough for his mother. *I'm sure there was a good reason for what she did; I only wish I knew what it was.*

One other thing bothered him: Who was his father? Selena had told no one, and whoever it might be had never come looking for Eragon. He wished that he knew who it was, if only to have a name. It would be nice to know his heritage.

He sighed and went to the nightstand, where he splashed his face, shivering as the water ran down his neck. Refreshed, he retrieved the stone from under the bed and set it on a shelf. The morning light caressed it, throwing a warm shadow on the wall. He touched it one more time, then hurried to the kitchen, eager to see his family. Garrow and Roran were already there, eating chicken. As Eragon greeted them, Roran stood with a grin.

Roran was two years older than Eragon, muscular, sturdy, and careful with his movements. They could not have been closer even if they had been real brothers.

Roran smiled. "I'm glad you're back. How was the trip?"

"Hard," replied Eragon. "Did Uncle tell you what happened?" He helped himself to a piece of chicken, which he devoured hungrily.

"No," said Roran, and the story was quickly told. At Roran's insistence, Eragon left his food to show him the stone. This elicited a satisfactory amount of awe, but Roran soon asked nervously, "Were you able to talk with Katrina?"

"No, there wasn't an opportunity after the argument with Sloan. But she'll expect you when the traders come. I gave the message to Horst; he will get it to her."

"You told Horst?" said Roran incredulously. "That was private. If I wanted everyone to know about it, I could have built a bonfire and used smoke signals to communicate. If Sloan finds out, he won't let me see her again."

"Horst will be discreet," assured Eragon. "He

won't let anyone fall prey to Sloan, least of all you." Roran seemed unconvinced, but argued no more. They returned to their meals in the taciturn presence of Garrow. When the last bites were finished, all three went to work in the fields.

The sun was cold and pale, providing little comfort. Under its watchful eye, the last of the barley was stored in the barn. Next, they gathered prickly vined squash, then the rutabagas, beets, peas, turnips, and beans, which they packed into the root cellar. After hours of labor, they stretched their cramped muscles, pleased that the harvest was finished.

The following days were spent pickling, salting, shelling, and preparing the food for winter.

Nine days after Eragon's return, a vicious blizzard blew out of the mountains and settled over the valley. The snow came down in great sheets, blanketing the countryside in white. They only dared leave the house for firewood and to feed the animals, for they feared getting lost in the howling wind and featureless landscape. They spent their time huddled over the stove as gusts rattled the heavy window shutters. Days later the storm finally passed, revealing an alien world of soft white drifts.

"I'm afraid the traders may not come this year, with conditions this bad," said Garrow. "They're late as it is. We'll give them a chance and wait before going to Carvahall. But if they don't show

30

soon, we'll have to buy any spare supplies from the townspeople." His countenance was resigned.

They grew anxious as the days crept by without sign of the traders. Talk was sparse, and depression hung over the house.

On the eighth morning, Roran walked to the road and confirmed that the traders had not yet passed. The day was spent readying for the trip into Carvahall, scrounging with grim expressions for saleable items. That evening, out of desperation, Eragon checked the road again. He found deep ruts cut into the snow, with numerous hoofprints between them. Elated, he ran back to the house whooping, bringing new life to their preparations.

They packed their surplus produce into the wagon before sunrise. Garrow put the year's money in a leather pouch that he carefully fastened to his belt. Eragon set the wrapped stone between bags of grain so it would not roll when the wagon hit bumps.

After a hasty breakfast, they harnessed the horses and cleared a path to the road. The traders' wagons had already broken the drifts, which sped their progress. By noon they could see Carvahall.

In daylight, it was a small earthy village filled with shouts and laughter. The traders had made camp in an empty field on the outskirts of town.

Groups of wagons, tents, and fires were randomly spread across it, spots of color against the snow. The troubadours' four tents were garishly decorated. A steady stream of people linked the camp to the village.

Crowds churned around a line of bright tents and booths clogging the main street. Horses whinnied at the noise. The snow had been pounded flat, giving it a glassy surface; elsewhere, bonfires had melted it. Roasted hazelnuts added a rich aroma to the smells wafting around them.

Garrow parked the wagon and picketed the horses, then drew coins from his pouch. "Get yourselves some treats. Roran, do what you want, only be at Horst's in time for supper. Eragon, bring that stone and come with me." Eragon grinned at Roran and pocketed the money, already planning how to spend it.

Roran departed immediately with a determined expression on his face. Garrow led Eragon into the throng, shouldering his way through the bustle. Women were buying cloth, while nearby their husbands examined a new latch, hook, or tool. Children ran up and down the road, shrieking with excitement. Knives were displayed here, spices there, and pots were laid out in shiny rows next to leather harnesses.

Eragon stared at the traders curiously. They seemed less prosperous than last year. Their children had a frightened, wary look, and their clothes were patched. The gaunt men carried swords and daggers with a new familiarity, and even the women had poniards belted at their waists.

What could have happened to make them like this? And why are they so late? wondered Eragon. He remembered the traders as being full of good cheer, but there was none of that now. Garrow pushed down the street, searching for Merlock, a trader who specialized in odd trinkets and pieces of jewelry.

They found him behind a booth, displaying brooches to a group of women. As each new piece was revealed, exclamations of admiration followed. Eragon guessed that more than a few purses would soon be depleted. Merlock seemed to flourish and grow every time his wares were complimented. He wore a goatee, held himself with ease, and seemed to regard the rest of the world with slight contempt.

The excited group prevented Garrow and Eragon from getting near the trader, so they settled on a step and waited. As soon as Merlock was unoccupied, they hurried over.

"And what might you sirs want to look at?" asked Merlock. "An amulet or trinket for a lady?" With a twirl he pulled out a delicately carved silver rose of excellent workmanship. The polished metal caught Eragon's attention, and he eyed it appreciatively. The trader continued, "Not even three crowns, though it has come all the way from the famed craftsmen of Belatona."

Garrow spoke in a quiet voice. "We aren't looking to buy, but to sell." Merlock immediately covered the rose and looked at them with new interest.

"I see. Maybe, if this item is of any value, you would like to trade it for one or two of these exquisite pieces." He paused for a moment while Eragon and his uncle stood uncomfortably, then continued, "You did *bring* the object of consideration?"

"We have it, but we would rather show it to you elsewhere," said Garrow in a firm voice.

Merlock raised an eyebrow, but spoke smoothly. "In that case, let me invite you to my tent." He gathered up his wares and gently laid them in an iron-bound chest, which he locked. Then he ushered them up the street and into the temporary camp. They wound between the wagons to a tent removed from the rest of the traders'. It was crimson at the top and sable at the bottom, with thin triangles of colors stabbing into each other. Merlock untied the opening and swung the flap to one side.

Small trinkets and strange pieces of furniture, such as a round bed and three seats carved from tree stumps, filled the tent. A gnarled dagger with a ruby in the pommel rested on a white cushion.

Merlock closed the flap and turned to them.

"Please, seat yourselves." When they had, he said, "Now show me why we are meeting in private." Eragon unwrapped the stone and set it between the two men. Merlock reached for it with a gleam in his eye, then stopped and asked, "May I?" When Garrow indicated his approval, Merlock picked it up.

He put the stone in his lap and reached to one side for a thin box. Opened, it revealed a large set of copper scales, which he set on the ground. After weighing the stone, he scrutinized its surface under a jeweler's glass, tapped it gently with a wooden mallet, and drew the point of a tiny clear stone over it. He measured its length and diameter, then recorded the figures on a slate. He considered the results for a while. "Do you know what this is worth?"

"No," admitted Garrow. His cheek twitched, and he shifted uncomfortably on the seat.

Merlock grimaced. "Unfortunately, neither do I. But I can tell you this much: the white veins are the same material as the blue that surrounds them, only a different color. What that material might be, though, I haven't a clue. It's harder than any rock I have seen, harder even than diamond. Whoever shaped it used tools I have never seen—or magic. Also, it's hollow."

"What?" exclaimed Garrow.

An irritated edge crept into Merlock's voice. "Did you ever hear a rock sound like this?" He grabbed the dagger from the cushion and slapped the stone with the flat of the blade. A pure note filled the air, then faded away smoothly. Eragon was alarmed, afraid that the stone had been damaged. Merlock tilted the stone toward them. "You will find no scratches or blemishes where the dagger struck. I doubt I could do anything to harm this stone, even if I took a hammer to it."

Garrow crossed his arms with a reserved expression. A wall of silence surrounded him. Eragon was puzzled. *I knew that the stone appeared in the Spine through magic, but made by magic? What for and why?* He blurted, "But what is it worth?"

"I can't tell you that," said Merlock in a pained voice. "I am sure there are people who would pay dearly to have it, but none of them are in Carvahall. You would have to go to the southern cities to find a buyer. This is a curiosity for most people—not an item to spend money on when practical things are needed."

Garrow stared at the tent ceiling like a gambler calculating the odds. "Will you buy it?"

The trader answered instantly, "It's not worth the risk. I might be able to find a wealthy buyer during my spring travels, but I can't be certain. Even if I did, you wouldn't be paid until I returned next year. No, you will have to find someone else to trade with. I am curious, however . . . Why did you insist on talking to me in private?"

Eragon put the stone away before answering. "Because," he glanced at the man, wondering if he would explode like Sloan, "I found this in the Spine, and folks around here don't like that."

Merlock gave him a startled look. "Do you know why my fellow merchants and I were late this year?"

Eragon shook his head.

"Our wanderings have been dogged with misfortune. Chaos seems to rule Alagaësia. We could not avoid illness, attacks, and the most cursed black luck. Because the Varden's attacks have increased, Galbatorix has forced cities to send more soldiers to the borders, men who are needed to combat the Urgals. The brutes have been migrating southeast, toward the Hadarac Desert. No one knows why and it wouldn't concern us, except that they're passing through populated areas. They've been spotted on roads and near cities. Worst of all are reports of a Shade, though the stories are unconfirmed. Not many people survive such an encounter."

"Why haven't we heard of this?" cried Eragon.

"Because," said Merlock grimly, "it only began a few months ago. Whole villages have been forced to move because Urgals destroyed their fields and starvation threatens."

"Nonsense," growled Garrow. "We haven't seen any Urgals; the only one around here has his horns mounted in Morn's tavern."

Merlock arched an eyebrow. "Maybe so, but this is a small village hidden by mountains. It's not surprising that you've escaped notice. However, I wouldn't expect that to last. I only mentioned this because strange things are happening here as well if you found such a stone in the Spine." With that sobering statement, he bid them farewell with a bow and slight smile.

Garrow headed back to Carvahall with Eragon trailing behind. "What do you think?" asked Eragon.

"I'm going to get more information before I make up my mind. Take the stone back to the wagon, then do what you want. I'll meet you for dinner at Horst's."

Eragon dodged through the crowd and happily dashed back to the wagon. Trading would take his uncle hours, time that he planned to enjoy fully. He hid the stone under the bags, then set out into town with a cocky stride.

He walked from one booth to another, evaluating the goods with a buyer's eye, despite his meager supply of coins. When he talked with the merchants, they confirmed what Merlock had said about the instability in Alagaësia. Over and over the message was repeated: last year's security has deserted us; new dangers have appeared, and nothing is safe.

Later in the day he bought three sticks of malt candy and a small piping-hot cherry pie. The hot food felt good after hours of standing in the snow. He licked the sticky syrup from his fingers regretfully, wishing for more, then sat on the edge of a porch and nibbled a piece of candy. Two boys from Carvahall wrestled nearby, but he felt no inclination to join them.

As the day descended into late afternoon, the traders took their business into people's homes. Eragon was impatient for evening, when the troubadours would come out to tell stories and perform tricks. He loved hearing about magic, gods, and, if they were especially lucky, the Dragon Riders. Carvahall had its own storyteller, Brom—a friend of Eragon's—but his tales grew old over the years, whereas the troubadours always had new ones that he listened to eagerly.

Eragon had just broken off an icicle from the underside of the porch when he spotted Sloan nearby. The butcher had not seen him, so Eragon ducked his head and bolted around a corner toward Morn's tavern.

The inside was hot and filled with greasy smoke from sputtering tallow candles. The shiny-black Urgal horns, their twisted span as great as his outstretched arms, were mounted over the door. The bar was long and low, with a stack of staves on one end for customers to carve. Morn tended the bar, his sleeves rolled up to his elbows. The bottom half of his face was short and mashed, as if he had rested his chin on a grinding wheel. People crowded solid oak tables and listened to two traders who had finished their business early and had come in for beer.

Morn looked up from a mug he was cleaning. "Eragon! Good to see you. Where's your uncle?"

"Buying," said Eragon with a shrug. "He's going to be a while."

"And Roran, is he here?" asked Morn as he swiped the cloth through another mug.

"Yes, no sick animals to keep him back this year."

"Good, good."

Eragon gestured at the two traders. "Who are they?"

"Grain buyers. They bought everyone's seed at ridiculously low prices, and now they're telling wild stories, expecting us to believe them."

Eragon understood why Morn was so upset. *People need that money. We can't get by without it.* "What kind of stories?"

Morn snorted. "They say the Varden have formed a pact with the Urgals and are massing an army to attack us. *Supposedly*, it's only through the grace of our king that we've been protected for so long—as if Galbatorix would care if we burned to the ground. . . . Go listen to them. I have enough on my hands without explaining their lies."

The first trader filled a chair with his enormous girth; his every movement caused it to protest loudly. There was no hint of hair on his face, his pudgy hands were baby smooth, and he had pouting lips that curled petulantly as he sipped from a flagon. The second man had a florid face. The skin around his jaw was dry and corpulent, filled with lumps of hard fat, like cold butter gone rancid. Contrasted with his neck and jowls, the rest of his body was unnaturally thin.

The first trader vainly tried to pull back his expanding borders to fit within the chair. He said, "No, no, you don't understand. It is only through the king's unceasing efforts on your behalf that you are able to argue with us in safety. If he, in all his wisdom, were to withdraw that support, woe unto you!"

Someone hollered, "Right, why don't you also tell us the Riders have returned and you've each killed a hundred elves. Do you think we're children to believe in your tales? We can take care of ourselves." The group chuckled.

The trader started to reply when his thin companion intervened with a wave of his hand. Gaudy jewels flashed on his fingers. "You misunderstand. We know the Empire cannot care for each of us personally, as you may want, but it can keep Urgals and other abominations from overrunning this," he searched vaguely for the right term, "place."

The trader continued, "You're angry with the Empire for treating people unfairly, a legitimate concern, but a government cannot please everyone. There will inevitably be arguments and conflicts. However, the majority of us have nothing to complain about. Every country has some small group of malcontents who aren't satisfied with the balance of power."

"Yeah," called a woman, "if you're willing to call the Varden small!"

The fat man sighed. "We already explained that the Varden have no interest in helping you. That's only a falsehood perpetuated by the traitors in an attempt to disrupt the Empire and convince us that the real threat is inside—not outside—our borders. All they want to do is overthrow the king and take possession of our land. They have spies everywhere as they prepare to invade. You never know who might be working for them."

Eragon did not agree, but the traders' words were smooth, and people were nodding. He stepped forward and said, "How do you know this? I can say that clouds are green, but that doesn't mean it's true. Prove you aren't lying." The two men glared at him while the villagers waited silently for the answer.

The thin trader spoke first. He avoided Eragon's eyes. "Aren't your children taught respect? Or do you let boys challenge men whenever they want to?"

The listeners fidgeted and stared at Eragon. Then a man said, "Answer the question."

"It's only common sense," said the fat one, sweat beading on his upper lip. His reply riled the villagers, and the dispute resumed.

Eragon returned to the bar with a sour taste in his mouth. He had never before met anyone who favored the Empire and tore down its enemies. There was a deep-seated hatred of the Empire in Carvahall, almost hereditary in nature. The Empire never helped them during harsh years when they nearly starved, and its tax collectors were heartless. He felt justified in disagreeing with the traders regarding the king's mercy, but he did speculate about the Varden.

The Varden were a rebel group that constantly raided and attacked the Empire. It was a mystery who their leader was or who had formed them in the years following Galbatorix's rise to power over a century ago. The group had garnered much sympathy as they eluded Galbatorix's efforts to destroy them. Little was known about the Varden except that if you were a fugitive and had to hide, or if you hated the Empire, they would accept you. The only problem was finding them.

Morn leaned over the bar and said, "Incredible, isn't it? They're worse than vultures circling a dying animal. There's going to be trouble if they stay much longer."

"For us or for them?"

"Them," said Morn as angry voices filled the tavern. Eragon left when the argument threatened to become violent. The door thudded shut behind him, cutting off the voices. It was early evening, and the sun was sinking rapidly; the houses cast long shadows on the ground. As Eragon headed down the street, he noticed Roran and Katrina standing in an alley.

Roran said something Eragon could not hear. Katrina looked down at her hands and answered in an undertone, then leaned up on her tiptoes and kissed him before darting away. Eragon trotted to Roran and teased, "Having a good time?" Roran grunted noncommittally as he paced away.

"Have you heard the traders' news?" asked Eragon, following. Most of the villagers were indoors, talking to traders or waiting until it was dark enough for the troubadours to perform.

"Yes." Roran seemed distracted. "What do you think of Sloan?"

"I thought it was obvious."

"There'll be blood between us when he finds out about Katrina and me," stated Roran. A snowflake landed on Eragon's nose, and he looked up. The sky had turned gray. He could think of nothing appropriate to say; Roran was right. He clasped his cousin on the shoulder as they continued down the byway.

Dinner at Horst's was hearty. The room was full of conversation and laughter. Sweet cordials and heavy ales were consumed in copious amounts, adding to the boisterous atmosphere.

When the plates were empty, Horst's guests left the house and strolled to the field where the traders were camped. A ring of poles topped with candles had been stuck into the ground around a large clearing. Bonfires blazed in the background, painting the ground with dancing shadows. The villagers slowly gathered around the circle and waited expectantly in the cold.

The troubadours came tumbling out of their tents, dressed in tasseled clothing, followed by older and more stately minstrels. The minstrels provided music and narration as their younger counterparts acted out the stories. The first plays were pure entertainment: bawdy and full of jokes, pratfalls, and ridiculous characters. Later, however, when the candles sputtered in their sockets and everyone was drawn together into a tight circle, the old storyteller Brom stepped forward. A knotted white beard rippled over his chest, and a long black cape was wrapped around his bent shoulders, obscuring his body. He spread his arms with hands that reached out like talons and recited thus:

"The sands of time cannot be stopped. Years pass whether we will them or not . . . but we can remember. What has been lost may yet live on in memories. That which you will hear is imperfect and fragmented, yet treasure it, for without you it does not exist. I give you now a memory that has been forgotten, hidden in the dreamy haze that lies behind us."

His keen eyes inspected their interested faces. His gaze lingered on Eragon last of all.

"Before your grandfathers' fathers were born, and yea, even before their fathers, the Dragon Riders were formed. To protect and guard was their mission, and for thousands of years they succeeded. Their prowess in battle was unmatched, for each had the strength of ten men. They were immortal unless blade or poison took them. For good only were their powers used, and under their tutelage tall cities and towers were built out of the living stone. While they kept peace, the land flourished. It was a golden time. The elves were our allies, the dwarves our friends. Wealth flowed into our cities, and men prospered. But weep . . . for it could not last."

Brom looked down silently. Infinite sadness resonated in his voice.

"Though no enemy could destroy them, they could not guard against themselves. And it came to pass at the height of their power that a boy, Galbatorix by name, was born in the province of Inzilbêth, which is no more. At ten he was tested, as was the custom, and it was found that great power resided in him. The Riders accepted him as their own.

"Through their training he passed, exceeding all others in skill. Gifted with a sharp mind and strong body, he quickly took his place among the Riders' ranks. Some saw his abrupt rise as dangerous and warned the others, but the Riders had grown arrogant in their power and ignored caution. Alas, sorrow was conceived that day.

"So it was that soon after his training was finished, Galbatorix took a reckless trip with two friends. Far north they flew, night and day, and passed into the Urgals' remaining territory, foolishly thinking their new powers would protect them. There on a thick sheet of ice, unmelted even in summer, they were ambushed in their sleep. Though his friends and their dragons were butchered and he suffered great wounds, Galbatorix slew his attackers. Tragically, during the fight a stray arrow pierced his dragon's heart. Without the arts to save her, she died in his arms. Then were the seeds of madness planted."

The storyteller clasped his hands and looked around slowly, shadows flickering across his worn face. The next words came like the mournful toll of a requiem.

"Alone, bereft of much of his strength and half mad with loss, Galbatorix wandered without hope in that desolate land, seeking death. It did not come to him, though he threw himself without fear against any living thing. Urgals and other monsters soon fled from his haunted form. During this time he came to realize that the Riders might grant him another dragon. Driven by this thought, he began the arduous journey, on foot, back through the Spine. Territory he had soared over effortlessly on a dragon's back now took him months to traverse. He could hunt with magic, but oftentimes he walked in places where animals did not travel. Thus when his feet finally left the mountains, he was close to death. A farmer found him collapsed in the mud and summoned the Riders.

"Unconscious, he was taken to their holdings, and his body healed. He slept for four days. Upon awakening he gave no sign of his fevered mind. When he was brought before a council convened to judge him, Galbatorix demanded another dragon. The desperation of the request revealed his dementia, and the council saw him for what he truly was. Denied his hope, Galbatorix, through the twisted mirror of his madness, came to believe it was the Riders' fault his dragon had died. Night after night he brooded on that and formulated a plan to exact revenge."

Brom's words dropped to a mesmerizing whisper.

"He found a sympathetic Rider, and there his insidious words took root. By persistent reasoning and the use of dark secrets learned from a Shade, he inflamed the Rider against their elders. Together they treacherously lured and killed an elder. When the foul deed was done, Galbatorix turned on his ally and slaughtered him without warning. The Riders found him, then, with blood dripping from his hands. A scream tore from his lips, and he fled into the night. As he was cunning in his madness, they could not find him.

"For years he hid in wastelands like a hunted animal, always watching for pursuers. His atrocity was not forgotten, but over time searches ceased. Then through some ill fortune he met a young Rider, Morzan—strong of body, but weak of mind. Galbatorix convinced Morzan to leave a gate unbolted in the citadel Ilirea, which is now called Urû'baen. Through this gate Galbatorix entered and stole a dragon hatchling.

"He and his new disciple hid themselves in an evil place where the Riders dared not venture. There Morzan entered into a dark apprenticeship, learning secrets and forbidden magic that should never have been revealed. When his instruction was finished and Galbatorix's black dragon, Shruikan, was fully grown, Galbatorix revealed himself to the world, with Morzan at his side. Together they fought any Rider they met. With each kill their strength grew. Twelve of the Riders joined Galbatorix out of desire for power and revenge against perceived wrongs. Those twelve, with Morzan, became the Thirteen Forsworn. The Riders were unprepared and fell beneath the onslaught. The elves, too, fought bitterly against Galbatorix, but they were overthrown and forced to flee to their secret places, from whence they come no more.

"Only Vrael, leader of the Riders, could resist

Galbatorix and the Forsworn. Ancient and wise, he struggled to save what he could and keep the remaining dragons from falling to his enemies. In the last battle, before the gates of Doru Araeba, Vrael defeated Galbatorix, but hesitated with the final blow. Galbatorix seized the moment and smote him in the side. Grievously wounded, Vrael fled to Utgard Mountain, where he hoped to gather strength. But it was not to be, for Galbatorix found him. As they fought, Galbatorix kicked Vrael in the fork of his legs. With that underhanded blow, he gained dominance over Vrael and removed his head with a blazing sword.

"Then as power rushed through his veins, Galbatorix anointed himself king over all Alagaësia.

"And from that day, he has ruled us."

With the completion of the story, Brom shuffled away with the troubadours. Eragon thought he saw a tear shining on his cheek. People murmured quietly to each other as they departed. Garrow said to Eragon and Roran, "Consider yourselves fortunate. I have heard this tale only twice in my life. If the Empire knew that Brom had recited it, he would not live to see a new month."

FATE'S GIFT

The evening after their return from Carvahall, Eragon decided to test the stone as
Merlock had. Alone in his room, he set it
on his bed and laid three tools next to it. He
started with a wooden mallet and lightly tapped
the stone. It produced a subtle ringing. Satisfied,
he picked up the next tool, a heavy leather hammer. A mournful peal reverberated when it
struck. Lastly, he pounded a small chisel against
it. The metal did not chip or scratch the stone,
but it produced the clearest sound yet. As the final note died away, he thought he heard a faint
squeak.

*Merlock said the stone was hollow; there could be
something of value inside. I don't know how to open
it, though. There must have been a good reason for
someone to shape it, but whoever sent the stone into
the Spine hasn't taken the trouble to retrieve it or*

51

doesn't know where it is. But I don't believe that a magician with enough power to transport the stone wouldn't be able to find it again. So was I meant to have it? He could not answer the question. Resigned to an unsolvable mystery, he picked up the tools and returned the stone to its shelf.

That night he was abruptly roused from sleep. He listened carefully. All was quiet. Uneasy, he slid his hand under the mattress and grasped his knife. He waited a few minutes, then slowly sank back to sleep.

A squeak pierced the silence, tearing him back to wakefulness. He rolled out of bed and yanked the knife from its sheath. Fumbling with a tinderbox, he lit a candle. The door to his room was closed. Though the squeak was too loud for a mouse or rat, he still checked under the bed. Nothing. He sat on the edge of the mattress and rubbed the sleep from his eyes. Another squeak filled the air, and he started violently.

Where was the noise coming from? Nothing could be in the floor or walls; they were solid wood. The same went for his bed, and he would have noticed if anything had crawled into his straw mattress during the night. His eyes settled on the stone. He took it off the shelf and absently cradled it as he studied the room. A squeak rang in his ears and reverberated through his fingers; it came from the stone.

The stone had given him nothing but frustration and anger, and now it would not even let him sleep! It ignored his furious glare and sat solidly, occasionally peeping. Then it gave one very loud squeak and fell silent. Eragon warily put it away and got back under the sheets. Whatever secret the stone held, it would have to wait until morning.

The moon was shining through his window when he woke again. The stone was rocking rapidly on the shelf, knocking against the wall. It was bathed in cool moonlight that bleached its surface. Eragon jumped out of bed, knife in hand. The motion stopped, but he remained tense. Then the stone started squeaking and rocking faster than ever.

With an oath, he began dressing. He did not care how valuable the stone might be; he was going to take it far away and bury it. The rocking stopped; the stone became quiet. It quivered, then rolled forward and dropped onto the floor with a loud thump. He inched toward the door in alarm as the stone wobbled toward him.

Suddenly a crack appeared on the stone. Then another and another. Transfixed, Eragon leaned forward, still holding the knife. At the top of the stone, where all the cracks met, a small piece wobbled, as if it were balanced on something, then rose and toppled to the floor. After another series of squeaks, a small dark head poked out of

53

the hole, followed by a weirdly angled body. Eragon gripped the knife tighter and held very still. Soon the creature was all the way out of the stone. It stayed in place for a moment, then skittered into the moonlight.

Eragon recoiled in shock. Standing in front of him, licking off the membrane that encased it, was a dragon.

AWAKENING

The dragon was no longer than his forearm, yet it was dignified and noble. Its scales were deep sapphire blue, the same color as the stone. But not a stone, he realized, an egg. The dragon fanned its wings; they were what had made it appear so contorted. The wings were several times longer than its body and ribbed with thin fingers of bone that extended from the wing's front edge, forming a line of widely spaced talons. The dragon's head was roughly triangular. Two diminutive white fangs curved down out of its upper jaw. They looked very sharp. Its claws were also white, like polished ivory, and slightly serrated on the inside curve. A line of small spikes ran down the creature's spine from the base of its head to the tip of its tail. A hollow where its neck and shoulders joined created a larger-than-normal gap between the spikes.

Eragon shifted slightly, and the dragon's head snapped around. Hard, ice-blue eyes fixed on him. He kept very still. It might be a formidable enemy if it decided to attack.

The dragon lost interest in Eragon and awkwardly explored the room, squealing as it bumped into a wall or furniture. With a flutter of wings, it leapt onto the bed and crawled to his pillow, squeaking. Its mouth was open pitifully, like a young bird's, displaying rows of pointed teeth. Eragon sat cautiously on the end of the bed. The dragon smelled his hand, nibbled his sleeve. He pulled his arm back.

A smile tugged at Eragon's lips as he looked at the small creature. Tentatively, he reached out with his right hand and touched its flank. A blast of icy energy surged into his hand and raced up his arm, burning in his veins like liquid fire. He fell back with a wild cry. An iron clang filled his ears, and he heard a soundless scream of rage. Every part of his body seared with pain. He struggled to move, but was unable to. After what seemed like hours, warmth seeped back into his limbs, leaving them tingling. Shivering uncontrollably, he pushed himself upright. His hand was numb, his fingers paralyzed. Alarmed, he watched as the middle of his palm shimmered and formed a diffused white oval. The skin itched and burned like a spider bite. His heart pounded frantically.

Eragon blinked, trying to understand what

had occurred. Something brushed against his consciousness, like a finger trailing over his skin. He felt it again, but this time it solidified into a tendril of thought through which he could feel a growing curiosity. It was as if an invisible wall surrounding his thoughts had fallen away, and he was now free to reach out with his mind. He was afraid that without anything to hold him back, he would float out of his body and be unable to return, becoming a spirit of the ether. Scared, he pulled away from the contact. The new sense vanished as if he had closed his eyes. He glared suspiciously at the motionless dragon.

A scaly leg scraped against his side, and he jerked back. But the energy did not shock him again. Puzzled, he rubbed the dragon's head with his right hand. A light tingling ran up his arm. The dragon nuzzled him, arching its back like a cat. He slid a finger over its thin wing membranes. They felt like old parchment, velvety and warm, but still slightly damp. Hundreds of slender veins pulsed through them.

Again the tendril touched his mind, but this time, instead of curiosity, he sensed an overpowering, ravenous hunger. He got up with a sigh. This was a dangerous animal, of that he was sure. Yet it seemed so helpless crawling on his bed, he could only wonder if there was any harm in keeping it. The dragon wailed in a reedy tone as it looked for food. Eragon quickly scratched its head to keep it quiet. *I'll think about this later*, he decided, and left the room, carefully closing the door.

Returning with two strips of dried meat, he found the dragon sitting on the windowsill, watching the moon. He cut the meat into small squares and offered one to the dragon. It smelled the square cautiously, then jabbed its head forward like a snake and snatched the meat from his fingers, swallowing it whole with a peculiar jerk. The dragon prodded Eragon's hand for more food.

He fed it, careful to keep his fingers out of the way. By the time there was only one square left, the dragon's belly was bulging. He proffered the last piece; the dragon considered it for a moment, then lazily snapped it up. Done eating, it crawled onto his arm and curled against his chest. Then it snorted, a puff of dark smoke rising from its nostrils. Eragon looked at it with wonder.

Just when he thought the dragon was asleep, a low humming came from its vibrating throat. Gently, he carried it to the bed and set it by his pillow. The dragon, eyes closed, wrapped its tail around the bedpost contentedly. Eragon lay next to it, flexing his hand in the near darkness.

He faced a painful dilemma: By raising a dragon, he could become a Rider. Myths and stories about Riders were treasured, and being one would automatically place him among those legends. However, if the Empire discovered the dragon, he and his family would be put to death unless he joined the king. No one could—or would—help them. The simplest solution was just to kill the dragon, but the idea was repugnant, and he rejected it. Dragons were too revered for him to even consider that. *Besides, what could betray us?* he thought. *We live in a remote area and have done nothing to draw attention.*

The problem was convincing Garrow and Roran to let him keep the dragon. Neither of them would care to have a dragon around. *I could raise it in secret. In a month or two it will be too large for Garrow to get rid of, but will he accept it? Even if he does, can I get enough food for the dragon while it's hiding? It's no larger than a small cat, but it ate an entire handful of meat! I suppose it'll be able to hunt for itself eventually, but how long until then? Will it be able to survive the cold outside?* All the same, he wanted the dragon. The more he thought about it, the surer he was. However things might work out with Garrow, Eragon would do everything he could to protect it. Determined, he fell asleep with the dragon cradled against him.

When dawn came, the dragon was sitting atop his bedpost, like an ancient sentinel welcoming the new day. Eragon marveled at its color. He had never seen such a clear, hard blue. Its scales were like hundreds of small gemstones. He noticed that the white oval on his palm, where he had touched the dragon, had a silvery sheen. He hoped he could hide it by keeping his hands dirty.

The dragon launched off the post and glided to the floor. Eragon gingerly picked it up and left the quiet house, pausing to grab meat, several leather strips, and as many rags as he could carry. The crisp morning was beautiful; a fresh layer of snow covered the farm. He smiled as the small creature looked around with interest from the safety of his arms.

Hurrying across the fields, he walked silently into the dark forest, searching for a safe place for the dragon to stay. Eventually he found a rowan tree standing alone on a barren knoll, its branches snow-tipped gray fingers that reached toward the sky. He set the dragon down by the base of the trunk and shook the leather onto the ground.

With a few deft movements, he made a noose and slipped it over the dragon's head as it explored the snowy clumps surrounding the tree. The leather was worn, but it would hold. He watched the dragon crawl around, then untied the noose from its neck and fashioned a makeshift harness for its legs so the dragon would not strangle itself. Next he gathered an armful of sticks and built a crude hut high in the branches, layering the inside with rags and stashing the meat. Snow fell on his face as the tree swayed. He hung more rags over the front of the shelter to keep heat inside. Pleased, he surveyed his work.

"Time to show you your new home," he said, and lifted the dragon up into the branches. It wriggled, trying to get free, then clambered into the hut, where it ate a piece of meat, curled up, and blinked coyly at him. "You'll be fine as long as you stay in here," he instructed. The dragon blinked again.

Sure that it had not understood him, Eragon groped with his mind until he felt the dragon's consciousness. Again he had the terrible feeling of *openness*—of a space so large it pressed down on him like a heavy blanket. Summoning his strength, he focused on the dragon and tried to impress on it one idea: *Stay here.* The dragon stopped moving and cocked its head at him. He pushed harder: *Stay here.* A dim acknowledgment came tentatively through the link, but Eragon wondered if it really understood. *After all, it's only an animal.* He retreated from the contact with relief and felt the safety of his own mind envelop him.

Eragon left the tree, casting glances backward. The dragon stuck its head out of the shelter and watched with large eyes as he left.

After a hurried walk home, he sneaked back into his room to dispose of the egg fragments. He was sure Garrow and Roran would not notice the egg's absence—it had faded from their thoughts after they learned it could not be sold. When his family got up, Roran mentioned that he had heard some noises during the night but, to Eragon's relief, did not pursue the issue.

Eragon's enthusiasm made the day go by quickly. The mark on his hand proved easy to hide, so he soon stopped worrying about it. Before long he headed back to the rowan, carrying sausages he had pilfered from the cellar. With apprehension, he approached the tree. *Is the dragon able to survive outside in winter?*

His fears were groundless. The dragon was perched on a branch, gnawing on something between its front legs. It started squeaking excitedly when it saw him. He was pleased to see that it had remained in the tree, above the reach of large predators. As soon as he dropped the sausages at the base of the trunk, the dragon glided down. While it voraciously tore apart the food, Eragon examined the shelter. All the meat he had left was gone, but the hut was intact, and tufts of feathers littered the floor. *Good. It can get its own food.*

It struck him that he did not know if the dragon was a he or a she. He lifted and turned it over, ignoring its squeals of displeasure, but was unable to find any distinguishing marks. *It seems like it won't give up any secrets without a struggle.*

He spent a long time with the dragon. He untied it, set it on his shoulder, and went to explore the woods. The snow-laden trees watched over them like solemn pillars of a great cathedral. In that isolation, Eragon showed the dragon what he knew about the forest, not caring if it under-

stood his meaning. It was the simple act of shar-
ing that mattered. He talked to it continuously.
The dragon gazed back at him with bright eyes,
drinking in his words. For a while he just sat with
it resting in his arms and watched it with wonder,
still stunned by recent events. Eragon started for
home at sunset, conscious of two hard blue eyes
drilling into his back, indignant at being left behind.

That night he brooded about all the things
that could happen to a small and unprotected animal. Thoughts of ice storms and vicious animals
tormented him. It took hours for him to find
sleep. His dreams were of foxes and black wolves
tearing at the dragon with bloody teeth.

In the sunrise glow, Eragon ran from the house
with food and scraps of cloth—extra insulation
for the shelter. He found the dragon awake and
safe, watching the sunrise from high in the tree.
He fervently thanked all the gods, known and
unknown. The dragon came down to the ground
as he approached and leapt into his arms, hud-
dling close to his chest. The cold had not harmed
it, but it seemed frightened. A puff of dark smoke
blew out of its nostrils. He stroked it comfort-
ingly and sat with his back to the rowan, mur-
muring softly. He kept still as the dragon buried
its head in his coat. After a while it crawled out
of his embrace and onto his shoulder. He fed it,
then wrapped the new rags around the hut. They

played together for a time, but Eragon had to return to the house before long.

A smooth routine was quickly established. Every morning Eragon ran out to the tree and gave the dragon breakfast before hurrying back. During the day he attacked his chores until they were finished and he could visit the dragon again. Both Garrow and Roran noted his behavior and asked why he spent so much time outside. Eragon just shrugged and started checking to make sure he was not followed to the tree.

After the first few days he stopped worrying that a mishap would befall the dragon. Its growth was explosive; it would soon be safe from most dangers. The dragon doubled in size in the first week. Four days later it was as high as his knee. It no longer fit inside the hut in the rowan, so Eragon was forced to build a hidden shelter on the ground. The task took him three days.

When the dragon was a fortnight old, Eragon was compelled to let it roam free because it needed so much food. The first time he untied it, only the force of his will kept it from following him back to the farm. Every time it tried, he pushed it away with his mind until it learned to avoid the house and its other inhabitants.

And he impressed on the dragon the importance of hunting only in the Spine, where there was less chance of being seen. Farmers would notice if game started disappearing from Palancar Valley. It made him feel both safer and uneasy when the dragon was so far away.

The mental contact he shared with the dragon waxed stronger each day. He found that although it did not comprehend words, he could communicate with it through images or emotions. It was an imprecise method, however, and he was often misunderstood. The range at which they could touch each other's thoughts expanded rapidly. Soon Eragon could contact the dragon anywhere within three leagues. He often did so, and the dragon, in turn, would lightly brush against his mind. These mute conversations filled his working hours. There was always a small part of him connected to the dragon, ignored at times, but never forgotten. When he talked with people, the contact was distracting, like a fly buzzing in his ear.

As the dragon matured, its squeaks deepened to a roar and the humming became a low rumble, yet the dragon did not breathe fire, which concerned him. He had seen it blow smoke when it was upset, but there was never a hint of flame.

When the month ended, Eragon's elbow was level with the dragon's shoulder. In that brief span, it had transformed from a small, weak animal into a powerful beast. Its hard scales were as tough as chain-mail armor, its teeth like daggers.

Eragon took long walks in the evening with

the dragon padding beside him. When they found a clearing, he would settle against a tree and watch the dragon soar through the air. He loved to see it fly and regretted that it was not yet big enough to ride. He often sat beside the dragon and rubbed its neck, feeling sinews and corded muscles flex under his hands.

Despite Eragon's efforts, the forest around the farm filled with signs of the dragon's existence. It was impossible to erase all the huge four-clawed footprints sunk deep in the snow, and he refused even to try to hide the giant dung heaps that were becoming far too common. The dragon had rubbed against trees, stripping off the bark, and had sharpened its claws on dead logs, leaving gashes inches deep. If Garrow or Roran went too far beyond the farm's boundaries, they would discover the dragon. Eragon could imagine no worse way for the truth to come out, so he decided to preempt it by explaining everything to them.

He wanted to do two things first, though: give the dragon a suitable name and learn more about dragons in general. To that end he needed to talk with Brom, master of epics and legends—the only places where dragonlore survived.

So when Roran went to get a chisel repaired in Carvahall, Eragon volunteered to go with him.

The evening before they left, Eragon went to a small clearing in the forest and called the dragon with his mind. After a moment he saw a fast-moving speck in the dusky sky. The dragon dived toward him, pulled up sharply, then leveled off above the trees. He heard a low-pitched whistle as air rushed over its wings. It banked slowly to his left and spiraled gently down to the ground. The dragon back-flapped for balance with a deep, muffled *thwump* as it landed.

Eragon opened his mind, still uncomfortable with the strange sensation, and told the dragon that he was leaving. It snorted with unease. He attempted to soothe it with a calming mental picture, but the dragon whipped its tail, unsatisfied. He rested his hand on its shoulder and tried to radiate peace and serenity. Scales bumped under his fingers as he patted it gently.

A single word rang in his head, deep and clear. *Eragon.*

It was solemn and sad, as if an unbreakable pact were being sealed. He stared at the dragon and a cold tingle ran down his arm.

Eragon.

A hard knot formed in his stomach as unfathomable sapphire eyes gazed back at him. For the first time he did not think of the dragon as an animal. It was something else, something . . . different. He raced home, trying to escape the dragon. My *dragon.*

Eragon.

TEA FOR TWO

Roran and Eragon parted at the outskirts of Carvahall. Eragon walked slowly to Brom's house, engrossed in his thoughts. He stopped at the doorstep and raised his hand to knock.

A voice rasped, "What do you want, boy?"

He whirled around. Behind him Brom leaned on a twisted staff embellished with strange carvings. He wore a brown hooded robe like a friar. A pouch hung from the scuffed leather belt clasped around his waist. Above his white beard, a proud eagle nose hooked over his mouth and dominated his face. He peered at Eragon with deep-set eyes shadowed by a gnarled brow and waited for his reply.

"To get information," Eragon said. "Roran is getting a chisel fixed and I had free time, so I came to see if you could answer a few questions."

The old man grunted and reached for the door. Eragon noticed a gold ring on his right hand. Light glinted off a sapphire, highlighting a strange symbol carved on its face. "You might as well come in; we'll be talking awhile. Your questions never seem to end." Inside, the house was darker than charcoal, an acrid smell heavy in the air. "Now, for a light." Eragon heard the old man move around, then a low curse as something crashed to the floor. "Ah, here we go." A white spark flashed; a flame wavered into existence.

Brom stood with a candle before a stone fireplace. Stacks of books surrounded a high-backed, deeply carved wooden chair that faced the mantel; the four legs were shaped like eagle claws, and the seat and back were padded with leather embossed with a swirling rose pattern. A cluster of lesser chairs held piles of scrolls. Ink pots and pens were scattered across a writing desk. "Make room for yourself, but by the lost kings, be *careful*. This stuff is valuable."

Eragon stepped over pages of parchment covered with angular runes. He gently lifted cracking scrolls off a chair and placed them on the floor. A cloud of dust flew into the air as he sat. He stifled a sneeze.

Brom bent down and lit the fire with his candle. "Good! Nothing like sitting by a fire for conversation." He threw back his hood to reveal hair that was not white, but silver, then hung a kettle over the flames and settled into the high-backed chair.

"Now, what do you want?" He addressed Eragon roughly, but not unkindly.

"Well," said Eragon, wondering how best to approach the subject, "I keep hearing about the Dragon Riders and their supposed accomplishments. Most everyone seems to want them to return, but I've never heard tell of how they were started, where the dragons came from, or what made the Riders special—aside from the dragons."

"A vast subject to tell about," grumbled Brom. He peered at Eragon alertly. "If I told you their whole story, we would still be sitting here when winter comes again. It will have to be reduced to a manageable length. But before we start properly, I need my pipe."

Eragon waited patiently as Brom tamped down the tobacco. He liked Brom. The old man was irascible at times, but he never seemed to mind taking time for Eragon. Eragon had once asked him where he came from, and Brom had laughed, saying, "A village much like Carvahall, only not quite as interesting." Curiosity aroused, Eragon asked his uncle. But Garrow could only tell him that Brom had bought a house in Carvahall nearly fifteen years ago and had lived there quietly ever since.

Brom used a tinderbox to light the pipe. He

puffed a few times, then said, "There . . . we won't have to stop, except for the tea. Now, about the Riders, or the Shur'tugal, as they are called by the elves. Where to start? They spanned countless years and, at the height of their power, held sway over twice the Empire's lands. Numerous stories have been told about them, most nonsense. If you believed everything said, you would expect them to have the powers of a lesser god. Scholars have devoted entire lives to separating these fictions from fact, but it's doubtful any of them will succeed. However, it isn't an impossible task if we confine ourselves to the three areas you specified: how the Riders began, why they were so highly regarded, and where dragons came from. I shall start with the last item." Eragon settled back and listened to the man's mesmerizing voice.

"Dragons have no beginning, unless it lies with the creation of Alagaësia itself. And if they have an end, it will be when this world perishes, for they suffer as the land does. They, the dwarves, and a few others are the true inhabitants of this land. They lived here before all others, strong and proud in their elemental glory. Their world was unchanging until the first elves sailed over the sea on their silver ships."

"Where did the elves come from?" interrupted Eragon. "And why are they called the fair folk? Do they really exist?"

Brom scowled. "Do you want your original

questions answered or not? They won't be if you want to explore every obscure piece of knowledge."

"Sorry," said Eragon. He dipped his head and tried to look contrite.

"No, you're not," said Brom with some amusement. He shifted his gaze to the fire and watched it lick the underside of the kettle. "If you must know, elves are not legends, and they are called the fair folk because they are more graceful than any of the other races. They come from what they call Alalëa, though none but they know what, or even where, it is.

"Now," he glared from under his bushy eyebrows to make sure there would be no more interruptions, "the elves were a proud race then, and strong in magic. At first they regarded dragons as mere animals. From that belief rose a deadly mistake. A brash elven youth hunted down a dragon, as he would a stag, and killed it. Outraged, the dragons ambushed and slaughtered the elf. Unfortunately, the bloodletting did not stop there. The dragons massed together and attacked the entire elven nation. Dismayed by the terrible misunderstanding, the elves tried to end the hostilities, but couldn't find a way to communicate with the dragons.

"Thus, to greatly abbreviate a complicated series of occurrences, there was a very long and very bloody war, which both sides later regretted.

At the beginning the elves fought only to defend themselves, for they were reluctant to escalate the fighting, but the dragons' ferocity eventually forced them to attack for their own survival. This lasted for five years and would have continued for much longer if an elf called Eragon hadn't found a dragon egg." Eragon blinked in surprise. "Ah, I see you didn't know of your namesake," said Brom.

"No." The teakettle whistled stridently. *Why was I named after an elf?*

"Then you should find this all the more interesting," said Brom. He hooked the kettle out of the fire and poured boiling water into two cups. Handing one to Eragon, he warned, "These leaves don't need to steep long, so drink it quickly before it gets too strong." Eragon tried a sip, but scalded his tongue. Brom set his own cup aside and continued smoking the pipe.

"No one knows why that egg was abandoned. Some say the parents were killed in an elven attack. Others believe the dragons purposefully left it there. Either way, Eragon saw the value of raising a friendly dragon. He cared for it secretly and, in the custom of the ancient language, named him Bid'Daum. When Bid'Daum had grown to a good size, they traveled together among the dragons and convinced them to live in peace with the elves. Treaties were formed between the two races. To ensure that war would never break out again, they decided that it was necessary to establish the Riders.

"At first the Riders were intended merely as a means of communication between the elves and dragons. However, as time passed, their worth was recognized and they were given ever more authority. Eventually they took the island Vroengard for their home and built a city on it—Doru Araeba. Before Galbatorix overthrew them, the Riders held more power than all the kings in Alagaësia. Now I believe I have answered two of your questions."

"Yes," said Eragon absently. It seemed like an incredible coincidence that he had been named after the first Rider. For some reason his name did not feel the same anymore. "What does *Eragon* mean?"

"I don't know," said Brom. "It's very old. I doubt anyone remembers except the elves, and fortune would have to smile greatly before you talked with one. It is a good name to have, though; you should be proud of it. Not everyone has one so honorable."

Eragon brushed the matter from his mind and focused on what he had learned from Brom; there was something missing. "I don't understand. Where were we when the Riders were created?"

"We?" asked Brom, raising an eyebrow.

"You know, all of us." Eragon waved his hands vaguely. "Humans in general."

Brom laughed. "We are no more native to this land than the elves. It took our ancestors another three centuries to arrive here and join the Riders."

"That can't be," protested Eragon. "We've always lived in Palancar Valley."

"That might be true for a few generations, but beyond that, no. It isn't even true for you, Eragon," said Brom gently. "Though you consider yourself part of Garrow's family, and rightly so, your sire was not from here. Ask around and you'll find many people who haven't been here that long. This valley is old and hasn't always belonged to us."

Eragon scowled and gulped at the tea. It was still hot enough to burn his throat. This was his home, regardless of who his father was! "What happened to the dwarves after the Riders were destroyed?"

"No one really knows. They fought with the Riders through the first few battles, but when it became clear Galbatorix was going to win, they sealed all the known entrances to their tunnels and disappeared underground. As far as I know, not one has been seen since."

"And the dragons?" he asked. "What of them? Surely they weren't all killed."

Brom answered sorrowfully, "That is the greatest mystery in Alagaësia nowadays: How many dragons survived Galbatorix's murderous slaughter? He spared those who agreed to serve him, but only the twisted dragons of the Forsworn would assist his madness. If any dragons aside from Shruikan are still alive, they have hidden themselves so they will never be found by the Empire."

So where did *my dragon come from?* wondered Eragon. "Were the Urgals here when the elves came to Alagaësia?" he asked.

"No, they followed the elves across the sea, like ticks seeking blood. They were one of the reasons the Riders became valued for their battle prowess and ability to keep the peace. . . . Much can be learned from this history. It's a pity the king makes it a delicate subject," reflected Brom.

"Yes, I heard your story the last time I was in town."

"Story!" roared Brom. Lightning flashed in his eyes. "If it is a story, then the rumors of my death are true and you are speaking with a ghost! Respect the past; you never know how it may affect you."

Eragon waited until Brom's face mellowed before he dared ask, "How big were the dragons?"

A dark plume of smoke swirled above Brom like a miniature thunderstorm. "Larger than a house. Even the small ones had wingspans over a hundred feet; they never stopped growing. Some of the ancient ones, before the Empire killed them, could have passed for large hills."

Dismay swept through Eragon. *How can I hide*

my dragon in the years to come? He raged silently, but kept his voice calm. "When did they mature?"

"Well," said Brom, scratching his chin, "they couldn't breathe fire until they were around five to six months old, which was about when they could mate. The older a dragon was, the longer it could breathe fire. Some of them could keep at it for minutes." Brom blew a smoke ring and watched it float up to the ceiling.

"I heard that their scales shone like gems."

Brom leaned forward and growled, "You heard right. They came in every color and shade. It was said that a group of them looked like a living rainbow, constantly shifting and shimmering. But who told you that?"

Eragon froze for a second, then lied, "A trader."

"What was his name?" asked Brom. His tangled eyebrows met in a thick white line; the wrinkles deepened on his forehead. Unnoticed, the pipe smoldered out.

Eragon pretended to think. "I don't know. He was talking in Morn's, but I never found out who he was."

"I wish you had," muttered Brom.

"He also said a Rider could hear his dragon's thoughts," said Eragon quickly, hoping that the fictitious trader would protect him from suspicion.

Brom's eyes narrowed. Slowly he took out a

tinderbox and struck the flint. Smoke rose, and he took a long pull from the pipe, exhaling slowly. In a flat voice he said, "He was wrong. It isn't in any of the stories, and I know them all. Did he say anything else?"

Eragon shrugged. "No." Brom was too interested in the trader for him to continue the falsehood. Casually he inquired, "Did dragons live very long?"

Brom did not respond at once. His chin sank to his chest while his fingers tapped the pipe thoughtfully, light reflecting off his ring. "Sorry, my mind was elsewhere. Yes, a dragon will live for quite a while, forever, in fact, as long as it isn't killed and its Rider doesn't die."

"How does anyone know that?" objected Eragon. "If dragons die when their Riders do, they could only live to be sixty or seventy. You said during your . . . narration that Riders lived for hundreds of years, but that's impossible." It troubled him to think of outliving his family and friends.

A quiet smile curled Brom's lips as he said slyly, "What is possible is subjective. Some would say that you cannot travel through the Spine and live, yet you do. It's a matter of perspective. You must be very wise to know so much at such a young age." Eragon flushed, and the old man chuckled. "Don't be angry; you can't be expected to know such things. You forget that the dragons were magical—they affected everything around them in strange ways. The Riders were closest to them and experienced this the most. The most common side effect was an extended life. Our king has lived long enough to make that apparent, but most people attribute it to his own magical abilities. There were also other, less noticeable changes. All the Riders were stronger of body, keener of mind, and truer of sight than normal men. Along with this, a human Rider would slowly acquire pointed ears, though they were never as prominent as an elf's."

Eragon had to stop his hand from reaching up to feel the tips of his ears. *How else will this dragon change my life? Not only has it gotten inside my head, but it's altering my body as well!* "Were dragons very smart?"

"Didn't you pay attention to what I told you earlier!" demanded Brom. "How could the elves form agreements and peace treaties with dumb brutes? They were as intelligent as you or I."

"But they were animals," persisted Eragon.

Brom snorted. "They were no more animals than we are. For some reason people praise everything the Riders did, yet ignore the dragons, assuming that they were nothing more than an exotic means to get from one town to another. They weren't. The Riders' great deeds were only possible because of the dragons. How many men would draw their swords if they knew a giant fire-breathing lizard—one with more natural cunning and wisdom than even a king could hope for—would soon be there to stop the violence? Hmm?" He blew another smoke ring and watched it waft away.

"Did you ever see one?"

"Nay," said Brom, "it was long before my time."

And now for a name. "I've been trying to recall the name of a certain dragon, but it keeps eluding me. I think I heard it when the traders were in Carvahall, but I'm not sure. Could you help me?"

Brom shrugged and quickly listed a stream of names. "There was Jura, Hírador, and Fundor—who fought the giant sea snake. Galzra, Briam, Ohen the Strong, Gretiem, Beroan, Roslarb . . ." He added many others. At the very end, he uttered so softly Eragon almost did not hear, ". . . and Saphira." Brom quietly emptied his pipe. "Was it any of those?"

"I'm afraid not," said Eragon. Brom had given him much to think about, and it was getting late. "Well, Roran's probably finished with Horst. I should get back, though I'd rather not."

Brom raised an eyebrow. "What, is that it? I expected to be answering your questions until he came looking for you. No queries about dragon battle tactics or requests for descriptions of breathtaking aerial combat? Are we done?"

"For now," laughed Eragon. "I learned what I

wanted to and more." He stood and Brom followed.

"Very well, then." He ushered Eragon to the door. "Goodbye. Take care. And don't forget, if you remember who that trader was, tell me."

"I will. Thank you." Eragon stepped into the glaring winter sunlight, squinting. He slowly paced away, pondering what he had heard.

A NAME OF POWER

On the way home Roran said, "There was a stranger from Therinsford at Horst's today."

"What's his name?" asked Eragon. He sidestepped a patch of ice and continued walking at a brisk pace. His cheeks and eyes burned from the cold.

"Dempton. He came here to have Horst forge him some sockets," said Roran. His stocky legs plowed through a drift, clearing the way for Eragon.

"Doesn't Therinsford have its own smith?"

"Yes," replied Roran, "but he isn't skilled enough." He glanced at Eragon. With a shrug he added, "Dempton needs the sockets for his mill. He's expanding it and offered me a job. If I accept, I'll leave with him when he picks up the sockets."

Millers worked all year. During winter they

ground whatever people brought them, but in harvest season they bought grain and sold it as flour. It was hard, dangerous work; workers often lost fingers or hands to the giant millstones. "Are you going to tell Garrow?" asked Eragon.

"Yes." A grimly amused smile played across Roran's face.

"What for? You know what he thinks about us going away. It'll only cause trouble if you say anything. Forget about it so we can eat tonight's dinner in peace."

"I can't. I'm going to take the job."

Eragon halted. "Why?" They faced each other, their breath visible in the air. "I know money is hard to come by, but we always manage to survive. You don't have to leave."

"No, I don't. But the money is for myself." Roran tried to resume walking, but Eragon refused to budge.

"What do you need it for?" he demanded.

Roran's shoulders straightened slightly. "I want to marry."

Bewilderment and astonishment overwhelmed Eragon. He remembered seeing Katrina and Roran kissing during the traders' visit, but marriage? "Katrina?" he asked weakly, just to confirm. Roran nodded. "Have you asked her?"

"Not yet, but come spring, when I can raise a house, I will."

"There's too much work on the farm for you to

leave now," protested Eragon. "Wait until we're ready for planting."

"No," said Roran, laughing slightly. "Spring's the time I'll be needed the most. The ground will have to be furrowed and sown. The crops must be weeded—not to mention all the other chores. No, this is the best time for me to go, when all we really do is wait for the seasons to change. You and Garrow can make do without me. If all goes well, I'll soon be back working on the farm, with a wife."

Eragon reluctantly conceded that Roran made sense. He shook his head, but whether with amazement or anger, he knew not. "I guess I can only wish you the best of luck. But Garrow may take this with ill humor."

"We will see."

They resumed walking, the silence a barrier between them. Eragon's heart was disturbed. It would take time before he could look upon this development with favor. When they arrived home, Roran did not tell Garrow of his plans, but Eragon was sure that he soon would.

Eragon went to see the dragon for the first time since it had spoken to him. He approached apprehensively, aware now that it was an equal.

Eragon.

"Is that all you can say?" he snapped.

Yes.

His eyes widened at the unexpected reply, and he sat down roughly. *Now it has a sense of humor. What next?* Impulsively, he broke a dead branch with his foot. Roran's announcement had put him in a foul mood. A questioning thought came from the dragon, so he told it what had happened. As he talked his voice grew steadily louder until he was yelling pointlessly into the air. He ranted until his emotions were spent, then ineffectually punched the ground.

"I don't want him to go, that's all," he said helplessly. The dragon watched impassively, listening and learning. Eragon mumbled a few choice curses and rubbed his eyes. He looked at the dragon thoughtfully. "You need a name. I heard some interesting ones today; perhaps you'll like one." He mentally ran through the list Brom had given him until he found two names that struck him as heroic, noble, and pleasing to the ear. "What do you think of Vanilor or his successor, Eridor? Both were great dragons."

No, said the dragon. It sounded amused with his efforts. *Eragon.*

"That's *my* name; you can't have it," he said, rubbing his chin. "Well, if you don't like those, there are others." He continued through the list, but the dragon rejected every one he proposed. It seemed to be laughing at something Eragon did not understand, but he ignored it and kept suggesting names. "There was Ingothold, he slew the . . ." A revelation stopped him. *That's the problem! I've been choosing male names. You are a she!*

Yes. The dragon folded her wings smugly.

Now that he knew what to look for, he came up with half a dozen names. He toyed with Miremel, but that did not fit—after all, it was the name of a brown dragon. Opheila and Lenora were also discarded. He was about to give up when he remembered the last name Brom had muttered. Eragon liked it, but would the dragon?

He asked.

"Are you Saphira?" She looked at him with intelligent eyes. Deep in his mind he felt her satisfaction.

Yes. Something clicked in his head and her voice echoed, as if from a great distance. He grinned in response. Saphira started humming.

A MILLER-TO-BE

The sun had set by the time dinner was served. A blustery wind howled outside, shaking the house. Eragon eyed Roran closely and waited for the inevitable. Finally: "I was offered a job at Therinsford's mill . . . which I plan to take."

Garrow finished his mouthful of food with deliberate slowness and laid down his fork. He leaned back in his chair, then interlaced his fingers behind his head and uttered one dry word, "Why?"

Roran explained while Eragon absently picked at his food.

"I see," was Garrow's only comment. He fell silent and stared at the ceiling. No one moved as they awaited his response. "Well, when do you leave?"

"What?" asked Roran.

Garrow leaned forward with a twinkle in his eye. "Did you think I would stop you? I'd hoped you would marry soon. It will be good to see this family growing again. Katrina will be lucky to have you." Astonishment raced over Roran's face, then he settled into a relieved grin. "So when do you leave?" Garrow asked.

Roran regained his voice. "When Dempton returns to get the sockets for the mill."

Garrow nodded. "And that will be in . . . ?"

"Two weeks."

"Good. That will give us time to prepare. It'll be different to have the house to ourselves. But if nothing goes amiss, it shouldn't be for too long." He looked over the table and asked, "Eragon, did you know of this?"

He shrugged ruefully. "Not until today. . . . It's madness."

Garrow ran a hand over his face. "It's life's natural course." He pushed himself up from the chair. "All will be fine; time will settle everything. For now, though, let's clean the dishes." Eragon and Roran helped him in silence.

The next few days were trying. Eragon's temper was frayed. Except for curtly answering direct questions, he spoke with no one. There were small reminders everywhere that Roran was leaving: Garrow making him a pack, things missing from the walls, and a strange emptiness that filled the house. It was almost a week before he realized that distance had grown between Roran and him. When they spoke, the words did not come easily and their conversations were uncomfortable.

Saphira was a balm for Eragon's frustration. He could talk freely with her; his emotions were completely open to her mind, and she understood him better than anyone else. During the weeks before Roran's departure, she went through another growth spurt. She gained twelve inches at the shoulder, which was now higher than Eragon's. He found that the small hollow where her neck joined her shoulders was a perfect place to sit. He often rested there in the evenings and scratched her neck while he explained the meanings of different words. Soon she understood everything he said and frequently commented on it.

For Eragon, this part of his life was delightful. Saphira was as real and complex as any person. Her personality was eclectic and at times completely alien, yet they understood each other on a profound level. Her actions and thoughts constantly revealed new aspects of her character. Once she caught an eagle and, instead of eating it, released it, saying, *No hunter of the sky should end his days as prey. Better to die on the wing than pinned to the ground.*

Eragon's plan to let his family see Saphira was dispelled by Roran's announcement and Saphira's own cautionary words. She was reluctant to be seen, and he, partly out of selfishness, agreed. The moment her existence was divulged, he knew that shouts, accusations, and fear would be directed at him . . . so he procrastinated. He told himself to wait for a sign that it was the right time.

The night before Roran was to leave, Eragon went to talk with him. He stalked down the hallway to Roran's open door. An oil lamp rested on a nightstand, painting the walls with warm flickering light. The bedposts cast elongated shadows on empty shelves that rose to the ceiling. Roran—his eyes shaded and the back of his neck tense—was rolling blankets around his clothes and belongings. He paused, then picked up something from the pillow and bounced it in his hand. It was a polished rock Eragon had given him years ago. Roran started to tuck it into the bundle, then stopped and set it on a shelf. A hard lump formed in Eragon's throat, and he left.

STRANGERS IN
CARVAHALL

Breakfast was cold, but the tea was hot. Ice inside the windows had melted with the morning fire and soaked into the wood floor, staining it with dark puddles. Eragon looked at Garrow and Roran by the kitchen stove and reflected that this would be the last time he saw them together for many months.

Roran sat in a chair, lacing his boots. His full pack rested on the floor next to him. Garrow stood between them with his hands stuck deep into his pockets. His shirt hung loosely; his skin looked drawn. Despite the young men's cajoling, he refused to go with them. When pressed for a reason, he only said that it was for the best.

"Do you have everything?" Garrow asked Roran.

"Yes."

He nodded and took a small pouch from his

pocket. Coins clinked as he handed it to Roran. "I've been saving this for you. It isn't much, but if you wish to buy some bauble or trinket, it will suffice."

"Thank you, but I won't be spending my money on trifles," said Roran.

"Do what you will; it is yours," said Garrow. "I've nothing else to give you, except a father's blessing. Take it if you wish, but it is worth little."

Roran's voice was thick with emotion. "I would be honored to receive it."

"Then do, and go in peace," said Garrow, and kissed him on the forehead. He turned and said in a louder voice, "Do not think that I have forgotten you, Eragon. I have words for both of you. It's time I said them, as you are entering the world. Heed them and they will serve you well." He bent his gaze sternly on them. "First, let no one rule your mind or body. Take special care that your thoughts remain unfettered. One may be a free man and yet be bound tighter than a slave. Give men your ear, but not your heart. Show respect for those in power, but don't follow them blindly. Judge with logic and reason, but comment not.

"Consider none your superior, whatever their rank or station in life. Treat all fairly or they will seek revenge. Be careful with your money. Hold fast to your beliefs and others will listen." He continued at a slower pace, "Of the affairs of love . . . my only advice is to be honest. That's your most powerful tool to unlock a heart or gain forgiveness. That is all I have to say." He seemed slightly self-conscious of his speech.

He hoisted Roran's pack. "Now you must go. Dawn is approaching, and Dempton will be waiting."

Roran shouldered the pack and hugged Garrow. "I will return as soon as I can," he said.

"Good!" replied Garrow. "But now go and don't worry about us."

They parted reluctantly. Eragon and Roran went outside, then turned and waved. Garrow raised a bony hand, his eyes grave, and watched as they trudged to the road. After a long moment he shut the door. As the sound carried through the morning air, Roran halted.

Eragon looked back and surveyed the land. His eyes lingered on the lone buildings. They looked pitifully small and fragile. A thin finger of smoke trailing up from the house was the only proof that the snowbound farm was inhabited.

"There is our whole world," Roran observed somberly.

Eragon shivered impatiently and grumbled, "A good one too." Roran nodded, then straightened his shoulders and headed into his new future. The house disappeared from view as they descended the hill.

It was still early when they reached Carvahall, but they found the smithy doors already open.

The air inside was pleasantly warm. Baldor slowly worked two large bellows attached to the side of a stone forge filled with sparkling coals. Before the forge stood a black anvil and an iron-bound barrel filled with brine. From a line of neck-high poles protruding from the walls hung rows of items: giant tongs, pliers, hammers in every shape and weight, chisels, angles, center punches, files, rasps, lathes, bars of iron and steel waiting to be shaped, vises, shears, picks, and shovels. Horst and Dempton stood next to a long table.

Dempton approached with a smile beneath his flamboyant red mustache. "Roran! I'm glad you came. There's going to be more work than I can handle with my new grindstones. Are you ready to go?"

Roran hefted his pack. "Yes. Do we leave soon?"

"I've a few things to take care of first, but we'll be off within the hour." Eragon shifted his feet as Dempton turned to him, tugging at the corner of his mustache. "You must be Eragon. I would offer you a job too, but Roran got the only one. Maybe in a year or two, eh?"

Eragon smiled uneasily and shook his hand. The man was friendly. Under other circumstances Eragon would have liked him, but right then, he sourly wished that the miller had never come to Carvahall. Dempton huffed. "Good, very good." He returned his attention to Roran and started to explain how a mill worked.

"They're ready to go," interrupted Horst, gesturing at the table where several bundles rested. "You can take them whenever you want to." They shook hands, then Horst left the smithy, beckoning to Eragon on the way out.

Interested, Eragon followed. He found the smith standing in the street with his arms crossed. Eragon thrust his thumb back toward the miller and asked, "What do you think of him?"

Horst rumbled, "A good man. He'll do fine with Roran." He absently brushed metal filings off his apron, then put a massive hand on Eragon's shoulder. "Lad, do you remember the fight you had with Sloan?"

"If you're asking about payment for the meat, I haven't forgotten."

"No, I trust you, lad. What I wanted to know is if you still have that blue stone."

Eragon's heart fluttered. *Why does he want to know? Maybe someone saw Saphira!* Struggling not to panic, he said, "I do, but why do you ask?"

"As soon as you return home, get rid of it." Horst overrode Eragon's exclamation. "Two men arrived here yesterday. Strange fellows dressed in black and carrying swords. It made my skin crawl just to look at them. Last evening they started asking people if a stone like yours had been found. They're at it again today." Eragon blanched. "No one with any sense said anything. They know trouble when they see it, but I could name a few people who will talk."

Dread filled Eragon's heart. Whoever had sent the stone into the Spine had finally tracked it down. Or perhaps the Empire had learned of Saphira. He did not know which would be worse. *Think! Think! The egg is gone. It's impossible for them to find it now. But if they know what it was, it'll be obvious what happened. . . . Saphira might be in danger!* It took all of his self-control to retain a casual air. "Thanks for telling me. Do you know where they are?" He was proud that his voice barely trembled.

"I didn't warn you because I thought you needed to meet those men! Leave Carvahall. Go home."

"All right," said Eragon to placate the smith, "if you think I should."

"I do." Horst's face softened. "I may be over-reacting, but these strangers give me a bad feeling. It would be better if you stay home until they leave. I'll try to keep them away from your farm, though it may not do any good."

Eragon looked at him gratefully. He wished he could tell him about Saphira. "I'll leave now," he said, and hurried back to Roran. Eragon clasped his cousin's arm and bade him farewell.

"Aren't you going to stay awhile?" Roran asked with surprise.

Eragon almost laughed. For some reason, the

question struck him as funny. "There's nothing for me to do, and I'm not going to stand around until you go."

"Well," said Roran doubtfully, "I guess this is the last time we'll see each other for a few months."

"I'm sure it won't seem that long," said Eragon hastily. "Take care and come back soon." He hugged Roran, then left. Horst was still in the street. Aware that the smith was watching, Eragon headed to the outskirts of Carvahall. Once the smithy was out of sight, he ducked behind a house and sneaked back through the village.

Eragon kept to the shadows as he searched each street, listening for the slightest noise. His thoughts flashed to his room, where his bow hung; he wished that it was in his hand. He prowled across Carvahall, avoiding everyone until he heard a sibilant voice from around a house. Although his ears were keen, he had to strain to hear what was being said.

"When did this happen?" The words were smooth, like oiled glass, and seemed to worm their way through the air. Underlying the speech was a strange hiss that made his scalp prickle.

"About three months ago," someone else answered. Eragon identified him as Sloan.

Shade's blood, he's telling them. . . . He resolved to punch Sloan the next time they met.

A third person spoke. The voice was deep and

moist. It conjured up images of creeping decay, mold, and other things best left untouched. "Are you sure? We would hate to think you had made a mistake. If that were so, it would be most . . . unpleasant." Eragon could imagine only too well what they might do. Would anyone but the Empire dare threaten people like that? Probably not, but whoever sent the egg might be powerful enough to use force with impunity.

"Yeah, I'm sure. He had it then. I'm not lying. Plenty of people know about it. Go ask them." Sloan sounded shaken. He said something else that Eragon did not catch.

"They have been . . . rather uncooperative." The words were derisive. There was a pause. "Your information has been helpful. We will not forget you." Eragon believed him.

Sloan muttered something, then Eragon heard someone hurrying away. He peered around the corner to see what was happening. Two tall men stood in the street. Both were dressed in long black cloaks that were lifted by sheaths poking past their legs. On their shirts were insignias intricately wrought with silver thread. Hoods shaded their faces, and their hands were covered by gloves. Their backs were oddly humped, as though their clothes were stuffed with padding.

Eragon shifted slightly to get a better view. One of the strangers stiffened and grunted peculiarly to his companion. They both swiveled around and sank into crouches. Eragon's breath caught. Mortal fear clenched him. His eyes locked onto their hidden faces, and a stifling power fell over his mind, keeping him in place. He struggled against it and screamed to himself, *Move!* His legs swayed, but to no avail. The strangers stalked toward him with a smooth, noiseless gait. He knew they could see his face now. They were almost to the corner, hands grasping at swords. . . .

"Eragon!" He jerked as his name was called. The strangers froze in place and hissed. Brom hurried toward him from the side, head bare and staff in hand. The strangers were blocked from the old man's view. Eragon tried to warn him, but his tongue and arms would not stir. "Eragon!" cried Brom again. The strangers gave Eragon one last look, then slipped away between the houses.

Eragon collapsed to the ground, shivering. Sweat beaded on his forehead and made his palms sticky. The old man offered Eragon a hand and pulled him up with a strong arm. "You look sick; is all well?"

Eragon gulped and nodded mutely. His eyes flickered around, searching for anything unusual. "I just got dizzy all of a sudden . . . it's passed. It was very odd—I don't know why it happened."

"You'll recover," said Brom, "but perhaps it would be better if you went home."

Yes, I have to get home! Have to get there before

they do. "I think you're right. Maybe I'm getting ill."

"Then home is the best place for you. It's a long walk, but I'm sure you will feel better by the time you arrive. Let me escort you to the road." Eragon did not protest as Brom took his arm and led him away at a quick pace. Brom's staff crunched in the snow as they passed the houses.

"Why were you looking for me?"

Brom shrugged. "Simple curiosity. I learned you were in town and wondered if you had remembered the name of that trader."

Trader? What's he talking about? Eragon stared blankly; his confusion caught the attention of Brom's probing eyes. "No," he said, and then amended himself, "I'm afraid I still don't remember."

Brom sighed gruffly, as if something had been confirmed, and rubbed his eagle nose. "Well, then . . . if you do, come tell me. I am most interested in this trader who pretends to know so much about dragons." Eragon nodded with a distracted air. They walked in silence to the road, then Brom said, "Hasten home. I don't think it would be a good idea to tarry on the way." He offered a gnarled hand.

Eragon shook it, but as he let go something in Brom's hand caught on his mitt and pulled it off. It fell to the ground. The old man picked it up. "Clumsy of me," he apologized, and handed it back. As Eragon took the mitt, Brom's strong fingers wrapped around his wrist and twisted sharply. His palm briefly faced upward, revealing the silvery mark. Brom's eyes glinted, but he let Eragon yank his hand back and jam it into the mitt.

"Goodbye," Eragon forced out, perturbed, and hurried down the road. Behind him he heard Brom whistling a merry tune.

FLIGHT OF DESTINY

Eragon's mind churned as he sped on his way. He ran as fast as he could, refusing to stop even when his breath came in great gasps. As he pounded down the cold road, he cast out with his mind for Saphira, but she was too far away for him to contact. He thought about what to say to Garrow. There was no choice now; he would have to reveal Saphira.

He arrived home, panting for air and heart pounding. Garrow stood by the barn with the horses. Eragon hesitated. *Should I talk to him now? He won't believe me unless Saphira is here—I'd better find her first*. He slipped around the farm and into the forest. *Saphira!* he shouted with his thoughts.

I come, was the dim reply. Through the words he sensed her alarm. He waited impatiently, though it was not long before the sound of her wings filled the air. She landed amid a gout of smoke. *What happened?* she queried.

He touched her shoulder and closed his eyes. Calming his mind, he quickly told her what had occurred. When he mentioned the strangers, Saphira recoiled. She reared and roared deafeningly, then whipped her tail over his head. He scrambled back in surprise, ducking as her tail hit a snowdrift. Bloodlust and fear emanated from her in great sickening waves. *Fire! Enemies! Death! Murderers!*

What's wrong? He put all of his strength into the words, but an iron wall surrounded her mind, shielding her thoughts. She let out another roar and gouged the earth with her claws, tearing the frozen ground. *Stop it! Garrow will hear!*

103

Oaths betrayed, souls killed, eggs shattered! Blood everywhere. Murderers!

Frantic, he blocked out Saphira's emotions and watched her tail. When it flicked past him, he dashed to her side and grabbed a spike on her back. Clutching it, he pulled himself into the small hollow at the base of her neck and held on tightly as she reared again. "Enough, Saphira!" he bellowed. Her stream of thoughts ceased abruptly. He ran a hand over her scales. "Everything's going to be all right." She crouched and her wings rushed upward. They hung there for an instant, then drove down as she flung herself into the sky.

Eragon yelled as the ground dropped away and

they rose above the trees. Turbulence buffeted him, snatching the breath out of his mouth. Saphira ignored his terror and banked toward the Spine. Underneath, he glimpsed the farm and the Anora River. His stomach convulsed. He tightened his arms around Saphira's neck and concentrated on the scales in front of his nose, trying not to vomit as she continued to climb. When she leveled off, he gained the courage to glance around.

The air was so cold that frost accumulated on his eyelashes. They had reached the mountains faster than he thought possible. From the air, the peaks looked like giant razor-sharp teeth waiting to slash them to ribbons. Saphira wobbled unexpectedly, and Eragon heaved over her side. He wiped his lips, tasting bile, and buried his head against her neck.

We have to go back, he pleaded. *The strangers are coming to the farm. Garrow has to be warned. Turn around!* There was no answer. He reached for her mind, but was blocked by a barrier of roiling fear and anger. Determined to make her turn around, he grimly wormed into her mental armor. He pushed at its weak places, undermined the stronger sections, and fought to make her listen, but to no avail.

Soon mountains surrounded them, forming tremendous white walls broken by granite cliffs. Blue glaciers sat between the summits like frozen rivers. Long valleys and ravines opened beneath them. He heard the dismayed screech of birds far below as Saphira soared into view. He saw a herd of woolly goats bounding from ledge to ledge on a rocky bluff.

Eragon was battered by swirling gusts from Saphira's wings, and whenever she moved her neck, he was tossed from side to side. She seemed tireless. He was afraid she was going to fly through the night. Finally, as darkness fell, she tilted into a shallow dive.

He looked ahead and saw that they were headed for a small clearing in a valley. Saphira spiraled down, leisurely drifting over the tree-tops. She pulled back as the ground neared, filled her wings with air, and landed on her rear legs. Her powerful muscles rippled as they absorbed the shock of impact. She dropped to all fours and skipped a step to keep her balance. Eragon slid off without waiting for her to fold her wings.

As he struck the ground, his knees buckled, and his cheek slammed against the snow. He gasped as excruciating pain seared through his legs, sending tears to his eyes. His muscles, cramped from clenching for so long, shook vio- lently. He rolled onto his back, shivering, and stretched his limbs as best he could. Then he forced himself to look down. Two large blots darkened his wool pants on the insides of his thighs. He touched the fabric. It was wet.

Alarmed, he peeled off the pants and grimaced. The insides of his legs were raw and bloody. The skin was gone, rubbed off by Saphira's hard scales. He gingerly felt the abrasions and winced. Cold bit into him as he pulled the pants back on, and he cried out as they scraped against the sensitive wounds. He tried to stand, but his legs would not support him.

The deepening night obscured his surroundings; the shaded mountains were unfamiliar. *I'm in the Spine, I don't know where, during the middle of winter, with a crazed dragon, unable to walk or find shelter. Night is falling. I have to get back to the farm tomorrow. And the only way to do that is to fly, which I can't endure anymore.* He took a deep breath. *Oh, I wish Saphira could breathe fire.* He turned his head and saw her next to him, crouched low to the ground. He put a hand on her side and found it trembling. The barrier in her mind was gone. Without it, her fear scorched through him. He clamped down on it and slowly soothed her with gentle images. *Why do the strangers frighten you?*

Murderers, she hissed.

Garrow is in danger and you kidnap me on this ridiculous journey! Are you unable to protect me? She growled deeply and snapped her jaws. *Ah, but if you think you can, why run?*

Death is a poison.

He leaned on one elbow and stifled his frustration. *Saphira, look where we are! The sun is down, and your flight has stripped my legs as easily as I would scale a fish. Is that what you wanted?*

No.

Then why did you do it? he demanded. Through his link with Saphira, he felt her regret for his pain, but not for her actions. She looked away and refused to answer. The icy temperature deadened Eragon's legs; although it lessened the pain, he knew that his condition was not good. He changed tack. *I'm going to freeze unless you make me a shelter or hollow so I can stay warm. Even a pile of pine needles and branches would do.*

She seemed relieved that he had stopped interrogating her. *There is no need. I will curl around you and cover you with my wings—the fire inside me will stay the cold.*

Eragon let his head thump back on the ground. *Fine, but scrape the snow off the ground. It'll be more comfortable.* In answer, Saphira razed a drift with her tail, clearing it with one powerful stroke. She swept over the site again to remove the last few inches of hardened snow. He eyed the exposed dirt with distaste. *I can't walk over there. You'll have to help me to it.* Her head, larger than his torso, swung over him and came to rest by his side. He stared at her large, sapphire-colored eyes and wrapped his hands around one of her ivory spikes. She lifted her head and slowly dragged him to the bare spot. *Gently, gently.* Stars danced in his eyes as he slid over a rock, but he managed to hold on. After he let go, Saphira rolled on her side, exposing her warm belly. He huddled against the smooth scales of her underside. Her right wing extended over him and enclosed him in complete darkness, forming a living tent. Almost immediately the air began to lose its frigidity.

He pulled his arms inside his coat and tied the empty sleeves around his neck. For the first time he noticed that hunger gnawed at his stomach. But it did not distract him from his main worry: Could he get back to the farm before the strangers did? And if not, what would happen? *Even if I can force myself to ride Saphira again, it'll be at least midafternoon before we get back. The strangers could be there long before that.* He closed his eyes and felt a single tear slide down his face. *What have I done?*

THE DOOM OF
INNOCENCE

When Eragon opened his eyes in the morning, he thought the sky had fallen. An unbroken plane of blue stretched over his head and slanted to the ground. Still half asleep, he reached out tentatively and felt a thin membrane under his fingers. It took him a long minute to realize what he was staring at. He bent his neck slightly and glared at the scaly haunch his head rested on. Slowly he pushed his legs out from his fetal curl, scabs cracking. The pain had subsided some from yesterday, but he shrank from the thought of walking. Burning hunger reminded him of his missed meals. He summoned the energy to move and pounded weakly on Saphira's side. "Hey! Wake up!" he yelled.

She stirred and lifted her wing to admit a torrent of sunshine. He squinted as the snow momentarily blinded him. Beside him Saphira stretched like a cat and yawned, flashing rows of white teeth. When Eragon's eyes adjusted, he examined where they were. Imposing and unfamiliar mountains surrounded them, casting deep shadows on the clearing. Off to one side, he saw a trail cut through the snow and into the forest, where he could hear the muffled gurgling of a creek.

Groaning, he stood and swayed, then stiffly hobbled to a tree. He grabbed one of its branches and threw his weight against it. It held, then broke with a loud crack. He ripped off the twigs, fit one end of the branch under his arm, and planted the other firmly in the ground. With the help of his improvised crutch, he limped to the iced-over creek. He broke through the hard shell and cupped the clear, bitter water. Sated, he returned to the clearing. As he emerged from the trees, he finally recognized the mountains and the lay of the land.

This was where, amid deafening sound, Saphira's egg had first appeared. He sagged against a rough trunk. There could be no mistake, for now he saw the gray trees that had been stripped of their needles in the explosion. *How did Saphira know where this was? She was still in the egg. My memories must have given her enough information to find it.* He shook his head in silent astonishment.

Saphira was waiting patiently for him. *Will you*

take me home? he asked her. She cocked her head. *I know you don't want to, but you must. Both of us carry an obligation to Garrow. He has cared for me and, through me, you. Would you ignore that debt? What will be said of us in years to come if we don't return—that we hid like cowards while my uncle was in danger? I can hear it now, the story of the Rider and his craven dragon! If there will be a fight, let's face it and not shy away. You are a dragon! Even a Shade would run from you! Yet you crouch in the mountains like a frightened rabbit.*

Eragon meant to anger her, and he succeeded. A growl rippled in her throat as her head jabbed within a few inches of his face. She bared her fangs and glared at him, smoke trailing from her nostrils. He hoped that he had not gone too far. Her thoughts reached him, red with anger. *Blood will meet blood. I will fight. Our wyrds—our fates— bind us, but try me not. I will take you because of debt owed, but into foolishness we fly.*

"Foolishness or not," he said into the air, "there is no choice—we must go." He ripped his shirt in half and stuffed a piece into each side of his pants. Gingerly, he hoisted himself onto Saphira and took a tight hold on her neck. *This time,* he told her, *fly lower and faster. Time is of the essence.*

Don't let go, she cautioned, then surged into the sky. They rose above the forest and leveled out immediately, barely staying above the branches.

Eragon's stomach lurched; he was glad it was empty.

Faster, faster, he urged. She said nothing, but the beat of her wings increased. He screwed his eyes shut and hunched his shoulders. He had hoped that the extra padding of his shirt would protect him, but every movement sent pangs through his legs. Soon lines of hot blood trickled down his calves. Concern emanated from Saphira. She went even faster now, her wings straining. The land sped past, as if it were being pulled out from under them. Eragon imagined that to someone on the ground, they were just a blur.

By early afternoon, Palancar Valley lay before them. Clouds obscured his vision to the south; Carvahall was to the north. Saphira glided down while Eragon searched for the farm. When he spotted it, fear jolted him. A black plume with orange flames dancing at its base rose from the farm.

Saphira! He pointed. *Get me down there. Now!*

She locked her wings and tilted into a steep dive, hurtling groundward at a frightening rate. Then she altered her dive slightly so they sped toward the forest. He yelled over the screaming air, "Land in the fields!" He held on tighter as they plummeted. Saphira waited until they were only a hundred feet off the ground before driving her wings downward in several powerful strokes.

She landed heavily, breaking his grip. He crashed to the ground, then staggered upright, gasping for breath.

The house had been blasted apart. Timbers and boards that had been walls and roof were strewn across a wide area. The wood was pulverized, as if a giant hammer had smashed it. Sooty shingles lay everywhere. A few twisted metal plates were all that remained of the stove. The snow was perforated with smashed white crockery and chunks of bricks from the chimney. Thick, oily smoke billowed from the barn, which burned fiercely. The farm animals were gone, either killed or frightened away.

"Uncle!" Eragon ran to the wreckage, hunting through the destroyed rooms for Garrow. There was no sign of him. "Uncle!" Eragon cried again. Saphira walked around the house and came to his side.

Sorrow breeds here, she said.

"This wouldn't have happened if you hadn't run away with me!"

You would not be alive if we had stayed.

"Look at this!" he screamed. "We could've warned Garrow! It's your fault he didn't get away!" He slammed his fist against a pole, splitting the skin on his knuckles. Blood dripped down his fingers as he stalked out of the house. He stumbled to the path that led to the road and bent down to examine the snow. Several tracks were before him, but his vision was blurry and he could barely see. *Am I going blind?* he wondered. With a shaking hand, he touched his cheeks and found them wet.

A shadow fell on him as Saphira loomed overhead, sheltering him with her wings. *Take comfort; all may not be lost.* He looked up at her, searching for hope. *Examine the trail; my eyes see only two sets of prints. Garrow could not have been taken from here.*

He focused on the trampled snow. The faint imprints of two pairs of leather boots headed toward the house. On top of those were traces of the same two sets of boots leaving. And whoever had made the departing tracks had been carrying the same weight as when they arrived. *You're right, Garrow has to be here!* He leapt to his feet and hurried back to the house.

I will search around the buildings and in the forest, said Saphira.

Eragon scrambled into the remains of the kitchen and frantically started digging through a pile of rubble. Pieces of debris that he could not have moved normally now seemed to shift on their own accord. A cupboard, mostly intact, stymied him for a second, then he heaved and sent it flying. As he pulled on a board, something rattled behind him. He spun around, ready for an attack.

A hand extended from under a section of collapsed roof. It moved weakly, and he grasped it with a cry. "Uncle, can you hear me?" There was no response. Eragon tore at pieces of wood, heedless of the splinters that pierced his hands. He quickly exposed an arm and shoulder, but was barred by a heavy beam. He threw his shoulder at it and shoved with every fiber of his being, but it defied his efforts. "Saphira! I need you!"

She came immediately. Wood cracked under her feet as she crawled over the ruined walls. Without a word she nosed past him and set her side against the beam. Her claws sank into what was left of the floor; her muscles strained. With a grating sound, the beam lifted, and Eragon rushed under it. Garrow lay on his stomach, his clothes mostly torn off. Eragon pulled him out of the rubble. As soon as they were clear, Saphira released the beam, leaving it to crash to the floor.

Eragon dragged Garrow out of the destroyed house and eased him to the ground. Dismayed, he touched his uncle gently. His skin was gray, lifeless, and dry, as if a fever had burned off any sweat. His lip was split, and there was a long scrape on his cheekbone, but that was not the worst. Deep, ragged burns covered most of his body. They were chalky white and oozed clear liquid. A cloying, sickening smell hung over him—the odor of rotting fruit. His breath came in short jerks, each one sounding like a death rattle.

115

Murderers, hissed Saphira.

Don't say that. He can still be saved! We have to get him to Gertrude. I can't carry him to Carvahall, though.

Saphira presented an image of Garrow hanging under her while she flew.

Can you lift both of us?

I must.

Eragon dug through the rubble until he found a board and leather thongs. He had Saphira pierce a hole with a claw at each of the board's corners, then he looped a piece of leather through each hole and tied them to her forelegs. After checking to make sure the knots were secure, he rolled Garrow onto the board and lashed him down. As he did, a scrap of black cloth fell from his uncle's hand. It matched the strangers' clothing. He angrily stuffed it in a pocket, mounted Saphira, and closed his eyes as his body settled into a steady throb of pain. *Now!*

She leapt up, hind legs digging into the ground. Her wings clawed at the air as she slowly climbed. Tendons strained and popped as she battled gravity. For a long, painful second, nothing happened, but then she lunged forward powerfully and they rose higher. Once they were over the forest, Eragon told her, *Follow the road. It'll give you enough room if you have to land.*

I might be seen.

It doesn't matter anymore! She argued no further as she veered to the road and headed for Carvahall. Garrow swung wildly underneath them; only the slender leather cords kept him from falling.

The extra weight slowed Saphira. Before long her head sagged, and there was froth at her mouth. She struggled to continue, yet they were almost a league from Carvahall when she locked her wings and sank toward the road.

Her hind feet touched with a shower of snow. Eragon tumbled off her, landing heavily on his side to avoid hurting his legs. He struggled to his feet and worked to untie the leather from Saphira's legs. Her thick panting filled the air. *Find a safe place to rest*, he said. *I don't know how long I'll be gone, so you're going to have to take care of yourself for a while.*

I will wait, she said.

He gritted his teeth and began to drag Garrow down the road. The first few steps sent an explosion of agony through him. "I can't do this!" he howled at the sky, then took a few more steps. His mouth locked into a snarl. He stared at the ground between his feet as he forced himself to hold a steady pace. It was a fight against his unruly body—a fight he refused to lose. The minutes crawled by at an excruciating rate. Each yard he covered seemed many times that. With desperation he wondered if Carvahall still existed or if the strangers had burnt it down, too. After a time, through a haze of pain, he heard shouting and looked up.

Brom was running toward him—eyes large, hair awry, and one side of his head caked with dried blood. He waved his arms wildly before dropping his staff and grabbing Eragon's shoulders, saying something in a loud voice. Eragon blinked uncomprehendingly. Without warning, the ground rushed up to meet him. He tasted blood, then blacked out.

118

DEATHWATCH

Dreams roiled in Eragon's mind, breeding and living by their own laws. *He watched as a group of people on proud horses approached a lonely river. Many had silver hair and carried tall lances. A strange, fair ship waited for them, shining under a bright moon. The figures slowly boarded the vessel; two of them, taller than the rest, walked arm in arm. Their faces were obscured by cowls, but he could tell that one was a woman. They stood on the deck of the ship and faced the shore. A man stood alone on the pebble beach, the only one who had not boarded the ship. He threw back his head and let out a long, aching cry. As it faded, the ship glided down the river, without a breeze or oars, out into the flat, empty land. The vision clouded, but just before it disappeared, Eragon glimpsed two dragons in the sky.*

* * *

Eragon was first aware of the creaking: back and forth, back and forth. The persistent sound made him open his eyes and stare at the underside of a thatched roof. A rough blanket was draped over him, concealing his nakedness. Someone had bandaged his legs and tied a clean rag around his knuckles.

He was in a single-room hut. A mortar and pestle sat on a table with bowls and plants. Rows of dried herbs hung from the walls and suffused the air with strong, earthy aromas. Flames writhed inside a fireplace, before which sat a rotund woman in a wicker rocking chair—the town healer, Gertrude. Her head lolled, eyes closed. A pair of knitting needles and a ball of wool thread rested in her lap.

Though Eragon felt drained of willpower, he made himself sit up. That helped to clear his mind. He sifted through his memories of the last two days. His first thought was of Garrow, and his second was of Saphira. *I hope she's in a safe place.* He tried to contact her but could not. Wherever she was, it was far from Carvahall. *At least Brom got me to Carvahall. I wonder what happened to him? There was all that blood.*

Gertrude stirred and opened her sparkling eyes. "Oh," she said. "You're awake. Good!" Her voice was rich and warm. "How do you feel?"

"Well enough. Where's Garrow?"

Gertrude dragged the chair close to the bed.

"Over at Horst's. There wasn't enough room to keep both of you here. And let me tell you, it's kept me on my toes, having to run back and forth, checking to see if the two of you were all right."

Eragon swallowed his worries and asked, "How is he?"

There was a long delay as she examined her hands. "Not good. He has a fever that refuses to break, and his injuries aren't healing."

"I have to see him." He tried to get up.

"Not until you eat," she said sharply, pushing him down. "I didn't spend all this time sitting by your side so you can get back up and hurt yourself. Half the skin on your legs was torn off, and your fever broke only last night. Don't worry yourself about Garrow. He'll be fine. He's a tough man." Gertrude hung a kettle over the fire, then began chopping parsnips for soup.

"How long have I been here?"

"Two full days."

Two days! That meant his last meal had been four mornings ago! Just thinking about it made Eragon feel weak. *Saphira's been on her own this entire time; I hope she's all right.*

"The whole town wants to know what happened. They sent men down to your farm and found it destroyed." Eragon nodded; he had expected that. "Your barn was burned down. . . . Is that how Garrow was injured?"

"I . . . I don't know," said Eragon. "I wasn't there when it happened."

"Well, no matter. I'm sure it'll all get untangled." Gertrude resumed knitting while the soup cooked. "That's quite a scar on your palm."

He reflexively clenched his hand. "Yes."

"How did you get it?"

Several possible answers came to mind. He chose the simplest one. "I've had it ever since I can remember. I never asked Garrow where it came from."

"Mmm." The silence remained unbroken until the soup reached a rolling boil. Gertrude poured it in a bowl and handed it to Eragon with a spoon. He accepted it gratefully and took a cautious sip. It was delicious.

When he finished, he asked, "Can I visit Garrow now?"

Gertrude sighed. "You're a determined one, aren't you? Well, if you really want to, I won't stop you. Put on your clothes and we'll go."

She turned her back as he struggled into his pants, wincing as they dragged over the bandages, and then slipped on his shirt. Gertrude helped him stand. His legs were weak, but they did not pain him like before.

"Take a few steps," she commanded, then dryly observed, "At least you won't have to crawl there."

Outside, a blustery wind blew smoke from the

adjacent buildings into their faces. Storm clouds hid the Spine and covered the valley while a curtain of snow advanced toward the village, obscuring the foothills. Eragon leaned heavily on Gertrude as they made their way through Carvahall.

Horst had built his two-story house on a hill so he could enjoy a view of the mountains. He had lavished all of his skill on it. The shale roof shadowed a railed balcony that extended from a tall window on the second floor. Each waterspout was a snarling gargoyle, and every window and door was framed by carvings of serpents, harts, ravens, and knotted vines.

The door was opened by Elain, Horst's wife, a small, willowy woman with refined features and silky blond hair pinned into a bun. Her dress was demure and neat, and her movements graceful. "Please, come in," she said softly. They stepped over the threshold into a large well-lit room. A staircase with a polished balustrade curved down to the floor. The walls were the color of honey. Elain gave Eragon a sad smile, but addressed Gertrude. "I was just about to send for you. He isn't doing well. You should see him right away."

"Elain, you'll have to help Eragon up the stairs," Gertrude said, then hurried up them two at a time.

"It's okay, I can do it myself."

"Are you sure?" asked Elain. He nodded, but she looked doubtful. "Well . . . as soon as you're done come visit me in the kitchen. I have a fresh-baked pie you might enjoy." As soon as she left, he sagged against the wall, welcoming the support. Then he started up the stairs, one painful step at a time. When he reached the top, he looked down a long hallway dotted with doors. The last one was open slightly. Taking a breath, he lurched toward it.

Katrina stood by a fireplace, boiling rags. She looked up, murmured a condolence, and then returned to her work. Gertrude stood beside her, grinding herbs for a poultice. A bucket by her feet held snow melting into ice water.

Garrow lay on a bed piled high with blankets. Sweat covered his brow, and his eyeballs flickered blindly under their lids. The skin on his face was shrunken like a cadaver's. He was still, save for subtle tremors from his shallow breathing. Eragon touched his uncle's forehead with a feeling of unreality. It burned against his hand. He apprehensively lifted the edge of the blankets and saw that Garrow's many wounds were bound with strips of cloth. Where the bandages were being changed, the burns were exposed to the air. They had not begun to heal. Eragon looked at Gertrude with hopeless eyes. "Can't you do anything about these?"

She pressed a rag into the bucket of ice water,

then draped the cool cloth over Garrow's head. "I've tried everything: salves, poultices, tinctures, but nothing works. If the wounds closed, he would have a better chance. Still, things may turn for the better. He's hardy and strong."

Eragon moved to a corner and sank to the floor. *This isn't the way things are supposed to be!* Silence swallowed his thoughts. He stared blankly at the bed. After a while he noticed Katrina kneeling beside him. She put an arm around him. When he did not respond, she diffidently left.

Sometime later the door opened and Horst came in. He talked to Gertrude in a low voice, then approached Eragon. "Come on. You need to get out of here." Before Eragon could protest, Horst dragged him to his feet and shepherded him out the door.

"I want to stay," he complained.

"You need a break and fresh air. Don't worry, you can go back soon enough," consoled Horst.

Eragon grudgingly let the smith help him downstairs into the kitchen. Heady smells from half a dozen dishes—rich with spices and herbs— filled the air. Albriech and Baldor were there, talking with their mother as she kneaded bread. The brothers fell silent as they saw Eragon, but he had heard enough to know that they were discussing Garrow.

"Here, sit down," said Horst, offering a chair. Eragon sank into it gratefully. "Thank you."

His hands were shaking slightly, so he clasped them in his lap. A plate, piled high with food, was set before him.

"You don't have to eat," said Elain, "but it's there if you want." She returned to her cooking as he picked up a fork. He could barely swallow a few bites.

"How do you feel?" asked Horst.

"Terrible."

The smith waited a moment. "I know this isn't the best time, but we need to know . . . what happened?"

"I don't really remember."

"Eragon," said Horst, leaning forward, "I was one of the people who went out to your farm. Your house didn't just fall apart—something tore it to pieces. Surrounding it were tracks of a gigantic beast I've never seen nor heard of before. Others saw them too. Now, if there's a Shade or a monster roaming around, we have to know. You're the only one who can tell us."

Eragon knew he had to lie. "When I left Carvahall . . . ," he counted up the time, "four days ago, there were . . . strangers in town asking about a stone like the one I found." He gestured at Horst. "You talked to me about them, and because of that, I hurried home." All eyes were upon him. He licked his lips. "Nothing . . . nothing happened that night. The next morning I finished my chores and went walking in the forest.

Before long I heard an explosion and saw smoke above the trees. I rushed back as fast as I could, but whoever did it was already gone. I dug through the wreckage and . . . found Garrow."

"So then you put him on the plank and dragged him back?" asked Albriech.

"Yes," said Eragon, "but before I left, I looked at the path to the road. There were two pairs of tracks on it, both of them men's." He dug in his pocket and pulled out the scrap of black fabric. "This was clenched in Garrow's hand. I think it matches what those strangers were wearing." He set it on the table.

"It does," said Horst. He looked both thoughtful and angry. "And what of your legs? How were they injured?"

"I'm not sure," said Eragon, shaking his head. "I think it happened when I dug Garrow out, but I don't know. It wasn't until the blood started dripping down my legs that I noticed it."

"That's horrible!" exclaimed Elain.

"We should pursue those men," stated Albriech hotly. "They can't get away with this! With a pair of horses we could catch them tomorrow and bring them back here."

"Put that foolishness out of your head," said Horst. "They could probably pick you up like a baby and throw you in a tree. Remember what happened to the house? We don't want to get in the way of those people. Besides, they have what they want now." He looked at Eragon. "They did take the stone, didn't they?"

"It wasn't in the house."

"Then there's no reason for them to return now that they have it." He gave Eragon a piercing look. "You didn't mention anything about those strange tracks. Do you know where they came from?"

Eragon shook his head. "I didn't see them."

Baldor abruptly spoke. "I don't like this. Too much of this rings of wizardry. Who are those men? Are they Shades? Why did they want the stone, and how could they have destroyed the house except with dark powers? You may be right, Father, the stone might be all they wanted, but I think we will see them again."

Silence followed his words.

Something had been overlooked, though Eragon was not sure what. Then it struck him. With a sinking heart, he voiced his suspicion. "Roran doesn't know, does he?" *How could I have forgotten him?*

Horst shook his head. "He and Dempton left a little while after you. Unless they ran into some difficulty on the road, they've been in Therinsford for a couple of days now. We were going to send a message, but the weather was too cold yesterday and the day before."

"Baldor and I were about to leave when you woke up," offered Albriech.

Horst ran a hand through his beard. "Go on, both of you. I'll help you saddle the horses."

Baldor turned to Eragon. "I'll break it to him gently," he promised, then followed Horst and Albriech out of the kitchen.

Eragon remained at the table, his eyes focused on a knot in the wood. Every excruciating detail was clear to him: the twisting grain, an asymmetrical bump, three little ridges with a fleck of color. The knot was filled with endless detail; the closer he looked, the more he saw. He searched for answers in it, but if there were any, they eluded him.

A faint call broke through his pounding thoughts. It sounded like yelling from outside. He ignored it. *Let someone else deal with it.* Several minutes later he heard it again, louder than before. Angrily, he blocked it out. *Why can't they be quiet? Garrow's resting.* He glanced at Elain, but she did not seem to be bothered by the noise.

ERAGON! The roar was so strong he almost fell out of the chair. He peered around in alarm, but nothing had changed. He suddenly realized that the shouts had been inside his head.

Saphira? he asked anxiously.

There was a pause. *Yes, stone ears.*

Relief seeped into him. *Where are you?*

She sent him an image of a small clump of trees. *I tried to contact you many times, but you were beyond reach.*

129

I was sick . . . but I'm better now. Why couldn't I sense you earlier?

After two nights of waiting, hunger bested me. I had to hunt.

Did you catch anything?

A young buck. He was wise enough to guard against the predators of land, but not those of sky. When I first caught him in my jaws, he kicked vigorously and tried to escape. I was stronger, though, and when defeat became unavoidable, he gave up and died. Does Garrow also fight the inevitable?

I don't know. He told her the particulars, then said, *It'll be a long time, if ever, before we can go home. I won't be able to see you for at least a couple of days. You might as well make yourself comfortable.*

Unhappily, she said, *I will do as you say. But do not take too long.*

They parted reluctantly. He looked out a window and was surprised to see that the sun had set. Feeling very tired, he limped to Elain, who was wrapping meat pies with oilcloth. "I'm going back to Gertrude's house to sleep," he said.

She finished with the packages and asked, "Why don't you stay with us? You'll be closer to your uncle, and Gertrude can have her bed back."

"Do you have enough room?" he asked, wavering.

"Of course." She wiped her hands. "Come

with me; I'll get everything ready." She escorted him upstairs to an empty room. He sat on the edge of the bed. "Do you need anything else?" she asked. He shook his head. "In that case, I'll be downstairs. Call me if you need help." He listened as she descended the stairs. Then he opened the door and slipped down the hallway to Garrow's room. Gertrude gave him a small smile over her darting knitting needles.

"How is he?" whispered Eragon.

Her voice rasped with fatigue. "He's weak, but the fever's gone down a little and some of the burns look better. We'll have to wait and see, but this could mean he'll recover."

That lightened Eragon's mood, and he returned to his room. The darkness seemed unfriendly as he huddled under the blankets. Eventually he fell asleep, healing the wounds his body and soul had suffered.

THE MADNESS OF
LIFE

It was dark when Eragon jolted upright in bed, breathing hard. The room was chilly; goose bumps formed on his arms and shoulders. It was a few hours before dawn—the time when nothing moves and life waits for the first warm touches of sunlight.

His heart pounded as a terrible premonition gripped him. It felt like a shroud lay over the world, and its darkest corner was over his room. He quietly got out of bed and dressed. With apprehension he hurried down the hallway. Alarm shot through him when he saw the door to Garrow's room open and people clustered inside.

Garrow lay peacefully on the bed. He was dressed in clean clothes, his hair had been combed back, and his face was calm. He might have been sleeping if not for the silver amulet clasped around his neck and the sprig of dried

132

hemlock on his chest, the last gifts from the living to the dead.

Katrina stood next to the bed, face pale and eyes downcast. He heard her whisper, "I had hoped to call him *Father* one day. . . ."

Call him Father, he thought bitterly, *a right even I don't have.* He felt like a ghost, drained of all vitality. Everything was insubstantial except for Garrow's face. Tears flooded Eragon's cheeks. He stood there, shoulders shaking, but did not cry out. Mother, aunt, uncle—he had lost them all. The weight of his grief was crushing, a monstrous force that left him tottering. Someone led him back to his room, uttering consolations.

He fell on the bed, wrapped his arms around his head, and sobbed convulsively. He felt Saphira contact him, but he pushed her aside and let himself be swept away by sorrow. He could not accept that Garrow was gone. If he did, what was left to believe in? Only a merciless, uncaring world that snuffed lives like candles before a wind. Frustrated and terrified, he turned his tear-dampened face toward the heavens and shouted, "What god would do this? Show yourself!" He heard people running to his room, but no answer came from above. "He didn't deserve this!"

Comforting hands touched him, and he was aware of Elain sitting next to him. She held him as he cried, and eventually, exhausted, he slipped unwillingly into sleep.

133

A RIDER'S BLADE

Anguish enveloped Eragon as he awoke.
Though he kept his eyes closed, they could
not stop a fresh flow of tears. He searched
for some idea or hope to help him keep his sanity.
I can't live with this, he moaned.

Then don't. Saphira's words reverberated in his
head.

*How? Garrow is gone forever! And in time, I
must meet the same fate. Love, family, accomplishments—they are all torn away, leaving nothing.
What is the worth of anything we do?*

*The worth is in the act. Your worth halts when you
surrender the will to change and experience life. But
options are before you; choose one and dedicate
yourself to it. The deeds will give you new hope and
purpose.*

But what can I do?

*The only true guide is your heart. Nothing less
than its supreme desire can help you.*

134

She left him to ponder her statements. Eragon examined his emotions. It surprised him that, more than grief, he found a searing anger. *What do you want me to do . . . pursue the strangers?*

Yes.

Her frank answer confused him. He took a deep, trembling breath. *Why?*

Remember what you said in the Spine? How you reminded me of my duty as dragon, and I returned with you despite the urging of my instinct? So, too, must you control yourself. I thought long and deep the past few days, and I realized what it means to be dragon and Rider: It is our destiny to attempt the impossible, to accomplish great deeds regardless of fear. It is our responsibility to the future.

I don't care what you say; those aren't reasons to leave! cried Eragon.

Then here are others. My tracks have been seen, and people are alert to my presence. Eventually I will be exposed. Besides, there is nothing here for you. No farm, no family, and—

Roran's not dead! he said vehemently.

But if you stay, you'll have to explain what really happened. He has a right to know how and why his father died. What might he do once he knows of me?

Saphira's arguments whirled around in Eragon's head, but he shrank from the idea of forsaking Palancar Valley; it was his home. Yet the thought of enacting vengeance on the strangers was fiercely comforting. *Am I strong enough for this?*

You have me.

Doubt besieged him. It would be such a wild, desperate thing to do. Contempt for his indecision rose, and a harsh smile danced on his lips. Saphira was right. Nothing mattered anymore except the act itself. *The doing is the thing.* And what would give him more satisfaction than hunting down the strangers? A terrible energy and strength began to grow in him. It grabbed his emotions and forged them into a solid bar of anger with one word stamped on it: revenge. His head pounded as he said with conviction, *I will do it.*

He severed the contact with Saphira and rolled out of bed, his body tense like a coiled spring. It was still early morning; he had only slept a few hours. *Nothing is more dangerous than an enemy with nothing to lose*, he thought. *Which is what I have become.*

Yesterday he had had difficulty walking upright, but now he moved confidently, held in place by his iron will. The pain his body sent him was defied and ignored.

As he crept out of the house, he heard the murmur of two people talking. Curious, he stopped and listened. Elain was saying in her gentle voice, ". . . place to stay. We have room." Horst answered inaudibly in his bass rumble. "Yes, the poor boy," replied Elain.

This time Eragon could hear Horst's response.

"Maybe . . ." There was a long pause. "I've been thinking about what Eragon said, and I'm not sure he told us everything."

"What do you mean?" asked Elain. There was concern in her voice.

"When we started for their farm, the road was scraped smooth by the board he dragged Garrow on. Then we reached a place where the snow was all trampled and churned up. His footprints and signs of the board stopped there, but we also saw the same giant tracks from the farm. And what about his legs? I can't believe he didn't notice losing that much skin. I didn't want to push him for answers earlier, but now I think I will."

"Maybe what he saw scared him so much that he doesn't want to talk about it," suggested Elain. "You saw how distraught he was."

"That still doesn't explain how he managed to get Garrow nearly all the way here without leaving any tracks."

Saphira was right, thought Eragon. *It's time to leave. Too many questions from too many people. Sooner or later they'll find the answers.* He continued through the house, tensing whenever the floor creaked.

The streets were clear; few people were up at this time of day. He stopped for a minute and forced himself to focus. *I don't need a horse. Saphira will be my steed, but she needs a saddle. She can hunt for both of us, so I don't have to worry*

about food—though I should get some anyway.
Whatever else I need I can find buried in our house.

He went to Gedric's tanning vats on the outskirts of Carvahall. The vile smell made him cringe, but he kept moving, heading for a shack set into the side of a hill where the cured hides were stored. He cut down three large ox hides from the rows of skins hanging from the ceiling. The thievery made him feel guilty, but he reasoned, *It's not really stealing. I'll pay Gedric back someday, along with Horst.* He rolled up the thick leather and took it to a stand of trees away from the village. He wedged the hides between the branches of a tree, then returned to Carvahall.

Now for food. He went to the tavern, intending to get it there, but then smiled tightly and reversed direction. If he was going to steal, it might as well be from Sloan. He sneaked up to the butcher's house. The front door was barred whenever Sloan was not there, but the side door was secured with only a thin chain, which he broke easily. The rooms inside were dark. He fumbled blindly until his hands came upon hard piles of meat wrapped in cloth. He stuffed as many of them as he could under his shirt, then hurried back to the street and furtively closed the door.

A woman shouted his name nearby. He clasped the bottom of his shirt to keep the meat from falling out and ducked behind a corner. He

138

shivered as Horst walked between two houses not ten feet away.

Eragon ran as soon as Horst was out of sight. His legs burned as he pounded down an alley and back to the trees. He slipped between the tree trunks, then turned to see if he was being pursued. No one was there. Relieved, he let out his breath and reached into the tree for the leather. It was gone.

"Going somewhere?"

Eragon whirled around. Brom scowled angrily at him, an ugly wound on the side of his head. A short sword hung at his belt in a brown sheath. The hides were in his hands.

Eragon's eyes narrowed in irritation. How had the old man managed to sneak up on him? Everything had been so quiet, he would have sworn that no one was around. "Give them back," he snapped.

"Why? So you can run off before Garrow is even buried?" The accusation was sharp.

"It's none of your business!" he barked, temper flashing. "Why did you follow me?"

"I didn't," grunted Brom. "I've been waiting for you here. Now where are you going?"

"Nowhere." Eragon lunged for the skins and grabbed them from Brom's hands. Brom did nothing to stop him.

"I hope you have enough meat to feed your dragon."

Eragon froze. "What are you talking about?"

Brom crossed his arms. "Don't fool with me. I know where that mark on your hand, the gedwëy ignasia, the *shining palm,* comes from: you have touched a dragon hatchling. I know why you came to me with those questions, and I know that once more the Riders live."

Eragon dropped the leather and meat. *It's finally happened . . . I have to get away! I can't run faster than him with my injured legs, but if . . . Saphira!* he called.

For a few agonizing seconds she did not answer, but then, *Yes.*

We've been discovered! I need you! He sent her a picture of where he was, and she took off immediately. Now he just had to stall Brom. "How did you find out?" he asked in a hollow voice.

Brom stared into the distance and moved his lips soundlessly as if he were talking to someone else. Then he said, "There were clues and hints everywhere; I had only to pay attention. Anyone with the right knowledge could have done the same. Tell me, how is your dragon?"

"She," said Eragon, "is fine. We weren't at the farm when the strangers came."

"Ah, your legs. You were flying?"

How did Brom figure that out? What if the strangers coerced him into doing this? Maybe they want him to discover where I'm going so they can ambush us. And where is Saphira? He reached out

with his mind and found her circling far overhead. *Come!*

No, I will watch for a time.

Why!

Because of the slaughter at Doru Araeba.

What?

Brom leaned against a tree with a slight smile.
"I have talked with her, and she has agreed to
stay above us until we settle our differences. As
you can see, you really don't have any choice but
to answer my questions. Now tell me, where are
you going?"

Bewildered, Eragon put a hand to his temple.
How could Brom speak to Saphira? The back of his
head throbbed and ideas whirled through his
mind, but he kept reaching the same conclusion:
he had to tell the old man something. He said, "I
was going to find a safe place to stay while I heal."

"And after that?"

The question could not be ignored. The
throbbing in his head grew worse. It was impossible to think; nothing seemed clear anymore. All
he wanted to do was tell someone about the
events of the past few months. It tore at him that
his secret had caused Garrow's death. He gave up
and said tremulously, "I was going to hunt down
the strangers and kill them."

"A mighty task for one so young," Brom said in
a normal tone, as if Eragon had proposed the
most obvious and suitable thing to do. "Certainly

a worthy endeavor and one you are fit to carry out, yet it strikes me that help would not be unwelcome." He reached behind a bush and pulled out a large pack. His tone became gruff. "Anyway, I'm not going to stay behind while some stripling gets to run around with a dragon."

Is he really offering help, or is it a trap? Eragon was afraid of what his mysterious enemies could do. *But Brom convinced Saphira to trust him, and they've talked through the mind touch. If she isn't worried . . .* He decided to put his suspicions aside for the present. "I don't need help," said Eragon, then grudgingly added, "but you can come."

"Then we had best be going," said Brom. His face blanked for a moment. "I think you'll find that your dragon will listen to you again."

Saphira? asked Eragon.

Yes.

He resisted the urge to question her. *Will you meet us at the farm?*

Yes. So you reached an agreement?

I guess so. She broke contact and soared away. He glanced at Carvahall and saw people running from house to house. "I think they're looking for me."

Brom raised an eyebrow. "Probably. Shall we go?"

Eragon hesitated. "I'd like to leave a message for Roran. It doesn't seem right to run off without telling him why."

"It's been taken care of," assured Brom. "I left a letter for him with Gertrude, explaining a few things. I also cautioned him to be on guard for certain dangers. Is that satisfactory?"

Eragon nodded. He wrapped the leather around the meat and started off. They were careful to stay out of sight until they reached the road, then quickened their pace, eager to distance themselves from Carvahall. Eragon plowed ahead determinedly, his legs burning. The mindless rhythm of walking freed his mind to think. *Once we get home, I won't travel any farther with Brom until I get some answers,* he told himself firmly. *I hope that he can tell me more about the Riders and whom I'm fighting.*

As the wreckage of the farm came into view, Brom's eyebrows beetled with anger. Eragon was dismayed to see how swiftly nature was reclaiming the farm. Snow and dirt were already piled inside the house, concealing the violence of the strangers' attack. All that remained of the barn was a rapidly eroding rectangle of soot.

Brom's head snapped up as the sound of Saphira's wings drifted over the trees. She dived past them from behind, almost brushing their heads. They staggered as a wall of air buffeted them. Saphira's scales glittered as she wheeled over the farm and landed gracefully.

Brom stepped forward with an expression both solemn and joyous. His eyes were shining, and a

143

tear shone on his cheek before it disappeared into his beard. He stood there for a long while, breathing heavily as he watched Saphira, and she him. Eragon heard him muttering and edged closer to listen.

"So . . . it starts again. But how and where will it end? My sight is veiled; I cannot tell if this be tragedy or farce, for the elements of both are here. . . . However it may be, my station is unchanged, and I . . ."

Whatever else he might have said faded away as Saphira proudly approached them. Eragon passed Brom, pretended he had heard nothing, and greeted her. There was something different between them now, as if they knew each other even more intimately, yet were still strangers. He rubbed her neck, and his palm tingled as their minds touched. A strong curiosity came from her.

I've seen no humans except you and Garrow, and he was badly injured, she said.

You've viewed people through my eyes.

It's not the same. She came closer and turned her long head so that she could inspect Brom with one large blue eye. *You really are queer creatures,* she said critically, and continued to stare at him. Brom held still as she sniffed the air, and then he extended a hand to her. Saphira slowly bowed her head and allowed him to touch her on the brow. With a snort, she jerked back and retreated behind Eragon. Her tail flicked over the ground.

What is it? he asked. She did not answer.

Brom turned to him and asked in an undertone, "What's her name?"

"Saphira." A peculiar expression crossed Brom's face. He ground the butt of his staff into the earth with such force his knuckles turned white. "Of all the names you gave me, it was the only one she liked. I think it fits," Eragon added quickly.

"Fit it does," said Brom. There was something in his voice Eragon could not identify. Was it loss, wonder, fear, envy? He was not sure; it could have been none of them or all. Brom raised his voice and said, "Greetings, Saphira. I am honored to meet you." He twisted his hand in a strange gesture and bowed.

I like him, said Saphira quietly.

Of course you do; everyone enjoys flattery. Eragon touched her on the shoulder and went to the ruined house. Saphira trailed behind with Brom. The old man looked vibrant and alive.

Eragon climbed into the house and crawled under a door into what was left of his room. He barely recognized it under the piles of shattered wood. Guided by memory, he searched where the inside wall had been and found his empty pack. Part of the frame was broken, but the damage could be easily repaired. He kept rummaging and eventually uncovered the end of his bow, which was still in its buckskin tube.

Though the leather was scratched and scuffed, he was pleased to see that the oiled wood was unharmed. *Finally, some luck.* He strung the bow and pulled on the sinew experimentally. It bent smoothly, without any snaps or creaks. Satisfied, he hunted for his quiver, which he found buried nearby. Many of the arrows were broken.

He unstrung the bow and handed it and the quiver to Brom, who said, "It takes a strong arm to pull that." Eragon took the compliment silently. He picked through the rest of the house for other useful items and dumped the collection next to Brom. It was a meager pile. "What now?" asked Brom. His eyes were sharp and inquisitive. Eragon looked away.

"We find a place to hide."

"Do you have somewhere in mind?"

"Yes." He wrapped all the supplies, except for his bow, into a tight bundle and tied it shut. Hefting it onto his back, he said, "This way," and headed into the forest. *Saphira, follow us in the air. Your footprints are too easily found and tracked.*

Very well. She took off behind them.

Their destination was nearby, but Eragon took a circuitous route in an effort to baffle any pursuers. It was well over an hour before he finally stopped in a well-concealed bramble.

The irregular clearing in the center was just

large enough for a fire, two people, and a dragon. Red squirrels scampered into the trees, chattering in protest at their intrusion. Brom extricated himself from a vine and looked around with interest. "Does anyone else know of this?" he asked.

"No. I found it when we first moved here. It took me a week to dig into the center, and another week to clear out all the deadwood." Saphira landed beside them and folded her wings, careful to avoid the thorns. She curled up, snapping twigs with her hard scales, and rested her head on the ground. Her unreadable eyes followed them closely.

Brom leaned against his staff and fixed his gaze on her. His scrutiny made Eragon nervous.

Eragon watched them until hunger forced him to action. He built a fire, filled a pot with snow, and then set it over the flames to melt. When the water was hot, he tore off chunks of meat and dropped them into the pot with a lump of salt. *Not much of a meal,* he thought grimly, *but it'll do. I'll probably be eating this for some time to come, so I might as well get used to it.*

The stew simmered quietly, spreading a rich aroma through the clearing. The tip of Saphira's tongue snaked out and tasted the air. When the meat was tender, Brom came over and Eragon served the food. They ate silently, avoiding each other's eyes. Afterward, Brom pulled out his pipe and lit it leisurely.

"Why do you want to travel with me?" asked Eragon.

A cloud of smoke left Brom's lips and spiraled up through the trees until it disappeared. "I have a vested interest in keeping you alive," he said.

"What do you mean?" demanded Eragon.

"To put it bluntly, I'm a storyteller and I happen to think that you will make a fine story. You're the first Rider to exist outside of the king's control for over a hundred years. What will happen? Will you perish as a martyr? Will you join the Varden? Or will you kill King Galbatorix? All fascinating questions. And I will be there to see every bit of it, no matter what I have to do."

A knot formed in Eragon's stomach. He could not see himself doing any of those things, least of all becoming a martyr. *I want my vengeance, but for the rest . . . I have no ambition.* "That may be, but tell me, how can you talk with Saphira?"

Brom took his time putting more tobacco in his pipe. Once it was relit and firmly in his mouth, he said, "Very well, if it's answers you want, it's answers you'll get, but they may not be to your liking." He got up, brought his pack over to the fire, and pulled out a long object wrapped in cloth. It was about three and a half feet long and, from the way he handled it, rather heavy.

He peeled away the cloth, strip by strip, like a mummy being unswathed. Eragon gazed, transfixed, as a sword was revealed. The gold pommel was teardrop shaped with the sides cut away to reveal a ruby the size of a small egg. The hilt was wrapped in silver wire, burnished until it gleamed like starlight. The sheath was wine red and smooth as glass, adorned solely by a strange black symbol etched into it. Next to the sword was a leather belt with a heavy buckle. The last strip fell away, and Brom passed the weapon to Eragon.

The handle fit Eragon's hand as if it had been made for him. He slowly drew the sword; it slid soundlessly from the sheath. The flat blade was iridescent red and shimmered in the firelight. The keen edges curved gracefully to a sharp point. A duplicate of the black symbol was inscribed on the metal. The balance of the sword was perfect; 149 it felt like an extension of his arm, unlike the rude farm tools he was used to. An air of power lay over it, as if an unstoppable force resided in its core. It had been created for the violent convulsions of battle, to end men's lives, yet it held a terrible beauty.

"This was once a Rider's blade," said Brom gravely. "When a Rider finished his training, the elves would present him with a sword. Their methods of forging have always remained secret. However, their swords are eternally sharp and will never stain. The custom was to have the blade's color match that of the Rider's dragon, but I think we can make an exception in this case. This sword is named Zar'roc. I don't know what it means, probably something personal to the Rider who owned it." He watched Eragon swing the sword.

"Where did you get it?" asked Eragon. He reluctantly slipped the blade back into the sheath and attempted to hand the sword back, but Brom made no move to take it.

"It doesn't matter," said Brom. "I will only say that it took me a series of nasty and dangerous adventures to attain it. Consider it yours. You have more of a claim to it than I do, and before all is done, I think you will need it."

The offer caught Eragon off guard. "It is a princely gift, thank you." Unsure of what else to say, he slid his hand down the sheath. "What is this symbol?" he asked.

"That was the Rider's personal crest." Eragon tried to interrupt, but Brom glared at him until he was quiet. "Now, if you must know, anyone can learn how to speak to a dragon if they have the proper training. And," he raised a finger for emphasis, "it doesn't mean anything if they can. I know more about the dragons and their abilities than almost anyone else alive. On your own it might take years to learn what I can teach you. I'm offering my knowledge as a shortcut. As for how I know so much, I will keep *that* to myself."

Saphira pulled herself up as he finished speaking and prowled over to Eragon. He pulled out the blade and showed her the sword. *It has power,* she said, touching the point with her nose. The metal's iridescent color rippled like water as it met her scales. She lifted her head with a satisfied snort, and the sword resumed its normal appearance. Eragon sheathed it, troubled.

Brom raised an eyebrow. "That's the sort of thing I'm talking about. Dragons will constantly amaze you. Things . . . happen around them, mysterious things that are impossible anywhere else. Even though the Riders worked with dragons for centuries, they never completely understood their abilities. Some say that even the dragons don't know the full extent of their own powers. They are linked with this land in a way that lets them overcome great obstacles. What Saphira just did illustrates my earlier point: there is much you don't know."

There was a long pause. "That may be," said Eragon, "but I can learn. And the strangers are the most important thing I need to know about right now. Do you have any idea who they are?"

Brom took a deep breath. "They are called the Ra'zac. No one knows if that's the name of their race or what they have chosen to call themselves. Either way, if they have individual names, they keep them hidden. The Ra'zac were never seen before Galbatorix came to power. He must have found them during his travels and enlisted them in his service. Little or nothing is known about them. However, I can tell you this: they aren't human. When I glimpsed one's head, it appeared to have something resembling a beak and black eyes as large as my fist—though how they manage our speech is a mystery to me. Doubtless the rest of their bodies are just as twisted. That is why they cover themselves with cloaks at all times, regardless of the weather.

"As for their powers, they are stronger than any man and can jump incredible heights, but they cannot use magic. Be thankful for that, because if they could, you would already be in their grasp. I also know they have a strong aversion to sunlight, though it won't stop them if they're determined. Don't make the mistake of underestimating a Ra'zac, for they are cunning and full of guile."

"How many of them are there?" asked Eragon, wondering how Brom could possibly know so much.

"As far as I know, only the two you saw. There might be more, but I've never heard of them. Perhaps they're the last of a dying race. You see, they are the king's personal dragon hunters. Whenever rumors reach Galbatorix of a dragon in the land, he sends the Ra'zac to investigate. A trail of death often follows them." Brom blew a series of smoke rings and watched them float up between the brambles. Eragon ignored the rings until he noticed that they were changing color and darting around. Brom winked slyly.

Eragon was sure that no one had seen Saphira, so how could Galbatorix have heard about her? When he voiced his objections, Brom said, "You're right, it seems unlikely that anyone from Carvahall could have informed the king. Why don't you tell me where you got the egg and how you raised Saphira—that might clarify the issue."

Eragon hesitated, then recounted all the events since he had found the egg in the Spine. It felt wonderful to finally confide in someone. Brom asked a few questions, but most of the time he listened intently. The sun was about to set when Eragon finished his tale. Both of them were quiet as the clouds turned a soft pink. Eragon eventually broke the silence. "I just wish I knew where she came from. And Saphira doesn't remember."

Brom cocked his head. "I don't know. . . . You've made many things clear to me. I am sure that no one besides us has seen Saphira. The Ra'zac must have had a source of information outside of this valley, one who is probably dead by now. . . . You have had a hard time and done much. I'm impressed."

Eragon stared blankly into the distance, then asked, "What happened to your head? It looks like you were hit with a rock."

"No, but that's a good guess." He took a deep pull on the pipe. "I was sneaking around the Ra'zac's camp after dark, trying to learn what I could, when they surprised me in the shadows. It was a good trap, but they underestimated me, and I managed to drive them away. Not, however," he said wryly, "without this token of my stupidity. Stunned, I fell to the ground and didn't regain consciousness until the next day. By then they had already arrived at your farm. It was too late to stop them, but I set out after them anyway. That's when we met on the road."

Who is he to think that he could take on the Ra'zac alone? They ambushed him in the dark, and he was only stunned? Unsettled, Eragon asked hotly, "When you saw the mark, the gedwëy ignasia, on my palm, why didn't you tell me who the Ra'zac were? I would have warned Garrow instead of going to Saphira first, and the three of us could have fled."

Brom sighed. "I was unsure of what to do at the time. I thought I could keep the Ra'zac away from you and, once they had left, confront you about Saphira. But they outsmarted me. It's a mistake that I deeply regret, and one that has cost you dearly."

"Who are you?" demanded Eragon, suddenly bitter. "How come a mere village storyteller happens to have a Rider's sword? How do you know about the Ra'zac?"

Brom tapped his pipe. "I thought I made it clear I wasn't going to talk about that."

"My uncle is dead because of this. *Dead!*" exclaimed Eragon, slashing a hand through the air. "I've trusted you this far because Saphira respects you, but no more! You're not the person I've known in Carvahall for all of these years. Explain yourself!"

For a long time Brom stared at the smoke swirling between them, deep lines creasing his forehead. When he stirred, it was only to take another puff. Finally he said, "You've probably never thought about it, but most of my life has been spent outside of Palancar Valley. It was only in Carvahall that I took up the mantle of storyteller. I have played many roles to different people—I've a complicated past. It was partly through a desire to escape it that I came here. So no, I'm not the man you think I am."

"Ha!" snorted Eragon. "Then who are you?"

Brom smiled gently. "I am one who is here to help you. Do not scorn those words—they are the truest I've ever spoken. But I'm not going to answer your questions. At this point you don't need to hear my history, nor have you yet earned that right. Yes, I have knowledge Brom the storyteller wouldn't, but I'm more than he. You'll have to learn to live with that fact and the fact that I don't hand out descriptions of my life to anyone who asks!"

Eragon glared at him sullenly. "I'm going to sleep," he said, leaving the fire.

Brom did not seem surprised, but there was sorrow in his eyes. He spread his bedroll next to the fire as Eragon lay beside Saphira. An icy silence fell over the camp.

SADDLEMAKING

When Eragon's eyes opened, the memory of Garrow's death crashed down on him. He pulled the blankets over his head and cried quietly under their warm darkness. It felt good just to lie there . . . to hide from the world outside. Eventually the tears stopped. He cursed Brom. Then he reluctantly wiped his cheeks and got up.

Brom was making breakfast. "Good morning," he said. Eragon grunted in reply. He jammed his cold fingers in his armpits and crouched by the fire until the food was ready. They ate quickly, trying to consume the food before it lost its warmth. When he finished, Eragon washed his bowl with snow, then spread the stolen leather on the ground.

"What are you going to do with that?" asked Brom. "We can't carry it with us."

"I'm going to make a saddle for Saphira."

"Mmm," said Brom, moving forward. "Well, dragons used to have two kinds of saddles. The first was hard and molded like a horse's saddle. But those take time and tools to make, neither of which we have. The other was thin and lightly padded, nothing more than an extra layer between the Rider and dragon. Those saddles were used whenever speed and flexibility were important, though they weren't nearly as comfortable as the molded ones."

"Do you know what they looked like?" asked Eragon.

"Better, I can make one."

"Then please do," said Eragon, standing aside.

"Very well, but pay attention. Someday you may have to do this for yourself." With Saphira's permission, Brom measured her neck and chest. Then he cut five bands out of the leather and outlined a dozen or so shapes on the hides. Once the pieces had been sliced out, he cut what remained of the hides into long cords.

Brom used the cords to sew everything together, but for each stitch, two holes had to be bored through the leather. Eragon helped with that. Intricate knots were rigged in place of buckles, and every strap was made extra long so the saddle would still fit Saphira in the coming months.

The main part of the saddle was assembled

from three identical sections sewn together with padding between them. Attached to the front was a thick loop that would fit snugly around one of Saphira's neck spikes, while wide bands sewn on either side would wrap around her belly and tie underneath. Taking the place of stirrups were a series of loops running down both bands. Tightened, they would hold Eragon's legs in place. A long strap was constructed to pass between Saphira's front legs, split in two, and then come up behind her front legs to rejoin with the saddle.

While Brom worked, Eragon repaired his pack and organized their supplies. The day was spent by the time their tasks were completed. Weary from his labor, Brom put the saddle on Saphira and checked to see that the straps fit. He made a few small adjustments, then took it off, satisfied.

159

"You did a good job," Eragon acknowledged grudgingly.

Brom inclined his head. "One tries his best. It should serve you well; the leather's sturdy enough."

Aren't you going to try it out? asked Saphira.

Maybe tomorrow, said Eragon, storing the saddle with his blankets. *It's too late now.* In truth he was not eager to fly again—not after the disastrous outcome of his last attempt.

Dinner was made quickly. It tasted good even though it was simple. While they ate, Brom looked over the fire at Eragon and asked, "Will we leave tomorrow?"

"There isn't any reason to stay."

"I suppose not. . . ." He shifted. "Eragon, I must apologize about how events have turned out. I never wished for this to happen. Your family did not deserve such a tragedy. If there were anything I could do to reverse it, I would. This is a terrible situation for all of us." Eragon sat in silence, avoiding Brom's gaze, then Brom said, "We're going to need horses."

"Maybe you do, but I have Saphira."

Brom shook his head. "There isn't a horse alive that can outrun a flying dragon, and Saphira is too young to carry us both. Besides, it'll be safer if we stay together, and riding is faster than walking."

"But that'll make it harder to catch the Ra'zac," protested Eragon. "On Saphira, I could probably find them within a day or two. On horses, it'll take much longer—if it's even possible to overtake their lead on the ground!"

Brom said slowly, "That's a chance you'll have to take if I'm to accompany you."

Eragon thought it over. "All right," he grumbled, "we'll get horses. But you have to buy them. I don't have any money, and I don't want to steal again. It's wrong."

"That depends on your point of view," corrected Brom with a slight smile. "Before you set out on this venture, remember that your enemies, the Ra'zac, are the king's servants. They will be protected wherever they go. Laws do not stop them. In cities they'll have access to abundant resources and willing servants. Also keep in mind that nothing is more important to Galbatorix than recruiting or killing you—though word of your existence probably hasn't reached him yet. The longer you evade the Ra'zac, the more desperate he'll become. He'll know that every day you'll be growing stronger and that each passing moment will give you another chance to join his enemies. You must be very careful, as you may easily turn from the hunter into the hunted."

Eragon was subdued by the strong words. Pensive, he rolled a twig between his fingers. "Enough talk," said Brom. "It's late and my bones ache. We can say more tomorrow." Eragon nodded and banked the fire.

THERINSFORD

awn was gray and overcast with a cutting wind. The forest was quiet. After a light breakfast, Brom and Eragon doused the fire and shouldered their packs, preparing to leave. Eragon hung his bow and quiver on the side of his pack where he could easily reach them. Saphira wore the saddle; she would have to carry it until they got horses. Eragon carefully tied Zar'roc onto her back, too, as he did not want the extra weight. Besides, in his hands the sword would be no better than a club.

Eragon had felt safe inside the bramble, but outside, wariness crept into his movements. Saphira took off and circled overhead. The trees thinned as they returned to the farm.

I will see this place again, Eragon insisted to himself, looking at the ruined buildings. *This cannot, will not, be a permanent exile. Someday when it's safe, I'll return.* . . . Throwing back his shoulders, he faced south and the strange, barbaric lands that lay there.

As they walked, Saphira veered west toward the mountains and out of sight. Eragon felt uncomfortable as he watched her go. Even now, with no one around, they could not spend their days together. She had to stay hidden in case they met a fellow traveler.

The Ra'zac's footprints were faint on the eroding snow, but Eragon was unconcerned. It was unlikely that they had forsaken the road, which was the easiest way out of the valley, for the wilderness. Once outside the valley, however, the road divided in several places. It would be difficult to ascertain which branch the Ra'zac had taken.

They traveled in silence, concentrating on speed. Eragon's legs continued to bleed where the scabs had cracked. To take his mind off the discomfort, he asked, "So what exactly can dragons do? You said that you knew something of their abilities."

Brom laughed, his sapphire ring flashing in the air as he gestured. "Unfortunately, it's a pitiful amount compared to what I would like to know. Your question is one people have been trying to answer for centuries, so understand that what I tell you is by its very nature incomplete. Dragons have always been mysterious, though maybe not on purpose.

163

"Before I can truly answer your question, you need a basic education on the subject of dragons. It's hopelessly confusing to start in the middle of such a complex topic without understanding the foundation on which it stands. I'll begin with the life cycle of dragons, and if that doesn't wear you out, we can continue to another topic."

Brom explained how dragons mate and what it took for their eggs to hatch. "You see," he said, "when a dragon lays an egg, the infant inside is ready to hatch. But it waits, sometimes for years, for the right circumstances. When dragons lived in the wild, those circumstances were usually dictated by the availability of food. However, once they formed an alliance with the elves, a certain number of their eggs, usually no more than one or two, were given to the Riders each year. These eggs, or rather the infants inside, wouldn't hatch until the person destined to be its Rider came into their presence—though how they sensed that isn't known. People used to line up to touch the eggs, hoping that one of them might be picked."

"Do you mean that Saphira might not have hatched for me?" asked Eragon.

"Quite possibly, if she hadn't liked you."

He felt honored that of all the people in Alagaësia, she had chosen him. He wondered how long she had been waiting, then shuddered at the thought of being cramped inside an egg, surrounded by darkness.

Brom continued his lecture. He explained what and when dragons ate. A fully grown sedentary dragon could go for months without food, but in mating season they had to eat every week. Some plants could heal their sicknesses, while others would make them ill. There were various ways to care for their claws and clean their scales.

He explained the techniques to use when attacking from a dragon and what to do if you were fighting one, whether on foot, horseback, or with another dragon. Their bellies were armored; their armpits were not. Eragon constantly interrupted to ask questions, and Brom seemed pleased by the inquiries. Hours passed unheeded as they talked.

When evening came, they were near Therinsford. As the sky darkened and they searched for a place to camp, Eragon asked, "Who was the Rider that owned Zar'roc?"

"A mighty warrior," said Brom, "who was much feared in his time and held great power."

"What was his name?"

"I'll not say." Eragon protested, but Brom was firm. "I don't want to keep you ignorant, far from it, but certain knowledge would only prove dangerous and distracting for you right now. There isn't any reason for me to trouble you with such things until you have the time and the power to deal with them. I only wish to protect you from those who would use you for evil."

Eragon glared at him. "You know what? I think you just enjoy speaking in riddles. I've half a mind to leave you so I don't have to be bothered with them. If you're going to say something, then say it instead of dancing around with vague phrases!"

"Peace. All will be told in time," Brom said gently. Eragon grunted, unconvinced.

They found a comfortable place to spend the night and set up camp. Saphira joined them as dinner was being set on the fire. *Did you have time to hunt for food?* asked Eragon.

She snorted with amusement. *If the two of you were any slower, I would have time to fly across the sea and back without falling behind.*

You don't have to be insulting. Besides, we'll go faster once we have horses.

She let out a puff of smoke. *Maybe, but will it be enough to catch the Ra'zac? They have a lead of several days and many leagues. And I'm afraid they may suspect we're following them. Why else would they have destroyed the farm in such a spectacular manner, unless they wished to provoke you into chasing them?*

I don't know, said Eragon, disturbed. Saphira curled up beside him, and he leaned against her belly, welcoming the warmth. Brom sat on the other side of the fire, whittling two long sticks. He suddenly threw one at Eragon, who grabbed it out of reflex as it whirled over the crackling flames.

"Defend yourself!" barked Brom, standing.

Eragon looked at the stick in his hand and saw that it was shaped in the crude likeness of a sword. Brom wanted to fight him? What chance did the old man stand? *If he wants to play this game, so be it, but if he thinks to beat me, he's in for a surprise.*

He rose as Brom circled the fire. They faced each other for a moment, then Brom charged, swinging his stick. Eragon tried to block the attack but was too slow. He yelped as Brom struck him on the ribs, and stumbled backward.

Without thinking, he lunged forward, but Brom easily parried the blow. Eragon whipped the stick toward Brom's head, twisted it at the last moment, and then tried to hit his side. The solid smack of wood striking wood resounded through the camp. "Improvisation—good!" exclaimed Brom, eyes gleaming. His arm moved in a blur, and there was an explosion of pain on the side of Eragon's head. He collapsed like an empty sack, dazed.

A splash of cold water roused him to alertness, and he sat up, sputtering. His head was ringing, and there was dried blood on his face. Brom stood over him with a pan of melted snow water. "You didn't have to do that," said Eragon angrily, pushing himself up. He felt dizzy and unsteady.

Brom arched an eyebrow. "Oh? A real enemy wouldn't soften his blows, and neither will I. Should I pander to your . . . incompetence so

167

you'll feel better? I don't think so." He picked up the stick that Eragon had dropped and held it out. "Now, defend yourself."

Eragon stared blankly at the piece of wood, then shook his head. "Forget it; I've had enough." He turned away and stumbled as he was whacked loudly across the back. He spun around, growling.

"Never turn your back to the enemy!" snapped Brom, then tossed the stick at him and attacked. Eragon retreated around the fire, beneath the onslaught. "Pull your arms in. Keep your knees bent," shouted Brom. He continued to give instructions, then paused to show Eragon exactly how to execute a certain move. "Do it again, but this time *slowly*!" They slid through the forms with exaggerated motions before returning to their furious battle. Eragon learned quickly, but no matter what he tried, he could not hold Brom off for more than a few blows.

When they finished, Eragon flopped on his blankets and groaned. He hurt everywhere—Brom had not been gentle with his stick. Saphira let out a long, coughing growl and curled her lip until a formidable row of teeth showed.

What's wrong with you? he demanded irritably.

Nothing, she replied. *It's funny to see a hatchling like you beaten by the old one*. She made the sound again, and Eragon turned red as he realized that she was laughing. Trying to preserve some dignity, he rolled onto his side and fell asleep.

He felt even worse the next day. Bruises covered his arms, and he was almost too sore to move. Brom looked up from the mush he was serving and grinned. "How do you feel?" Eragon grunted and bolted down the breakfast.

Once on the road, they traveled swiftly so as to reach Therinsford before noon. After a league, the road widened and they saw smoke in the distance. "You'd better tell Saphira to fly ahead and wait for us on the other side of Therinsford," said Brom. "She has to be careful here, otherwise people are bound to notice her."

"Why don't you tell her yourself?" challenged Eragon.

"It's considered bad manners to interfere with another's dragon."

"You didn't have a problem with it in Carvahall."

Brom's lips twitched with a smile. "I did what I had to."

Eragon eyed him darkly, then relayed the instructions. Saphira warned, *Be careful; the Empire's servants could be hiding anywhere.*

As the ruts in the road deepened, Eragon noticed more footprints. Farms signaled their approach to Therinsford. The village was larger than Carvahall, but it had been constructed haphazardly, the houses aligned in no particular order.

"What a mess," said Eragon. He could not see Dempton's mill. *Baldor and Albriech have surely fetched Roran by now.* Either way, Eragon had no wish to face his cousin.

"It's ugly, if nothing else," agreed Brom.

The Anora River flowed between them and the town, spanned by a stout bridge. As they approached it, a greasy man stepped from behind a bush and barred their way. His shirt was too short, and his dirty stomach spilled over a rope belt. Behind his cracked lips, his teeth looked like crumbling tombstones. "You c'n stop right there. This's my bridge. Gotta pay t' get over."

"How much?" asked Brom in a resigned voice. He pulled out a pouch, and the bridgekeeper brightened.

"Five crowns," he said, pulling his lips into a broad smile. Eragon's temper flared at the exorbitant price, and he started to complain hotly, but Brom silenced him with a quick look. The coins were wordlessly handed over. The man put them into a sack hanging from his belt. "Thank'ee much," he said in a mocking tone, and stood out of the way.

As Brom stepped forward, he stumbled and caught the bridgekeeper's arm to support himself. "Watch y're step," snarled the grimy man, sidling away.

"Sorry," apologized Brom, and continued over the bridge with Eragon.

"Why didn't you haggle? He skinned you alive!" exclaimed Eragon when they were out of earshot. "He probably doesn't even own the bridge. We could have pushed right past him."

"Probably," agreed Brom.

"Then why pay him?"

"Because you can't argue with all of the fools in the world. It's easier to let them have their way, then trick them when they're not paying attention." Brom opened his hand, and a pile of coins glinted in the light.

"You cut his purse!" said Eragon incredulously.

Brom pocketed the money with a wink. "And it held a surprising amount. He should know better than to keep all these coins in one place." There was a sudden howl of anguish from the other side of the river. "I'd say our friend has just discovered his loss. If you see any watchmen, tell me." He grabbed the shoulder of a young boy running between the houses and asked, "Do you know where we can buy horses?" The child stared at them with solemn eyes, then pointed to a large barn near the edge of Therinsford. "Thank you," said Brom, tossing him a small coin.

The barn's large double doors were open, revealing two long rows of stalls. The far wall was covered with saddles, harnesses, and other paraphernalia. A man with muscular arms stood at the end, brushing a white stallion. He raised a hand and beckoned for them to come over.

As they approached, Brom said, "That's a beautiful animal."

"Yes indeed. His name's Snowfire. Mine's Haberth." Haberth offered a rough palm and shook hands vigorously with Eragon and Brom. There was a polite pause as he waited for their names in return. When they were not forthcoming, he asked, "Can I help you?"

Brom nodded. "We need two horses and a full set of tack for both. The horses have to be fast and tough; we'll be doing a lot of traveling."

Haberth was thoughtful for a moment. "I don't have many animals like that, and the ones I do aren't cheap." The stallion moved restlessly; he calmed it with a few strokes of his fingers.

"Price is no object. I'll take the best you have," said Brom. Haberth nodded and silently tied the stallion to a stall. He went to the wall and started pulling down saddles and other items. Soon he had two identical piles. Next he walked up the line of stalls and brought out two horses. One was a light bay, the other a roan. The bay tugged against his rope.

"He's a little spirited, but with a firm hand you won't have any problems," said Haberth, handing the bay's rope to Brom.

Brom let the horse smell his hand; it allowed him to rub its neck. "We'll take him," he said, then eyed the roan. "The other one, however, I'm not so sure of."

"There are some good legs on him."

"Mmm . . . What will you take for Snowfire?"

Haberth looked fondly at the stallion. "I'd rather not sell him. He's the finest I've ever bred— I'm hoping to sire a whole line from him."

"If you were willing to part with him, how much would all of this cost me?" asked Brom.

Eragon tried to put his hand on the bay like Brom had, but it shied away. He automatically reached out with his mind to reassure the horse, stiffening with surprise as he touched the animal's consciousness. The contact was not clear or sharp like it was with Saphira, but he could communicate with the bay to a limited degree. Tentatively, he made it understand that he was a friend. The horse calmed and looked at him with liquid brown eyes.

Haberth used his fingers to add up the price of the purchase. "Two hundred crowns and no less," he said with a smile, clearly confident that no one would pay that much. Brom silently opened his pouch and counted out the money.

"Will this do?" he asked.

There was a long silence as Haberth glanced between Snowfire and the coins. A sigh, then, "He is yours, though I go against my heart."

"I will treat him as if he had been sired by Gildintor, the greatest steed of legend," said Brom.

"Your words gladden me," answered Haberth, bowing his head slightly. He helped them saddle the horses. When they were ready to leave, he said, "Farewell, then. For the sake of Snowfire, I hope that misfortune does not befall you."

"Do not fear; I will guard him well," promised Brom as they departed. "Here," he said, handing Snowfire's reins to Eragon, "go to the far side of Therinsford and wait there."

"Why?" asked Eragon, but Brom had already slipped away. Annoyed, he exited Therinsford with the two horses and stationed himself beside the road. To the south he saw the hazy outline of Utgard, sitting like a giant monolith at the end of the valley. Its peak pierced the clouds and rose out of sight, towering over the lesser mountains that surrounded it. Its dark, ominous look made Eragon's scalp tingle.

174   Brom returned shortly and gestured for Eragon to follow. They walked until Therinsford was hidden by trees. Then Brom said, "The Ra'zac definitely passed this way. Apparently they stopped here to pick up horses, as we did. I was able to find a man who saw them. He described them with many shudders and said that they galloped out of Therinsford like demons fleeing a holy man."

"They left quite an impression."

"Quite."

Eragon patted the horses. "When we were in the barn, I touched the bay's mind by accident. I didn't know it was possible to do that."

Brom frowned. "It's unusual for one as young

as you to have the ability. Most Riders had to train for years before they were strong enough to contact anything other than their dragon." His face was thoughtful as he inspected Snowfire. Then he said, "Take everything from your pack, put it into the saddlebags, and tie the pack on top." Eragon did so while Brom mounted Snowfire.

Eragon gazed doubtfully at the bay. It was so much smaller than Saphira that for an absurd moment he wondered if it could bear his weight. With a sigh, he awkwardly got into the saddle. He had only ridden horses bareback and never for any distance. "Is this going to do the same thing to my legs as riding Saphira?" he asked.

"How do they feel now?"

"Not too bad, but I think any hard riding will open them up again."

"We'll take it easy," promised Brom. He gave Eragon a few pointers, then they started off at a gentle pace. Before long the countryside began to change as cultivated fields yielded to wilder land. Brambles and tangled weeds lined the road, along with huge rosebushes that clung to their clothes. Tall rocks slanted out of the ground— gray witnesses to their presence. There was an unfriendly feel in the air, an animosity that resisted intruders.

Above them, growing larger with every step, loomed Utgard, its craggy precipices deeply furrowed with snowy canyons. The black rock of the mountain absorbed light like a sponge and dimmed the surrounding area. Between Utgard and the line of mountains that formed the east side of Palancar Valley was a deep cleft. It was the only practical way out of the valley. The road led toward it.

The horses' hooves clacked sharply over gravel, and the road dwindled to a skinny trail as it skirted the base of Utgard. Eragon glanced up at the peak looming over them and was startled to see a steepled tower perched upon it. The turret was crumbling and in disrepair, but it was still a stern sentinel over the valley. "What is that?" he asked, pointing.

Brom did not look up, but said sadly and with bitterness, "An outpost of the Riders—one that has lasted since their founding. That was where Vrael took refuge, and where, through treachery, he was found and defeated by Galbatorix. When Vrael fell, this area was tainted. Edoc'sil, 'Unconquerable,' was the name of this bastion, for the mountain is so steep none may reach the top unless they can fly. After Vrael's death the commoners called it Utgard, but it has another name, Ristvak'baen—the 'Place of Sorrow.' It was known as such to the last Riders before they were killed by the king."

Eragon stared with awe. Here was a tangible remnant of the Riders' glory, tarnished though it was by the relentless pull of time. It struck him then just how old the Riders were. A legacy of tradition and heroism that stretched back to antiquity had fallen upon him.

They traveled for long hours around Utgard. It formed a solid wall to their right as they entered the breach that divided the mountain range. Eragon stood in his stirrups; he was impatient to see what lay outside of Palancar, but it was still too far away. For a while they were in a sloped pass, winding over hill and gully, following the Anora River. Then, with the sun low behind their backs, they mounted a rise and saw over the trees.

Eragon gasped. On either side were mountains, but below them stretched a huge plain that extended to the distant horizon and fused into the sky. The plain was a uniform tan, like the color of dead grass. Long, wispy clouds swept by overhead, shaped by fierce winds.

He understood now why Brom had insisted on horses. It would have taken them weeks or months to cover that vast distance on foot. Far above he saw Saphira circling, high enough to be mistaken for a bird.

"We'll wait until tomorrow to make the descent," said Brom. "It's going to take most of the day, so we should camp now."

"How far across is the plain?" Eragon asked, still amazed.

"Two or three days to over a fortnight, depending on which direction we go. Aside from the nomad tribes that roam this section of the plains, it's almost as uninhabited as the Hadarac Desert to the east. So we aren't going to find many villages. However, to the south the plains are less arid and more heavily populated."

They left the trail and dismounted by the Anora River. As they unsaddled the horses, Brom gestured at the bay. "You should name him."

Eragon considered it as he picketed the bay. "Well, I don't have anything as noble as Snowfire, but maybe this will do." He placed his hand on the bay and said, "I name you Cadoc. It was my grandfather's name, so bear it well." Brom nodded in approval, but Eragon felt slightly foolish.

When Saphira landed, he asked, *How do the plains look?*

Dull. There's nothing but rabbits and scrub in every direction.

After dinner, Brom stood and barked, "Catch!" Eragon barely had time to raise his arm and grab the piece of wood before it hit him on the head. He groaned as he saw another makeshift sword.

"Not again," he complained. Brom just smiled and beckoned with one hand. Eragon reluctantly got to his feet. They whirled around in a flurry of smacking wood, and he backed away with a stinging arm.

The training session was shorter than the first, but it was still long enough for Eragon to amass a new collection of bruises. When they finished sparring, he threw down the stick in disgust and stalked away from the fire to nurse his injuries.

THUNDER ROAR AND LIGHTNING CRACKLE

The next morning Eragon avoided bringing to mind any of the recent events; they were too painful for him to consider. Instead, he focused his energies on figuring out how to find and kill the Ra'zac. *I'll do it with my bow,* he decided, imagining how the cloaked figures would look with arrows sticking out of them.

He had difficulty even standing up. His muscles cramped with the slightest movement, and one of his fingers was hot and swollen. When they were ready to leave, he mounted Cadoc and said acidly, "If this keeps up, you're going to batter me to pieces."

"I wouldn't push you so hard if I didn't think you were strong enough."

"For once, I wouldn't mind being thought less of," muttered Eragon.

Cadoc pranced nervously as Saphira approached. Saphira eyed the horse with something close to disgust and said, *There's nowhere to hide on the plains, so I'm not going to bother trying to stay out of sight. I'll just fly above you from now on.*

She took off, and they began the steep descent. In many places the trail all but disappeared, leaving them to find their own way down. At times they had to dismount and lead the horses on foot, holding on to trees to keep from falling down the slope. The ground was scattered with loose rocks, which made the footing treacherous. The ordeal left them hot and irritable, despite the cold.

They stopped to rest when they reached the bottom near midday. The Anora River veered to their left and flowed northward. A biting wind scoured the land, whipping them unmercifully. The soil was parched, and dirt flew into their eyes.

It unnerved Eragon how flat everything was; the plains were unbroken by hummocks or mounds. He had lived his entire life surrounded by mountains and hills. Without them he felt exposed and vulnerable, like a mouse under an eagle's keen eye.

The trail split in three once it reached the plains. The first branch turned north, toward Ceunon, one of the greatest northern cities; the second one led straight across the plains; and the last went south. They examined all three for traces of the Ra'zac and eventually found their tracks, heading directly into the grasslands.

"It seems they've gone to Yazuac," said Brom with a perplexed air.

"Where's that?"

"Due east and four days away, if all goes well. It's a small village situated by the Ninor River." He gestured at the Anora, which streamed away from them to the north. "Our only supply of water is here. We'll have to replenish our waterskins before attempting to cross the plains. There isn't another pool or stream between here and Yazuac."

The excitement of the hunt began to rise within Eragon. In a few days, maybe less than a week, he would use his arrows to avenge Garrow's death. *And then . . .* He refused to think about what might happen afterward.

They filled the waterskins, watered the horses, and drank as much as they could from the river. Saphira joined them and took several gulps of water. Fortified, they turned eastward and started across the plains.

Eragon decided that it would be the wind that drove him crazy first. Everything that made him miserable—his chapped lips, parched tongue, and burning eyes—stemmed from it. The ceaseless gusting followed them throughout the day. Evening only strengthened the wind, instead of subduing it.

Since there was no shelter, they were forced to camp in the open. Eragon found some scrub brush, a short tough plant that thrived on harsh conditions, and pulled it up. He made a careful pile and tried to light it, but the woody stems only smoked and gave off a pungent smell. Frustrated, he tossed the tinderbox to Brom. "I can't make it burn, especially with this blasted wind. See if you can get it going: otherwise dinner will be cold."

Brom knelt by the brush and looked at it critically. He rearranged a couple of branches, then struck the tinderbox, sending a cascade of sparks onto the plants. There was smoke, but nothing else. Brom scowled and tried again, but his luck was no better than Eragon's. "Brisingr!" he swore angrily, striking the flint again. Flames suddenly appeared, and he stepped back with a pleased expression. "There we go. It must have been smoldering inside."

They sparred with mock swords while the food cooked. Fatigue made it hard on both of them, so they kept the session short. After they had eaten, they lay next to Saphira and slept, grateful for her shelter.

The same cold wind greeted them in the morning, sweeping over the dreadful flatness. Eragon's lips had cracked during the night; every time he smiled or talked, beads of blood covered them. Licking them only made it worse. It was the same for Brom. They let the horses drink sparingly from their supply of water before mounting them. The day was a monotonous trek of endless plodding.

On the third day, Eragon woke well rested. That, coupled with the fact that the wind had stopped, put him in a cheery humor. His high spirits were dampened, however, when he saw the sky ahead of them was dark with thunderheads.

Brom looked at the clouds and grimaced. "Normally I wouldn't go into a storm like that, but we're in for a battering no matter what we do, so we might as well get some distance covered."

It was still calm when they reached the storm front. As they entered its shadow, Eragon looked up. The thundercloud had an exotic structure, forming a natural cathedral with a massive arched roof. With some imagination he could see pillars, windows, soaring tiers, and snarling gargoyles. It was a wild beauty.

As Eragon lowered his gaze, a giant ripple raced toward them through the grass, flattening it. It took him a second to realize that the wave was a tremendous blast of wind. Brom saw it too, and they hunched their shoulders, preparing for the storm.

The gale was almost upon them when Eragon had a horrible thought and twisted in his saddle, yelling, both with his voice and mind, *Saphira!*

Land!" Brom's face grew pale. Overhead, they saw her dive toward the ground. *She's not going to make it!*

Saphira angled back the way they had come, to gain time. As they watched, the tempest's wrath struck them like a hammer blow. Eragon gasped for breath and clenched the saddle as a frenzied howling filled his ears. Cadoc swayed and dug his hooves into the ground, mane snapping in the air. The wind tore at their clothes with invisible fingers while the air darkened with billowing clouds of dust.

Eragon squinted, searching for Saphira. He saw her land heavily and then crouch, clenching the ground with her talons. The wind reached her just as she started to fold her wings. With an angry yank, it unfurled them and dragged her into the air. For a moment she hung there, suspended by the storm's force. Then it slammed her down on her back.

With a savage wrench, Eragon yanked Cadoc around and galloped back up the trail, goading the horse with both heels and mind. *Saphira!* he shouted. *Try to stay on the ground. I'm coming!* He felt a grim acknowledgment from her. As they neared Saphira, Cadoc balked, so Eragon leapt down and ran toward her.

His bow banged against his head. A strong gust pushed him off balance and he flew forward, landing on his chest. He skidded, then got back up with a snarl, ignoring the deep scrapes in his skin.

Saphira was only three yards away, but he could get no closer because of her flailing wings. She struggled to fold them against the overpowering gale. He rushed at her right wing, intending to hold it down, but the wind caught her and she somersaulted over him. The spines on her back missed his head by inches. Saphira clawed at the ground, trying to stay down.

Her wings began to lift again, but before they could flip her, Eragon threw himself at the left one. The wing crumpled in at the joints and Saphira tucked it firmly against her body. Eragon vaulted over her back and tumbled onto the other wing. Without warning it was blown upward, sending him sliding to the ground. He broke his fall with a roll, then jumped up and grabbed the wing again. Saphira started to fold it, and he pushed with all of his strength. The wind battled with them for a second, but with one last surge they overcame it.

Eragon leaned against Saphira, panting. *Are you all right?* He could feel her trembling.

She took a moment to answer. *I . . . I think so.* She sounded shaken. *Nothing's broken—I couldn't do anything; the wind wouldn't let me go. I was helpless.* With a shudder, she fell silent.

He looked at her, concerned. *Don't worry, you're safe now.* He spotted Cadoc a ways off, standing with his back to the wind. With his mind, Eragon instructed the horse to return to Brom. He then got onto Saphira. She crept up the road, fighting the gale while he clung to her back and kept his head down.

When they reached Brom, he shouted over the storm, "Is she hurt?"

Eragon shook his head and dismounted. Cadoc trotted over to him, nickering. As he stroked the horse's long cheek, Brom pointed at a dark curtain of rain sweeping toward them in rippling gray sheets. "What else?" cried Eragon, pulling his clothes tighter. He winced as the torrent reached them. The stinging rain was cold as ice; before long they were drenched and shivering.

Lightning lanced through the sky, flickering in and out of existence. Mile-high blue bolts streaked across the horizon, followed by peals of thunder that shook the ground below. It was beautiful, but dangerously so. Here and there, grass fires were ignited by strikes, only to be extinguished by the rain.

The wild elements were slow to abate, but as the day passed, they wandered elsewhere. Once again the sky was revealed, and the setting sun glowed with brilliance. As beams of light tinted the clouds with blazing colors, everything gained a sharp contrast: brightly lit on one side, deeply shadowed on the other. Objects had a unique sense of mass; grass stalks seemed sturdy as marble pillars. Ordinary things took on an unearthly beauty; Eragon felt as if he were sitting inside a painting.

The rejuvenated earth smelled fresh, clearing their minds and raising their spirits. Saphira stretched, craning her neck, and roared happily. The horses skittered away from her, but Eragon and Brom smiled at her exuberance.

Before the light faded, they stopped for the night in a shallow depression. Too exhausted to spar, they went straight to sleep.

REVELATION AT
YAZUAC

Although they had managed to partially refill the waterskins during the storm, they drank the last of their water that morning. "I hope we're going in the right direction," said Eragon, crunching up the empty water bag, "because we'll be in trouble if we don't reach Yazuac today."

Brom did not seem disturbed. "I've traveled this way before. Yazuac will be in sight before dusk."

Eragon laughed doubtfully. "Perhaps you see something I don't. How can you know that when everything looks exactly the same for leagues around?"

"Because I am guided not by the land, but by the stars and sun. They will not lead us astray. Come! Let us be off. It is foolish to conjure up woe where none exists. Yazuac will be there."

His words proved true. Saphira spotted the village first, but it was not until later in the day that the rest of them saw it as a dark bump on the horizon. Yazuac was still very far away; it was only visible because of the plain's uniform flatness. As they rode closer, a dark winding line appeared on either side of the town and disappeared in the distance.

"The Ninor River," said Brom, pointing at it.

Eragon pulled Cadoc to a stop. "Saphira will be seen if she stays with us much longer. Should she hide while we go into Yazuac?"

Brom scratched his chin and looked at the town. "See that bend in the river? Have her wait there. It's far enough from Yazuac so no one should find her, but close enough that she won't be left behind. We'll go through the town, get what we need, and then meet her."

I don't like it, said Saphira when Eragon had explained the plan. *This is irritating, having to hide all the time like a criminal.*

You know what would happen if we were revealed. She grumbled but gave in and flew away low to the ground.

They kept a swift pace in anticipation of the food and drink they would soon enjoy. As they approached the small houses, they could see smoke from a dozen chimneys, but there was no one in the streets. An abnormal silence enveloped the village. By unspoken consent they stopped before the first house. Eragon abruptly said, "There aren't any dogs barking."

"No."

"Doesn't mean anything, though."

". . . No."

Eragon paused. "Someone should have seen us by now."

"Yes."

"Then why hasn't anyone come out?"

Brom squinted at the sun. "Could be afraid."

"Could be," said Eragon. He was quiet for a moment. "And if it's a trap? The Ra'zac might be waiting for us."

"We need provisions and water."

"There's the Ninor."

"Still need provisions."

"True." Eragon looked around. "So we go in?"

Brom flicked his reins. "Yes, but not like fools. This is the main entrance to Yazuac. If there's an ambush, it'll be along here. No one will expect us to arrive from a different direction."

"Around to the side, then?" asked Eragon. Brom nodded and pulled out his sword, resting the bare blade across his saddle. Eragon strung his bow and nocked an arrow.

They trotted quietly around the town and entered it cautiously. The streets were empty, except for a small fox that darted away as they came near. The houses were dark and foreboding, with shattered windows. Many of the doors swung on

191

broken hinges. The horses rolled their eyes nervously. Eragon's palm tingled, but he resisted the urge to scratch it. As they rode into the center of town, he gripped his bow tighter, blanching. "Gods above," he whispered.

A mountain of bodies rose above them, the corpses stiff and grimacing. Their clothes were soaked in blood, and the churned ground was stained with it. Slaughtered men lay over the women they had tried to protect, mothers still clasped their children, and lovers who had tried to shield each other rested in death's cold embrace. Black arrows stuck out of them all. Neither young nor old had been spared. But worst of all was the barbed spear that rose out of the peak of the pile, impaling the white body of a baby.

Tears blurred Eragon's vision and he tried to look away, but the dead faces held his attention. He stared at their open eyes and wondered how life could have left them so easily. *What does our existence mean when it can end like this?* A wave of hopelessness overwhelmed him.

A crow dipped out of the sky, like a black shadow, and perched on the spear. It cocked its head and greedily scrutinized the infant's corpse. "Oh no you don't," snarled Eragon as he pulled back the bowstring and released it with a twang. With a puff of feathers, the crow fell over backward, the arrow protruding from its chest. Eragon fit another arrow to the string, but nausea rose from his stomach and he threw up over Cadoc's side.

Brom patted him on the back. When Eragon was done, Brom asked gently, "Do you want to wait for me outside Yazuac?"

"No . . . I'll stay," said Eragon shakily, wiping his mouth. He avoided looking at the gruesome sight before them. "Who could have done . . ." He could not force out the words.

Brom bowed his head. "Those who love the pain and suffering of others. They wear many faces and go by many disguises, but there is only one name for them: evil. There is no understanding it. All we can do is pity and honor the victims."

He dismounted Snowfire and walked around, inspecting the trampled ground carefully. "The Ra'zac passed this way," he said slowly, "but this wasn't their doing. This is Urgal work; the spear is of their make. A company of them came through here, perhaps as many as a hundred. It's odd; I know of only a few instances when they have gathered in such . . ." He knelt and examined a footprint intently. With a curse he ran back to Snowfire and leapt onto him.

"Ride!" he hissed tightly, spurring Snowfire forward. "There are still Urgals here!" Eragon jammed his heels into Cadoc. The horse jumped forward and raced after Snowfire. They dashed past the houses and were almost to the edge of

Yazuac when Eragon's palm tingled again. He saw a flicker of movement to his right, then a giant fist smashed him out of the saddle. He flew back over Cadoc and crashed into a wall, holding on to his bow only by instinct. Gasping and stunned, he staggered upright, hugging his side.

An Urgal stood over him, face set in a gross leer. The monster was tall, thick, and broader than a doorway, with gray skin and yellow piggish eyes. Muscles bulged on his arms and chest, which was covered by a too small breastplate. An iron cap rested over the pair of ram's horns curling from his temples, and a roundshield was bound to one arm. His powerful hand held a short, wicked sword.

194 Behind him, Eragon saw Brom rein in Snowfire and start back, only to be stopped by the appearance of a second Urgal, this one with an ax. "Run, you fool!" Brom cried to Eragon, cleaving at his enemy. The Urgal in front of Eragon roared and swung his sword mightily. Eragon jerked back with a startled yelp as the weapon whistled past his cheek. He spun around and fled toward the center of Yazuac, heart pounding wildly.

The Urgal pursued him, heavy boots thudding. Eragon sent a desperate cry for help to Saphira, then forced himself to go even faster. The Urgal rapidly gained ground despite Eragon's efforts; large fangs separated in a soundless bellow. With the Urgal almost upon him, Eragon strung an arrow, spun to a stop, took aim, and released. The Urgal snapped up his arm and caught the quivering bolt on his shield. The monster collided with Eragon before he could shoot again, and they fell to the ground in a confused tangle.

Eragon sprang to his feet and rushed back to Brom, who was trading fierce blows with his opponent from Snowfire's back. *Where are the rest of the Urgals?* wondered Eragon frantically. *Are these two the only ones in Yazuac?* There was a loud smack, and Snowfire reared, whinnying. Brom doubled over in his saddle, blood streaming down his arm. The Urgal beside him howled in triumph and raised his ax for the death blow.

A deafening scream tore out of Eragon as he charged the Urgal, headfirst. The Urgal paused in astonishment, then faced him contemptuously, swinging his ax. Eragon ducked under the two-handed blow and clawed the Urgal's side, leaving bloody furrows. The Urgal's face twisted with rage. He slashed again, but missed as Eragon dived to the side and scrambled down an alley.

Eragon concentrated on leading the Urgals away from Brom. He slipped into a narrow passageway between two houses, saw it was a dead end, and slid to a stop. He tried to back out, but the Urgals had already blocked the entrance. They advanced, cursing him in their gravelly voices. Eragon swung his head from side to side, searching for a way out, but there was none.

As he faced the Urgals, images flashed in his mind: dead villagers piled around the spear and an innocent baby who would never grow to adulthood. At the thought of their fate, a burning, fiery power gathered from every part of his body. It was more than a desire for justice. It was his entire being rebelling against the fact of death—that he would cease to exist. The power grew stronger and stronger until he felt ready to burst from the contained force.

He stood tall and straight, all fear gone. He raised his bow smoothly. The Urgals laughed and lifted their shields. Eragon sighted down the shaft, as he had done hundreds of times, and aligned the arrowhead with his target. The energy inside him burned at an unbearable level. He had to release it, or it would consume him. A word suddenly leapt unbidden to his lips. He shot, yelling, "Brisingr!"

The arrow hissed through the air, glowing with a crackling blue light. It struck the lead Urgal on the forehead, and the air resounded with an explosion. A blue shock wave blasted out of the monster's head, killing the other Urgal instantly. It reached Eragon before he had time to react, and it passed through him without harm, dissipating against the houses.

Eragon stood panting, then looked at his icy

palm. The gedwëy ignasia was glowing like white-hot metal, yet even as he watched, it faded back to normal. He clenched his fist, then a wave of exhaustion washed over him. He felt strange and feeble, as if he had not eaten for days. His knees buckled, and he sagged against a wall.

ADMONISHMENTS

Once a modicum of strength returned to him, Eragon staggered out of the alley, skirting the dead monsters. He did not get far before Cadoc trotted to his side. "Good, you weren't hurt," mumbled Eragon. He noticed, without particularly caring, that his hands were shaking violently and his movements were jerky. He felt detached, as if everything he saw were happening to someone else.

Eragon found Snowfire, nostrils flared and ears flat against his head, prancing by the corner of a house, ready to bolt. Brom was still slumped motionless in the saddle. Eragon reached out with his mind and soothed the horse. Once Snowfire relaxed, Eragon went to Brom.

There was a long, blood-soaked cut on the old man's right arm. The wound bled profusely, but it was neither deep nor wide. Still, Eragon knew it had to be bound before Brom lost too much blood. He stroked Snowfire for a moment, then slid Brom out of the saddle. The weight proved too much for him, and Brom dropped heavily to the ground. Eragon was shocked by his own weakness.

A scream of rage filled his head. Saphira dived out of the sky and landed fiercely in front of him, keeping her wings half raised. She hissed angrily, eyes burning. Her tail lashed, and Eragon winced as it snapped overhead. *Are you hurt?* she asked, rage boiling in her voice.

"No," he assured her as he laid Brom on his back.

She growled and exclaimed, *Where are the ones who did this? I will tear them apart!*

He wearily pointed in the direction of the al- ley. "It'll do no good; they're already dead."

You killed them? Saphira sounded surprised.

He nodded. "Somehow." With a few terse words, he told her what had happened while he searched his saddlebags for the rags in which Zar'roc had been wrapped.

Saphira said gravely, *You have grown.*

Eragon grunted. He found a long rag and carefully rolled back Brom's sleeve. With a few deft strokes he cleaned the cut and bandaged it tightly. *I wish we were still in Palancar Valley,* he said to Saphira. *There, at least, I knew what plants were good for healing. Here, I don't have any idea what will help him.* He retrieved Brom's sword from the ground, wiped it, then returned it to the sheath on Brom's belt.

We should leave, said Saphira. *There may be more Urgals lurking about.*

Can you carry Brom? Your saddle will hold him in place, and you can protect him.

Yes, but I'm not leaving you alone.

Fine, fly next to me, but let's get out of here. He tied the saddle onto Saphira, then put his arms around Brom and tried to lift him, but again his diminished strength failed him. *Saphira—help.*

She snaked her head past him and caught the back of Brom's robe between her teeth. Arching her neck, she lifted the old man off the ground, like a cat would a kitten, and deposited him onto her back. Then Eragon slipped Brom's legs through the saddle's straps and tightened them. He looked up when the old man moaned and shifted.

Brom blinked blearily, putting a hand to his head. He gazed down at Eragon with concern. "Did Saphira get here in time?"

Eragon shook his head. "I'll explain it later. Your arm is injured. I bandaged it as best I could, but you need a safe place to rest."

"Yes," said Brom, gingerly touching his arm. "Do you know where my sword . . . Ah, I see you found it."

Eragon finished tightening the straps. "Saphira's going to take you and follow me by air."

"Are you sure you want me to ride her?" asked Brom. "I can ride Snowfire."

"Not with that arm. This way, even if you faint, you won't fall off."

Brom nodded. "I'm honored." He wrapped his good arm around Saphira's neck, and she took off in a flurry, springing high into the sky. Eragon backed away, buffeted by the eddies from her wings, and returned to the horses.

He tied Snowfire behind Cadoc, then left Yazuac, returning to the trail and following it southward. It led through a rocky area, veered left, and continued along the bank of the Ninor River. Ferns, mosses, and small bushes dotted the side of the path. It was refreshingly cool under the trees, but Eragon did not let the soothing air lull him into a sense of security. He stopped briefly to fill the waterskins and let the horses drink. Glancing down, he saw the Ra'zac's spoor. *At least we're going in the right direction.* Saphira circled overhead, keeping a keen eye on him.

It disturbed him that they had seen only two Urgals. The villagers had been killed and Yazuac ransacked by a large horde, yet where was it? *Perhaps the ones we encountered were a rear guard or a trap left for anyone who was following the main force.*

His thoughts turned to how he had killed the Urgals. An idea, a revelation, slowly wormed its way through his mind. He, Eragon—farm boy of

201

Palancar Valley—had used magic. *Magic!* It was the only word for what had happened. It seemed impossible, but he could not deny what he had seen. *Somehow I've become a sorcerer or wizard!* But he did not know how to use this new power again or what its limits and dangers might be. *How can I have this ability? Was it common among the Riders? And if Brom knew of it, why didn't he tell me?* He shook his head in wonder and bewilderment.

He conversed with Saphira to check on Brom's condition and to share his thoughts. She was just as puzzled as he was about the magic. *Saphira, can you find us a place to stay? I can't see very far down here.* While she searched, he continued along the Ninor.

202   The summons reached him just as the light was fading. *Come.* Saphira sent him an image of a secluded clearing in the trees by the river. Eragon turned the horses in the new direction and nudged them into a trot. With Saphira's help it was easy to find, but it was so well hidden that he doubted anyone else would notice it.

A small, smokeless fire was already burning when he entered the clearing. Brom sat next to it, tending his arm, which he held at an awkward angle. Saphira was crouched beside him, her body tense. She looked intently at Eragon and asked, *Are you sure you aren't hurt?*

Not on the outside . . . but I'm not sure about the rest of me.

I should have been there sooner.

Don't feel bad. We all made mistakes today. Mine was not staying closer to you. Her gratitude for that remark washed over him. He looked at Brom. "How are you?"

The old man glanced at his arm. "It's a large scratch and hurts terribly, but it should heal quickly enough. I need a fresh bandage; this one didn't last as long as I'd hoped." They boiled water to wash Brom's wound. Then Brom tied a fresh rag to his arm and said, "I must eat, and you look hungry as well. Let's have dinner first, then talk."

When their bellies were full and warm, Brom lit his pipe. "Now, I think it's time for you to tell me what transpired while I was unconscious. I am most curious." His face reflected the flickering firelight, and his bushy eyebrows stuck out fiercely.

Eragon nervously clasped his hands and told the story without embellishment. Brom remained silent throughout it, his face inscrutable. When Eragon finished, Brom looked down at the ground. For a long time the only sound was the snapping fire. Brom finally stirred. "Have you used this power before?"

"No. Do you know anything about it?"

"A little." Brom's face was thoughtful. "It seems I owe you a debt for saving my life. I hope I can return the favor someday. You should be proud; few escape unscathed from slaying their first Urgal. But the manner in which you did it was very dangerous. You could have destroyed yourself and the whole town."

"It wasn't as if I had a choice," said Eragon defensively. "The Urgals were almost upon me. If I had waited, they would have chopped me into pieces!"

Brom stamped his teeth vigorously on the pipe stem. "You didn't have any idea what you were doing."

"Then tell me," challenged Eragon. "I've been searching for answers to this mystery, but I can't make sense of it. What happened? How could I have possibly used magic? No one has ever instructed me in it or taught me spells."

204   Brom's eyes flashed. "This isn't something you should be taught—much less use!"

"Well, I *have* used it, and I may need it to fight again. But I won't be able to if you don't help me. What's wrong? Is there some secret I'm not supposed to learn until I'm old and wise? Or maybe you don't know anything about magic!"

"Boy!" roared Brom. "You demand answers with an insolence rarely seen. If you knew what you asked for, you would not be so quick to inquire. Do not try me." He paused, then relaxed into a kinder countenance. "The knowledge you ask for is more complex than you understand."

Eragon rose hotly in protest. "I feel as though I've been thrust into a world with strange rules that no one will explain."

"I understand," said Brom. He fiddled with a piece of grass. "It's late and we should sleep, but I will tell you a few things now, to stop your badgering. This magic—for it is magic—has rules like the rest of the world. If you break the rules, the penalty is death, without exception. Your deeds are limited by your strength, the words you know, and your imagination."

"What do you mean by words?" asked Eragon.

"More questions!" cried Brom. "For a moment I had hoped you were empty of them. But you are quite right in asking. When you shot the Urgals, didn't you say something?"

"Yes, *brisingr*." The fire flared, and a shiver ran through Eragon. Something about the word made him feel incredibly alive.

"I thought so. *Brisingr* is from an ancient language that all living things used to speak. However, it was forgotten over time and went unspoken for eons in Alagaësia, until the elves brought it back over the sea. They taught it to the other races, who used it for making and doing powerful things. The language has a name for everything, if you can find it."

"But what does that have to do with magic?" interrupted Eragon.

"Everything! It is the basis for all power. The language describes the true nature of things, not the superficial aspects that everyone sees. For example, fire is called *brisingr*. Not only is that *a* name for fire, it is *the* name for fire. If you are strong enough, you can use *brisingr* to direct fire to do whatever you will. And that is what happened today."

Eragon thought about it for a moment. "Why was the fire blue? How come it did exactly what I wanted, if all I said was *fire?*"

"The color varies from person to person. It depends on who says the word. As to why the fire did what you wanted, that's a matter of practice. Most beginners have to spell out exactly what they want to happen. As they gain more experience, it isn't as necessary. A true master could just say *water* and create something totally unrelated, like a gemstone. You wouldn't be able to understand how he had done it, but the master would have seen the connection between *water* and the gem and would have used that as the focal point for his power. The practice is more of an art than anything else. What you did was extremely difficult."

Saphira interrupted Eragon's thoughts. *Brom is a magician! That's how he was able to light the fire on the plains. He doesn't just know about magic; he can use it himself!*

Eragon's eyes widened. *You're right!*

Ask him about this power, but be careful of what you say. It is unwise to trifle with those who have such abilities. If he is a wizard or sorcerer, who knows what his motives might have been for settling in Carvahall?

Eragon kept that in mind as he said carefully, "Saphira and I just realized something. You can use this magic, can't you? That's how you started the fire our first day on the plains."

Brom inclined his head slightly. "I am proficient to some degree."

"Then why didn't you fight the Urgals with it? In fact, I can think of many times when it would have been useful—you could have shielded us from the storm and kept the dirt out of our eyes."

After refilling his pipe, Brom said, "Some simple reasons, really. I am not a Rider, which means that, even at your weakest moment, you are stronger than I. And I have outlived my youth; I'm not as strong as I used to be. Every time I reach for magic, it gets a little harder."

Eragon dropped his eyes, abashed. "I'm sorry."

"Don't be," said Brom as he shifted his arm. "It happens to everyone."

"Where did you learn to use magic?"

"That is one fact I'll keep to myself. . . . Suffice it to say, it was in a remote area and from a very good teacher. I can, at the very least, pass on his lessons." Brom snuffed his pipe with a small rock. "I know that you have more questions, and I will answer them, but they must wait until morning."

He leaned forward, eyes gleaming. "Until then, I will say this to discourage any experiments: magic takes just as much energy as if you used your arms and back. That is why you felt tired after destroying the Urgals. And that is why I was angry. It was a dreadful risk on your part. If the magic had used more energy than was in your body, it would have killed you. You should use magic only for tasks that can't be accomplished the mundane way."

"How do you know if a spell will use all your energy?" asked Eragon, frightened.

Brom raised his hands. "Most of the time you don't. That's why magicians have to know their limits well, and even then they are cautious. Once you commit to a task and release the magic, you can't pull it back, even if it's going to kill you. I mean this as a warning: don't try anything until you've learned more. Now, enough of this for tonight."

208

As they spread out their blankets, Saphira commented with satisfaction, *We are becoming more powerful, Eragon, both of us. Soon no one will be able to stand in our way.*

Yes, but which way shall we choose?

Whichever one we want, she said smugly, settling down for the night.

MAGIC IS THE
SIMPLEST THING

"Why do you think those two Urgals were still in Yazuac?" asked Eragon, after they had been on the trail for a while. "There doesn't seem to be any reason for them to have stayed behind."

"I suspect they deserted the main group to loot the town. What makes it odd is that, as far as I know, Urgals have gathered in force only two or three times in history. It's unsettling that they are doing it now."

"Do you think the Ra'zac caused the attack?"

"I don't know. The best thing we can do is continue away from Yazuac at the fastest pace we can muster. Besides, this is the direction the Ra'zac went: south."

Eragon agreed. "We still need provisions, however. Is there another town nearby?"

Brom shook his head. "No, but Saphira can

hunt for us if we must survive on meat alone. This swath of trees may look small to you, but there are plenty of animals in it. The river is the only source of water for many miles around, so most of the plains animals come here to drink. We won't starve."

Eragon remained quiet, satisfied with Brom's answer. As they rode, loud birds darted around them, and the river rushed by peacefully. It was a noisy place, full of life and energy. Eragon asked, "How did that Urgal get you? Things were happening so fast, I didn't see."

"Bad luck, really," grumbled Brom. "I was more than a match for him, so he kicked Snowfire. The idiot of a horse reared and threw me off balance. That was all the Urgal needed to give me this gash." He scratched his chin. "I suppose you're still wondering about this magic. The fact that you've discovered it presents a thorny problem. Few know it, but every Rider could use magic, though with differing strengths. They kept the ability secret, even at the height of their power, because it gave them an advantage over their enemies. Had everyone known about it, dealing with common people would have been difficult. Many think the king's magical powers come from the fact that he is a wizard or sorcerer. That's not true; it is because he's a Rider."

"What's the difference? Doesn't the fact that I used magic make me a sorcerer?"

"Not at all! A sorcerer, like a Shade, uses spirits to accomplish his will. That is totally different from your power. Nor does that make you a magician, whose powers come without the aid of spirits or a dragon. And you're certainly not a witch or wizard, who get their powers from various potions and spells.

"Which brings me back to my original point: the problem you've presented. Young Riders like yourself were put through a strict regimen designed to strengthen their bodies and increase their mental control. This regimen continued for many months, occasionally years, until the Riders were deemed responsible enough to handle magic. Up until then, not one student was told of his potential powers. If one of them discovered magic by accident, he or she was immediately taken away for private tutoring. It was rare for anyone to discover magic on his own," he inclined his head toward Eragon, "though they were never put under the same pressure you were."

"Then how were they finally trained to use magic?" asked Eragon. "I don't see how you could teach it to anyone. If you had tried to explain it to me two days ago, it wouldn't have made any sense."

"The students were presented with a series of pointless exercises designed to frustrate them. For example, they were instructed to move piles of stones using only their feet, fill ever draining tubs full of water, and other impossibilities. After a time, they would get infuriated enough to use magic. Most of the time it succeeded.

"What this means," Brom continued, "is that you will be disadvantaged if you ever meet an enemy who has received this training. There are still some alive who are that old: the king for one, not to mention the elves. Any one of those could tear you apart with ease."

"What can I do, then?"

"There isn't time for formal instruction, but we can do much while we travel," said Brom. "I know many techniques you can practice that will give you strength and control, but you cannot gain the discipline the Riders had overnight. You," he looked at Eragon humorously, "will have to amass it on the run. It will be hard in the beginning, but the rewards will be great. It may please you to know that no Rider your age ever used magic the way you did yesterday with those two Urgals."

Eragon smiled at the praise. "Thank you. Does this language have a name?"

Brom laughed. "Yes, but no one knows it. It would be a word of incredible power, something by which you could control the entire language and those who use it. People have long searched for it, but no one has ever found it."

"I still don't understand how this magic works," said Eragon. "Exactly how do I use it?"

Brom looked astonished. "I haven't made that clear?"

"No."

Brom took a deep breath and said, "To work with magic, you must have a certain innate power, which is very rare among people nowadays. You also have to be able to summon this power at will. Once it is called upon, you have to use it or let it fade away. Understood? Now, if you wish to employ the power, you must utter the word or phrase of the ancient language that describes your intent. For example, if you hadn't said *brisingr* yesterday, nothing would have happened."

"So I'm limited by my knowledge of this language?"

"Exactly," crowed Brom. "Also, while speaking it, it's impossible to practice deceit."

Eragon shook his head. "That can't be. People always lie. The sounds of the ancient words can't stop them from doing that."

Brom cocked an eyebrow and said, "Fethrblaka, eka weohnata néiat haina ono. Blaka eom iet lam." A bird suddenly flitted from a branch and landed on his hand. It trilled lightly and looked at them with beady eyes. After a moment he said, "Eitha," and it fluttered away.

"How did you do that?" asked Eragon in wonder.

"I promised not to harm him. He may not have known exactly what I meant, but in the language of power, the meaning of my words was evident. The bird trusted me because he knows what all animals do, that those who speak in that tongue are bound by their word."

"And the elves speak this language?"

"Yes."

"So they never lie?"

"Not quite," admitted Brom. "They maintain that they don't, and in a way it's true, but they have perfected the art of saying one thing and meaning another. You never know exactly what their intent is, or if you have fathomed it correctly. Many times they only reveal part of the truth and withhold the rest. It takes a refined and subtle mind to deal with their culture."

Eragon considered that. "What do personal names mean in this language? Do they give power over people?"

Brom's eyes brightened with approval. "Yes, they do. Those who speak the language have two names. The first is for everyday use and has little authority. But the second is their true name and is shared with only a few trusted people. There was a time when no one concealed his true name, but this age isn't as kind. Whoever knows your true name gains enormous power over you. It's like putting your life into another person's hands. Everyone has a hidden name, but few know what it is."

"How do you find your true name?" asked Eragon.

"Elves instinctively know theirs. No one else has that gift. The human Riders usually went on quests to discover it—or found an elf who would tell them, which was rare, for elves don't distribute that knowledge freely," replied Brom.

"I'd like to know mine," Eragon said wistfully.

Brom's brow darkened. "Be careful. It can be a terrible knowledge. To know who you are without any delusions or sympathy is a moment of revelation that no one experiences unscathed. Some have been driven to madness by that stark reality. Most try to forget it. But as much as the name will give others power, so you may gain power over yourself, if the truth doesn't break you."

And I'm sure that it would not, stated Saphira.

"I still wish to know," said Eragon, determined.

215

"You are not easily dissuaded. That is good, for only the resolute find their identity, but I cannot help you with this. It is a search that you will have to undertake on your own." Brom moved his injured arm and grimaced uncomfortably.

"Why can't you or I heal that with magic?" asked Eragon.

Brom blinked. "No reason—I just never considered it because it's beyond my strength. You could probably do it with the right word, but I don't want you to exhaust yourself."

"I could save you a lot of trouble and pain," protested Eragon.

"I'll live with it," said Brom flatly. "Using magic to heal a wound takes just as much energy as it would to mend on its own. I don't want you tired for the next few days. You shouldn't attempt such a difficult task yet."

"Still, if it's possible to fix your arm, could I bring someone back from the dead?"

The question surprised Brom, but he answered quickly, "Remember what I said about projects that will kill you? That is one of them. Riders were forbidden to try to resurrect the dead, for their own safety. There is an abyss beyond life where magic means nothing. If you reach into it, your strength will flee and your soul will fade into darkness. Wizards, sorcerers, and Riders—all have failed and died on that threshold. Stick with what's possible—cuts, bruises, maybe some broken bones—but definitely not dead people."

Eragon frowned. "This is a lot more complex than I thought."

"Exactly!" said Brom. "And if you don't understand what you're doing, you'll try something too big and die." He twisted in his saddle and swooped down, grabbing a handful of pebbles from the ground. With effort, he righted himself, then discarded all but one of the rocks. "See this pebble?"

"Yes."

"Take it." Eragon did and stared at the unremarkable lump. It was dull black, smooth, and as large as the end of his thumb. There were count-less stones like it on the trail. "This is your train-ing."

Eragon looked back at him, confused. "I don't understand."

"Of course you don't," said Brom impatiently. "That's why I'm teaching you and not the other way around. Now stop talking or we'll never get anywhere. What I want you to do is lift the rock off your palm and hold it in the air for as long as you can. The words you're going to use are *stenr reisa*. Say them."

"Stenr reisa."

"Good. Go ahead and try."

Eragon focused sourly on the pebble, search-ing his mind for any hint of the energy that had burned in him the day before. The stone re-mained motionless as he stared at it, sweating and frustrated. *How am I supposed to do this?* Fi-nally, he crossed his arms and snapped, "This is impossible."

"No," said Brom gruffly. "*I'll* say when it's im-possible or not. Fight for it! Don't give in this easily. Try again."

Frowning, Eragon closed his eyes, setting aside all distracting thoughts. He took a deep breath and reached into the farthest corners of his con-sciousness, trying to find where his power resided. Searching, he found only thoughts and memories until he felt something different—a small bump that was a part of him and yet not of him. Excited, he dug into it, seeking what it hid. He felt resistance, a barrier in his mind, but knew that the power lay on the other side. He tried to breach it, but it held firm before his efforts. Growing angry, Eragon drove into the barrier, ramming against it with all of his might until it shattered like a thin pane of glass, flooding his mind with a river of light.

"Stenr reisa," he gasped. The pebble wobbled into the air over his faintly glowing palm. He struggled to keep it floating, but the power slipped away and faded back behind the barrier. The pebble dropped to his hand with a soft plop, and his palm returned to normal. He felt a little tired, but grinned from his success.

"Not bad for your first time," said Brom.

"Why does my hand do that? It's like a little lantern."

"No one's sure," Brom admitted. "The Riders always preferred to channel their power through whichever hand bore the gedwëy ignasia. You can use your other palm, but it isn't as easy." He looked at Eragon for a minute. "I'll buy you some gloves at the next town, if it isn't gutted. You hide the mark pretty well on your own, but we don't want anyone to see it by accident. Besides, there may be times when you won't want the glow to alert an enemy."

"Do you have a mark of your own?"

"No. Only Riders have them," said Brom.

"Also, you should know that magic is affected by distance, just like an arrow or a spear. If you try to lift or move something a mile away, it'll take more energy than if you were closer. So if you see enemies racing after you from a league away, let them approach before using magic. Now, back to work! Try to lift the pebble again."

"Again?" asked Eragon weakly, thinking of the effort it had taken to do it just once.

"Yes! And this time be quicker about it."

They continued with the exercises throughout most of the day. When Eragon finally stopped, he was tired and ill-tempered. In those hours, he had come to hate the pebble and everything about it. He started to throw it away, but Brom said, "Don't. Keep it." Eragon glared at him, then reluctantly 219 tucked the stone into a pocket.

"We're not done yet," warned Brom, "so don't get comfortable." He pointed at a small plant. "This is called *delois*." From there on he instructed Eragon in the ancient language, giving him words to memorize, from *vöndr*, a thin, straight stick, to the morning star, *Aiedail*.

That evening they sparred around the fire. Though Brom fought with his left hand, his skill was undiminished.

The days followed the same pattern. First, Eragon struggled to learn the ancient words and to manipulate the pebble. Then, in the evening, he trained against Brom with the fake swords.

Eragon was in constant discomfort, but he gradually began to change, almost without noticing. Soon the pebble no longer wobbled when he lifted it. He mastered the first exercises Brom gave him and undertook harder ones, and his knowledge of the ancient language grew.

In their sparring, Eragon gained confidence and speed, striking like a snake. His blows became heavier, and his arm no longer trembled when he warded off attacks. The clashes lasted longer as he learned how to fend off Brom. Now, when they went to sleep, Eragon was not the only one with bruises.

Saphira continued to grow as well, but more slowly than before. Her extended flights, along with periodic hunts, kept her fit and healthy. She was taller than the horses now, and much longer. Because of her size and the way her scales sparkled, she was altogether too visible. Brom and Eragon worried about it, but they could not convince her to allow dirt to obscure her scintillating hide.

They continued south, tracking the Ra'zac. It frustrated Eragon that no matter how fast they went, the Ra'zac always stayed a few days ahead of them. At times he was ready to give up, but then they would find some mark or print that would renew his hope.

There were no signs of habitation along the Ninor or in the plains, leaving the three companions undisturbed as the days slipped by. Finally, they neared Daret, the first village since Yazuac.

The night before they reached the village, Eragon's dreams were especially vivid.

He saw Garrow and Roran at home, sitting in the destroyed kitchen. They asked him for help rebuilding the farm, but he only shook his head with a pang of longing in his heart. "I'm tracking your killers," he whispered to his uncle.

Garrow looked at him askance and demanded, "Do I look dead to you?"

"I can't help you," said Eragon softly, feeling tears in his eyes.

There was a sudden roar, and Garrow transformed into the Ra'zac. "Then die," they hissed, and leapt at Eragon.

He woke up feeling ill and watched the stars slowly turn in the sky.

All will be well, little one, said Saphira gently.

DARET

D aret was on the banks of the Ninor River—
as it had to be to survive. The village was
small and wild-looking, without any signs
of inhabitants. Eragon and Brom approached it
with great caution. Saphira hid close to the town
this time; if trouble arose, she would be at their
sides within seconds.

They rode into Daret, striving to be silent.
Brom gripped his sword with his good hand, eyes
flashing everywhere. Eragon kept his bow partially drawn as they passed between the silent
houses, glancing at each other with apprehension. *This doesn't look good*, commented Eragon to
Saphira. She did not answer, but he felt her prepare to rush after them. He looked at the ground
and was reassured to see the fresh footprints of
children. *But where are they?*

Brom stiffened as they entered the center of

Daret and found it empty. Wind blew through the desolate town, and dust devils swirled sporadically. Brom wheeled Snowfire about. "Let's get out of here. I don't like the feel of this." He spurred Snowfire into a gallop. Eragon followed him, urging Cadoc onward.

They advanced only a few strides before wagons toppled out from behind the houses and blocked their way. Cadoc snorted and dug in his hooves, sliding to a stop next to Snowfire. A swarthy man hopped over the wagon and planted himself before them, a broadsword slung at his side and a drawn bow in his hands. Eragon swung his own bow up and pointed it at the stranger, who commanded, "Halt! Put your weapons down. You're surrounded by sixty archers. They'll shoot if you move." As if on cue, a row of men stood up on the roofs of the surrounding houses.

Stay away, Saphira! cried Eragon. *There are too many. If you come, they'll shoot you out of the sky. Stay away!* She heard, but he was unsure if she would obey. He prepared to use magic. *I'll have to stop the arrows before they hit me or Brom.*

"What do you want?" asked Brom calmly.

"Why have you come here?" demanded the man.

"To buy supplies and hear the news. Nothing more. We're on the way to my cousin's house in Dras-Leona."

"You're armed pretty heavily."

"So are you," said Brom. "These are dangerous times."

"True." The man looked at them carefully. "I don't think you mean us ill, but we've had too many encounters with Urgals and bandits for me to trust you only on your word."

"If it doesn't matter what we say, what happens now?" countered Brom. The men on top of the houses had not moved. By their very stillness, Eragon was sure that they were either highly disciplined . . . or frightened for their lives. He hoped it was the latter.

"You say that you only want supplies. Would you agree to stay here while we bring what you need, then pay us and leave immediately?"

"Yes."

"All right," said the man, lowering his bow, though he kept it ready. He waved at one of the archers, who slid to the ground and ran over. "Tell him what you want."

Brom recited a short list and then added, "Also, if you have a spare pair of gloves that would fit my nephew, I'd like to buy those too." The archer nodded and ran off.

"The name's Trevor," said the man standing in front of them. "Normally I'd shake your hand, but under the circumstances, I think I'll keep my distance. Tell me, where are you from?"

"North," said Brom, "but we haven't lived in any place long enough to call it home. Have Urgals forced you to take these measures?"

"Yes," said Trevor, "and worse fiends. Do you have any news from other towns? We receive word from them rarely, but there have been reports that they are also beleaguered."

Brom turned grave. "I wish it wasn't our lot to bring you these tidings. Nearly a fortnight ago we passed through Yazuac and found it pillaged. The villagers had been slaughtered and piled together. We would have tried to give them a decent burial, but two Urgals attacked us."

Shocked, Trevor stepped back and looked down with tears in his eyes. "Alas, this is indeed a dark day. Still, I don't see how two Urgals could have defeated all of Yazuac. The people there were good fighters—some were my friends."

"There were signs that a band of Urgals had ravaged the town," stated Brom. "I think the ones we encountered were deserters."

"How large was the company?"

Brom fiddled with his saddlebags for a minute. "Large enough to wipe out Yazuac, but small enough to go unnoticed in the countryside. No more than a hundred, and no less than fifty. If I'm not mistaken, either number would prove fatal to you." Trevor wearily agreed. "You should consider leaving," Brom continued. "This area has become far too perilous for anyone to live in peace."

"I know, but the people here refuse to consider moving. This is their home—as well as mine, though I have only been here a couple years—and they place its worth above their own lives." Trevor looked at him seriously. "We have repulsed individual Urgals, and that has given the townspeople a confidence far beyond their abilities. I fear that we will all wake up one morning with our throats slashed."

The archer hurried out of a house with a pile of goods in his arms. He set them next to the horses, and Brom paid him. As the man left, Brom asked, "Why did they choose you to defend Daret?"

Trevor shrugged. "I was in the king's army for some years."

Brom dug through the items, handed Eragon the pair of gloves, and packed the rest of the supplies into their saddlebags. Eragon pulled the gloves on, being careful to keep his palm facing down, and flexed his hands. The leather felt good and strong, though it was scarred from use. "Well," said Brom, "as I promised, we will go now."

Trevor nodded. "When you enter Dras-Leona, would you do us this favor? Alert the Empire to our plight and that of the other towns. If word of this hasn't reached the king by now, it's cause for worry. And if it has, but he has chosen to do nothing, that too is cause for worry."

"We will carry your message. May your swords stay sharp," said Brom.

"And yours."

The wagons were pulled out of their way, and they rode from Daret into the trees along the Ninor River. Eragon sent his thoughts to Saphira. *We're on our way back. Everything turned out all right.* Her only response was simmering anger.

Brom pulled at his beard. "The Empire is in worse condition than I had imagined. When the traders visited Carvahall, they brought reports of unrest, but I never believed that it was this widespread. With all these Urgals around, it seems that the Empire itself is under attack, yet no troops or soldiers have been sent out. It's as if the king doesn't care to defend his domain."

"It is strange," agreed Eragon.

Brom ducked under a low-hanging branch. "Did you use any of your powers while we were in Daret?"

"There was no reason to."

"Wrong," corrected Brom. "You could have sensed Trevor's intentions. Even with my limited abilities, I was able to do that. If the villagers had been bent on killing us, I wouldn't have just sat there. However, I felt there was a reasonable chance of talking our way out of there, which is what I did."

"How could I know what Trevor was thinking?" asked Eragon. "Am I supposed to be able to see into people's minds?"

"Come now," chided Brom, "you should know the answer to that. You could have discovered

Trevor's purpose in the same way that you communicate with Cadoc or Saphira. The minds of men are not so different from a dragon's or horse's. It's a simple thing to do, but it's a power you must use sparingly and with great caution. A person's mind is his last sanctuary. You must never violate it unless circumstances force you to. The Riders had very strict rules regarding this. If they were broken without due cause, the punishment was severe."

"And you can do this even though you aren't a Rider?" asked Eragon.

"As I said before, with the right instruction anyone can talk with their minds, but with differing amounts of success. Whether it's magic, though, is hard to tell. Magical abilities will certainly trigger the talent—or becoming linked with a dragon—but I've known plenty who learned it on their own. Think about it: you can communicate with any sentient being, though the contact may not be very clear. You could spend the entire day listening to a bird's thoughts or understanding how an earthworm feels during a rainstorm. But I've never found birds very interesting. I suggest starting with a cat; they have unusual personalities."

Eragon twisted Cadoc's reins in his hands, considering the implications of what Brom had said. "But if I can get into someone's head, doesn't that mean that others can do the same to me? How do I know if someone's prying in my mind? Is there a way to stop that?" *How do I know if Brom can tell what I'm thinking right now?*

"Why, yes. Hasn't Saphira ever blocked you from her mind?"

"Occasionally," admitted Eragon. "When she took me into the Spine, I couldn't talk to her at all. It wasn't that she was ignoring me; I don't think she could even hear me. There were walls around her mind that I couldn't get through."

Brom worked on his bandage for a moment, shifting it higher on his arm. "Only a few people can tell if someone is in their mind, and of those, only a handful could stop you from entering. It's a matter of training and of how you think. Because of your magical power, you'll always know if someone is in your mind. Once you do, blocking them is a simple matter of concentrating on one thing to the exclusion of all else. For instance, if you only think about a brick wall, that's all the enemy will find in your mind. However, it takes a huge amount of energy and discipline to block someone for any length of time. If you're distracted by even the slightest thing, your wall will waver and your opponent will slip in through the weakness."

"How can I learn to do this?" asked Eragon.

"There is only one thing for it: practice, practice, and yet more practice. Picture something in your mind and hold it there to the exclusion of all else for as long as you can. It is a very advanced ability; only a handful ever master it," said Brom.

"I don't need perfection, just safety." *If I can get into someone's mind, can I change how he thinks? Every time I learn something new about magic, I grow more wary of it.*

When they reached Saphira, she startled them by thrusting her head at them. The horses backstepped nervously. Saphira looked Eragon over carefully and gave a low hiss. Her eyes were flinty. Eragon threw a concerned look at Brom—he had never seen Saphira this angry—then asked, *What's wrong?*

You, she growled. *You are the problem.*

Eragon frowned and got off Cadoc. As soon as his feet touched the ground, Saphira swept his legs out from under him with her tail and pinned him with her talons. "What are you doing?" he yelled, struggling to get up, but she was too strong for him. Brom watched attentively from Snowfire.

Saphira swung her head over Eragon until they were eye to eye. He squirmed under her unwavering glare. *You! Every time you leave my sight you get into trouble. You're like a new hatchling, sticking your nose into everything. And what happens when you stick it into something that bites back? How will you survive then? I cannot help you when I'm miles away. I've stayed hidden so that no one*

230

*would see me, but no longer! Not when it may cost
you your life.*

I can understand why you're upset, said Eragon,
*but I'm much older than you and can take care of
myself. If anything, you're the one who needs to be
protected.*

She snarled and snapped her teeth by his ear.
Do you really believe that? she asked. *Tomorrow
you will ride me—not that pitiful deer-animal you
call a horse—or else I will carry you in my claws.
Are you a Dragon Rider or not? Don't you care
for me?*

The question burned in Eragon, and he
dropped his gaze. He knew she was right, but he
was scared of riding her. Their flights had been
the most painful ordeal he had ever endured.

"Well?" demanded Brom.

"She wants me to ride her tomorrow," said
Eragon lamely.

Brom considered it with twinkling eyes.
"Well, you have the saddle. I suppose that if the
two of you stay out of sight, it won't be a problem." Saphira switched her gaze to him, then returned it to Eragon.

"But what if you're attacked or there's an accident? I won't be able to get there in time and—"

Saphira pressed harder on his chest, stopping
his words. *Exactly my point, little one.*

Brom seemed to hide a smile. "It's worth the
risk. You need to learn how to ride her anyway.

Think about it this way: with you flying ahead and looking at the ground, you'll be able to spot any traps, ambushes, or other unwelcome surprises."

Eragon looked back at Saphira and said, *Okay, I'll do it. But let me up.*

Give me your word.

Is that really necessary? he demanded. She blinked. *Very well. I give you my word that I will fly with you tomorrow. Satisfied?*

I am content.

Saphira let him up and, with a push of her legs, took off. A small shiver ran through Eragon as he watched her twist through the air. Grumbling, he returned to Cadoc and followed Brom.

It was nearly sundown when they made camp. As usual, Eragon dueled with Brom before dinner. In the midst of the fight, Eragon delivered such a powerful blow that he snapped both of their sticks like twigs. The pieces whistled into the darkness in a cloud of splintered fragments. Brom tossed what remained of his stick into the fire and said, "We're done with these; throw yours in as well. You have learned well, but we've gone as far as we can with branches. There is nothing more you can gain from them. It is time for you to use the blade." He removed Zar'roc from Eragon's bag and gave it to him.

"We'll cut each other to ribbons," protested Eragon.

"Not so. Again you forget magic," said Brom. He held up his sword and turned it so that fire-light glinted off the edge. He put a finger on either side of the blade and focused intensely, deepening the lines on his forehead. For a moment nothing happened, then he uttered, "Gëuloth du knífr!" and a small red spark jumped between his fingers. As it flickered back and forth, he ran his fingers down the length of the sword. Then he twirled it and did the same thing on the other side. The spark vanished the moment his fingers left the metal.

Brom held his hand out, palm up, and slashed it with the sword. Eragon jumped forward but was too slow to stop him. He was astonished when Brom raised his unharmed hand with a smile. "What did you do?" asked Eragon.

"Feel the edge," said Brom. Eragon touched it and felt an invisible surface under his fingers. The barrier was about a quarter inch wide and very slippery. "Now do the same on Zar'roc," instructed Brom. "Your block will be a bit different than mine, but it should accomplish the same thing."

He told Eragon how to pronounce the words and coached him through the process. It took Eragon a few tries, but he soon had Zar'roc's edge protected. Confident, he took his fighting stance. Before they started, Brom admonished, "These swords won't cut us, but they can still break bones. I would prefer to avoid that, so don't flail around like you normally do. A blow to the neck could prove fatal."

Eragon nodded, then struck without warning. Sparks flew off his blade, and the clash of metal filled their campsite as Brom parried. The sword felt slow and heavy to Eragon after fighting with sticks for so long. Unable to move Zar'roc fast enough, he received a sharp rap on his knee.

They both had large welts when they stopped, Eragon more so than Brom. He marveled that Zar'roc had not been scratched or dented by the vigorous pounding it had received.

THROUGH A
DRAGON'S EYE

The next morning Eragon woke with stiff limbs and purple bruises. He saw Brom carry the saddle to Saphira and tried to quell his uneasiness. By the time breakfast was ready, Brom had strapped the saddle onto Saphira and hung Eragon's bags from it.

When his bowl was empty, Eragon silently picked up his bow and went to Saphira. Brom said, "Now remember, grip with your knees, guide her with your thoughts, and stay as flat as you can on her back. Nothing will go wrong if you don't panic." Eragon nodded, sliding his unstrung bow into its leather tube, and Brom boosted him into the saddle.

Saphira waited impatiently while Eragon tightened the bands around his legs. *Are you ready?* she asked.

He sucked in the fresh morning air. *No, but*

let's do it! She agreed enthusiastically. He braced himself as she crouched. Her powerful legs surged and the air whipped past him, snatching his breath away. With three smooth strokes of her wings, she was in the sky, climbing rapidly.

The last time Eragon had ridden Saphira, every flap of her wings had been strained. Now she flew steadily and effortlessly. He clenched his arms around her neck as she turned on edge, banking. The river shrank to a wispy gray line beneath them. Clouds floated around them.

When they leveled off high above the plains, the trees below were no more than specks. The air was thin, chilly, and perfectly clear. "This is wonderfu—" His words were lost as Saphira tilted and rolled completely around. The ground spun in a dizzying circle, and vertigo clutched Eragon. "Don't do that!" he cried. "I feel like I'm going to fall off."

You must become accustomed to it. If I'm attacked in the air, that's one of the simplest maneuvers I will do, she replied. He could think of no rebuttal, so he concentrated on controlling his stomach. Saphira angled into a shallow dive and slowly approached the ground.

Although Eragon's stomach lurched with every wobble, he began to enjoy himself. He relaxed his arms a bit and stretched his neck back, taking in the scenery. Saphira let him enjoy the sights awhile, then said, *Let me show you what flying is really like.*

236

How? he asked.

Relax and do not be afraid, she said.

Her mind tugged at his, pulling him away from his body. Eragon fought for a moment, then surrendered control. His vision blurred, and he found himself looking through Saphira's eyes. Everything was distorted: colors had weird, exotic tints; blues were more prominent now, while greens and reds were subdued. Eragon tried to turn his head and body but could not. He felt like a ghost who had slipped out of the ether.

Pure joy radiated from Saphira as she climbed into the sky. She loved this freedom to go anywhere. When they were high above the ground, she looked back at Eragon. He saw himself as she did, hanging on to her with a blank look. He could feel her body strain against the air, using updrafts to rise. All her muscles were like his own. He felt her tail swinging through the air like a giant rudder to correct her course. It surprised him how much she depended on it.

Their connection grew stronger until there was no distinction between their identities. They clasped their wings together and dived straight down, like a spear thrown from on high. No terror of falling touched Eragon, engulfed as he was in Saphira's exhilaration. The air rushed past their face. Their tail whipped in the air, and their joined minds reveled in the experience.

Even as they plummeted toward the ground, there was no fear of collision. They snapped open their wings at just the right moment, pulling out of the dive with their combined strength. Slanting toward the sky, they shot up and continued back over into a giant loop.

As they leveled out, their minds began to diverge, becoming distinct personalities again. For a split second, Eragon felt both his body and Saphira's. Then his vision blurred and he again sat on her back. He gasped and collapsed on the saddle. It was minutes before his heart stopped hammering and his breathing calmed. Once he had recovered, he exclaimed, *That was incredible! How can you bear to land when you enjoy flying so much?*

I must eat, she said with some amusement. *But I am glad that you took pleasure in it.*

Those are spare words for such an experience. I'm sorry I haven't flown with you more; I never thought it could be like that. Do you always see so much blue?

It is the way I am. We will fly together more often now?

Yes! Every chance we get.

Good, she replied in a contented tone.

They exchanged many thoughts as she flew, talking as they had not for weeks. Saphira showed Eragon how she used hills and trees to hide and how she could conceal herself in the shadow of a cloud. They scouted the trail for Brom, which proved to be more arduous than Eragon expected. They could not see the path unless Saphira flew very close to it, in which case she risked being detected.

Near midday, an annoying buzz filled Eragon's ears, and he became aware of a strange pressure on his mind. He shook his head, trying to get rid of it, but the tension only grew stronger. Brom's words about how people could break into others' minds flashed through Eragon's head, and he frantically tried to clear his thoughts. He concentrated on one of Saphira's scales and forced himself to ignore everything else. The pressure faded for a moment and then returned, greater than ever. A sudden gust rocked Saphira, and Eragon's concentration slipped. Before he could marshal any defenses, the force broke through. But instead of the invasive presence of another mind, there were only the words, *What do you think you're doing? Get down here. I found something important.*

Brom? queried Eragon.

Yes, the old man said irritably. *Now get that oversized lizard of yours to land. I'm here. . . .* He sent a picture of his location. Eragon quickly told Saphira where to go, and she banked toward the river below. Meanwhile, he strung his bow and drew several arrows.

If there's trouble, I'll be ready for it.

As will I, said Saphira.

When they reached Brom, Eragon saw him standing in a clearing, waving his arms. Saphira

239

landed, and Eragon jumped off her and looked for danger. The horses were tied to a tree on the edge of the clearing, but otherwise Brom was alone. Eragon trotted over and asked, "What's wrong?"

Brom scratched his chin and muttered a string of curses. "Don't ever block me out like that again. It's hard enough for me to reach you without having to fight to make myself heard."

"Sorry."

He snorted. "I was farther down the river when I noticed that the Ra'zac's tracks had ceased. I backtracked until I found where they had disappeared. Look at the ground and tell me what you see."

Eragon knelt and examined the dirt and found a confusion of impressions that were difficult to decipher. Numerous Ra'zac footprints overlapped each other. Eragon guessed that the tracks were only a few days old. Superimposed over them were long, thick gouges torn into the ground. They looked familiar, but Eragon could not say why.

He stood, shaking his head. "I don't have any idea what . . ." Then his eyes fell on Saphira and he realized what had made the gouges. Every time she took off, her back claws dug into the ground and ripped it in the same manner. "This doesn't make any sense, but the only thing I can think of is that the Ra'zac flew off on dragons. Or else they got onto giant birds and disappeared into the heavens. Tell me you have a better explanation."

Brom shrugged. "I've heard reports of the Ra'zac moving from place to place with incredible speed, but this is the first evidence I've had of it. It will be almost impossible to find them if they have flying steeds. They aren't dragons—I know that much. A dragon would never consent to bear a Ra'zac."

"What do we do? Saphira can't track them through the sky. Even if she could, we would leave you far behind."

"There's no easy solution to this riddle," said Brom. "Let's have lunch while we think on it. Perhaps inspiration will strike us while we eat." Eragon glumly went to his bags for food. They ate in silence, staring at the empty sky.

Once again Eragon thought of home and wondered what Roran was doing. A vision of the burnt farm appeared before him and grief threatened to overwhelm him. *What will I do if we can't find the Ra'zac? What is my purpose then? I could return to Carvahall*—he plucked a twig from the ground and snapped it between two fingers—*or just travel with Brom and continue my training.* Eragon stared out at the plains, hoping to quiet his thoughts.

When Brom finished eating, he stood and threw back his hood. "I have considered every trick I know, every word of power within my grasp, and all the skills we have, but I still don't see how we can find the Ra'zac." Eragon slumped against Saphira in despair. "Saphira could show herself at some town. That would draw the Ra'zac like flies to honey. But it would be an extremely risky thing to attempt. The Ra'zac would bring soldiers with them, and the king might be interested enough to come himself, which would spell certain death for you and me."

"So what now?" asked Eragon, throwing his hands up. *Do you have any ideas, Saphira?*

No.

"That's up to you," said Brom. "This is your crusade."

Eragon ground his teeth angrily and stalked away from Brom and Saphira. Just as he was about to enter the trees, his foot struck something hard. Lying on the ground was a metal flask with a leather strap just long enough to hang off someone's shoulder. A silver insignia Eragon recognized as the Ra'zac's symbol was wrought into it.

Excited, he picked up the flask and unscrewed its cap. A cloying smell filled the air—the same one he had noticed when he found Garrow in the wreckage of their house. He tilted the flask, and a drop of clear, shiny liquid fell on his finger. Instantly Eragon's finger burned as if it were on fire. He yelped and scrubbed his hand on the ground. After a moment the pain subsided to a dull throbbing. A patch of skin had been eaten away.

Grimacing, he jogged back to Brom. "Look

what I found." Brom took the flask and examined it, then poured a bit of the liquid into the cap. Eragon started to warn him, "Watch out, it'll burn—"

"My skin, I know," said Brom. "And I suppose you went ahead and poured it all over your hand. Your finger? Well, at least you showed sense enough not to drink it. Only a puddle would have been left of you."

"What is it?" asked Eragon.

"Oil from the petals of the Seithr plant, which grows on a small island in the frigid northern seas. In its natural state, the oil is used for preserving pearls—it makes them lustrous and strong. But when specific words are spoken over the oil, along with a blood sacrifice, it gains the property to eat any flesh. That alone wouldn't make it special— there are plenty of acids that can dissolve sinew and bone—except for the fact that it leaves everything else untouched. You can dip anything into the oil and pull it out unharmed, unless it was once part of an animal or human. This has made it a weapon of choice for torture and assassination. It can be stored in wood, slathered on the point of a spear, or dripped onto sheets so that the next person to touch them will be burned. There are myriad uses for it, limited only by your ingenuity. Any injury caused by it is always slow to heal. It's rather rare and expensive, especially this converted form."

Eragon remembered the terrible burns that

had covered Garrow. *That's what they used on him*, he realized with horror. "I wonder why the Ra'zac left it behind if it's so valuable."

"It must have slipped off when they flew away."

"But why didn't they come back for it? I doubt that the king will be pleased that they lost it."

"No, he won't," said Brom, "but he would be even more displeased if they delayed bringing him news of you. In fact, if the Ra'zac have reached him by now, you can be sure that the king has learned your name. And that means we will have to be much more careful when we go into towns. There will be notices and alerts about you posted throughout the Empire."

244   Eragon paused to think. "This oil, how rare is it exactly?"

"Like diamonds in a pig trough," said Brom. He amended himself after a second, "Actually, the normal oil is used by jewelers, but only those who can afford it."

"So there are people who trade in it?"

"Perhaps one, maybe two."

"Good," said Eragon. "Now, do the cities along the coast keep shipping records?"

Brom's eyes brightened. "Of course they do. If we could get to those records, they would tell us who brought the oil south and where it went from there."

"And the record of the Empire's purchase will

tell us where the Ra'zac live!" concluded Eragon. "I don't know how many people can afford this oil, but it shouldn't be hard to figure out which ones aren't working for the Empire."

"Genius!" exclaimed Brom, smiling. "I wish I had thought of this years ago; it would have saved me many headaches. The coast is dotted with numerous cities and towns where ships can land. I suppose that Teirm would be the place to start, as it controls most of the trade." Brom paused. "The last I heard, my old friend Jeod lives there. We haven't seen each other for many years, but he might be willing to help us. And because he's a merchant, it's possible that he has access to those records."

"How do we get to Teirm?"

"We'll have to go southwest until we reach a high pass in the Spine. Once on the other side, we can head up the coast to Teirm," said Brom. A gentle wind pulled at his hair.

"Can we reach the pass within a week?"

"Easily. If we angle away from the Ninor and to our right, we might be able to see the mountains by tomorrow."

Eragon went to Saphira and mounted her. "I'll see you at dinner, then." When they were at a good height, he said, *I'm going to ride Cadoc tomorrow. Before you protest, know that I am only doing it because I want to talk with Brom.*

You should ride with him every other day. That

*way you can still receive your instruction, and I will
have time to hunt.*

You won't be troubled by it?

It is necessary.

When they landed for the day, he was pleased
to discover that his legs did not hurt. The saddle
had protected him well from Saphira's scales.

Eragon and Brom had their nightly fight, but it
lacked energy, as both were preoccupied with the
day's events. By the time they finished, Eragon's
arms burned from Zar'roc's unaccustomed weight.

246

A SONG FOR
THE ROAD

The next day while they were riding, Eragon asked Brom, "What is the sea like?"

"You must have heard it described before," said Brom.

"Yes, but what is it really like?"

Brom's eyes grew hazy, as if he looked upon some hidden scene. "The sea is emotion incarnate. It loves, hates, and weeps. It defies all attempts to capture it with words and rejects all shackles. No matter what you say about it, there is always that which you can't. Do you remember what I told you about how the elves came over the sea?"

"Yes."

"Though they live far from the coast, they retain a great fascination and passion for the ocean. The sound of crashing waves, the smell of salt air, it affects them deeply and has inspired many of their loveliest songs. There is one that tells of this love, if you want to hear it."

"I would," said Eragon, interested.

Brom cleared his throat and said, "I will translate it from the ancient language as best I can. It won't be perfect, but perhaps it will give you an idea of how the original sounds." He pulled Snowfire to a stop and closed his eyes. He was silent for a while, then chanted softly:

> O liquid temptress 'neath the azure sky,
> Your gilded expanse calls me, calls me.
> For I would sail ever on,
> Were it not for the elven maid,
> Who calls me, calls me.
> She binds my heart with a lily-white tie,
> Never to be broken, save by the sea,
> Ever to be torn twixt the trees and the waves.

248

The words echoed hauntingly in Eragon's head. "There is much more to that song, the 'Du Silbena Datia.' I have only recited one of its verses. It tells the sad tale of two lovers, Acallamh and Nuada, who were separated by longing for the sea. The elves find great meaning in the story."

"It's beautiful," said Eragon simply.

The Spine was a faint outline on the horizon when they halted that evening.

When they arrived at the Spine's foothills, they turned and followed the mountains south. Eragon was glad to be near the mountains again;

they placed comforting boundaries on the world. Three days later they came to a wide road rutted by wagon wheels. "This is the main road between the capital, Urû'baen, and Teirm," said Brom. "It's widely used and a favorite route for merchants. We have to be more cautious. This isn't the busiest time of year, but a few people are bound to be using the road."

Days passed quickly as they continued to trek along the Spine, searching for the mountain pass. Eragon could not complain of boredom. When not learning the elven language, he was either learning how to care for Saphira or practicing magic. Eragon also learned how to kill game with magic, which saved them time hunting. He would hold a small rock on his hand and shoot it at his prey. It was impossible to miss. The results of his efforts roasted over the fire each night. And after dinner, Brom and Eragon would spar with swords and, occasionally, fists.

The long days and strenuous work stripped Eragon's body of excess fat. His arms became corded, and his tanned skin rippled with lean muscles. *Everything about me is turning hard*, he thought dryly.

When they finally reached the pass, Eragon saw that a river rushed out of it and cut across the road. "This is the Toark," explained Brom. "We'll follow it all the way to the sea."

"How can we," laughed Eragon, "if it flows out

of the Spine in *this* direction? It won't end up in the ocean unless it doubles back on itself."

Brom twisted the ring on his finger. "Because in the middle of the mountains rests the Woadark Lake. A river flows from each end of it and both are called the Toark. We see the eastward one now. It runs to the south and winds through the brush until it joins Leona Lake. The other one goes to the sea."

After two days in the Spine, they came upon a rock ledge from which they could see clearly out of the mountains. Eragon noticed how the land flattened in the distance, and he groaned at the leagues they still had to traverse. Brom pointed. "Down there and to the north lies Teirm. It is an old city. Some say it's where the elves first landed in Alagaësia. Its citadel has never fallen, nor have its warriors ever been defeated." He spurred Snowfire forward and left the ledge.

It took them until noon the next day to descend through the foothills and arrive at the other side of the Spine, where the forested land quickly leveled out. Without the mountains to hide behind, Saphira flew close to the ground, using every hollow and dip in the land to conceal herself.

Beyond the forest, they noticed a change. The countryside was covered with soft turf and heather that their feet sank into. Moss clung to every stone and branch and lined the streams that laced the ground. Pools of mud pocked the road where horses had trampled the dirt. Before long both Brom and Eragon were splattered with grime.

"Why is everything green?" asked Eragon. "Don't they have winter here?"

"Yes, but the season is mild. Mist and fog roll in from the sea and keep everything alive. Some find it to their liking, but to me it's dreary and depressing."

When evening fell, they set up camp in the driest spot they could find. As they ate, Brom commented, "You should continue to ride Cadoc until we reach Teirm. It's likely that we'll meet other travelers now that we are out of the Spine, and it will be better if you are with me. An old man traveling alone will raise suspicion. With you at my side, no one will ask questions. Besides, I don't want to show up at the city and have someone who saw me on the trail wondering where you suddenly came from."

"Will we use our own names?" asked Eragon.

Brom thought about it. "We won't be able to deceive Jeod. He already knows my name, and I think I trust him with yours. But to everyone else, I will be Neal and you will be my nephew Evan. If our tongues slip and give us away, it probably won't make a difference, but I don't want our names in anyone's heads. People have an annoying habit of remembering things they shouldn't."

A TASTE OF TEIRM

After two days of traveling north toward the ocean, Saphira sighted Teirm. A heavy fog clung to the ground, obscuring Brom's and Eragon's sight until a breeze from the west blew the mist away. Eragon gaped as Teirm was suddenly revealed before them, nestled by the edge of the shimmering sea, where proud ships were docked with furled sails. The surf's dull thunder could be heard in the distance.

The city was contained behind a white wall—a hundred feet tall and thirty feet thick—with rows of rectangular arrow slits lining it and a walkway on top for soldiers and watchmen. The wall's smooth surface was broken by two iron portcullises, one facing the western sea, the other opening south to the road. Above the wall—and set against its northeast section—rose a huge citadel built of giant stones and turrets. In the highest tower, a lighthouse lantern gleamed brilliantly. The castle was the only thing visible over the fortifications.

Soldiers guarded the southern gate but held their pikes carelessly. "This is our first test," said Brom. "Let's hope they haven't received reports of us from the Empire and won't detain us. Whatever happens, don't panic or act suspiciously."

Eragon told Saphira, *You should land somewhere now and hide. We're going in.*

Sticking your nose where it doesn't belong. Again, she said sourly.

I know. But Brom and I do have some advantages most people don't. We'll be all right.

If anything happens, I'm going to pin you to my back and never let you off.

I love you too.

Then I will bind you all the tighter.

Eragon and Brom rode toward the gate, trying to appear casual. A yellow pennant bearing the outline of a roaring lion and an arm holding a lily blossom waved over the entrance. As they neared the wall, Eragon asked in amazement, "How big is this place?"

"Larger than any city you have ever seen," said Brom.

At the entrance to Teirm, the guards stood straighter and blocked the gate with their pikes. "Wha's yer name?" asked one of them in a bored tone.

253

"I'm called Neal," said Brom in a wheezy voice, slouching to one side, an expression of happy idiocy on his face.

"And who's th' other one?" asked the guard.

"Well, I wus gettin' to that. This'ed be m'nephew Evan. He's m'sister's boy, not a . . ."

The guard nodded impatiently. "Yeah, yeah. And yer business here?"

"He's visitin' an old friend," supplied Eragon, dropping his voice into a thick accent: "I'm along t' make sure he don't get lost, if y' get m'meaning. He ain't as young as he used to be—had a bit too much sun when he was young'r. Touch o' the brain fever, y' know." Brom bobbed his head pleasantly.

254 "Right. Go on through," said the guard, waving his hand and dropping the pike. "Just make sure he doesn't cause any trouble."

"Oh, he won't," promised Eragon. He urged Cadoc forward, and they rode into Teirm. The cobblestone street clacked under the horses' hooves.

Once they were away from the guards, Brom sat up and growled, "Touch of brain fever, eh?"

"I couldn't let you have all the fun," teased Eragon.

Brom harrumphed and looked away.

The houses were grim and foreboding. Small, deep windows let in only sparse rays of light. Narrow doors were recessed into the buildings. The tops of the roofs were flat—except for metal railings—and all were covered with slate shingles. Eragon noticed that the houses closest to Teirm's outer wall were no more than one story, but the buildings got progressively higher as they went in. Those next to the citadel were tallest of all, though insignificant compared to the fortress.

"This place looks ready for war," said Eragon.

Brom nodded. "Teirm has a history of being attacked by pirates, Urgals, and other enemies. It has long been a center of commerce. There will always be conflict where riches gather in such abundance. The people here have been forced to take extraordinary measures to keep themselves from being overrun. It also helps that Galbatorix gives them soldiers to defend their city."

255

"Why are some houses higher than others?"

"Look at the citadel," said Brom, pointing. "It has an unobstructed view of Teirm. If the outer wall were breached, archers would be posted on all the roofs. Because the houses in the front, by the outer wall, are lower, the men farther back could shoot over them without fear of hitting their comrades. Also, if the enemy were to capture those houses and put their own archers on them, it would be an easy matter to shoot them down."

"I've never seen a city planned like this," said Eragon in wonder.

"Yes, but it was only done after Teirm was

nearly burned down by a pirate raid," commented Brom. As they continued up the street, people gave them searching looks, but there was not an undue amount of interest.

Compared to our reception at Daret, we've been welcomed with open arms. Perhaps Teirm has escaped notice by the Urgals, thought Eragon. He changed his opinion when a large man shouldered past them, a sword hanging from his waist. There were other, subtler signs of adverse times: no children played in the streets, people bore hard expressions, and many houses were deserted, with weeds growing from cracks in their stone-covered yards. "It looks like they've had trouble," said Eragon.

"The same as everywhere else," said Brom grimly. "We have to find Jeod." They led their horses across the street to a tavern and tied them to the hitching post. "The Green Chestnut . . . wonderful," muttered Brom, looking at the battered sign above them as he and Eragon entered the building.

The dingy room felt unsafe. A fire smoldered in the fireplace, yet no one bothered to throw more wood on it. A few lonely people in the corners nursed their drinks with sullen expressions. A man missing two fingers sat at a far table, eyeing his twitching stumps. The bartender had a cynical twist to his lips and held a glass in his hand that he kept polishing, even though it was broken.

Brom leaned against the bar and asked, "Do you know where we can find a man called Jeod?" Eragon stood at his side, fiddling with the tip of his bow by his waist. It was slung across his back, but right then he wished that it were in his hands.

The bartender said in an overly loud voice, "Now, why would I know something like that? Do you think I keep track of the mangy louts in this forsaken place?" Eragon winced as all eyes turned toward them.

Brom kept talking smoothly. "Could you be enticed to remember?" He slid some coins onto the bar.

The man brightened and put his glass down. "Could be," he replied, lowering his voice, "but my memory takes a great deal of prodding." Brom's face soured, but he slid more coins onto the bar. The bartender sucked on one side of his cheek undecidedly. "All right," he finally said, and reached for the coins.

Before he touched them, the man missing two fingers called out from his table, "Gareth, what in th' blazes do you think you're doing? Anyone on the street could tell them where Jeod lives. What are you charging them for?"

Brom swept the coins back into his purse. Gareth shot a venomous look at the man at the table, then turned his back on them and picked up the glass again. Brom went to the stranger and said, "Thanks. The name's Neal. This is Evan."

The man raised his mug to them. "Martin, and of course you met Gareth." His voice was deep and rough. Martin gestured at some empty chairs. "Go ahead and sit down. I don't mind." Eragon took a chair and arranged it so his back was to the wall and he faced the door. Martin raised an eyebrow, but made no comment.

"You just saved me a few crowns," said Brom.

"My pleasure. Can't blame Gareth, though—business hasn't been doing so well lately." Martin scratched his chin. "Jeod lives on the west side of town, right next to Angela, the herbalist. Do you have business with him?"

"Of a sort," said Brom.

"Well, he won't be interested in buying anything; he just lost another ship a few days ago."

Brom latched onto the news with interest. "What happened? It wasn't Urgals, was it?"

"No," said Martin. "They've left the area. No one's seen 'em in almost a year. It seems they've all gone south and east. But they aren't the problem. See, most of our business is through sea trade, as I'm sure you know. Well," he stopped to drink from his mug, "starting several months ago, someone's been attacking our ships. It's not the usual piracy, because only ships that carry the goods of certain merchants are attacked. Jeod's one of 'em. It's gotten so bad that no captain will accept those merchants' goods, which makes life difficult around here. Especially because some of 'em run the largest shipping businesses in the Empire. They're being forced to send goods by land. It's driven costs painfully high, and their caravans don't always make it."

"Do you have any idea who's responsible? There must be witnesses," said Brom.

Martin shook his head. "No one survives the attacks. Ships go out, then disappear; they're never seen again." He leaned toward them and said in a confidential tone, "The sailors are saying that it's magic." He nodded and winked, then leaned back.

Brom seemed worried by his words. "What do you think?"

Martin shrugged carelessly. "I don't know. And I don't think I will unless I'm unfortunate enough to be on one of those captured ships."

"Are you a sailor?" asked Eragon.

"No," snorted Martin. "Do I look like one? The captains hire me to defend their ships against pirates. And those thieving scum haven't been very active lately. Still, it's a good job."

"But a dangerous one," said Brom. Martin shrugged again and downed the last of his beer. Brom and Eragon took their leave and headed to the west side of the city, a nicer section of Teirm. The houses were clean, ornate, and large. The people in the streets wore expensive finery and walked with authority. Eragon felt conspicuous and out of place.

AN OLD FRIEND

The herbalist's shop had a cheery sign and was easy to find. A short, curly-haired woman sat by the door. She was holding a frog in one hand and writing with the other. Eragon assumed that she was Angela, the herbalist. On either side of the store was a house. "Which one do you think is his?" he asked.

Brom deliberated, then said, "Let's find out." He approached the woman and asked politely, "Could you tell us which house Jeod lives in?"

"I could." She continued writing.

"Will you tell us?"

"Yes." She fell silent, but her pen scribbled faster than ever. The frog on her hand croaked and looked at them with baleful eyes. Brom and Eragon waited uncomfortably, but she said no more. Eragon was about to blurt something out when Angela looked up. "Of course I'll tell you!

All you have to do is ask. Your first question was whether or not I *could* tell you, and the second was if I *would* tell you. But you never actually put the question to me."

"Then let me ask properly," said Brom with a smile. "Which house is Jeod's? And why are you holding a frog?"

"Now we're getting somewhere," she bantered. "Jeod is on the right. And as for the frog, he's actually a toad. I'm trying to prove that toads don't exist—that there are only frogs."

"How can toads not exist if you have one on your hand right now?" interrupted Eragon. "Besides, what good will it do, proving that there are only frogs?"

The woman shook her head vigorously, dark curls bouncing. "No, no, you don't understand. If I prove toads don't exist, then this is a frog and never was a toad. Therefore, the toad you see now doesn't exist. And," she raised a small finger, "if I can prove there are only frogs, then toads won't be able to do anything bad—like make teeth fall out, cause warts, and poison or kill people. Also, witches won't be able to use any of their evil spells because, of course, there won't be any toads around."

"I see," said Brom delicately. "It sounds interesting, and I would like to hear more, but we have to meet Jeod."

"Of course," she said, waving her hand and returning to her writing.

Once they were out of the herbalist's hearing, Eragon said, "She's crazy!"

"It's possible," said Brom, "but you never know. She might discover something useful, so don't criticize. Who knows, toads might really be frogs!"

"And my shoes are made of gold," retorted Eragon.

They stopped before a door with a wrought-iron knocker and marble doorstep. Brom banged three times. No one answered. Eragon felt slightly foolish. "Maybe this is the wrong house. Let's try the other one," he said. Brom ignored him and knocked again, pounding loudly.

Again no one answered. Eragon turned away in exasperation, then heard someone run to the door. A young woman with a pale complexion and light blond hair cracked it open. Her eyes were puffy; it looked like she had been crying, but her voice was perfectly steady. "Yes, what do you want?"

"Does Jeod live here?" asked Brom kindly.

The woman dipped her head a little. "Yes, he is my husband. Is he expecting you?" She opened the door no farther.

"No, but we need to talk with him," said Brom.

"He is very busy."

"We have traveled far. It's very important that we see him."

Her face hardened. "He is busy."

Brom bristled, but his voice stayed pleasant. "Since he is unavailable, would you please give him a message?" Her mouth twitched, but she consented. "Tell him that a friend from Gil'ead is waiting outside."

The woman seemed suspicious, but said, "Very well." She closed the door abruptly. Eragon heard her footsteps recede.

"That wasn't very polite," he commented.

"Keep your opinions to yourself," snapped Brom. "And don't say anything. Let me do the talking." He crossed his arms and tapped his fingers. Eragon clamped his mouth shut and looked away.

The door suddenly flew open, and a tall man burst out of the house. His expensive clothes were rumpled, his gray hair wispy, and he had a mournful face with short eyebrows. A long scar stretched across his scalp to his temple.

At the sight of them, his eyes grew wide, and he sagged against the doorframe, speechless. His mouth opened and closed several times like a gasping fish. He asked softly, in an incredulous voice, "Brom . . . ?"

Brom put a finger to his lips and reached forward, clasping the man's arm. "It's good to see you, Jeod! I'm glad that memory has not failed you, but don't use that name. It would be unfortunate if anyone knew I was here."

Jeod looked around wildly, shock plain on his face. "I thought you were dead," he whispered. "What happened? Why haven't you contacted me before?"

"All things will be explained. Do you have a place where we can talk safely?"

Jeod hesitated, swinging his gaze between Eragon and Brom, face unreadable. Finally he said, "We can't talk here, but if you wait a moment, I'll take you somewhere we can."

"Fine," said Brom. Jeod nodded and vanished behind the door.

I hope I can learn something of Brom's past, thought Eragon.

There was a rapier at Jeod's side when he reappeared. An embroidered jacket hung loosely on his shoulders, matched by a plumed hat. Brom cast a critical eye at the finery, and Jeod shrugged self-consciously.

He took them through Teirm toward the citadel. Eragon led the horses behind the two men. Jeod gestured at their destination. "Risthart, the lord of Teirm, has decreed that all the business owners must have their headquarters in his castle. Even though most of us conduct our business elsewhere, we still have to rent rooms there. It's nonsense, but we abide by it anyway to keep him calm. We'll be free of eavesdroppers in there; the walls are thick."

They went through the fortress's main gate and into the keep. Jeod strode to a side door and pointed to an iron ring. "You can tie the horses there. No one will bother them." When Snowfire and Cadoc were safely tethered, he opened the door with an iron key and let them inside.

Within was a long, empty hallway lit by torches set into the walls. Eragon was surprised by how cold and damp it was. When he touched the wall, his fingers slid over a layer of slime. He shivered.

Jeod snatched a torch from its bracket and led them down the hall. They stopped before a heavy, wooden door. He unlocked it and ushered them into a room dominated by a bearskin rug laden with stuffed chairs. Bookshelves stacked with leather-bound tomes covered the walls.

Jeod piled wood in the fireplace, then thrust the torch under it. The fire quickly roared. "You, old man, have some explaining to do."

Brom's face crinkled with a smile. "Who are you calling an old man? The last time I saw you there was no gray in your hair. Now it looks like it's in the final stages of decomposition."

"And you look the same as you did nearly twenty years ago. Time seems to have preserved you as a crotchety old man just to inflict wisdom upon each new generation. Enough of this! Get on with the story. That's always what you were good at," said Jeod impatiently. Eragon's ears pricked up, and he waited eagerly to hear what Brom would say.

Brom relaxed into a chair and pulled out his

pipe. He slowly blew a smoke ring that turned green, darted into the fireplace, then flew up the chimney. "Do you remember what we were doing in Gil'ead?"

"Yes, of course," said Jeod. "That sort of thing is hard to forget."

"An understatement, but true nevertheless," said Brom dryly. "When we were . . . separated, I couldn't find you. In the midst of the turmoil I stumbled into a small room. There wasn't anything extraordinary in it—just crates and boxes—but out of curiosity, I rummaged around anyway. Fortune smiled on me that hour, for I found what we had been searching for." An expression of shock ran over Jeod's face. "Once it was in my hands, I couldn't wait for you. At any second I might have been discovered, and all lost. Disguising myself as best I could, I fled the city and ran to the . . ." Brom hesitated and glanced at Eragon, then said, "ran to our friends. They stored it in a vault, for safekeeping, and made me promise to care for whomever received it. Until the day when my skills would be needed, I had to disappear. No one could know that I was alive—not even you—though it grieved me to pain you unnecessarily. So I went north and hid in Carvahall."

Eragon clenched his jaw, infuriated that Brom was deliberately keeping him in the dark.

Jeod frowned and asked, "Then our . . . friends knew that you were alive all along?"

"Yes."

He sighed. "I suppose the ruse was unavoidable, though I wish they had told me. Isn't Carvahall farther north, on the other side of the Spine?" Brom inclined his head. For the first time, Jeod inspected Eragon. His gray eyes took in every detail. He raised his eyebrows and said, "I assume, then, that you are fulfilling your duty."

Brom shook his head. "No, it's not that simple. It was stolen a while ago—at least that's what I presume, for I haven't received word from our friends, and I suspect their messengers were waylaid—so I decided to find out what I could. Eragon happened to be traveling in the same direction. We have stayed together for a time now."

Jeod looked puzzled. "But if they haven't sent any messages, how could you know that it was—"

Brom overrode him quickly, saying, "Eragon's uncle was brutally killed by the Ra'zac. They burned his home and nearly caught him in the process. He deserves revenge, but they have left us without a trail to follow, and we need help finding them."

Jeod's face cleared. "I see. . . . But why have you come here? I don't know where the Ra'zac might be hiding, and anyone who does won't tell you."

Standing, Brom reached into his robe and pulled out the Ra'zac's flask. He tossed it to Jeod.

"There's Seithr oil in there—the dangerous kind. The Ra'zac were carrying it. They lost it by the trail, and we happened to find it. We need to see Teirm's shipping records so we can trace the Empire's purchases of the oil. That should tell us where the Ra'zac's lair is."

Lines appeared on Jeod's face as he thought. He pointed at the books on the shelves. "Do you see those? They are all records from my business. *One* business. You have gotten yourself into a project that could take months. There is another, greater problem. The records you seek are held in this castle, but only Brand, Risthart's administrator of trade, sees them on a regular basis. Traders such as myself aren't allowed to handle them. They fear that we will falsify the results, thus cheating the Empire of its precious taxes."

"I can deal with that when the time comes," said Brom. "But we need a few days of rest before we can think about proceeding."

Jeod smiled. "It seems that it is my turn to help you. My house is yours, of course. Do you have another name while you are here?"

"Yes," said Brom, "I'm Neal, and the boy is Evan."

"Eragon," said Jeod thoughtfully. "You have a unique name. Few have ever been named after the first Rider. In my life I've read about only three people who were called such." Eragon was startled that Jeod knew the origin of his name.

Brom looked at Eragon. "Could you go check on the horses and make sure they're all right? I don't think I tied Snowfire to the ring tightly enough."

They're trying to hide something from me. The moment I leave they're going to talk about it. Eragon shoved himself out of the chair and left the room, slamming the door shut. Snowfire had not moved; the knot that held him was fine. Scratching the horses' necks, Eragon leaned sullenly against the castle wall.

It's not fair, he complained to himself. *If only I could hear what they are saying.* He jolted upright, electrified. Brom had once taught him some words that would enhance his hearing. *Keen ears aren't exactly what I want, but I should be able to make the words work. After all, look what I could do with* brisingr!

He concentrated intensely and reached for his power. Once it was within his grasp, he said, "Thverr stenr un atra eka hórna!" and imbued the words with his will. As the power rushed out of him, he heard a faint whisper in his ears, but nothing more. Disappointed, he sank back, then started as Jeod said, "—and I've been doing that for almost eight years now."

Eragon looked around. No one was there except for a few guards standing against the far wall of the keep. Grinning, he sat on the courtyard and closed his eyes.

"I never expected you to become a merchant," said Brom. "After all the time you spent in books. And finding the passageway in that manner! What made you take up trading instead of remaining a scholar?"

"After Gil'ead, I didn't have much taste for sitting in musty rooms and reading scrolls. I decided to help Ajihad as best I could, but I'm no warrior. My father was a merchant as well—you may remember that. He helped me get started. However, the bulk of my business is nothing more than a front to get goods into Surda."

"But I take it that things have been going badly," said Brom.

"Yes, none of the shipments have gotten through lately, and Tronjheim is running low on supplies. Somehow the Empire—at least I think it's them—has discovered those of us who have been helping to support Tronjheim. But I'm still not convinced that it's the Empire. No one sees any soldiers. I don't understand it. Perhaps Galbatorix hired mercenaries to harass us."

"I heard that you lost a ship recently."

"The last one I owned," answered Jeod bitterly. "Every man on it was loyal and brave. I doubt I'll ever see them again. . . . The only option I have left is to send caravans to Surda or Gil'ead—which I know won't get there, no matter how many guards I hire—or charter someone else's ship to carry the goods. But no one will take them now."

"How many merchants have been helping you?" asked Brom.

"Oh, a good number up and down the seaboard. All of them have been plagued by the same troubles. I know what you are thinking; I've pondered it many a night myself, but I cannot bear the thought of a traitor with that much knowledge and power. If there is one, we're all in jeopardy. You should return to Tronjheim."

"And take Eragon there?" interrupted Brom. "They'd tear him apart. It's the worst place he could be right now. Maybe in a few months or, even better, a year. Can you imagine how the dwarves will react? Everyone will be trying to influence him, especially Islanzadí. He and Saphira won't be safe in Tronjheim until I at least get them through tuatha du orothrim."

Dwarves! thought Eragon excitedly. *Where is this Tronjheim? And why did he tell Jeod about Saphira? He shouldn't have done that without asking me!*

"Still, I have a feeling that they are in need of your power and wisdom."

"Wisdom," snorted Brom. "I'm just what you said earlier—a crotchety old man."

"Many would disagree."

"Let them. I've no need to explain myself. No, Ajihad will have to get along without me. What I'm doing now is much more important. But the prospect of a traitor raises troubling questions. I wonder if that's how the Empire knew where to be. . . ." His voice trailed off.

"And I wonder why I haven't been contacted about this," said Jeod.

"Maybe they tried. But if there's a traitor . . ." Brom paused. "I have to send word to Ajihad. Do you have a messenger you can trust?"

"I think so," said Jeod. "It depends on where he would have to go."

"I don't know," said Brom. "I've been isolated so long, my contacts have probably died or forgotten me. Could you send him to whoever receives your shipments?"

"Yes, but it'll be risky."

"What isn't these days? How soon can he leave?"

"He can go in the morning. I'll send him to Gil'ead. It will be faster," said Jeod. "What can he take to convince Ajihad the message comes from you?"

"Here, give your man my ring. And tell him that if he loses it, I'll personally tear his liver out. It was given to me by the queen."

"Aren't you cheery," commented Jeod.

Brom grunted. After a long silence he said, "We'd better go out and join Eragon. I get worried when he's alone. That boy has an unnatural propensity for being wherever there's trouble."

"Are you surprised?"

"Not really."

Eragon heard chairs being pushed back. He

quickly pulled his mind away and opened his eyes. "What's going on?" he muttered to himself. *Jeod and other traders are in trouble for helping people the Empire doesn't favor. Brom found something in Gil'ead and went to Carvahall to hide. What could be so important that he would let his own friend think he was dead for nearly twenty years? He mentioned a queen—when there aren't any queens in the known kingdoms—and dwarves, who, as he himself told me, disappeared underground long ago.*

He wanted answers! But he would not confront Brom now and risk jeopardizing their mission. No, he would wait until they left Teirm, and then he would persist until the old man explained his secrets. Eragon's thoughts were still whirling when the door opened.

273

"Were the horses all right?" asked Brom.

"Fine," said Eragon. They untied the horses and left the castle.

As they reentered the main body of Teirm, Brom said, "So, Jeod, you finally got married. And," he winked slyly, "to a lovely young woman. Congratulations."

Jeod did not seem happy with the compliment. He hunched his shoulders and stared down at the street. "Whether congratulations are in order is debatable right now. Helen isn't very happy."

"Why? What does she want?" asked Brom.

"The usual," said Jeod with a resigned shrug. "A good home, happy children, food on the table, and pleasant company. The problem is that she comes from a wealthy family; her father has invested heavily in my business. If I keep suffering these losses, there won't be enough money for her to live the way she's used to."

Jeod continued, "But please, my troubles are not your troubles. A host should never bother his guests with his own concerns. While you are in my house, I will let nothing more than an overfull stomach disturb you."

"Thank you," said Brom. "We appreciate the hospitality. Our travels have long been without comforts of any kind. Do you happen to know where we could find an inexpensive shop? All this riding has worn out our clothes."

274 "Of course. That's my job," said Jeod, lightening up. He talked eagerly about prices and stores until his house was in sight. Then he asked, "Would you mind if we went somewhere else to eat? It might be awkward if you came in right now."

"Whatever makes you feel comfortable," said Brom.

Jeod looked relieved. "Thanks. Let's leave your horses in my stable."

They did as he suggested, then followed him to a large tavern. Unlike the Green Chestnut, this one was loud, clean, and full of boisterous people. When the main course arrived—a stuffed suckling pig—Eragon eagerly dug into the meat, but he especially savored the potatoes, carrots, turnips, and sweet apples that accompanied it. It had been a long time since he had eaten much more than wild game.

They lingered over the meal for hours as Brom and Jeod swapped stories. Eragon did not mind. He was warm, a lively tune jangled in the background, and there was more than enough food. The spirited tavern babble fell pleasantly on his ears.

When they finally exited the tavern, the sun was nearing the horizon. "You two go ahead; I have to check on something," Eragon said. He wanted to see Saphira and make sure that she was safely hidden.

Brom agreed absently. "Be careful. Don't take too long."

"Wait," said Jeod. "Are you going outside Teirm?" Eragon hesitated, then reluctantly nodded. "Make sure you're inside the walls before dark. The gates close then, and the guards won't let you back in until morning."

"I won't be late," promised Eragon. He turned around and loped down a side street, toward Teirm's outer wall. Once out of the city, he breathed deeply, enjoying the fresh air. *Saphira!* he called. *Where are you?* She guided him off the road, to the base of a mossy cliff surrounded by maples. He saw her head poke out of the trees on the top and waved. *How am I supposed to get up there?*

If you find a clearing, I'll come down and get you.

No, he said, eyeing the cliff, *that won't be necessary. I'll just climb up.*

It's too dangerous.

And you worry too much. Let me have some fun.

Eragon pulled off his gloves and started climbing. He relished the physical challenge. There were plenty of handholds, so the ascent was easy. He was soon high above the trees. Halfway up, he stopped on a ledge to catch his breath.

Once his strength returned, he stretched up for the next handhold, but his arm was not long enough. Stymied, he searched for another crevice or ridge to grasp. There was none. He tried backing down, but his legs could not reach his last foothold. Saphira watched with unblinking eyes. He gave up and said, *I could use some help.*

This is your own fault.

Yes! I know. Are you going to get me down or not?

If I weren't around, you would be in a very bad situation.

Eragon rolled his eyes. *You don't have to tell me.*

You're right. After all, how can a mere dragon expect to tell a man like yourself what to do? In fact, everyone should stand in awe of your brilliance of finding the only dead end. Why, if you had started a few feet in either direction, the path to the top would have been clear. She cocked her head at him, eyes bright.

All right! I made a mistake. Now can you please

get me out of here? he pleaded. She pulled her head back from the edge of the cliff. After a moment he called, "Saphira?" Above him were only swaying trees. "Saphira! Come back!" he roared.

With a loud crash Saphira barreled off the top of the cliff, flipping around in midair. She floated down to Eragon like a huge bat and grabbed his shirt with her claws, scratching his back. He let go of the rocks as she yanked him up in the air. After a brief flight, she set him down gently on the top of the cliff and tugged her claws out of his shirt.

Foolishness, said Saphira gently.

Eragon looked away, studying the landscape. The cliff provided a wonderful view of their sur-roundings, especially the foaming sea, as well as protection against unwelcome eyes. Only birds would see Saphira here. It was an ideal location.

Is Brom's friend trustworthy? she asked.

I don't know. Eragon proceeded to recount the day's events. *There are forces circling us that we aren't aware of. Sometimes I wonder if we can ever understand the true motives of the people around us. They all seem to have secrets.*

It is the way of the world. Ignore all the schemes and trust in the nature of each person. Brom is good. He means us no harm. We don't have to fear his plans.

I hope so, he said, looking down at his hands.

This finding of the Ra'zac through writing is a

strange way of tracking, she remarked. *Would there be a way to use magic to see the records without being inside the room?*

I'm not sure. You would have to combine the word for seeing with distance . . . or maybe light and distance. Either way, it seems rather difficult. I'll ask Brom.

That would be wise. They lapsed into tranquil silence.

You know, we may have to stay here awhile.

Saphira's answer held a hard edge. *And as always, I will be left to wait outside.*

That is not how I want it. Soon enough we will travel together again.

May that day come quickly.

Eragon smiled and hugged her. He noticed then how rapidly the light was fading. *I have to go now, before I'm locked out of Teirm. Hunt tomorrow, and I will see you in the evening.*

She spread her wings. *Come, I will take you down.* He got onto her scaly back and held on tightly as she launched off the cliff, glided over the trees, then landed on a knoll. Eragon thanked her and ran back to Teirm.

He came into sight of the portcullis just as it was beginning to lower. Calling for them to wait, he put on a burst of speed and slipped inside seconds before the gateway slammed closed. "Ya cut that a little close," observed one of the guards.

"It won't happen again," assured Eragon,

bending over to catch his breath. He wound his way through the darkened city to Jeod's house. A lantern hung outside like a beacon.

A plump butler answered his knock and ushered him inside without a word. Tapestries covered the stone walls. Elaborate rugs dotted the polished wood floor, which glowed with the light from three gold candelabra hanging from the ceiling. Smoke drifted through the air and collected above.

"This way, sir. Your friend is in the study."

They passed scores of doorways until the butler opened one to reveal a study. Books covered the room's walls. But unlike those in Jeod's office, these came in every size and shape. A fireplace filled with blazing logs warmed the room. Brom **279** and Jeod sat before an oval writing desk, talking amiably. Brom raised his pipe and said in a jovial voice, "Ah, here you are. We were getting worried about you. How was your walk?"

I wonder what put him in such a good mood? Why doesn't he just come out and ask how Saphira is? "Pleasant, but the guards almost locked me outside the city. And Teirm is big. I had trouble finding this house."

Jeod chuckled. "When you have seen Dras-Leona, Gil'ead, or even Kuasta, you won't be so easily impressed by this small ocean city. I like it here, though. When it's not raining, Teirm is really quite beautiful."

Eragon turned to Brom. "Do you have any idea how long we'll be here?"

Brom spread his palms upward. "That's hard to tell. It depends on whether we can get to the records and how long it will take us to find what we need. We'll all have to help; it will be a huge job. I'll talk with Brand tomorrow and see if he'll let us examine the records."

"I don't think I'll be able to help," Eragon said, shifting uneasily.

"Why not?" asked Brom. "There will be plenty of work for you."

Eragon lowered his head. "I can't read."

Brom straightened with disbelief. "You mean Garrow never taught you?"

"He knew how to read?" asked Eragon, puzzled. Jeod watched them with interest.

"Of course he did," snorted Brom. "The proud fool—what was he thinking? I should have realized that he wouldn't have taught you. He probably considered it an unnecessary luxury." Brom scowled and pulled at his beard angrily. "This sets my plans back, but not irreparably. I'll just have to teach you how to read. It won't take long if you put your mind to it."

Eragon winced. Brom's lessons were usually intense and brutally direct. *How much more can I learn at one time?* "I suppose it's necessary," he said ruefully.

"You'll enjoy it. There is much you can learn

from books and scrolls," said Jeod. He gestured at the walls. "These books are my friends, my companions. They make me laugh and cry and find meaning in life."

"It sounds intriguing," admitted Eragon.

"Always the scholar, aren't you?" asked Brom.

Jeod shrugged. "Not anymore. I'm afraid I've degenerated into a bibliophile."

"A what?" asked Eragon.

"One who loves books," explained Jeod, and resumed conversing with Brom. Bored, Eragon scanned the shelves. An elegant book set with gold studs caught his attention. He pulled it off the shelf and stared at it curiously.

It was bound in black leather carved with mysterious runes. Eragon ran his fingers over the cover and savored its cool smoothness. The letters inside were printed with a reddish glossy ink. He let the pages slip past his fingers. A column of script, set off from the regular lettering, caught his eye. The words were long and flowing, full of graceful lines and sharp points.

Eragon took the book to Brom. "What is this?" he asked, pointing to the strange writing.

Brom looked at the page closely and raised his eyebrows in surprise. "Jeod, you've expanded your collection. Where did you get this? I haven't seen one in ages."

Jeod strained his neck to see the book. "Ah yes, the *Domia abr Wyrda*. A man came through here a few years ago and tried to sell it to a trader down by the wharves. Fortunately, I happened to be there and was able to save the book, along with his neck. He didn't have a clue what it was."

"It's odd, Eragon, that you should pick up this book, the *Dominance of Fate*," said Brom. "Of all the items in this house, it's probably worth the most. It details a complete history of Alagaësia— starting long before the elves landed here and ending a few decades ago. The book is very rare and is the best of its kind. When it was written, the Empire decried it as blasphemy and burned the author, Heslant the Monk. I didn't think any copies still existed. The lettering you asked about is from the ancient language."

"What does it say?" asked Eragon.

It took Brom a moment to read the writing. "It's part of an elven poem that tells of the years they fought the dragons. This excerpt describes one of their kings, Ceranthor, as he rides into battle. The elves love this poem and tell it regularly—though you need three days to do it properly—so that they won't repeat the mistakes of the past. At times they sing it so beautifully it seems the very rocks will cry."

Eragon returned to his chair, holding the book gently. *It's amazing that a man who is dead can talk to people through these pages. As long as this book survives, his ideas live. I wonder if it contains any information about the Ra'zac?*

He browsed through the book while Brom and Jeod spoke. Hours passed, and Eragon began to drowse. Out of pity for his exhaustion, Jeod bid them good night. "The butler will show you to your rooms."

On the way upstairs, the servant said, "If you need assistance, use the bellpull next to the bed." He stopped before a cluster of three doors, bowed, then backed away.

As Brom entered the room on the right, Eragon asked, "Can I talk to you?"

"You just did, but come in anyway."

Eragon closed the door behind himself. "Saphira and I had an idea. Is there—"

Brom stopped him with a raised hand and pulled the curtains shut over the window. "When you talk of such things, you would do well to make sure that no unwelcome ears are present."

"Sorry," said Eragon, berating himself for the slip. "Anyway, is it possible to conjure up an image of something that you can't see?"

Brom sat on the edge of his bed. "What you are talking about is called scrying. It is quite possible and extremely helpful in some situations, but it has a major drawback. You can only observe people, places, and things that you've already seen. If you were to scry the Ra'zac, you'd see them all right, but not their surroundings. There are other problems as well. Let's say that you wanted to view a page in a book, one that you'd already seen. You could only see the page if the book were open to it. If the book were closed when you tried this, the page would appear completely black."

"Why can't you view objects that you haven't seen?" asked Eragon. Even with those limitations, he realized, scrying could be very useful. *I wonder if I could view something leagues away and use magic to affect what was happening there?*

"Because," said Brom patiently, "to scry, you have to know what you're looking at and where to direct your power. Even if a stranger was described to you, it would still be nigh impossible to view him, not to mention the ground and whatever else might be around him. You have to know *what* you're going to scry before you *can* scry it. Does that answer your question?"

Eragon thought for a moment. "But how is it done? Do you conjure up the image in thin air?"

"Not usually," said Brom, shaking his white head. "That takes more energy than projecting it onto a reflective surface like a pool of water or a mirror. Some Riders used to travel everywhere they could, trying to see as much as possible. Then, whenever war or some other calamity occurred, they would be able to view events throughout Alagaësia."

"May I try it?" asked Eragon.

Brom looked at him carefully. "No, not now. You're tired, and scrying takes lots of strength.

I will tell you the words, but you must promise not to attempt it tonight. And I'd rather you wait until we leave Teirm; I have more to teach you."

Eragon smiled. "I promise."

"Very well." Brom bent over and very quietly whispered, "Draumr kópa" into Eragon's ear.

Eragon took a moment to memorize the words. "Maybe after we've left Teirm, I can scry Roran. I would like to know how he's doing. I'm afraid that the Ra'zac might go after him."

"I don't mean to frighten you, but that's a distinct possibility," said Brom. "Although Roran was gone most of the time the Ra'zac were in Carvahall, I'm sure that they asked questions about him. Who knows, they may have even met him while they were in Therinsford. Either way, I doubt their curiosity is sated. You're on the loose, after all, and the king is probably threatening them with terrible punishment if you aren't found. If they get frustrated enough, they'll go back and interrogate Roran. It's only a matter of time."

"If that's true, then the only way to keep Roran safe is to let the Ra'zac know where I am so that they'll come after me instead of him."

"No, that won't work either. You're not thinking," admonished Brom. "If you can't understand your enemies, how can you expect to anticipate them? Even if you exposed your location, the

Ra'zac would *still* chase Roran. Do you know why?"

Eragon straightened and tried to consider every possibility. "Well, if I stay in hiding long enough, they might get frustrated and capture Roran to force me to reveal myself. If that didn't work, they'd kill him just to hurt me. Also, if I become a public enemy of the Empire, they might use him as bait to catch me. And if I met with Roran and they found out about it, they would torture him to find out where I was."

"Very good. You figured that out quite nicely," said Brom.

"But what's the solution? I can't let him be killed!"

Brom clasped his hands loosely. "The solution is quite obvious. Roran is going to have to learn how to defend himself. That may sound hard-hearted, but as you pointed out, you cannot risk meeting with him. You may not remember this— you were half delirious at the time—but when we left Carvahall, I told you that I had left a warning letter for Roran so he won't be totally unprepared for danger. If he has any sense at all, when the Ra'zac show up in Carvahall again, he'll take my advice and flee."

"I don't like this," said Eragon unhappily.

"Ah, but you forget something."

"What?" he demanded.

"There is some good in all of this. The king

cannot afford to have a Rider roaming around that he does not control. Galbatorix is the only known Rider alive besides yourself, but he would like another one under his command. Before he tries to kill you or Roran, he will offer you the chance to serve him. Unfortunately, if he ever gets close enough to make that proposition, it will be far too late for you to refuse and still live."

"You call that some good!"

"It's all that's protecting Roran. As long as the king doesn't know which side you've chosen, he won't risk alienating you by harming your cousin. Keep that firmly in mind. The Ra'zac killed Garrow, but I think it was an ill-considered decision on their part. From what I know of Galbatorix, he would not have approved it unless he gained something from it."

"And how will I be able to deny the king's wishes when he is threatening me with death?" asked Eragon sharply.

Brom sighed. He went to his nightstand and dipped his fingers in a basin of rose water. "Galbatorix wants your willing cooperation. Without that, you're worse than useless to him. So the question becomes, If you are ever faced with this choice, are you willing to die for what you believe in? For that is the only way you will deny him."

The question hung in the air.

Brom finally said, "It's a difficult question and not one you can answer until you're faced with it. Keep in mind that many people have died for their beliefs; it's actually quite common. The real courage is in living and suffering for what you believe."

THE WITCH AND
THE WERECAT

It was late in the morning when Eragon woke. He dressed, washed his face in the basin, then held the mirror up and brushed his hair into place. Something about his reflection made him stop and look closer. His face had changed since he had run out of Carvahall just a short while ago. Any baby fat was gone now, stripped away by traveling, sparring, and training. His cheekbones were more prominent, and the line of his jaw was sharper. There was a slight cast to his eyes that, when he looked closely, gave his face a wild, alien appearance. He held the mirror at arm's length, and his face resumed its normal semblance—but it still did not seem quite his own.

A little disturbed, he slung his bow and quiver across his back, then left the room. Before he had reached the end of the hall, the butler caught up with him and said, "Sir, Neal left with my master for the castle earlier. He said that you could do whatever you want today because he will not return until this evening."

Eragon thanked him for the message, then eagerly began exploring Teirm. For hours he wandered the streets, entering every shop that struck his fancy and chatting with various people. Eventually he was forced back to Jeod's by his empty stomach and lack of money.

When he reached the street where the merchant lived, he stopped at the herbalist's shop next door. It was an unusual place for a store. The other shops were down by the city wall, not crammed between expensive houses. He tried to look in the windows, but they were covered with a thick layer of crawling plants on the interior. Curious, he went inside.

At first he saw nothing because the store was so dark, but then his eyes adjusted to the faint greenish light that filtered through the windows. A colorful bird with wide tail feathers and a sharp, powerful beak looked at Eragon inquisitively from a cage near the window. The walls were covered with plants; vines clung to the ceiling, obscuring all but an old chandelier, and on the floor was a large pot with a yellow flower. A collection of mortars, pestles, metal bowls, and a clear crystal ball the size of Eragon's head rested on a long counter.

He walked to the counter, carefully stepping

around complex machines, crates of rocks, piles of scrolls, and other objects he did not recognize. The wall behind the counter was covered with drawers of every size. Some of them were no larger than his smallest finger, while others were big enough for a barrel. There was a foot-wide gap in the shelves far above.

A pair of red eyes suddenly flashed from the dark space, and a large, fierce cat leapt onto the counter. It had a lean body with powerful shoulders and oversized paws. A shaggy mane surrounded its angular face; its ears were tipped with black tufts. White fangs curved down over its jaw. Altogether, it did not look like any cat Eragon had ever seen. It inspected him with shrewd eyes, then flicked its tail dismissively.

On a whim, Eragon reached out with his mind and touched the cat's consciousness. Gently, he prodded it with his thoughts, trying to make it understand that he was a friend.

You don't have to do that.

Eragon looked around in alarm. The cat ignored him and licked a paw. *Saphira? Where are you?* he asked. No one answered. Puzzled, he leaned against the counter and reached for what looked like a wood rod.

That wouldn't be wise.

Stop playing games, Saphira, he snapped, then picked up the rod. A shock of electricity exploded through his body, and he fell to the floor, writing. The pain slowly faded, leaving him gasping for air. The cat jumped down and looked at him.

You aren't very smart for a Dragon Rider. I did warn you.

You said that! exclaimed Eragon. The cat yawned, then stretched and sauntered across the floor, weaving its way between objects.

Who else?

But you're just a cat! he objected.

The cat yowled and stalked back to him. It jumped on his chest and crouched there, looking down at him with gleaming eyes. Eragon tried to sit up, but it growled, showing its fangs. *Do I look like other cats?*

292   *No . . .*

Then what makes you think I am one? Eragon started to say something, but the creature dug its claws into his chest. *Obviously your education has been neglected. I—to correct your mistake—am a werecat. There aren't many of us left, but I think even a farm boy should have heard of us.*

I didn't know you were real, said Eragon, fascinated. A werecat! He was indeed fortunate. They were always flitting around the edges of stories, keeping to themselves and occasionally giving advice. If the legends were true, they had magical powers, lived longer than humans, and usually knew more than they told.

The werecat blinked lazily. *Knowing is independent of being. I did not know you existed before you bumbled in here and ruined my nap. Yet that doesn't mean you weren't real before you woke me.*

Eragon was lost by its reasoning. *I'm sorry I disturbed you.*

I was getting up anyway, it said. It leapt back onto the counter and licked its paw. *If I were you, I wouldn't hold on to that rod much longer. It's going to shock you again in a few seconds.*

He hastily put the rod back where he had found it. *What is it?*

A common and boring artifact, unlike myself.

But what's it for?

Didn't you find out? The werecat finished cleaning its paw, stretched once more, then jumped back up to its sleeping place. It sat down, tucked its paws under its breast, and closed its eyes, purring.

Wait, said Eragon, *what's your name?*

One of the werecat's slanted eyes cracked open. *I go by many names. If you are looking for my proper one, you will have to seek elsewhere.* The eye closed. Eragon gave up and turned to leave. *However, you may call me Solembum.*

Thank you, said Eragon seriously. Solembum's purring grew louder.

The door to the shop swung open, letting in a beam of sunlight. Angela entered with a cloth bag full of plants. Her eyes flickered at Solembum and she looked startled. "He says you talked with him."

"You can talk with him, too?" asked Eragon.

She tossed her head. "Of course, but that doesn't mean he'll say anything back." She set her plants on the counter, then walked behind it and faced him. "He likes you. That's unusual. Most of the time Solembum doesn't show himself to customers. In fact, he says that you show some promise, given a few years of work."

"Thanks."

"It's a compliment, coming from him. You're only the third person to come in here who has been able to speak with him. The first was a woman, many years ago; the second was a blind beggar; and now you. But I don't run a store just so I can prattle on. Is there anything you want? Or did you only come in to look?"

"Just to look," said Eragon, still thinking about the werecat. "Besides, I don't really need any herbs."

"That's not all I do," said Angela with a grin. "The rich fool lords pay me for love potions and the like. I never claim that they work, but for some reason they keep coming back. But I don't think you need those chicaneries. Would you like your fortune told? I do that, too, for all the rich fool ladies."

Eragon laughed. "No, I'm afraid my fortune is pretty much unreadable. And I don't have any money."

Angela looked at Solembum curiously. "I think . . ." She gestured at the crystal ball resting on the counter. "That's only for show anyway—it doesn't do anything. But I do have . . . Wait here; I'll be right back." She hurried into a room at the back of the shop.

She came back, breathless, holding a leather pouch, which she set on the counter. "I haven't used these for so long, I almost forgot where they were. Now, sit across from me and I'll show you why I went to all this trouble." Eragon found a stool and sat. Solembum's eyes glowed from the gap in the drawers.

Angela laid a thick cloth on the counter, then poured a handful of smooth bones, each slightly longer than a finger, onto it. Runes and symbols were inscribed along their sides. "These," she said, touching them gently, "are the knuckle-bones of a dragon. Don't ask where I got them; it is a secret I won't reveal. But unlike tea leaves, crystal balls, or even divining cards, these have true power. They do not lie, though understanding what they say is . . . complicated. If you wish, I will cast and read them for you. But understand that to know one's fate can be a terrible thing. You must be sure of your decision."

Eragon looked at the bones with a feeling of dread. *There lies what was once one of Saphira's kin. To know one's fate . . . How can I make this decision when I don't know what lies in wait for me and whether I will like it? Ignorance is indeed bliss.* "Why do you offer this?" he asked.

"Because of Solembum. He may have been rude, but the fact that he spoke to you makes you special. He *is* a werecat, after all. I offered to do this for the other two people who talked with him. Only the woman agreed to it. Selena was her name. Ah, she regretted it, too. Her fortune was bleak and painful. I don't think she believed it—not at first."

Emotion overcame Eragon, bringing tears to his eyes. "Selena," he whispered to himself. His mother's name. *Could it have been her? Was her destiny so horrible that she had to abandon me?* "Do you remember anything about her fortune?" he asked, feeling sick.

Angela shook her head and sighed. "It was so long ago that the details have melted into the rest of my memory, which isn't as good as it used to be. Besides, I'll not tell you what I do remember. That was for her and her alone. It was sad, though; I've never forgotten the look on her face."

Eragon closed his eyes and struggled to regain control of his emotions. "Why do you complain about your memory?" he asked to distract himself. "You're not that old."

Dimples appeared on Angela's cheeks. "I'm flattered, but don't be deceived; I'm much older than I look. The appearance of youth probably comes from having to eat my own herbs when times are lean."

Smiling, Eragon took a deep breath. *If that was*

my mother and she could bear to have her fortune told, I can too. "Cast the bones for me," he said solemnly.

Angela's face became grave as she grasped the bones in each hand. Her eyes closed, and her lips moved in a soundless murmur. Then she said powerfully, *"Manin! Wyrda! Hügin!"* and tossed the bones onto the cloth. They fell all jumbled together, gleaming in the faint light.

The words rang in Eragon's ears; he recognized them from the ancient language and realized with apprehension that to use them for magic, Angela must be a witch. She had not lied; this was a true fortunetelling. Minutes slowly passed as she studied the bones.

Finally, Angela leaned back and heaved a long sigh. She wiped her brow and pulled out a wineskin from under the counter. "Do you want some?" she asked. Eragon shook his head. She shrugged and drank deeply. "This," she said, wiping her mouth, "is the hardest reading I've ever done. You were right. Your future is nigh impossible to see. I've never known of anyone's fate being so tangled and clouded. I was, however, able to wrestle a few answers from it."

Solembum jumped onto the counter and settled there, watching them both. Eragon clenched his hands as Angela pointed to one of the bones. "I will start here," she said slowly, "because it is the clearest to understand."

The symbol on the bone was a long horizontal

line with a circle resting on it. "Infinity or long life," said Angela quietly. "This is the first time I have ever seen it come up in someone's future. Most of the time it's the aspen or the elm, both signs that a person will live a normal span of years. Whether this means that you will live forever or that you will only have an extraordinarily long life, I'm not sure. Whatever it foretells, you may be sure that many years lie ahead of you."

No surprises there—I am a Rider, thought Eragon. Was Angela only going to tell him things he already knew?

"Now the bones grow harder to read, as the rest are in a confused pile." Angela touched three of them. "Here the wandering path, lightning bolt, and sailing ship all lie together—a pattern I've never seen, only heard of. The wandering path shows that there are many choices in your future, some of which you face even now. I see great battles raging around you, some of them fought for your sake. I see the mighty powers of this land struggling to control your will and destiny. Countless possible futures await you—all of them filled with blood and conflict—but only one will bring you happiness and peace. Beware of losing your way, for you are one of the few who are truly free to choose their own fate. That freedom is a gift, but it is also a responsibility more binding than chains."

Then her face grew sad. "And yet, as if to

counteract that, here is the lightning bolt. It is a terrible omen. There is a doom upon you, but of what sort I know not. Part of it lies in a death— one that rapidly approaches and will cause you much grief. But the rest awaits in a great journey. Look closely at this bone. You can see how its end rests on that of the sailing ship. That is impossible to misunderstand. Your fate will be to leave this land forever. Where you will end up I know not, but you will never again stand in Alagaësia. This is inescapable. It will come to pass even if you try to avoid it."

Her words frightened Eragon. *Another death . . . who must I lose now?* His thoughts immediately went to Roran. Then he thought about his homeland. *What could ever force me to leave? And where would I go? If there are lands across the sea or to the east, only the elves know of them.*

Angela rubbed her temples and breathed deeply. "The next bone is easier to read and perhaps a bit more pleasant." Eragon examined it and saw a rose blossom inscribed between the horns of a crescent moon.

Angela smiled and said, "An epic romance is in your future, extraordinary, as the moon indicates—for that is a magical symbol—and strong enough to outlast empires. I cannot say if this passion will end happily, but your love is of noble birth and heritage. She is powerful, wise, and beautiful beyond compare."

Of noble birth, thought Eragon in surprise. *How could that ever happen? I have no more standing than the poorest of farmers.*

"Now for the last two bones, the tree and the hawthorn root, which cross each other strongly. I wish that this were not so—it can only mean more trouble—but betrayal is clear. And it will come from within your family."

"Roran wouldn't do that!" objected Eragon abruptly.

"I wouldn't know," said Angela carefully. "But the bones have never lied, and that is what they say."

Doubt wormed into Eragon's mind, but he tried to ignore it. What reason would there ever be for Roran to turn on him? Angela put a comforting hand on his shoulder and offered him the wineskin again. This time Eragon accepted the drink, and it made him feel better.

"After all that, death might be welcome," he joked nervously. *Betrayal from Roran? It couldn't happen! It won't!*

"It might be," said Angela solemnly, then laughed slightly. "But you shouldn't fret about what has yet to occur. The only way the future can harm us is by causing worry. I guarantee that you'll feel better once you're out in the sun."

"Perhaps." *Unfortunately*, he reflected wryly, *nothing she said will make sense until it has already happened. If it really does*, he amended himself. "You used words of power," he noted quietly.

Angela's eyes flashed. "What I wouldn't give to see how the rest of your life plays out. You can speak to werecats, know of the ancient language, and have a most interesting future. Also, few young men with empty pockets and rough traveling clothes can expect to be loved by a noblewoman. Who are you?"

Eragon realized that the werecat must not have told Angela that he was a Rider. He almost said, "Evan," but then changed his mind and simply stated, "I am Eragon."

Angela arched her eyebrows. "Is that who you are or your name?" she asked.

"Both," said Eragon with a small smile, thinking of his namesake, the first Rider.

"Now I'm all the more interested in seeing how your life will unfold. Who was the ragged man with you yesterday?"

Eragon decided that one more name couldn't hurt. "His name is Brom."

A guffaw suddenly burst out of Angela, doubling her over in mirth. She wiped her eyes and took a sip of wine, then fought off another attack of merriment. Finally, gasping for breath, she forced out, "Oh . . . that one! I had no idea!"

"What is it?" demanded Eragon.

"No, no, don't be upset," said Angela, hiding a smile. "It's only that—well, he is known by those in my profession. I'm afraid that the poor man's doom, or future if you will, is something of a joke with us."

"Don't insult him! He's a better man than any you could find!" snapped Eragon.

"Peace, peace," chided Angela with amusement. "I know that. If we meet again at the right time I'll be sure to tell you about it. But in the meantime you should—" She stopped speaking as Solembum padded between them. The werecat stared at Eragon with unblinking eyes.

Yes? Eragon asked, irritated.

Listen closely and I will tell you two things. When the time comes and you need a weapon, look under the roots of the Menoa tree. Then, when all seems lost and your power is insufficient, go to the Rock of Kuthian and speak your name to open the Vault of Souls.

Before Eragon could ask what Solembum meant, the werecat walked away, waving his tail ever so gracefully. Angela tilted her head, coils of dense hair shadowing her forehead. "I don't know what he said, and I don't want to know. He spoke to you and only you. Don't tell anyone else."

"I think I have to go," said Eragon, shaken.

"If you want to," said Angela, smiling again. "You are welcome to stay here as long as you like, especially if you buy some of my goods. But go if you wish; I'm sure that we've given you enough to ponder for a while."

"Yes." Eragon quickly made his way to the door. "Thank you for reading my future." *I think.*

"You're welcome," said Angela, still smiling.

Eragon exited the shop and stood in the street, squinting until his eyes adjusted to the brightness. It was a few minutes before he could think calmly about what he had learned. He started walking, his steps unconsciously quickening until he dashed out of Teirm, feet flying as he headed to Saphira's hiding place.

He called to her from the base of the cliff. A minute later she soared down and bore him up to the cliff top. When they were both safely on the ground, Eragon told her about his day. *And so,* he concluded, *I think Brom's right; I always seem to be where there's trouble.*

You should remember what the werecat told you. It's important.

How do you know? he asked curiously.

I'm not sure, but the names he used feel powerful. Kuthian, she said, rolling the word around. *No, we should not forget what he said.*

Do you think I should tell Brom?

It's your choice, but think of this: he has no right to know your future. To tell him of Solembum and his words will only raise questions you may not want to answer. And if you decided to only ask him what those words mean, he will want to know where you learned them. Do you think you can lie convincingly to him?

No, admitted Eragon. *Maybe I won't say anything. Still, this might be too important to hide. They* talked until there was nothing more to say. Then they sat together companionably, watching the trees until dusk.

Eragon hurried back to Teirm and was soon knocking on Jeod's door. "Is Neal back?" he asked the butler.

"Yes sir. I believe he's in the study right now."

"Thank you," said Eragon. He strode to the room and peeked inside. Brom was sitting before the fire, smoking. "How did it go?" asked Eragon.

"Bloody awful!" growled Brom around his pipe.

"So you talked to Brand?"

"Not that it did any good. This *administrator* of trade is the worst sort of bureaucrat. He abides by every rule, delights in making his own whenever it can inconvenience someone, and at the same time believes that he's doing good."

"Then he won't let us see the records?" asked Eragon.

"No," snapped Brom, exasperated. "Nothing I could say would sway him. He even refused bribes! Substantial ones, too. I didn't think I would ever meet a noble who wasn't corrupt. Now that I have, I find that I prefer them when they're greedy bastards." He puffed furiously on his pipe and mumbled a steady stream of curses.

When he seemed to have calmed, Eragon asked tentatively, "So, what now?"

"I'm going to take the next week and teach you how to read."

"And after that?"

A smile split Brom's face. "After that, we're going to give Brand a nasty surprise." Eragon pestered him for details, but Brom refused to say more.

Dinner was held in a sumptuous dining room. Jeod sat at one end of the table, a hard-eyed Helen at the other. Brom and Eragon were seated between them, which Eragon felt was a dangerous place to be. Empty chairs were on either side of him, but he didn't mind the space. It helped to protect him from the glares of their hostess.

The food was served quietly, and Jeod and Helen wordlessly began eating. Eragon followed suit, thinking, *I've had cheerier meals at funerals.* And he had, in Carvahall. He remembered many burials that had been sad, yes, but not unduly so. This was different; he could feel simmering resentment pouring from Helen throughout the dinner.

OF READING AND PLOTS

Brom scratched a rune on parchment with charcoal, then showed it to Eragon. "This is the letter *a*," he said. "Learn it."

With that, Eragon began the task of becoming literate. It was difficult and strange and pushed his intellect to its limits, but he enjoyed it. Without anything else to do and with a good—if sometimes impatient—teacher, he advanced rapidly.

A routine was soon established. Every day Eragon got up, ate in the kitchen, then went to the study for his lessons, where he labored to memorize the sounds of the letters and the rules of writing. It got so that when he closed his eyes, letters and words danced in his mind. He thought of little else during that time.

Before dinner, he and Brom would go behind Jeod's house and spar. The servants, along with a

306

small crowd of wide-eyed children, would come and watch. If there was any time afterward, Eragon would practice magic in his room, with the curtains securely closed.

His only worry was Saphira. He visited her every evening, but it was not enough time together for either of them. During the day, Saphira spent most of her time leagues away searching for food; she could not hunt near Teirm without arousing suspicion. Eragon did what he could to help her, but he knew that the only solution for both her hunger and loneliness was to leave the city far behind.

Every day more grim news poured into Teirm. Arriving merchants told of horrific attacks along the coast. There were reports of powerful people disappearing from their houses in the night and their mangled corpses being discovered in the morning. Eragon often heard Brom and Jeod discussing the events in an undertone, but they always stopped when he came near.

The days passed quickly, and soon a week had gone by. Eragon's skills were rudimentary, but he could now read whole pages without asking Brom's help. He read slowly, but he knew that speed would come with time. Brom encouraged him, "No matter, you'll do fine for what I have planned."

It was afternoon when Brom summoned both Jeod and Eragon to the study. Brom gestured at

Eragon. "Now that you can help us, I think it's time to move ahead."

"What do you have in mind?" asked Eragon.

A fierce smile danced on Brom's face. Jeod groaned. "I know that look; it's what got us into trouble in the first place."

"A slight exaggeration," said Brom, "but not unwarranted. Very well, this is what we'll do. . . ."

We leave tonight or tomorrow, Eragon told Saphira from within his room.

This is unexpected. Will you be safe during this venture?

Eragon shrugged. *I don't know. We may end up fleeing Teirm with soldiers on our heels.* He felt her worry and tried to reassure her. *It'll be all right. Brom and I can use magic, and we're good fighters.*

He lay on the bed and stared at the ceiling. His hands shook slightly, and there was a lump in his throat. As sleep overcame him, he felt a wave of confusion. *I don't want to leave Teirm,* he suddenly realized. *The time I've spent here has been— almost normal. What I would give not to keep uprooting myself. To stay here and be like everyone else would be wonderful.* Then, another thought raged through him, *But I'll never be able to while Saphira is around. Never.*

Dreams owned his consciousness, twisting and directing it to their whims. At times he quaked with fear; at others he laughed with pleasure.

Then something changed—it was as though his eyes had been opened for the first time—and a dream came to him that was clearer than any before.

He saw a young woman, bent over by sorrow, chained in a cold, hard cell. A beam of moonlight shone through a barred window set high in the wall and fell on her face. A single tear rolled down her cheek, like a liquid diamond.

Eragon rose with a start and found himself crying uncontrollably before sinking back into a fitful sleep.

THIEVES IN THE CASTLE

Eragon woke from his nap to a golden sunset. Red and orange beams of light streamed into the room and fell across the bed. They warmed his back pleasantly, making him reluctant to move. He dozed, but the sunlight crept off him, and he grew cold. The sun sank below the horizon, lighting the sea and sky with color. *Almost time!*

He slung his bow and quiver on his back, but left Zar'roc in the room; the sword would only slow him, and he was averse to using it. If he had to disable someone, he could use magic or an arrow. He pulled his jerkin over his shirt and laced it securely.

He waited nervously in his room until the light faded. Then he entered the hallway and shrugged so the quiver settled comfortably across his back. Brom joined him, carrying his sword and staff.

Jeod, dressed in a black doublet and hose, was waiting for them outside. From his waist swung an elegant rapier and a leather pouch. Brom eyed the rapier and observed, "That toad sticker is too thin for any real fighting. What will you do if someone comes after you with a broadsword or a flamberge?"

"Be realistic," said Jeod. "None of the guards has a flamberge. Besides, this *toad sticker* is faster than a broadsword."

Brom shrugged. "It's your neck."

They walked casually along the street, avoiding watchmen and soldiers. Eragon was tense and his heart pounded. As they passed Angela's shop, a flash of movement on the roof caught his attention, but he saw no one. His palm tingled. He looked at the roof again, but it was still empty.

Brom led them along Teirm's outer wall. By the time they reached the castle, the sky was black. The sealed walls of the fortress made Eragon shiver. He would hate to be imprisoned there. Jeod silently took the lead and strode up to the gates, trying to look at ease. He pounded on the gate and waited.

A small grille slid open and a surly guard peered out. "Ya?" he grunted shortly. Eragon could smell rum on his breath.

"We need to get in," said Jeod.

The guard peered at Jeod closer. "Wha' for?"

"The boy here left something very valuable in

my office. We have to retrieve it immediately."
Eragon hung his head, shamefaced.

The guard frowned, clearly impatient to get
back to his bottle. "Ah, wha'ever," he said,
swinging his arm. "Jus' make sure 'n give 'im a
good beating f'r me."

"I'll do that," assured Jeod as the guard unbolted a small door set into the gate. They entered the keep, then Brom handed the guard a
few coins.

"Thank'ee," mumbled the man, tottering
away. As soon as he was gone, Eragon pulled his
bow from its tube and strung it. Jeod quickly let
them into the main part of the castle. They hurried toward their destination, listening carefully
for any soldiers on patrol. At the records room,
Brom tried the door. It was locked. He put his
hand against the door and muttered a word that
Eragon did not recognize. It swung open with a
faint click. Brom grabbed a torch from the wall,
and they darted inside, closing the door quietly.

The squat room was filled with wooden racks
piled high with scrolls. A barred window was set
in the far wall. Jeod threaded his way between
the racks, running his eyes over the scrolls. He
halted at the back of the room. "Over here," he
said. "These are the shipping records for the past
five years. You can tell the date by the wax seals
on the corner."

"So what do we do now?" asked Eragon,

pleased that they had made it so far without being discovered.

"Start at the top and work down," said Jeod. "Some scrolls only deal with taxes. You can ignore those. Look for anything that mentions Seithr oil." He took a length of parchment from his pouch and stretched it out on the floor, then set a bottle of ink and a quill pen next to it. "So we can keep track of whatever we find," he explained.

Brom scooped an armful of scrolls from the top of the rack and piled them on the floor. He sat and unrolled the first one. Eragon joined him, positioning himself so he could see the door. The tedious work was especially difficult for him, as the cramped script on the scrolls was different from the printing Brom had taught him.

By looking only for the names of ships that sailed in the northern areas, they winnowed out many of the scrolls. Even so, they moved down the rack slowly, recording each shipment of Seithr oil as they located it.

It was quiet outside the room, except for the occasional watchman. Suddenly, Eragon's neck prickled. He tried to keep working, but the uneasy feeling remained. Irritated, he looked up and jerked with surprise—a small boy crouched on the windowsill. His eyes were slanted, and a sprig of holly was woven into his shaggy black hair.

Do you need help? asked a voice in Eragon's

head. His eyes widened with shock. It sounded like Solembum.

Is that you? he asked incredulously.

Am I someone else?

Eragon gulped and concentrated on his scroll. *If my eyes don't deceive me, you are.*

The boy smiled slightly, revealing pointed teeth. *What I look like doesn't change who I am. You don't think I'm called a werecat for nothing, do you?*

What are you doing here? Eragon asked.

The werecat tilted his head and considered whether the question was worth an answer. *That depends on what you are doing here. If you are reading those scrolls for entertainment, then I suppose there isn't any reason for my visit. But if what you are doing is unlawful and you don't want to be discovered, I might be here to warn you that the guard whom you bribed just told his replacement about you and that this second official of the Empire has sent soldiers to search for you.*

Thank you for telling me, said Eragon.

Told you something, did I? I suppose I did. And I suggest you make use of it.

The boy stood and tossed back his wild hair. Eragon asked quickly, *What did you mean last time about the tree and the vault?*

Exactly what I said.

Eragon tried to ask more, but the werecat vanished through the window. He announced abruptly, "There are soldiers looking for us."

"How do you know?" asked Brom sharply.

"I listened in on the guard. His replacement just sent men to search for us. We have to get out of here. They've probably already discovered that Jeod's office is empty."

"Are you sure?" asked Jeod.

"Yes!" said Eragon impatiently. "They're on their way."

Brom snatched another scroll from the rack. "No matter. We have to finish this now!" They worked furiously for the next minute, scanning the records as fast as they could. As the last scroll was finished, Brom threw it back onto the rack, and Jeod jammed his parchment, ink, and pen into his pouch. Eragon grabbed the torch.

They raced from the room and shut the door, but just as it closed they heard the heavy tramp of soldiers' boots at the end of the hall. They turned to leave, but Brom hissed furiously, "Damnation! It's not locked." He put his hand against the door. The lock clicked at the same time three armed soldiers came into view.

"Hey! Get away from that door!" shouted one of them. Brom stepped back, assuming a surprised expression. The three men marched up to them. The tallest one demanded, "Why are you trying to get into the records?" Eragon gripped his bow tighter and prepared to run.

"I'm afraid we lost our way." The strain was evident in Jeod's voice. A drop of sweat rolled down his neck.

The soldier glared at them suspiciously.

"Check inside the room," he ordered one of his men.

Eragon held his breath as the soldier stepped up to the door, tried to open it, then pounded on it with his mailed fist. "It's locked, sir."

The leader scratched his chin. "Ar'right, then. I don't know what you were up to, but as long as the door's locked, I guess you're free to go. Come on." The soldiers surrounded them and marched them back to the keep.

I can't believe it, thought Eragon. *They're helping us get away!*

At the main gates, the soldier pointed and said, "Now, you walk through those and don't try anything. We'll be watching. If you have to come back, wait until morning."

"Of course," promised Jeod.

Eragon could feel the guards' eyes boring into their backs as they hurried out of the castle. The moment that the gates closed behind them, a triumphant grin stretched across his face, and he jumped into the air. Brom shot him a cautioning look and growled, "Walk back to the house normally. You can celebrate there."

Chastised, Eragon adopted a staid demeanor, but inside he still bubbled with energy. Once they had hurried back to the house and into the study, Eragon exclaimed, "We did it!"

"Yes, but now we have to figure out if it was worth the trouble," said Brom. Jeod took a map of

Alagaësia from the shelves and unrolled it on the desk.

On the left side of the map, the ocean extended to the unknown west. Along the coast stretched the Spine, an immense length of mountains. The Hadarac Desert filled the center of the map—the east end was blank. Somewhere in that void hid the Varden. To the south was Surda, a small country that had seceded from the Empire after the Riders' fall. Eragon had been told that Surda secretly supported the Varden.

Near Surda's eastern border was a mountain range labeled Beor Mountains. Eragon had heard of them in many stories—they were supposed to be ten times the height of the Spine, though he privately believed that was exaggeration. The map was empty to the east of the Beors.

Five islands rested off the coast of Surda: Nía, Parlim, Uden, Illium, and Beirland. Nía was no more than an outcropping of rock, but Beirland, the largest, had a small town. Farther up, near Teirm, was a jagged island called Sharktooth. And high to the north was one more island, immense and shaped like a knobby hand. Eragon knew its name without even looking: Vroengard, the ancestral home of the Riders—once a place of glory, but now a looted, empty shell haunted by strange beasts. In the center of Vroengard was the abandoned city of Doru Araeba.

Carvahall was a small dot at the top of Palancar Valley. Level with it, but across the plains, sprawled the forest Du Weldenvarden. Like the Beor Mountains, its eastern end was unmapped. Parts of Du Weldenvarden's western edge had been settled, but its heart lay mysterious and un-explored. The forest was wilder than the Spine; the few who braved its depths often came back raving mad, or not at all.

Eragon shivered as he saw Urû'baen in the center of the Empire. King Galbatorix ruled from there with his black dragon, Shruikan, by his side. Eragon put his finger on Urû'baen. "The Ra'zac are sure to have a hiding place here."

"You had better hope that that isn't their only sanctuary," said Brom flatly. "Otherwise you'll never get near them." He pushed the rustling map flat with his wrinkled hands.

Jeod took the parchment out of his pouch and said, "From what I saw in the records, there have been shipments of Seithr oil to every major city in the Empire over the past five years. As far as I can tell, all of them might have been ordered by wealthy jewelers. I'm not sure how we can narrow down the list without more information."

Brom swept a hand over the map. "I think we can eliminate some cities. The Ra'zac have to travel wherever the king wants, and I'm sure he keeps them busy. If they're expected to go any-where at anytime, the only reasonable place for them to stay is at a crossroads where they can reach every part of the country fairly easily." He was excited now and paced the room. "This crossroads has to be large enough so the Ra'zac will be inconspicuous. It also has to have enough trade so any unusual requests—special food for their mounts, for example—will go unnoticed."

"That makes sense," said Jeod, nodding. "Under those conditions, we can ignore most of the cities in the north. The only big ones are Teirm, Gil'ead, and Ceunon. I know they're not in Teirm, and I doubt that the oil has been shipped farther up the coast to Narda—it's too small. Ceunon is too isolated . . . only Gil'ead remains."

"The Ra'zac might be there," conceded Brom. "It would have a certain irony."

"It would at that," Jeod acknowledged softly.

"What about southern cities?" asked Eragon.

"Well," said Jeod. "There's obviously Urû'baen, but that's an unlikely destination. If someone were to die from Seithr oil in Galbatorix's court, it would be all too easy for an earl or some other lord to discover that the Empire had been buying large amounts of it. That still leaves many others, any one of which could be the one we want."

"Yes," said Eragon, "but the oil wasn't sent to all of them. The parchment only lists Kuasta, Dras-Leona, Aroughs, and Belatona. Kuasta wouldn't work for the Ra'zac; it's on the coast and surrounded by mountains. Aroughs is isolated like Ceunon, though it is a center of trade. That leaves Belatona and Dras-Leona, which are rather close together. Of the two, I think Dras-Leona is the likelier. It's larger and better situated."

"And that's where nearly all the goods of the Empire pass through at one time or another, including Teirm's," said Jeod. "It would be a good place for the Ra'zac to hide."

"So . . . Dras-Leona," said Brom as he sat down and lit his pipe. "What do the records show?"

Jeod looked at the parchment. "Here it is. At the beginning of the year, three shipments of Seithr oil were sent to Dras-Leona. Each shipment was only two weeks apart, and the records say they were all transported by the same merchant. The same thing happened last year and the year before that. I doubt any one jeweler, or even a group of them, has the money for so much oil."

"What about Gil'ead?" asked Brom, raising an eyebrow.

"It doesn't have the same access to the rest of the Empire. And," Jeod tapped the parchment, "they've only received the oil twice in recent years." He thought for a moment, then said, "Besides, I think we forgot something—Helgrind."

Brom nodded. "Ah yes, the Dark Gates. It's been many years since I've thought of it. You're right, that would make Dras-Leona perfect for the Ra'zac. I guess it's decided, then; that's where we'll go."

Eragon sat abruptly, too drained of emotion to even ask what Helgrind was. *I thought I would be happy to resume the hunt. Instead, I feel like an abyss has opened up before me. Dras-Leona! It's so far away. . . .*

The parchment crackled as Jeod slowly rolled up the map. He handed it to Brom and said, "You'll need this, I'm afraid. Your expeditions often take you into obscure regions." Nodding, Brom accepted the map. Jeod clapped him on the shoulder. "It doesn't feel right that you will leave without me. My heart expects to go along, but the rest of me reminds me of my age and responsibilities."

"I know," said Brom. "But you have a life in Teirm. It is time for the next generation to take up the standard. You've done your part; be happy."

"What of you?" asked Jeod. "Does the road ever end for you?"

A hollow laugh escaped Brom's lips. "I see it coming, but not for a while." He extinguished his pipe, and they left for their rooms, exhausted. Before he fell asleep, Eragon contacted Saphira to relate the night's adventures.

A COSTLY MISTAKE

In the morning Eragon and Brom retrieved their saddlebags from the stable and prepared to depart. Jeod greeted Brom while Helen watched from the doorway. With grave looks, the two men clasped hands. "I'll miss you, old man," said Jeod.

"And you I," said Brom thickly. He bowed his white head and then turned to Helen. "Thank you for your hospitality; it was most gracious." Her face reddened. Eragon thought she was going to slap him. Brom continued, unperturbed, "You have a good husband; take care of him. There are few men as brave and as determined as he is. But even he cannot weather difficult times without support from those he loves." He bowed again and said gently, "Only a suggestion, dear lady."

Eragon watched as indignation and hurt crossed Helen's face. Her eyes flashed as she shut the door brusquely. Sighing, Jeod ran his fingers through his hair. Eragon thanked him for all his help, then mounted Cadoc. With the last farewells said, he and Brom departed.

At Teirm's south gate, the guards let them through without a second glance. As they rode under the giant outer wall, Eragon saw movement in a shadow. Solembum was crouched on the ground, tail twitching. The werecat followed them with inscrutable eyes. As the city receded into the distance, Eragon asked, "What are werecats?"

Brom looked surprised at the question. "Why the sudden curiosity?"

"I heard someone mention them in Teirm. They're not real, are they?" said Eragon, pretending ignorance.

323

"They are quite real. During the Riders' years of glory, they were as renowned as the dragons. Kings and elves kept them as companions—yet the werecats were free to do what they chose. Very little has ever been known about them. I'm afraid that their race has become rather scarce recently."

"Could they use magic?" asked Eragon.

"No one's sure, but they could certainly do unusual things. They always seemed to know what was going on and somehow or another manage to get themselves involved." Brom pulled his hood up to block a chill wind.

"What's Helgrind?" asked Eragon, after a moment's thought.

"You'll see when we get to Dras-Leona."

When Teirm was out of sight, Eragon reached out with his mind and called, *Saphira!* The force of his mental shout was so strong that Cadoc flicked his ears in annoyance.

Saphira answered and sped toward them with all of her strength. Eragon and Brom watched as a dark blur rushed from a cloud, then heard a dull roar as Saphira's wings flared open. The sun shone behind the thin membranes, turning them translucent and silhouetting the dark veins. She landed with a blast of air.

Eragon tossed Cadoc's reins to Brom. "I'll join you for lunch."

Brom nodded, but seemed preoccupied. "Have a good time," he said, then looked at Saphira and smiled. "It's good to see you again."

And you too.

Eragon hopped onto Saphira's shoulders and held on tightly as she bounded upward. With the wind at her tail, Saphira sliced through the air. *Hold on*, she warned Eragon, and letting out a wild bugle, she soared in a great loop. Eragon yelled with excitement as he flung his arms in the air, holding on only with his legs.

I didn't know I could stay on while you did that without being strapped into the saddle, he said, grinning fiercely.

Neither did I, admitted Saphira, laughing in

her peculiar way. Eragon hugged her tightly, and they flew a level path, masters of the sky.

By noon his legs were sore from riding bareback, and his hands and face were numb from the cold air. Saphira's scales were always warm to the touch, but she could not keep him from getting chilled. When they landed for lunch, he buried his hands in his clothes and found a warm, sunny place to sit. As he and Brom ate, Eragon asked Saphira, *Do you mind if I ride Cadoc?* He had decided to question Brom further about his past.

No, but tell me what he says. Eragon was not surprised that Saphira knew his plans. It was nearly impossible to hide anything from her when they were mentally linked. When they finished eating, she flew away as he joined Brom on the trail. After a time, Eragon slowed Cadoc and said, "I need to talk to you. I wanted to do it when we first arrived in Teirm, but I decided to wait until now."

"About what?" asked Brom.

Eragon paused. "There's a lot going on that I don't understand. For instance, who are your 'friends,' and why were you hiding in Carvahall? I trust you with my life—which is why I'm still traveling with you—but I need to know more about who you are and what you are doing. What did you steal in Gil'ead, and what is the tuatha du orothrim that you're taking me through? I think that after all that's happened, I deserve an explanation."

"You eavesdropped on us."

"Only once," said Eragon.

"I see that you have yet to learn proper manners," said Brom grimly, tugging on his beard. "What makes you think that this concerns you?"

"Nothing, really," said Eragon shrugging. "Just it's an odd coincidence that you happened to be hiding in Carvahall when I found Saphira's egg *and* that you also know so much dragonlore. The more I think about it, the less likely it seems. There were other clues that I mostly ignored, but they're obvious now that I look back. Like how you knew of the Ra'zac in the first place and why they ran away when you approached. And I can't help but wonder if you had something to do with the appearance of Saphira's egg. There's a lot you haven't told us, and Saphira and I can't afford to ignore anything that might be dangerous."

Dark lines appeared on Brom's forehead as he reined Snowfire to a halt. "You won't wait?" he asked. Eragon shook his head mulishly. Brom sighed. "This wouldn't be a problem if you weren't so suspicious, but I suppose that you wouldn't be worth my time if you were otherwise." Eragon was unsure if he should take that as a compliment. Brom lit his pipe and slowly blew a plume of smoke into the air. "I'll tell you," he said, "but you have to understand that I cannot reveal everything." Eragon started to protest, but Brom cut him off. "It's not out of a desire to withhold information, but because I won't give away secrets that aren't mine. There are other stories woven in with this narrative. You'll have to talk with the others involved to find out the rest."

"Very well. Explain what you can," said Eragon.

"Are you sure?" asked Brom. "There are reasons for my secretiveness. I've tried to protect you by shielding you from forces that would tear you apart. Once you know of them and their purposes, you'll never have the chance to live quietly. You will have to choose sides and make a stand. Do you really want to know?"

"I cannot live my life in ignorance," said Eragon quietly.

"A worthy goal. . . . Very well: there is a war raging in Alagaësia between the Varden and the Empire. Their conflict, however, reaches far beyond any incidental armed clashes. They are locked in a titanic power struggle . . . centered around you."

"Me?" said Eragon, disbelieving. "That's impossible. I don't have anything to do with either of them."

"Not yet," said Brom, "but your very existence is the focus of their battles. The Varden and the Empire aren't fighting to control this land or its people. Their goal is to control the next generation of Riders, of whom you are the first. Whoever controls these Riders will become the undisputed master of Alagaësia."

Eragon tried to absorb Brom's statements. It seemed incomprehensible that so many people would be interested in him and Saphira. No one besides Brom had thought he was that important. The whole concept of the Empire and Varden fighting over him was too abstract for him to grasp fully. Objections quickly formed in his mind. "But all the Riders were killed except for the Forsworn, who joined Galbatorix. As far as I know, even those are now dead. And you told me in Carvahall that no one knows if there are still dragons in Alagaësia."

"I lied about the dragons," said Brom flatly. "Even though the Riders are gone, there are still three dragon eggs left—all of them in Galbatorix's possession. Actually there are only two now, since Saphira hatched. The king salvaged the three during his last great battle with the Riders."

"So there may soon be two new Riders, both of them loyal to the king?" asked Eragon with a sinking feeling.

"Exactly," said Brom. "There is a deadly race in progress. Galbatorix is desperately trying to find the people for whom his eggs will hatch, while the Varden are employing every means to kill his candidates or steal the eggs."

"But where did Saphira's egg come from? How could anyone have gotten it away from the king? And why do you know all of this?" asked Eragon, bewildered.

"So many questions," laughed Brom bitterly. "There is another chapter to all this, one that took place long before you were born. Back then I was a bit younger, though perhaps not as wise. I hated the Empire—for reasons I'll keep to myself—and wanted to damage it in any way I could. My fervor led me to a scholar, Jeod, who claimed to have discovered a book that showed a secret passageway into Galbatorix's castle. I eagerly brought Jeod to the Varden—who are my 'friends'—and they arranged to have the eggs stolen."

The Varden!

"However, something went amiss, and our thief got only one egg. For some reason he fled with it and didn't return to the Varden. When he wasn't found, Jeod and I were sent to bring him and the egg back." Brom's eyes grew distant, and he spoke in a curious voice. "That was the start of one of the greatest searches in history. We raced against the Ra'zac and Morzan, last of the Forsworn and the king's finest servant."

"Morzan!" interrupted Eragon. "But he was the one who betrayed the Riders to Galbatorix!" *And that happened so long ago! Morzan must have been ancient.* It disturbed him to be reminded of how long Riders lived.

"So?" asked Brom, raising an eyebrow. "Yes, he was old, but strong and cruel. He was one of the king's first followers and by far his most loyal. As there had been blood between us before, the hunt for the egg turned into a personal battle. When it was located in Gil'ead, I rushed there and fought Morzan for possession. It was a terrible contest, but in the end I slew him. During the conflict I was separated from Jeod. There was no time to search for him, so I took the egg and bore it to the Varden, who asked me to train whoever became the new Rider. I agreed and decided to hide in Carvahall—which I had been to several times before—until the Varden contacted me. I was never summoned."

"Then how did Saphira's egg appear in the Spine? Was another one stolen from the king?" asked Eragon.

Brom grunted. "Small chance of that. He has the remaining two guarded so thoroughly that it would be suicide to try and steal them. No, Saphira was taken from the Varden, and I think I know how. To protect the egg, its guardian must have tried to send it to me with magic.

"The Varden haven't contacted me to explain how they lost the egg, so I suspect that their runners were intercepted by the Empire and the Ra'zac were sent in their place. I'm sure they were quite eager to find me, as I've managed to foil many of their plans."

"Then the Ra'zac didn't know about me when they arrived in Carvahall," said Eragon with wonder.

"That's right," replied Brom. "If that ass Sloan

had kept his mouth shut, they might not have found out about you. Events could have turned out quite differently. In a way I have you to thank for my life. If the Ra'zac hadn't become so preoccupied with you, they might have caught me unawares, and that would have been the end of Brom the storyteller. The only reason they ran was because I'm stronger than the two of them, especially during the day. They must have planned to drug me during the night, then question me about the egg."

"You sent a message to the Varden, telling them about me?"

"Yes. I'm sure they'll want me to bring you to them as soon as possible."

"But you're not going to, are you?"

Brom shook his head. "No, I'm not."

"Why not? Being with the Varden must be safer than chasing after the Ra'zac, especially for a new Rider."

Brom snorted and looked at Eragon with fondness. "The Varden are dangerous people. If we go to them, you will be entangled in their politics and machinations. Their leaders may send you on missions just to make a point, even though you might not be strong enough for them. I want you to be well prepared before you go anywhere near the Varden. At least while we pursue the Ra'zac, I don't have to worry about someone poisoning your water. This is the lesser of two evils.

And," he said with a smile, "it keeps you happy while I train you. . . . Tuatha du orothrim is just a stage in your instruction. I *will* help you find—and perhaps even kill—the Ra'zac, for they are as much my enemies as yours. But then you will have to make a choice."

"And that would be . . . ?" asked Eragon warily.

"Whether to join the Varden," said Brom. "If you kill the Ra'zac, the only ways for you to escape Galbatorix's wrath will be to seek the Varden's protection, flee to Surda, or plead for the king's mercy and join his forces. Even if you don't kill the Ra'zac, you will still face this choice eventually."

Eragon knew the best way to gain sanctuary might be to join the Varden, but he did not want to spend his entire life fighting the Empire like they did. He mulled over Brom's comments, trying to consider them from every angle. "You still didn't explain how you know so much about dragons."

"No, I didn't, did I?" said Brom with a crooked smile. "That will have to wait for another time."

Why me? Eragon asked himself. What made him so special that he should become a Rider? "Did you ever meet my mother?" he blurted.

Brom looked grave. "Yes, I did."

"What was she like?"

The old man sighed. "She was full of dignity and pride, like Garrow. Ultimately it was her downfall, but it was one of her greatest gifts nevertheless. . . . She always helped the poor and the less fortunate, no matter what her situation."

"You knew her well?" asked Eragon, startled.

"Well enough to miss her when she was gone."

As Cadoc plodded along, Eragon tried to recall when he had thought that Brom was just a scruffy old man who told stories. For the first time Eragon understood how ignorant he had been.

He told Saphira what he had learned. She was intrigued by Brom's revelations, but recoiled from the thought of being one of Galbatorix's possessions. At last she said, *Aren't you glad that you didn't stay in Carvahall? Think of all the interesting experiences you would have missed!* Eragon groaned in mock distress.

When they stopped for the day, Eragon searched for water while Brom made dinner. He rubbed his hands together for warmth as he walked in a large circle, listening for a creek or spring. It was gloomy and damp between the trees.

He found a stream a ways from the camp, then crouched on the bank and watched the water splash over the rocks, dipping in his fingertips. The icy mountain water swirled around his skin, numbing it. *It doesn't care what happens to us, or anyone else,* thought Eragon. He shivered and stood.

An unusual print on the opposing stream bank

caught his attention. It was oddly shaped and very large. Curious, he jumped across the stream and onto a rock shelf. As he landed, his foot hit a patch of damp moss. He grabbed a branch for support, but it broke, and he thrust out his hand to break his fall. He felt his right wrist crack as he hit the ground. Pain lanced up his arm.

A steady stream of curses came out from behind his clenched teeth as he tried not to howl. Half blind with pain, he curled on the ground, cradling his arm. *Eragon!* came Saphira's alarmed cry. *What happened?*

Broke my wrist . . . did something stupid . . . fell.

I'm coming, said Saphira.

No—I can make it back. Don't . . . come. Trees too close for . . . wings.

She sent him a brief image of her tearing the forest apart to get at him, then said, *Hurry.*

Groaning, he staggered upright. The print was pressed deeply into the ground a few feet away. It was the mark of a heavy, nail-studded boot. Eragon instantly remembered the tracks that had surrounded the pile of bodies in Yazuac. "Urgal," he spat, wishing that Zar'roc was with him; he could not use his bow with only one hand. His head snapped up, and he shouted with his mind, *Saphira! Urgals! Keep Brom safe.*

Eragon leapt back over the stream and raced toward their camp, yanking out his hunting knife. He saw potential enemies behind every tree and bush. *I hope there's only one Urgal.* He burst into the camp, ducking as Saphira's tail swung overhead. "Stop. It's me!" he yelled.

Oops, said Saphira. Her wings were folded in front of her chest like a wall.

"Oops?" growled Eragon, running to her. "You could've killed me! Where's Brom?"

"I'm right here," snapped Brom's voice from behind Saphira's wings. "Tell your crazy dragon to release me; she won't listen to me."

"Let him go!" said Eragon, exasperated. "Didn't you tell him?"

No, she said sheepishly. *You just said to keep him safe*. She lifted her wings, and Brom stepped forward angrily.

"I found an Urgal footprint. And it's fresh."

Brom immediately turned serious. "Saddle the horses. We're leaving." He put out the fire, but Eragon did not move. "What's wrong with your arm?"

"My wrist is broken," he said, swaying.

Brom cursed and saddled Cadoc for him. He helped Eragon onto the horse and said, "We have to put a splint on your arm as soon as possible. Try not to move your wrist until then." Eragon gripped the reins tightly with his left hand. Brom said to Saphira, "It's almost dark; you might as well fly right overhead. If Urgals show up, they'll think twice about attacking with you nearby."

They'd better, or else they won't think again, remarked Saphira as she took off.

The light was disappearing quickly, and the

horses were tired, but they spurred them on without respite. Eragon's wrist, swollen and red, continued to throb. A mile from the camp, Brom halted. "Listen," he said.

Eragon heard the faint call of a hunting horn behind them. As it fell silent, panic gripped him. "They must have found where we were," said Brom, "and probably Saphira's tracks. They will chase us now. It's not in their nature to let prey escape." Then two horns winded. They were closer. A chill ran through Eragon. "Our only chance is to run," said Brom. He raised his head to the sky, and his face blanked as he called Saphira.

She rushed out of the night sky and landed. "Leave Cadoc. Go with her. You'll be safer," commanded Brom.

"What about you?" Eragon protested.

"I'll be fine. Now go!" Unable to muster the energy to argue, Eragon climbed onto Saphira while Brom lashed Snowfire and rode away with Cadoc. Saphira flew after him, flapping above the galloping horses.

Eragon clung to Saphira as best he could; he winced whenever her movements jostled his wrist. The horns blared nearby, bringing a fresh wave of terror. Brom crashed through the underbrush, forcing the horses to their limits. The horns trumpeted in unison close behind him, then were quiet.

Minutes passed. *Where are the Urgals?* wondered Eragon. A horn sounded, this time in the distance. He sighed in relief, resting against Saphira's neck, while on the ground Brom slowed his headlong rush. *That was close*, said Eragon.

Yes, but we cannot stop until— Saphira was interrupted as a horn blasted directly underneath them. Eragon jerked in surprise, and Brom resumed his frenzied retreat. Horned Urgals, shouting with coarse voices, barreled along the trail on horses, swiftly gaining ground. They were almost in sight of Brom; the old man could not outrun them. *We have to do something!* exclaimed Eragon.

What?

Land in front of the Urgals!

Are you crazy? demanded Saphira.

Land! I know what I'm doing, said Eragon. *There isn't time for anything else. They're going to overtake Brom!*

Very well. Saphira pulled ahead of the Urgals, then turned, preparing to drop onto the trail. Eragon reached for his power and felt the familiar resistance in his mind that separated him from the magic. He did not try to breach it yet. A muscle twitched in his neck.

As the Urgals pounded up the trail, he shouted, "Now!" Saphira abruptly folded her wings and dropped straight down from above the trees, landing on the trail in a spray of dirt and rocks.

The Urgals shouted with alarm and yanked on their horses' reins. The animals went stiff-legged and collided into each other, but the Urgals quickly untangled themselves to face Saphira with bared weapons. Hate crossed their faces as they glared at her. There were twelve of them, all ugly, jeering brutes. Eragon wondered why they did not flee. He had thought that the sight of Saphira would frighten them away. *Why are they waiting? Are they going to attack us or not?*

He was shocked when the largest Urgal advanced and spat, "Our master wishes to speak with you, human!" The monster spoke in deep, rolling gutturals.

It's a trap, warned Saphira before Eragon could say anything. *Don't listen to him.*

At least let's find out what he has to say, he reasoned, curious, but extremely wary. "Who is your master?" he asked.

The Urgal sneered. "His name does not deserve to be given to one as low as yourself. He rules the sky and holds dominance over the earth. You are no more than a stray ant to him. Yet he has decreed that you shall be brought before him, *alive*. Take heart that you have become worthy of such notice!"

"I'll never go with you nor any of my enemies!" declared Eragon, thinking of Yazuac. "Whether you serve Shade, Urgal, or some twisted fiend I've not heard of, I have no wish to parley with him."

"That is a grave mistake," growled the Urgal, showing his fangs. "There is no way to escape him. Eventually you will stand before our master. If you resist, he will fill your days with agony."

Eragon wondered who had the power to bring the Urgals under one banner. Was there a third great force loose in the land—along with the Empire and the Varden? "Keep your offer and tell your master that the crows can eat his entrails for all I care!"

Rage swept through the Urgals; their leader howled, gnashing his teeth. "We'll drag you to him, then!" He waved his arm and the Urgals rushed at Saphira. Raising his right hand, Eragon barked, "Jierda!"

No! cried Saphira, but it was too late.

The monsters faltered as Eragon's palm glowed. Beams of light lanced from his hand, striking each of them in the gut. The Urgals were thrown through the air and smashed into trees, falling senseless to the ground.

Fatigue suddenly drained Eragon of strength, and he tumbled off Saphira. His mind felt hazy and dull. As Saphira bent over him, he realized that he might have gone too far. The energy needed to lift and throw twelve Urgals was enormous. Fear engulfed him as he struggled to stay conscious.

At the edge of his vision he saw one of the Urgals stagger to his feet, sword in hand. Eragon tried to warn Saphira, but he was too weak.

No . . . , he thought feebly. The Urgal crept toward Saphira until he was well past her tail, then raised his sword to strike her neck. *No! . . .* Saphira whirled on the monster, roaring savagely. Her talons slashed with blinding speed. Blood spurted everywhere as the Urgal was rent in two.

Saphira snapped her jaws together with finality and returned to Eragon. She gently wrapped her bloody claws around his torso, then growled and jumped into the air. The night blurred into a pain-filled streak. The hypnotic sound of Saphira's wings put him in a bleary trance: up, down; up, down; up, down. . . .

When Saphira eventually landed, Eragon was dimly aware of Brom talking with her. Eragon could not understand what they said, but a decision must have been reached because Saphira took off again.

His stupor yielded to sleep that covered him like a soft blanket.

VISION OF PERFECTION

ragon twisted under the blankets, reluctant to open his eyes. He dozed, then a fuzzy thought entered his mind . . . *How did I get here?* Confused, he pulled the blankets tighter and felt something hard on his right arm. He tried to move his wrist. It zinged with pain. *The Urgals!* He bolted upright.

He lay in a small clearing that was empty save a small campfire heating a stew-filled pot. A squirrel chattered on a branch. His bow and quiver rested alongside the blankets. Attempting to stand made him grimace, as his muscles were feeble and sore. There was a heavy splint on his bruised right arm.

Where is everyone? he wondered forlornly. He tried to call Saphira, but to his alarm could not feel her. Ravenous hunger gripped him, so he ate the stew. Still hungry, he looked for the saddlebags, hoping to find a chunk of bread. Neither the saddlebags nor the horses were in the clearing. *I'm sure there's a good reason for this*, he thought, suppressing a surge of uneasiness.

He wandered about the clearing, then returned to his blankets and rolled them up. Without anything better to do, he sat against a tree and watched the clouds overhead. Hours passed, but Brom and Saphira did not show up. *I hope nothing's wrong.*

As the afternoon dragged on, Eragon grew bored and started to explore the surrounding forest. When he became tired, he rested under a fir tree that leaned against a boulder with a bowl-shaped depression filled with clear dew water.

Eragon stared at the water and thought about Brom's instructions for scrying. *Maybe I can see where Saphira is. Brom said that scrying takes a lot of energy, but I'm stronger than he is. . . .* He breathed deeply and closed his eyes. In his mind he formed a picture of Saphira, making it as lifelike as possible. It was more demanding than he expected. Then he said, "Draumr kópa!" and gazed at the water.

Its surface became completely flat, frozen by an invisible force. The reflections disappeared and the water became clear. On it shimmered an image of Saphira. Her surroundings were pure white, but Eragon could see that she was flying. Brom sat on her back, beard streaming, sword on his knees.

Eragon tiredly let the image fade. *At least they're safe.* He gave himself a few minutes to recuperate, then leaned back over the water. *Roran, how are you?* In his mind he saw his cousin clearly. Impulsively, he drew upon the magic and uttered the words.

The water grew still, then the image formed on its surface. Roran appeared, sitting on an invisible chair. Like Saphira, his surroundings were white. There were new lines on Roran's face—he looked more like Garrow than ever before. Eragon held the image in place as long as he could. *Is Roran in Therinsford? He's certainly nowhere I've been.*

The strain of using magic had brought beads of sweat to his forehead. He sighed and for a long time was content just to sit. Then an absurd notion struck him. *What if I tried to scry something I created with my imagination or saw in a dream?* He smiled. *Perhaps I'd be shown what my own consciousness looks like.*

It was too tempting an idea to pass by. He knelt by the water once again. *What shall I look for?* He considered a few things, but discarded them all when he remembered his dream about the woman in the cell.

After fixing the scene in his mind, he spoke the words and watched the water intently. He waited, but nothing happened. Disappointed, he was about to release the magic when inky blackness swirled across the water, covering the surface. The image of a lone candle flickered in the darkness, brightening to illuminate a stone cell. The woman from his dream was curled up on a cot in one corner. She lifted her head, dark hair falling back, and stared directly at Eragon. He froze, the force of her gaze keeping him in place. Chills ran up his spine as their eyes locked. Then the woman trembled and collapsed limply.

The water cleared. Eragon rocked back on his heels, gasping. "This can't be." *She shouldn't be real; I only dreamed about her! How could she know I was looking at her? And how could I have scryed into a dungeon that I've never seen?* He shook his head, wondering if any of his other dreams had been visions.

The rhythmic thump of Saphira's wings interrupted his thoughts. He hurried back to the clearing, arriving just as Saphira landed. Brom was on her back, as Eragon had seen, but his sword was now bloody. Brom's face was contorted; the edges of his beard were stained red. "What happened?" asked Eragon, afraid that he had been wounded.

"What happened?" roared the old man. "I've been trying to clean up your mess!" He slashed the air with the sword, flinging drops of blood along its arc. "Do you know what you did with that little trick of yours? Do you?"

"I stopped the Urgals from catching you," said Eragon, a pit forming in his stomach.

"Yes," growled Brom, "but that piece of magic nearly killed you! You've been sleeping for two days. There were twelve Urgals. *Twelve!* But that didn't stop you from trying to throw them all the way to Teirm, now did it? What were you thinking? Sending a rock through each of their heads would have been the smart thing to do. But no, you had to knock them unconscious so they could run away later. I've spent the last two days trying to track them down. Even with Saphira, three escaped!"

"I didn't want to kill them," said Eragon, feeling very small.

"It wasn't a problem in Yazuac."

"There was no choice then, and I couldn't control the magic. This time it just seemed . . . extreme."

"Extreme!" cried Brom. "It's not extreme when they wouldn't show you the same mercy. And why, oh why, did you *show* yourself to them?"

"You said that they had found Saphira's footprints. It didn't make any difference if they saw me," said Eragon defensively.

Brom stabbed his sword into the dirt and snapped, "I said they had *probably* found her tracks. We didn't know for certain. They might have believed they were chasing some stray travelers. But why would they think that now? After all, *you landed right in front of them!* And since you let them live, they're scrambling around the countryside with all sorts of fantastic tales! This might even get back to the Empire!" He threw his hands up. "You don't even deserve to be called a Rider after this, *boy*." Brom yanked his sword out of the ground and stomped to the fire. He took a rag from inside his robe and angrily began to clean the blade.

Eragon was stunned. He tried to ask Saphira for advice, but all she would say was, *Speak with Brom.*

Hesitantly, Eragon made his way to the fire and asked, "Would it help if I said I was sorry?"

Brom sighed and sheathed his sword. "No, it wouldn't. Your feelings can't change what happened." He jabbed his finger at Eragon's chest. "You made some very bad choices that could have dangerous repercussions. Not the least of which is that you almost died. Died, Eragon! From now on you're going to have to think. There's a reason why we're born with brains in our heads, not rocks."

Eragon nodded, abashed. "It's not as bad as you think, though; the Urgals already knew about me. They had orders to capture me."

Astonishment widened Brom's eyes. He stuck his unlit pipe in his mouth. "No, it's not as bad as I thought. It's worse! Saphira told me you had talked with the Urgals, but she didn't mention this." The words tumbled out of Eragon's mouth as he quickly described the confrontation. "So they have some sort of leader now, eh?" questioned Brom.

Eragon nodded.

"And you just defied his wishes, insulted him, and attacked his men?" Brom shook his head. "I didn't think it could get any worse. If the Urgals had been killed, your rudeness would have gone unnoticed, but now it'll be impossible to ignore. Congratulations, you just made enemies with one of the most powerful beings in Alagaësia."

"All right, I made a mistake," said Eragon sullenly.

"Yes, you did," agreed Brom, eyes flashing. "What has me worried, though, is who this Urgal leader is."

Shivering, Eragon asked softly, "What happens now?"

There was an uncomfortable pause. "Your arm is going to take at least a couple of weeks to heal. That time would be well spent forging some sense into you. I suppose this is partially my fault. I've been teaching you *how* to do things, but not whether you *should*. It takes discretion, something you obviously lack. All the magic in Alagaësia won't help you if you don't know when to use it."

"But we're still going to Dras-Leona, right?" asked Eragon.

Brom rolled his eyes. "Yes, we can keep looking for the Ra'zac, but even if we find them, it won't do any good until you've healed." He began unsaddling Saphira. "Are you well enough to ride?"

"I think so."

"Good, then we can still cover a few miles today."

"Where are Cadoc and Snowfire?"

Brom pointed off to the side. "Over there a ways. I picketed them where there was grass." Eragon prepared to leave, then followed Brom to the horses.

Saphira said pointedly, *If you had explained what you were planning to do, none of this would have happened. I would have told you it was a bad idea not to kill the Urgals. I only agreed to do what you asked because I assumed it was halfway reasonable!*

I don't want to talk about it.

As you wish, she sniffed.

As they rode, every bump and dip in the trail made Eragon grit his teeth with discomfort. If he had been alone, he would have stopped. With Brom there, he dared not complain. Also, Brom started drilling him with difficult scenarios involving Urgals, magic, and Saphira. The imagined fights were many and varied. Sometimes a Shade or other dragons were included. Eragon discovered that it was possible to torture his body and mind at the same time. He got most of the questions wrong and became increasingly frustrated.

When they stopped for the night, Brom grumbled shortly, "It was a start." Eragon knew that he was disappointed.

MASTER OF
THE BLADE

The next day was easier on both of them. Eragon felt better and was able to answer more of Brom's questions correctly. After an especially difficult exercise, Eragon mentioned his scrying of the woman. Brom pulled on his beard. "You say she was imprisoned?"

"Yes."

"Did you see her face?" asked Brom intently.

"Not very clearly. The lighting was bad, yet I could tell that she was beautiful. It's strange; I didn't have any problem seeing her eyes. And she did look at me."

Brom shook his head. "As far as I know, it's impossible for anyone to know if they're being scryed upon."

"Do you know who she might be?" asked Eragon, surprised by the eagerness in his own voice.

"Not really," admitted Brom. "If pressed, I suppose I could come up with a few guesses, but none of them would be very likely. This dream of yours is peculiar. Somehow you managed to scry in your sleep something that you'd never seen before—without saying the words of power. Dreams do occasionally touch the spirit realm, but this is different."

"Perhaps to understand this we should search every prison and dungeon until we find the woman," bantered Eragon. He actually thought it would be a good idea. Brom laughed and rode on.

Brom's strict training filled nearly every hour as the days slowly blended into weeks. Because of his splint, Eragon was forced to use his left hand whenever they sparred. Before long he could duel as well with his left hand as he had with his right.

By the time they crossed the Spine and came to the plains, spring had crept over Alagaësia, summoning a multitude of flowers. The bare deciduous trees were russet with buds, while new blades of grass began to push up between last year's dead stalks. Birds returned from their winter absence to mate and build nests.

The travelers followed the Toark River southeast, along the edge of the Spine. It grew steadily as tributaries flowed into it from every side, feeding its bulging girth. When the river was over a league wide, Brom pointed at the silt islands that dotted the water. "We're close to Leona Lake now," he said. "It's only about two leagues away."

"Do you think we can get there before nightfall?" asked Eragon.

"We can try."

Dusk soon made the trail hard to follow, but the sound of the river at their side guided them. When the moon rose, the bright disk provided enough light to see what lay ahead.

Leona Lake looked like a thin sheet of silver beaten over the land. The water was so calm and smooth it did not even seem to be liquid. Aside from a bright strip of moonlight reflecting off the surface, it was indistinguishable from the ground. Saphira was on the rocky shore, fanning her wings to dry them. Eragon greeted her and she said, *The water is lovely—deep, cool, and clear.*

Maybe I'll go swimming tomorrow, he responded. They set up camp under a stand of trees and were soon asleep.

At dawn, Eragon eagerly rushed out to see the lake in daylight. A whitecapped expanse of water rippled with fan-shaped patterns where wind brushed it. The pure size of it delighted him. He whooped and ran to the water. *Saphira, where are you? Let's have some fun!*

The moment Eragon climbed onto her, she jumped out over the water. They soared upward, circling over the lake, but even at that height the opposing shore was not visible. *Would you like to take a bath?* Eragon casually asked Saphira.

She grinned wolfishly. *Hold on!* She locked her wings and sank to the waves, clipping the crests with her claws. The water sparkled in the sunlight as they sailed over it. Eragon whooped again. Then Saphira folded her wings and dived into the lake, her head and neck entering it like a lance.

The water hit Eragon like an icy wall, knocking out his breath and almost tearing him off Saphira. He held on tightly as she swam to the surface. With three strokes of her feet, she breached it and sent a burst of shimmering water toward the sky. Eragon gasped and shook his hair as Saphira slithered across the lake, using her tail as a rudder.

Ready?

Eragon nodded and took a deep breath, tightening his arms. This time they slid gently under the water. They could see for yards through the unclouded liquid. Saphira twisted and turned in fantastic shapes, slipping through the water like an eel. Eragon felt as if he were riding a sea serpent of legend.

Just as his lungs started to cry for air, Saphira arched her back and pointed her head upward. An explosion of droplets haloed them as she leapt into the air, wings snapping open. With two powerful flaps she gained altitude.

Wow! That was fantastic, exclaimed Eragon.

Yes, said Saphira happily. *Though it's a pity you can't hold your breath longer.*

Nothing I can do about that, he said, pressing water out of his hair. His clothes were drenched, and the wind from Saphira's wings chilled him. He pulled at his splint—his wrist itched.

Once Eragon was dry, he and Brom saddled the horses and started around Leona Lake in high spirits while Saphira playfully dived in and out of the water.

Before dinner, Eragon blocked Zar'roc's edge in preparation for their usual sparring. Neither he nor Brom moved as they waited for the other to strike first. Eragon inspected their surroundings for anything that might give him an advantage. A stick near the fire caught his attention.

Eragon swooped down, grabbed the stick, and hurled it at Brom. The splint got in his way, though, and Brom easily sidestepped the piece of wood. The old man rushed forward, swinging his sword. Eragon ducked just as the blade whistled over his head. He growled and tackled Brom ferociously.

They pitched to the ground, each struggling to stay on top. Eragon rolled to the side and swept Zar'roc over the ground at Brom's shins. Brom parried the blow with the hilt of his sword, then jumped to his feet. Twisting as he stood, Eragon attacked again, guiding Zar'roc through a complex pattern. Sparks danced from their blades as they struck again and again. Brom blocked each blow, his face tight with concentration. But Eragon could tell that he was tiring. The relentless hammering continued as each sought an opening in the other's defenses.

Then Eragon felt the battle change. Blow by blow he gained advantage; Brom's parries slowed and he lost ground. Eragon easily blocked a stab from Brom. Veins pulsed on the old man's forehead and cords bulged in his neck from the effort.

Suddenly confident, Eragon swung Zar'roc faster than ever, weaving a web of steel around Brom's sword. With a burst of speed, he smashed the flat of his blade against Brom's guard and knocked the sword to the ground. Before Brom could react, Eragon flicked Zar'roc up to his throat.

They stood panting, the red sword tip resting on Brom's collarbone. Eragon slowly lowered his arm and backed away. It was the first time he had bested Brom without resorting to trickery. Brom picked up his sword and sheathed it. Still breathing hard, he said, "We're done for today."

"But we just started," said Eragon, startled.

Brom shook his head. "I can teach you nothing more of the sword. Of all the fighters I've met, only three of them could have defeated me like that, and I doubt any of them could have done it with their left hand." He smiled ruefully. "I may not be as young as I used to be, but I can tell that you're a talented and rare swordsman."

"Does this mean we're not going to spar every night?" asked Eragon.

"Oh, you're not getting out of it," laughed Brom. "But we'll go easier now. It's not as important if we miss a night here or there." He wiped his brow. "Just remember, if you ever have the misfortune to fight an elf—trained or not, female or male—expect to lose. They, along with dragons and other creatures of magic, are many times stronger than nature intended. Even the weakest elf could easily overpower you. The same goes for the Ra'zac—they are not human and tire much more slowly than we do."

"Is there any way to become their equal?" asked Eragon. He sat cross-legged by Saphira.

You fought well, she said. He smiled.

Brom seated himself with a shrug. "There are a few, but none are available to you now. Magic will let you defeat all but the strongest enemies. For those you'll need Saphira's help, plus a great deal of luck. Remember, when creatures of magic actually use magic, they can accomplish things that could kill a human, because of their enhanced abilities."

"How do you fight with magic?" asked Eragon.

"What do you mean?"

"Well," he said, leaning on an elbow. "Suppose I was attacked by a Shade. How could I block his magic? Most spells take place instantaneously, which makes it impossible to react in time. And even if I could, how would I nullify an enemy's magic? It seems I would have to know my opponent's intention *before* he acted." He paused. "I just don't see how it can be done. Whoever attacked first would win."

Brom sighed. "What you are talking about—a 'wizards' duel,' if you will—is extremely dangerous. Haven't you ever wondered how Galbatorix was able to defeat all of the Riders with the help of only a dozen or so traitors?"

"I never thought about it," acknowledged Eragon.

"There are several ways. Some you'll learn about later, but the main one is that Galbatorix was, and still is, a master of breaking into people's minds. You see, in a wizards' duel there are strict rules that each side must observe or else both contestants will die. To begin with, no one uses magic until one of the participants gains access to the other's mind."

Saphira curled her tail comfortably around Eragon and asked, *Why wait? By the time an enemy realizes that you've attacked, it will be too late for him to act.* Eragon repeated the question out loud.

Brom shook his head. "No, it won't. If I were to suddenly use my power against you, Eragon, you would surely die, but in the brief moment before you were destroyed, there would be time for a counterattack. Therefore, unless one combatant has a death wish, neither side attacks until one of them has breached the other's defenses."

"Then what happens?" Eragon inquired.

Brom shrugged and said, "Once you're inside your enemy's mind, it's easy enough to anticipate what he will do and prevent it. Even with that advantage, it's still possible to lose if you don't know how to counteract spells."

He filled and lit his pipe. "And that requires extraordinarily quick thinking. Before you can defend yourself, you have to understand the exact nature of the forces directed at you. If you're being attacked with heat, you have to know whether it is being conveyed to you through air, fire, light, or some other medium. Only once that's known can you combat the magic by, for instance, chilling the heated material."

"It sounds difficult."

"Extremely," confirmed Brom. A plume of smoke rose from his pipe. "Seldom can people survive such a duel for more than a few seconds. The enormous amount of effort and skill required condemns anyone without the proper training to a quick death. Once you've progressed, I'll start teaching you the necessary methods. In the meantime, if you ever find yourself facing a wizards' duel, I suggest you run away as fast as you can."

THE MIRE OF
DRAS-LEONA

They lunched at Fasaloft, a bustling lakeside village. It was a charming place set on a rise overlooking the lake. As they ate in the hostel's common room, Eragon listened intently to the gossip and was relieved to hear no rumors of him and Saphira.

The trail, now a road, had grown steadily worse over the past two days. Wagon wheels and iron-shod hooves had conspired to tear up the ground, making many sections impassable. An increase in travelers forced Saphira to hide during the day and then catch up with Brom and Eragon at night.

For days they continued south along Leona Lake's vast shore. Eragon began to wonder if they would ever get around it, so he was heartened when they met men who said that Dras-Leona was an easy day's ride ahead of them.

＊　＊　＊

Eragon rose early the following morning. His fingers twitched with anticipation at the thought of finally finding the Ra'zac. *The two of you must be careful*, said Saphira. *The Ra'zac could have spies watching for travelers that fit your description.*

We'll do our best to remain inconspicuous, he assured her.

She lowered her head until their eyes met. *Perhaps, but realize that I won't be able to protect you as I did with the Urgals. I will be too far away to come to your aid, nor would I survive long in the narrow streets your kind favor. Follow Brom's lead in this hunt; he is sensible.*

I know, he said somberly.

Will you go with Brom to the Varden? Once the Ra'zac are killed, he will want to take you to them. And since Galbatorix will be enraged by the Ra'zac's death, that may be the safest thing for us to do.

Eragon rubbed his arms. *I don't want to fight the Empire all the time like the Varden do. Life is more than constant war. There'll be time to consider it once the Ra'zac are gone.*

Don't be too sure, she warned, then went to hide herself until night.

The road was clogged with farmers taking their goods to market in Dras-Leona. Brom and Eragon were forced to slow their horses and wait for wagons that blocked the way.

Although they saw smoke in the distance before noon, it was another league before the city was clearly visible. Unlike Teirm, a planned city, Dras-Leona was a tangled mess that sprawled next to Leona Lake. Ramshackle buildings sat on crooked streets, and the heart of the city was surrounded by a dirty, pale yellow wall of daubed mud.

Several miles east, a mountain of bare rock speared the sky with spires and columns, a tenebrous nightmare ship. Near-vertical sides rose out of the ground like a jagged piece of the earth's bone.

Brom pointed. "*That* is Helgrind. It's the reason Dras-Leona was originally built. People are fascinated by it, even though it's an unhealthy and malevolent thing." He gestured at the buildings inside the city's wall. "We should go to the center of the city first."

As they crept along the road to Dras-Leona, Eragon saw that the highest building within the city was a cathedral that loomed behind the walls. It was strikingly similar to Helgrind, especially when its arches and flanged spires caught the light. "Who do they worship?" he asked.

Brom grimaced in distaste. "Their prayers go to Helgrind. It's a cruel religion they practice. They drink human blood and make flesh offerings. Their priests often lack body parts because they believe that the more bone and sinew you give up, the less you're attached to the mortal world. They spend much of their time arguing about which of Helgrind's three peaks is the highest and most important and whether the fourth—and lowest—should be included in their worship."

"That's horrible," said Eragon, shuddering.

"Yes," said Brom grimly, "but don't say that to a believer. You'll quickly lose a hand in 'penance.'"

At Dras-Leona's enormous gates, they led the horses through the crush of people. Ten soldiers were stationed on either side of the gates, casually scanning the crowd. Eragon and Brom passed into the city without incident.

362 The houses inside the city wall were tall and thin to compensate for the lack of space. Those next to the wall were braced against it. Most of the houses hung over the narrow, winding streets, covering the sky so that it was hard to tell if it was night or day. Nearly all the buildings were constructed of the same rough brown wood, which darkened the city even more. The air reeked like a sewer; the streets were filthy.

A group of ragged children ran between the houses, fighting over scraps of bread. Deformed beggars crouched next to the entrance gates, pleading for money. Their cries for help were like a chorus of the damned. *We don't even treat animals like this*, thought Eragon, eyes wide with anger. "I won't stay here," he said, rebelling against the sight.

"It gets better farther in," said Brom. "Right now we need to find an inn and form a strategy. Dras-Leona can be a dangerous place to even the most cautious. I don't want to remain on the streets any longer than necessary."

They forged deeper into Dras-Leona, leaving the squalid entrance behind. As they entered wealthier parts of the city, Eragon wondered, *How can these people live in ease when the suffering around them is so obvious?*

They found lodging at the Golden Globe, which was cheap but not decrepit. A narrow bed was crammed against one wall of the room, with a rickety table and a basin alongside it. Eragon took one look at the mattress and said, "I'm sleeping on the floor. There are probably enough bugs in that thing to eat me alive."

"Well, I wouldn't want to deprive them of a meal," said Brom, dropping his bags on the mattress. Eragon set his own on the floor and pulled off his bow.

"What now?" he asked.

"We find food and beer. After that, sleep. To-morrow we can start looking for the Ra'zac." Before they left the room, Brom warned, "No matter what happens, make sure that your tongue doesn't loosen. We'll have to leave immediately if we're given away."

The inn's food was barely adequate, but its beer was excellent. By the time they stumbled back to the room, Eragon's head was buzzing pleasantly. He unrolled his blankets on the floor and slid under them as Brom tumbled onto the bed.

Just before Eragon fell asleep, he contacted Saphira: *We're going to be here for a few days, but this shouldn't take as long as it did at Teirm. When we discover where the Ra'zac are, you might be able to help us get them. I'll talk to you in the morning. Right now I'm not thinking too clearly.*

You've been drinking, came the accusing thought. Eragon considered it for a moment and had to agree that she was absolutely right. Her disapproval was clear, but all she said was, *I won't envy you in the morning.*

No, groaned Eragon, *but Brom will. He drank twice as much as I did.*

TRAIL OF OIL

What was I thinking? wondered Eragon in the morning. His head was pounding and his tongue felt thick and fuzzy. As a rat skittered under the floor, Eragon winced at the noise.

How are we feeling? asked Saphira smugly.

Eragon ignored her.

A moment later, Brom rolled out of bed with a grumble. He doused his head in cold water from the basin, then left the room. Eragon followed him into the hallway. "Where are you going?" he asked.

"To recover."

"I'll come." At the bar, Eragon discovered that Brom's method of recovery involved imbibing copious amounts of hot tea and ice water and washing it all down with brandy. When they returned to the room, Eragon was able to function somewhat better.

Brom belted on his sword and smoothed the wrinkles out of his robe. "The first thing we need to do is ask some discreet questions. I want to find out where the Seithr oil was delivered in Dras-Leona and where it was taken from there. Most likely, soldiers or workmen were involved in transporting it. We have to find those men and get one to talk."

They left the Golden Globe and searched for warehouses where the Seithr oil might have been delivered. Near the center of Dras-Leona, the streets began to slant upward toward a palace of polished granite. It was built on a rise so that it towered above every building except the cathedral.

The courtyard was a mosaic of mother-of-pearl, and parts of the walls were inlaid with gold. Black statues stood in alcoves, with sticks of incense smoking in their cold hands. Soldiers stationed every four yards watched passersby keenly.

"Who lives there?" asked Eragon in awe.

"Marcus Tábor, ruler of this city. He answers only to the king and his own conscience, which hasn't been very active recently," said Brom. They walked around the palace, looking at the gated, ornate houses that surrounded it.

By midday they had learned nothing useful, so they stopped for lunch. "This city is too vast for us to comb it together," said Brom. "Search on your own. Meet me at the Golden Globe by dusk." He glowered at Eragon from under his bushy eyebrows. "I'm trusting you not to do anything stupid."

"I won't," promised Eragon. Brom handed him some coins, then strode away in the opposite direction.

Throughout the rest of the day, Eragon talked with shopkeepers and workers, trying to be as pleasant and charming as he could. His questions led him from one end of the city to the other and back again. No one seemed to know about the oil. Wherever he went, the cathedral stared down at him. It was impossible to escape its tall spires.

At last he found a man who had helped ship the Seithr oil and remembered to which warehouse it had been taken. Eragon excitedly went to look at the building, then returned to the Golden Globe. It was over an hour before Brom came back, slumped with fatigue. "Did you find anything?" asked Eragon.

Brom brushed back his white hair. "I heard a great deal of interesting things today, not the least of which is that Galbatorix will visit Dras-Leona within the week."

"What?" exclaimed Eragon.

Brom slouched against the wall, the lines on his forehead deepening. "It seems that Tábor has taken a few too many liberties with his power, so Galbatorix has decided to come teach him a lesson in humility. It's the first time the king has left Urû'baen in over ten years."

"Do you think he knows of us?" asked Eragon.

"Of course he *knows* of us, but I'm sure he hasn't been told our location. If he had, we would already be in the Ra'zac's grasp. However, this means that whatever we're going to do about the Ra'zac must be accomplished before Galbatorix arrives. We don't want to be anywhere within twenty leagues of him. The one thing in our favor is that the Ra'zac are sure to be here, preparing for his visit."

"I want to get the Ra'zac," said Eragon, his fists tightening, "but not if it means fighting the king. He could probably tear me to pieces."

That seemed to amuse Brom. "Very good: caution. And you're right; you wouldn't stand a chance against Galbatorix. Now tell me what you learned today. It might confirm what I heard."

Eragon shrugged. "It was mostly drivel, but I did talk with a man who knew where the oil was taken. It's just an old warehouse. Other than that, I didn't discover anything useful."

"My day was a little more fruitful than yours. I heard the same thing you did, so I went to the warehouse and talked with the workers. It didn't take much cajoling before they revealed that the cases of Seithr oil are always sent from the warehouse to the palace."

"And that's when you came back here," finished Eragon.

"No, it's not! Don't interrupt. After that, I went to the palace and got myself invited into the servants' quarters as a bard. For several hours I wandered about, amusing the maids and others with songs and poems—and asking questions all the while." Brom slowly filled his pipe with tobacco. "It's really amazing all the things servants find out. Did you know that one of the earls has *three* mistresses, and they all live in the same wing of the palace?" He shook his head and lit the pipe. "Aside from the fascinating tidbits, I was told, quite by accident, where the oil is taken from the palace."

"And that is . . . ?" asked Eragon impatiently.

Brom puffed on his pipe and blew a smoke ring. "Out of the city, of course. Every full moon two slaves are sent to the base of Helgrind with a month's worth of provisions. Whenever the Seithr oil arrives in Dras-Leona, they send it along with the provisions. The slaves are never seen again. And the one time someone followed them, he disappeared too."

"I thought the Riders demolished the slave trade," said Eragon.

"Unfortunately, it has flourished under the king's reign."

"So the Ra'zac are in Helgrind," said Eragon, thinking of the rock mountain.

"There or somewhere nearby."

"If they *are* in Helgrind, they'll be either at the bottom—and protected by a thick stone door—

or higher up where only their flying mounts, or Saphira, can reach. Top or bottom, their shelter will no doubt be disguised." He thought for a moment. "If Saphira and I go flying around Helgrind, the Ra'zac are sure to see us—not to mention all of Dras-Leona."

"It is a problem," agreed Brom.

Eragon frowned. "What if we took the place of the two slaves? The full moon isn't far off. It would give us a perfect opportunity to get close to the Ra'zac."

Brom tugged his beard thoughtfully. "That's chancy at best. If the slaves are killed from a distance, we'll be in trouble. We can't harm the Ra'zac if they aren't in sight."

"We don't know if the slaves are killed at all," Eragon pointed out.

"I'm sure they are," said Brom, his face grave. Then his eyes sparkled, and he blew another smoke ring. "Still, it's an intriguing idea. If it were done with Saphira hidden nearby and a . . ." His voice trailed off. "It might work, but we'll have to move quickly. With the king coming, there isn't much time."

"Should we go to Helgrind and look around? It would be good to see the land in daylight so we won't be surprised by any ambushes," said Eragon.

Brom fingered his staff. "That can be done later. Tomorrow I'll return to the palace and figure out how we can replace the slaves. I have to be careful not to arouse suspicion, though—I could easily be revealed by spies and courtiers who know about the Ra'zac."

"I can't believe it; we actually found them," said Eragon quietly. An image of his dead uncle and burned farm flashed through his mind. His jaw tightened.

"The toughest part is yet to come, but yes, we've done well," said Brom. "If fortune smiles on us, you may soon have your revenge and the Varden will be rid of a dangerous enemy. What comes after that will be up to you."

Eragon opened his mind and jubilantly told Saphira, *We found the Ra'zac's lair!*

Where? He quickly explained what they had discovered. *Helgrind,* she mused. *A fitting place for them.*

Eragon agreed. *When we're done here, maybe we could visit Carvahall.*

What is it you want? she asked, suddenly sour. *To go back to your previous life? You know that won't happen, so stop mooning after it! At a certain point you have to decide what to commit to. Will you hide for the rest of your life, or will you help the Varden? Those are the only options left to you, unless you join forces with Galbatorix, which I do not and never will accept.*

Softly, he said, *If I must choose, I cast my fate with the Varden, as you well know.*

Yes, but sometimes you have to hear yourself say it. She left him to ponder her words.

WORSHIPERS
OF HELGRIND

Eragon was alone in the room when he woke. Scrawled onto the wall with a charcoal stick was a note that read:

Eragon,

I will be gone until late tonight. Coins for food are under the mattress. Explore the city, enjoy yourself, but <u>stay unnoticed!</u>

Brom

P.S. Avoid the palace. Don't go anywhere without your bow! Keep it strung.

Eragon wiped the wall clean, then retrieved the money from under the bed. He slipped the bow across his back, thinking, *I wish I didn't have to go armed all the time.*

He left the Golden Globe and ambled through the streets, stopping to observe whatever interested him. There were many intriguing stores, but none quite as exciting as Angela's herb shop in Teirm. At times he glared at the dark, claustrophobic houses and wished that he were free of the city. When he grew hungry, he bought a wedge of cheese and a loaf of bread and ate them, sitting on a curb.

Later, in a far corner of Dras-Leona, he heard an auctioneer rattling off a list of prices. Curious, he headed toward the voice and arrived at a wide opening between two buildings. Ten men stood on a waist-high platform. Arrayed before them was a richly dressed crowd that was both colorful and boisterous. *Where are the goods for sale?* wondered Eragon.

The auctioneer finished his list and motioned for a young man behind the platform to join him. The man awkwardly climbed up, chains dragging at his hands and feet. "And here we have our first item," proclaimed the auctioneer. "A healthy male from the Hadarac Desert, captured just last month, and in excellent condition. Look at those arms and legs; he's strong as a bull! He'd be perfect as a shield bearer, or, if you don't trust him for that, hard labor. But let me tell you, lords and ladies, that would be a waste. He's bright as a nail, if you can get him to talk a civilized tongue!"

The crowd laughed, and Eragon ground his

teeth with fury. His lips started to form a word that would free the slave, and his arm, newly liberated from the splint, rose. The mark on his palm shimmered. He was about to release the magic when it struck him, *He'd never get away!* The slave would be caught before he reached the city walls. Eragon would only make the situation worse if he tried to help. He lowered his arm and quietly cursed. *Think! This is how you got into trouble with the Urgals.*

He watched helplessly as the slave was sold to a tall, hawk-nosed man. The next slave was a tiny girl, no more than six years old, wrenched from the arms of her crying mother. As the auctioneer started the bidding, Eragon forced himself to walk away, rigid with fury and outrage.

It was several blocks before the weeping was inaudible. *I'd like to see a thief try to cut my purse right now,* he thought grimly, almost wishing it would happen. Frustrated, he punched a nearby wall, bruising his knuckles.

That's the sort of thing I could stop by fighting the Empire, he realized. *With Saphira by my side I could free those slaves. I've been graced with special powers; it would be selfish of me not to use them for the benefit of others. If I don't, I might as well not be a Rider at all.*

It was a while before he took stock of his bearings and was surprised to find himself before the cathedral. Its twisted spires were covered with statues and scrollwork. Snarling gargoyles crouched along the eaves. Fantastic beasts writhed on the walls, and heroes and kings marched along their bottom edges, frozen in cold marble. Ribbed arches and tall stained-glass windows lined the cathedral's sides, along with columns of differing sizes. A lonely turret helmed the building like a mast.

Recessed in shadow at the cathedral's front was an iron-bound door inlaid with a row of silver script that Eragon recognized as the ancient language. As best he could tell, it read: *May thee who enter here understand thine impermanence and forget thine attachments to that which is beloved.*

The entire building sent a shiver down Eragon's spine. There was something menacing about it, as if it were a predator crouched in the city, waiting for its next victim.

A broad row of steps led to the cathedral's entrance. Eragon solemnly ascended them and stopped before the door. *I wonder if I can go in?* Almost guiltily he pushed on the door. It swung open smoothly, gliding on oiled hinges. He stepped inside.

The silence of a forgotten tomb filled the empty cathedral. The air was chill and dry. Bare walls extended to a vaulted ceiling that was so high Eragon felt no taller than an ant. Stained-glass windows depicting scenes of anger, hate, and remorse pierced the walls, while spectral beams of light washed sections of the granite pews with transparent hues, leaving the rest in shadow. His hands were shaded a deep blue.

Between the windows stood statues with rigid, pale eyes. He returned their stern gazes, then slowly trod up the center row, afraid to break the quiet. His leather boots padded noiselessly on the polished stone floor.

The altar was a great slab of stone devoid of adornment. A solitary finger of light fell upon it, illuminating motes of golden dust floating in the air. Behind the altar, the pipes of a wind organ pierced the ceiling and opened themselves to the elements. The instrument would play its music only when a gale rocked Dras-Leona.

376   Out of respect, Eragon knelt before the altar and bowed his head. He did not pray but paid homage to the cathedral itself. The sorrows of the lives it had witnessed, as well as the unpleasantness of the elaborate pageantry that played out between its walls, emanated from the stones. It was a forbidding place, bare and cold. In that chilling touch, though, came a glimpse of eternity and perhaps the powers that lay there.

Finally Eragon inclined his head and rose. Calm and grave, he whispered words to himself in the ancient language, then turned to leave. He froze. His heart jumped, hammering like a drum.

The Ra'zac stood at the cathedral's entrance, watching him. Their swords were drawn, keen edges bloody in a crimson light. A sibilant hiss came from the smaller Ra'zac. Neither of them moved.

Rage welled up in Eragon. He had chased the Ra'zac for so many weeks that the pain of their murderous deed had dulled within him. But his vengeance was at hand. His wrath exploded like a volcano, fueled even more by his pent-up fury at the slaves' plight. A roar broke from his lips, echoing like a thunderstorm as he snatched his bow from his back. Deftly, he fit an arrow to the string and loosed it. Two more followed an instant later.

The Ra'zac leapt away from the arrows with inhuman swiftness. They hissed as they ran up the aisle between the pews, cloaks flapping like raven wings. Eragon reached for another arrow, but caution stayed his hand. *If they knew where to find me, Brom is in danger as well! I must warn him!* Then, to Eragon's horror, a line of soldiers filed into the cathedral, and he glimpsed a field of uniforms jostling outside the doorway.

Eragon gazed hungrily at the charging Ra'zac, then swept around, searching for means of escape. A vestibule to the left of the altar caught his attention. He bounded through the archway and dashed down a corridor that led to a priory with a belfry. The patter of the Ra'zac's feet behind him made him quicken his pace until the hall abruptly ended with a closed door.

He pounded against it, trying to break it open, but the wood was too strong. The Ra'zac were nearly upon him. Frantic, he sucked in his breath and barked, "Jierda!" With a flash, the door splintered into pieces and fell to the floor. Eragon jumped into the small room and continued running.

He sped through several chambers, startling a group of priests. Shouts and curses followed him. The priory bell tolled an alarm. Eragon dodged through a kitchen, passed a pair of monks, then slipped through a side door. He skidded to stop in a garden surrounded by a high brick wall devoid of handholds. There were no other exits.

Eragon turned to leave, but there was a low hiss as the Ra'zac shouldered aside the door. Desperate, he rushed at the wall, arms pumping. Magic could not help him here—if he used it to break through the wall, he would be too tired to run.

He jumped. Even with his arms outstretched, only his fingertips cleared the edge of the wall. The rest of his body smashed against the bricks, driving out his breath. Eragon gasped and hung there, struggling not to fall. The Ra'zac prowled into the garden, swinging their heads from side to side like wolfhounds sniffing for prey.

Eragon sensed their approach and heaved with his arms. His shoulders shrieked with pain as he scrambled onto the wall and dropped to the other side. He stumbled, then regained his balance and darted down an alley just as the Ra'zac leapt over the wall. Galvanized, Eragon put on another burst of speed.

He ran for over a mile before he had to stop and catch his breath. Unsure if he had lost the Ra'zac, he found a crowded marketplace and dived under a parked wagon. *How did they find me?* he wondered, panting. *They shouldn't have known where I was . . . unless something happened to Brom!* He reached out with his mind to Saphira and said, *The Ra'zac found me. We're all in danger! Check if Brom's all right. If he is, warn him and have him meet me at the inn. And be ready to fly here as fast as you can. We may need your help to escape.*

She was silent, then said curtly, *He'll meet you at the inn. Don't stop moving; you're in great danger.* 379

"Don't I know it," muttered Eragon as he rolled out from under the wagon. He hurried back to the Golden Globe, quickly packed their belongings, saddled the horses, then led them to the street. Brom soon arrived, staff in hand, scowling dangerously. He swung onto Snowfire and asked, "What happened?"

"I was in the cathedral when the Ra'zac just appeared behind me," said Eragon, climbing onto Cadoc. "I ran back as fast as possible, but they could be here at any second. Saphira will join us once we're out of Dras-Leona."

"We have to get outside the city walls before

they close the gates, if they haven't already," said Brom. "If they're shut, it'll be nigh impossible for us to leave. Whatever you do, don't get separated from me." Eragon stiffened as ranks of soldiers marched down one end of the street.

Brom cursed, lashed Snowfire with his reins, and galloped away. Eragon bent low over Cadoc and followed. They nearly crashed several times during the wild, hazardous ride, plunging through masses of people that clogged the streets as they neared the city wall. When the gates finally came into view, Eragon pulled on Cadoc's reins with dismay. The gates were already half closed, and a double line of pikemen blocked their way.

"They'll cut us to pieces!" he exclaimed.

"We have to try and make it," said Brom, his voice hard. "I'll deal with the men, but you have to keep the gates open for us." Eragon nodded, gritted his teeth, and dug his heels into Cadoc.

They plowed toward the line of unwavering soldiers, who lowered their pikes toward the horses' chests and braced the weapons against the ground. Though the horses snorted with fear, Eragon and Brom held them in place. Eragon heard the soldiers shout but kept his attention on the gates inching shut.

As they neared the sharp pikes, Brom raised his hand and spoke. The words struck with precision; the soldiers fell to each side as if their legs had been cut out from under them. The gap between the gates shrank by the second. Hoping that the effort would not prove too much for him, Eragon drew on his power and shouted, "Du grind huildr!"

A deep grating sound emanated from the gates as they trembled, then ground to a stop. The crowd and guards fell silent, staring with amazement. With a clatter of the horses' hooves, Brom and Eragon shot out from behind Dras-Leona's wall. The instant they were free, Eragon released the gates. They shuddered, then boomed shut.

He swayed with the expected fatigue but managed to keep riding. Brom watched him with concern. Their flight continued through the outskirts of Dras-Leona as alarm trumpets sounded on the city wall. Saphira was waiting for them by the edge of the city, hidden behind some trees. Her eyes burned; her tail whipped back and forth. "Go, ride her," said Brom. "And this time stay in the air, no matter what happens to me. I'll head south. Fly nearby; I don't care if Saphira's seen." Eragon quickly mounted Saphira. As the ground dwindled away beneath him, he watched Brom gallop along the road.

Are you all right? asked Saphira.

Yes, said Eragon. *But only because we were very lucky.*

A puff of smoke blew from her nostrils. *All the time we've spent searching for the Ra'zac was useless.*

I know, he said, letting his head sag against her

scales. *If the Ra'zac had been the only enemies back there, I would have stayed and fought, but with all the soldiers on their side, it was hardly a fair match!*

You understand that there will be talk of us now? This was hardly an unobtrusive escape. Evading the Empire will be harder than ever. There was an edge to her voice that he was unaccustomed to.

I know.

They flew low and fast over the road. Leona Lake receded behind them; the land became dry and rocky and filled with tough, sharp bushes and tall cactuses. Clouds darkened the sky. Lightning flashed in the distance. As the wind began to howl, Saphira glided steeply down to Brom. He stopped the horses and asked, "What's wrong?"

"The wind's too strong."

"It's not that bad," objected Brom.

"It is up there," said Eragon, pointing at the sky.

Brom swore and handed him Cadoc's reins. They trotted away with Saphira following on foot, though on the ground she had difficulty keeping up with the horses.

The gale grew stronger, flinging dirt through the air and twisting like a dervish. They wrapped scarves around their heads to protect their eyes. Brom's robe flapped in the wind while his beard whipped about as if it had a life of its own. Though it would make them miserable, Eragon hoped it would rain so their tracks would be obliterated.

Soon darkness forced them to stop. With only the stars to guide them, they left the road and made camp behind two boulders. It was too dangerous to light a fire, so they ate cold food while Saphira sheltered them from the wind.

After the sparse dinner, Eragon asked bluntly, "How did they find us?"

Brom started to light his pipe, but thought better of it and put it away. "One of the palace servants warned me there were spies among them. Somehow word of me and my questions must have reached Tábor . . . and through him, the Ra'zac."

"We can't go back to Dras-Leona, can we?" asked Eragon.

Brom shook his head. "Not for a few years."

Eragon held his head between his hands. "Then should we draw the Ra'zac out? If we let Saphira be seen, they'll come running to wherever she is."

"And when they do, there will be fifty soldiers with them," said Brom. "At any rate, this isn't the time to discuss it. Right now we have to concentrate on staying alive. Tonight will be the most dangerous because the Ra'zac will be hunting us in the dark, when they are strongest. We'll have to trade watches until morning."

"Right," said Eragon, standing. He hesitated and squinted. His eyes had caught a flicker of movement, a small patch of color that stood out from the surrounding nightscape. He stepped toward the edge of their camp, trying to see it better.

"What is it?" asked Brom as he unrolled his blankets.

Eragon stared into the darkness, then turned back. "I don't know. I thought I saw something. It must have been a bird." Pain erupted in the back of his head, and Saphira roared. Then Eragon toppled to the ground, unconscious.

384

THE RA'ZAC'S
REVENGE

A dull throbbing roused Eragon. Every time blood pulsed through his head it brought a fresh wave of pain. He cracked his eyes open and winced; tears rushed to his eyes as he looked directly into a bright lantern. He blinked and looked away. When he tried to sit up, he realized that his hands were tied behind his back.

He turned lethargically and saw Brom's arms. Eragon was relieved to see that they were bound together. Why was that? He struggled to figure it out until the thought suddenly came to him, *They wouldn't tie up a dead man!* But then who were "they"? He swiveled his head further, then stopped as a pair of black boots entered his vision.

Eragon looked up, right into the cowled face of a Ra'zac. Fear jolted through him. He reached for the magic and started to voice a word that would kill the Ra'zac, but then halted, puzzled.

He could not remember the word. Frustrated, he tried again, only to feel it slip out of his grasp.

Above him the Ra'zac laughed chillingly. "The drug is working, yesss? I think you will not be bothering us again."

There was a rattle off to the left, and Eragon was appalled to see the second Ra'zac fit a muzzle over Saphira's head. Her wings were pinioned to her sides by black chains; there were shackles on her legs. Eragon tried to contact her, but felt nothing.

"She was most cooperative once we threatened to kill you," hissed the Ra'zac. Squatting by the lantern, he rummaged through Eragon's bags, examining and discarding various items until he removed Zar'roc. "What a pretty thing for one so . . . insignificant. Maybe I will keep it." He leaned closer and sneered, "Or maybe, if you behave, our master will let you polish it." His moist breath smelled like raw meat.

Then he turned the sword over in his hands and screeched as he saw the symbol on the scabbard. His companion rushed over. They stood over the sword, hissing and clicking. At last they faced Eragon. "You will serve our master very well, yesss."

Eragon forced his thick tongue to form words: "If I do, I will kill you."

They chuckled coldly. "Oh no, we are too valuable. But you . . . you are *disposable*." A deep snarl came from Saphira; smoke roiled from her nostrils. The Ra'zac did not seem to care.

Their attention was diverted when Brom groaned and rolled onto his side. One of the Ra'zac grabbed his shirt and thrust him effortlessly into the air. "It'sss wearing off."

"Give him more."

"Let'sss just kill him," said the shorter Ra'zac. "He has caused us much grief."

The taller one ran his finger down his sword. "A good plan. But remember, the king's instructions were to keep them *alive*."

"We can sssay he was killed when we captured them."

"And what of thisss one?" the Ra'zac asked, pointing his sword at Eragon. "If he talksss?"

His companion laughed and drew a wicked dagger. "He would not dare."

There was a long silence, then, "Agreed."

They dragged Brom to the center of the camp and shoved him to his knees. Brom sagged to one side. Eragon watched with growing fear. *I have to get free!* He wrenched at the ropes, but they were too strong to break. "None of that now," said the tall Ra'zac, poking him with a sword. He nosed the air and sniffed; something seemed to trouble him.

The other Ra'zac growled, yanked Brom's head back, and swept the dagger toward his exposed throat. At that very moment a low buzz sounded, followed by the Ra'zac's howl. An arrow protruded from his shoulder. The Ra'zac nearest Eragon dropped to the ground, barely avoiding a second arrow. He scuttled to his wounded companion, and they glared into the darkness, hissing angrily. They made no move to stop Brom as he blearily staggered upright. "Get down!" cried Eragon.

Brom wavered, then tottered toward Eragon. As more arrows hissed into the camp from the unseen attackers, the Ra'zac rolled behind some boulders. There was a lull, then arrows came from the opposite direction. Caught by surprise, the Ra'zac reacted slowly. Their cloaks were pierced in several places, and a shattered arrow buried itself in one's arm.

With a wild cry, the smaller Ra'zac fled toward the road, kicking Eragon viciously in the side as he passed. His companion hesitated, then grabbed the dagger from the ground and raced after him. As he left the camp, he hurled the knife at Eragon.

A strange light suddenly burned in Brom's eyes. He threw himself in front of Eragon, his mouth open in a soundless snarl. The dagger struck him with a soft thump, and he landed heavily on his shoulder. His head lolled limply.

"No!" screamed Eragon, though he was doubled over in pain. He heard footsteps, then his eyes closed and he knew no more.

MURTAGH

For a long while, Eragon was aware only of the burning in his side. Each breath was painful. It felt as though he had been the one stabbed, not Brom. His sense of time was skewed; it was hard to tell if weeks had gone by, or only a few minutes. When consciousness finally came to him, he opened his eyes and peered curiously at a campfire several feet away. His hands were still tied together, but the drug must have worn off because he could think clearly again. *Saphira, are you injured?*

No, but you and Brom are. She was crouched over Eragon, wings spread protectively on either side.

Saphira, you didn't make that fire, did you? And you couldn't have gotten out of those chains by yourself.

No.

I didn't think so. Eragon struggled to his knees and saw a young man sitting on the far side of the fire.

The stranger, dressed in battered clothes, exuded a calm, assured air. In his hands was a bow, at his side a long hand-and-a-half sword. A white horn bound with silver fittings lay in his lap, and the hilt of a dagger protruded from his boot. His serious face and fierce eyes were framed by locks of brown hair. He appeared to be a few years older than Eragon and perhaps an inch or so taller. Behind him a gray war-horse was picketed. The stranger watched Saphira warily.

"Who are you?" asked Eragon, taking a shallow breath.

The man's hands tightened on his bow. "Murtagh." His voice was low and controlled, but curiously emotional.

Eragon pulled his hands underneath his legs so they were in front of him. He clenched his teeth as his side flared with pain. "Why did you help us?"

"You aren't the only enemies the Ra'zac have. I was tracking them."

"You know who they are?"

"Yes."

Eragon concentrated on the ropes that bound his wrists and reached for the magic. He hesitated, aware of Murtagh's eyes on him, then decided it didn't matter. "Jierda!" he grunted. The ropes snapped off his wrists. He rubbed his hands to get the blood flowing.

Murtagh sucked in his breath. Eragon braced himself and tried to stand, but his ribs seared with agony. He fell back, gasping between clenched teeth. Murtagh tried to come to his aid, but Saphira stopped him with a growl. "I would have helped you earlier, but your dragon wouldn't let me near you."

"Her name's Saphira," said Eragon tightly. *Now let him by! I can't do this alone. Besides, he saved our lives.* Saphira growled again, but folded her wings and backed away. Murtagh eyed her flatly as he stepped forward.

He grasped Eragon's arm, gently pulling him to his feet. Eragon yelped and would have fallen without support. They went to the fire, where Brom lay on his back. "How is he?" asked Eragon.

"Bad," said Murtagh, lowering him to the ground. "The knife went right between his ribs. You can look at him in a minute, but first we'd better see how much damage the Ra'zac did to you." He helped Eragon remove his shirt, then whistled. "Ouch!"

"Ouch," agreed Eragon weakly. A blotchy bruise extended down his left side. The red, swollen skin was broken in several places. Murtagh put a hand on the bruise and pressed lightly. Eragon yelled, and Saphira growled a warning.

Murtagh glanced at Saphira as he grabbed a blanket. "I think you have some broken ribs. It's hard to tell, but at least two, maybe more. You're lucky you're not coughing up blood." He tore the blanket into strips and bound Eragon's chest.

Eragon slipped the shirt back on. "Yes . . . I'm lucky." He took a shallow breath, sidled over to Brom, and saw that Murtagh had cut open the side of his robe to bandage the wound. With trembling fingers, he undid the bandage.

"I wouldn't do that," warned Murtagh. "He'll bleed to death without it."

Eragon ignored him and pulled the cloth away from Brom's side. The wound was short and thin, belying its depth. Blood streamed out of it. As he had learned when Garrow was injured, a wound inflicted by the Ra'zac was slow to heal.

He peeled off his gloves while furiously searching his mind for the healing words Brom had taught him. *Help me, Saphira,* he implored. *I am too weak to do this alone.*

Saphira crouched next to him, fixing her eyes on Brom. *I am here, Eragon.* As her mind joined his, new strength infused his body. Eragon drew upon their combined power and focused it on the words. His hand trembled as he held it over the wound. "Waíse heill!" he said. His palm glowed, and Brom's skin flowed together, as if it had never been broken. Murtagh watched the entire process.

It was over quickly. As the light vanished, Eragon sat, feeling sick. *We've never done that before*, he said.

Saphira nodded. *Together we can cast spells that are beyond either of us.*

Murtagh examined Brom's side and asked, "Is he completely healed?"

"I can only mend what is on the surface. I don't know enough to fix whatever's damaged inside. It's up to him now. I've done all I can." Eragon closed his eyes for a moment, utterly weary. "My . . . my head seems to be floating in clouds."

"You probably need to eat," said Murtagh. "I'll make soup."

While Murtagh fixed the meal, Eragon wondered who this stranger was. His sword and bow were of the finest make, as was his horn. Either he was a thief or accustomed to money—and lots of it. *Why was he hunting the Ra'zac? What have they done to make him an enemy? I wonder if he works for the Varden?*

Murtagh handed him a bowl of broth. Eragon spooned it down and asked, "How long has it been since the Ra'zac fled?"

"A few hours."

"We have to go before they return with reinforcements."

"You might be able to travel," said Murtagh, then gestured at Brom, "but he can't. You don't get up and ride away after being stabbed between the ribs."

If we make a litter, can you carry Brom with your claws like you did with Garrow? Eragon asked Saphira.

Yes, but landing will be awkward.

As long as it can be done. Eragon said to Murtagh, "Saphira can carry him, but we need a litter. Can you make one? I don't have the strength."

"Wait here." Murtagh left the camp, sword drawn. Eragon hobbled to his bags and picked up his bow from where it had been thrown by the Ra'zac. He strung it, found his quiver, then retrieved Zar'roc, which lay hidden in shadow. Last, he got a blanket for the litter.

Murtagh returned with two saplings. He laid them parallel on the ground, then lashed the blanket between the poles. After he carefully tied Brom to the makeshift litter, Saphira grasped the saplings and laboriously took flight. "I never thought I would see a sight like that," Murtagh said, an odd note in his voice.

As Saphira disappeared into the dark sky, Eragon limped to Cadoc and hoisted himself painfully into the saddle. "Thanks for helping us. You should leave now. Ride as far away from us as you can. You'll be in danger if the Empire finds you with us. We can't protect you, and I wouldn't see harm come to you on our account."

"A pretty speech," said Murtagh, grinding out the fire, "but where will you go? Is there a place nearby that you can rest in safety?"

"No," admitted Eragon.

Murtagh's eyes glinted as he fingered the hilt of his sword. "In that case, I think I'll accompany you until you're out of danger. I've no better place to be. Besides, if I stay with you, I might get another shot at the Ra'zac sooner than if I were on my own. Interesting things are bound to happen around a Rider."

Eragon wavered, unsure if he should accept help from a complete stranger. Yet he was unpleasantly aware that he was too weak to force the issue either way. *If Murtagh proves untrustworthy, Saphira can always chase him away.* "Join us if you wish." He shrugged.

Murtagh nodded and mounted his gray warhorse. Eragon grabbed Snowfire's reins and rode away from the camp, into the wilderness. An oxbow moon provided wan light, but he knew that it would only make it easier for the Ra'zac to track them.

Though Eragon wanted to question Murtagh further, he kept silent, conserving his energy for riding. Near dawn Saphira said, *I must stop. My wings are tired and Brom needs attention. I discovered a good place to stay, about two miles ahead of where you are.*

They found her sitting at the base of a broad

sandstone formation that curved out of the ground like a great hill. Its sides were pocked with caves of varying sizes. Similar domes were scattered across the land. Saphira looked pleased with herself. *I found a cave that can't be seen from the ground. It's large enough for all of us, including the horses. Follow me.* She turned and climbed up the sandstone, her sharp claws digging into the rock. The horses had difficulty, as their shod hooves could not grip the sandstone. Eragon and Murtagh had to pull and shove the animals for almost an hour before they managed to reach the cave.

The cavern was a good hundred feet long and more than twenty feet wide, yet it had a small opening that would protect them from bad weather and prying eyes. Darkness swallowed the far end, clinging to the walls like mats of soft black wool.

"Impressive," said Murtagh. "I'll gather wood for a fire." Eragon hurried to Brom. Saphira had set him on a small rock ledge at the rear of the cave. Eragon clasped Brom's limp hand and anxiously watched his craggy face. After a few minutes, he sighed and went to the fire Murtagh had built.

They ate quietly, then tried to give Brom water, but the old man would not drink. Stymied, they spread out their bedrolls and slept.

LEGACY OF A RIDER

*W*ake up, Eragon. He stirred and groaned.

I need your help. Something is wrong! Eragon tried to ignore the voice and return to sleep.

Arise!

Go *away,* he grumbled.

Eragon! A bellow rang in the cave. He bolted upright, fumbling for his bow. Saphira was crouched over Brom, who had rolled off the ledge and was thrashing on the cave floor. His face was contorted in a grimace; his fists were clenched. Eragon rushed over, fearing the worst.

"Help me hold him down. He's going to hurt himself!" he cried to Murtagh, clasping Brom's arms. His side burned sharply as the old man spasmed. Together they restrained Brom until his convulsions ceased. Then they carefully returned him to the ledge.

Eragon touched Brom's forehead. The skin was so hot that the heat could be felt an inch away. "Get me water and a cloth," he said worriedly. Murtagh brought them, and Eragon gently bathed Brom's face, trying to cool him down. With the cave quiet again, he noticed the sun shining outside. *How long did we sleep?* he asked Saphira.

A good while. I've been watching Brom for most of that time. He was fine until a minute ago when he started thrashing. I woke you once he fell to the floor.

He stretched, wincing as his ribs twinged painfully. A hand suddenly gripped his shoulder. Brom's eyes snapped opened and fixed a glassy stare on Eragon. "You!" he gasped. "Bring me the wineskin!"

398

"Brom?" exclaimed Eragon, pleased to hear him talk. "You shouldn't drink wine; it'll only make you worse."

"Bring it, boy—just bring it . . . ," sighed Brom. His hand slipped off Eragon's shoulder.

"I'll be right back—hold on." Eragon dashed to the saddlebags and rummaged through them frantically. "I can't find it!" he cried, looking around desperately.

"Here, take mine," said Murtagh, holding out a leather skin.

Eragon grabbed it and returned to Brom. "I have the wine," he said, kneeling. Murtagh retreated to the cave's mouth so they could have privacy.

Brom's next words were faint and indistinct. "Good . . ." He moved his arm weakly. "Now . . . wash my right hand with it."

"What—" Eragon started to ask.

"No questions! I haven't time." Mystified, Eragon unstoppered the wineskin and poured the liquid onto Brom's palm. He rubbed it into the old man's skin, spreading it around the fingers and over the back of the hand. "More," croaked Brom. Eragon splashed wine onto his hand again. He scrubbed vigorously as a brown dye floated off Brom's palm, then stopped, his mouth agape with amazement. There on Brom's palm was the gedwëy ignasia.

"You're a Rider?" he asked incredulously.

A painful smile flickered on Brom's face. "Once upon a time that was true . . . but no more. When I was young . . . younger than you are now, I was chosen . . . chosen by the Riders to join their ranks. While they trained me, I became friends with another apprentice . . . Morzan, before he was a Forsworn." Eragon gasped—that had been over a hundred years ago. "But then he betrayed us to Galbatorix . . . and in the fighting at Doru Araeba—Vroengard's city—my young dragon was killed. Her name . . . was Saphira."

"Why didn't you tell me this before?" asked Eragon softly.

Brom laughed. "Because . . . there was no need to." He stopped. His breathing was labored; his hands were clenched. "I am old, Eragon . . . so old. Though my dragon was killed, my life has been longer than most. You don't know what it is to reach my age, look back, and realize that you don't remember much of it; then to look forward and know that many years still lie ahead of you. . . . After all this time I still grieve for my Saphira . . . and hate Galbatorix for what he tore from me." His feverish eyes drilled into Eragon as he said fiercely, "Don't let that happen to you. Don't! Guard Saphira with your life, for without her it's hardly worth living."

"You shouldn't talk like this. Nothing's going to happen to her," said Eragon, worried.

Brom turned his head to the side. "Perhaps I am rambling." His gaze passed blindly over Murtagh, then he focused on Eragon. Brom's voice grew stronger. "Eragon! I cannot last much longer. This . . . this is a grievous wound; it saps my strength. I have not the energy to fight it. . . . Before I go, will you take my blessing?"

"Everything will be all right," said Eragon, tears in his eyes. "You don't have to do this."

"It is the way of things . . . I must. Will you take my blessing?" Eragon bowed his head and nodded, overcome. Brom placed a trembling hand on his brow. "Then I give it to you. May the coming years bring you great happiness." He motioned for Eragon to bend closer. Very quietly, he whispered seven words from the ancient language, then even more softly told him what they meant. "That is all I can give you. . . . Use them only in great need."

Brom blindly turned his eyes to the ceiling. "And now," he murmured, "for the greatest adventure of all. . . ."

Weeping, Eragon held his hand, comforting him as best he could. His vigil was unwavering and steadfast, unbroken by food or drink. As the long hours passed, a gray pallor crept over Brom, and his eyes slowly dimmed. His hands grew icy; the air around him took on an evil humor. Powerless to help, Eragon could only watch as the Ra'zac's wound took its toll.

The evening hours were young and the shadows long when Brom suddenly stiffened. Eragon called his name and cried for Murtagh's help, but they could do nothing. As a barren silence dampened the air, Brom locked his eyes with Eragon's. Then contentment spread across the old man's face, and a whisper of breath escaped his lips. And so it was that Brom the storyteller died.

With shaking fingers, Eragon closed Brom's eyes and stood. Saphira raised her head behind him and roared mournfully at the sky, keening her lamentation. Tears rolled down Eragon's cheeks as a sense of horrible loss bled through him. Haltingly, he said, "We have to bury him."

"We might be seen," warned Murtagh.

"I don't care!"

Murtagh hesitated, then bore Brom's body out of the cave, along with his sword and staff. Saphira followed them. "To the top," Eragon said thickly, indicating the crown of the sandstone hill.

"We can't dig a grave out of stone," objected Murtagh.

"I can do it."

Eragon climbed onto the smooth hilltop, struggling because of his ribs. There, Murtagh lay Brom on the stone.

Eragon wiped his eyes and fixed his gaze on the sandstone. Gesturing with his hand, he said, "Moi stenr!" The stone rippled. It flowed like water, forming a body-length depression in the hilltop. Molding the sandstone like wet clay, he raised waist-high walls around it.

They laid Brom inside the unfinished sandstone vault with his staff and sword. Stepping back, Eragon again shaped the stone with magic. It joined over Brom's motionless face and flowed upward into a tall faceted spire. As a final tribute, Eragon set runes into the stone:

HERE LIES BROM
Who was a Dragon Rider
And like a father
To me.
May his name live on in glory.

Then he bowed his head and mourned freely. He stood like a living statue until evening, when light faded from the land.

That night he dreamed of the imprisoned woman again.

He could tell that something was wrong with her. Her breathing was irregular, and she shook—whether from cold or pain, he did not know. In the semidarkness of the cell, the only thing clearly illuminated was her hand, which hung over the edge of the cot. A dark liquid dripped from the tips of her fingers. Eragon knew it was blood.

DIAMOND TOMB

When Eragon woke, his eyes were gritty, his body stiff. The cave was empty except for the horses. The litter was gone; no sign of Brom remained. He walked to the entrance and sat on the pitted sandstone. *So the witch Angela was correct—there was a death in my future*, he thought, staring bleakly at the land. The topaz sun brought a desert heat to the early morning.

A tear slid down his listless face and evaporated in the sunlight, leaving a salty crust on his skin. He closed his eyes and absorbed the warmth, emptying his mind. With a fingernail, he aimlessly scratched the sandstone. When he looked, he saw that he had written *Why me?*

He was still there when Murtagh climbed up to the cave, carrying a pair of rabbits. Without a word he seated himself by Eragon. "How are you?" he asked.

"Very ill."

Murtagh considered him thoughtfully. "Will you recover?" Eragon shrugged. After a few minutes of reflection, Murtagh said, "I dislike asking this at such a time, but I must know . . . Is your Brom *the* Brom? The one who helped steal a dragon egg from the king, chased it across the Empire, and killed Morzan in a duel? I heard you say his name, and I read the inscription you put on his grave, but I must know for certain, Was that he?"

"It was," said Eragon softly. A troubled expression settled on Murtagh's face. "How do you know all that? You talk about things that are secret to most, and you were trailing the Ra'zac right when we needed help. Are you one of the Varden?"

Murtagh's eyes became inscrutable orbs. "I'm running away, like you." There was restrained sorrow in his words. "I do not belong to either the Varden or the Empire. Nor do I owe allegiance to any man but myself. As for my rescuing you, I will admit that I've heard whispered tales of a new Rider and reasoned that by following the Ra'zac I might discover if they were true."

"I thought you wanted to kill the Ra'zac," said Eragon.

Murtagh smiled grimly. "I do, but if I had, I never would have met you."

But Brom would still be alive. . . . I wish he were here. He would know whether to trust Murtagh. Eragon remembered how Brom had sensed Trevor's intentions in Daret and wondered if he could do the same with Murtagh. He reached for Murtagh's consciousness, but his probe abruptly ran into an iron-hard wall, which he tried to circumvent. Murtagh's entire mind was fortified. *How did he learn to do that? Brom said that few people, if any, could keep others out of their mind without training. So who is Murtagh to have this ability?* Pensive and lonely, Eragon asked, "Where is Saphira?"

406

"I don't know," said Murtagh. "She followed me for a time when I went hunting, then flew off on her own. I haven't seen her since before noon." Eragon rocked onto his feet and returned to the cave. Murtagh followed. "What are you going to do now?"

"I'm not sure." *And I don't want to think about it either.* He rolled up his blankets and tied them to Cadoc's saddlebags. His ribs hurt. Murtagh went to prepare the rabbits. As Eragon shifted things in his bags, he uncovered Zar'roc. The red sheath glinted brightly. He took out the sword . . . weighed it in his hands.

He had never carried Zar'roc nor used it in combat—except when he and Brom had sparred—because he had not wanted people to see it. That concerned Eragon no more. The Ra'zac had seemed surprised and frightened by the sword; that was more than enough reason for him to wear it. With a shudder he pulled off his bow and belted on Zar'roc. *From this moment on, I'll live by the sword. Let the whole world see what I am. I have no fear. I am a Rider now, fully and completely.*

He sorted through Brom's bags but found only clothes, a few odd items, and a small pouch of coins. Eragon took the map of Alagaësia and put the bags away, then crouched by the fire. Murtagh's eyes narrowed as he looked up from the rabbit he was skinning. "That sword. May I see it?" he asked, wiping his hands.

Eragon hesitated, reluctant to relinquish the weapon for even a moment, then nodded. Murtagh examined the symbol on the blade intently. His face darkened. "Where did you get this?"

"Brom gave it to me. Why?"

Murtagh shoved the sword back and crossed his arms angrily. He was breathing hard. "That sword," he said with emotion, "was once as well known as its owner. The last Rider to carry it was Morzan—a brutal, savage man. I thought you were a foe of the Empire, yet here I find you bearing one of the Forsworn's bloody swords!"

Eragon stared at Zar'roc with shock. He realized that Brom must have taken it from Morzan after they fought in Gil'ead. "Brom never told me where it came from," he said truthfully. "I had no idea it was Morzan's."

"He never told you?" asked Murtagh, a note of disbelief in his voice. Eragon shook his head. "That's strange. I can think of no reason for him to have concealed it."

"Neither can I. But then, he kept many secrets," said Eragon. It felt unsettling to hold the sword of the man who had betrayed the Riders to Galbatorix. *This blade probably killed many Riders in its time*, he thought with revulsion. *And worse, dragons!* "Even so, I'm going to carry it. I don't have a sword of my own. Until such time as I get one, I'll use Zar'roc."

Murtagh flinched as Eragon said the name. "It's your choice," he said. He returned to skinning, keeping his gaze focused downward.

When the meal was ready, Eragon ate slowly, though he was quite hungry. The hot food made him feel better. As they scraped out their bowls, he said, "I have to sell my horse."

"Why not Brom's?" asked Murtagh. He seemed to have gotten over his bad temper.

"Snowfire? Because Brom promised to take care of him. Since he . . . isn't around, I'll do it for him."

Murtagh set his bowl on his lap. "If that's what

you want, I'm sure we can find a buyer in some town or village."

"We?" asked Eragon.

Murtagh looked at him sideways in a calculating way. "You won't want to stay here for much longer. If the Ra'zac are nearby, Brom's tomb will be like a beacon for them." Eragon had not thought of that. "And your ribs are going to take time to heal. I know you can defend yourself with magic, but you need a companion who can lift things and use a sword. I'm asking to travel with you, at least for the time being. But I must warn you, the Empire is searching for me. There'll be blood over it eventually."

Eragon laughed weakly and found himself crying because it hurt so much. Once his breath was back, he said, "I don't care if the entire army is searching for you. You're right. I do need help. I would be glad to have you along, though I have to talk to Saphira about it. But I have to warn *you*, Galbatorix just *might* send the entire army after me. You won't be any safer with Saphira and me than if you were on your own."

"I know that," said Murtagh with a quick grin. "But all the same, it won't stop me."

"Good." Eragon smiled with gratitude.

While they spoke, Saphira crawled into the cave and greeted Eragon. She was glad to see him, but there was deep sadness in her thoughts and words. She laid her big blue head on the floor and asked, *Are you well again?*

Not quite.

I miss the old one.

As do I . . . I never suspected that he was a Rider. Brom! He really was an old man—as old as the Forsworn. Everything he taught me about magic he must have learned from the Riders themselves.

Saphira shifted slightly. *I knew what he was the moment he touched me at your farm.*

And you didn't tell me? Why?

He asked me not to, she said simply.

Eragon decided not to make an issue of it. Saphira never meant to hurt him. *Brom kept more than that secret,* he told her, then explained about Zar'roc and Murtagh's reaction to it. *I understand now why Brom didn't explain Zar'roc's origins when he gave it to me. If he had, I probably would have run away from him at the first opportunity.*

You would do well to rid yourself of that sword, she said with distaste. *I know it's a peerless weapon, but you would be better off with a normal blade rather than Morzan's butchery tool.*

Perhaps. Saphira, where does our path go from here? Murtagh offered to come with us. I don't know his past, but he seems honest enough. Should we go to the Varden now? Only I don't know how to find them. Brom never told us.

He told me, said Saphira.

Eragon grew angry. *Why did he trust you, but not me, with all this knowledge?*

Her scales rustled over the dry rock as she stood above him, eyes profound. *After we left Teirm and were attacked by the Urgals, he told me many things, some of which I will not speak of unless necessary. He was concerned about his own death and what would happen to you after it. One fact he imparted to me was the name of a man, Dormnad, who lives in Gil'ead. He can help us find the Varden. Brom also wanted you to know that of all the people in Alagaësia, he believed you were the best suited to inherit the Riders' legacy.*

Tears welled in Eragon's eyes. This was the highest praise he could have ever received from Brom. *A responsibility I will bear honorably.*

Good.

We will go to Gil'ead, then, stated Eragon, strength and purpose returning to him. *And what of Murtagh? Do you think he should come with us?*

We owe him our lives, said Saphira. *But even if that weren't so, he has seen both you and me. We should keep him close so he doesn't furnish the Empire with our location and descriptions, willingly or not.*

He agreed with her, then told Saphira about his dream. *What I saw disturbed me. I feel that time is running out for her; something dreadful is going to happen soon. She's in mortal danger—I'm sure of it—but I don't know how to find her! She could be anywhere.*

411

What does your heart say? asked Saphira.

My heart died a while back, said Eragon with a hint of black humor. *However, I think we should go north to Gil'ead. With any luck, one of the towns or cities along our path is where this woman is being held. I'm afraid that my next dream of her will show a grave. I couldn't stand that.*

Why?

I'm not sure, he said, shrugging. *It's just that when I see her, I feel as if she's precious and shouldn't be lost. . . . It's very strange.* Saphira opened her long mouth and laughed silently, fangs gleaming. *What is it?* snapped Eragon. She shook her head and quietly padded away.

Eragon grumbled to himself, then told Murtagh what they had decided. Murtagh said, "If you find this Dormnad and then continue on to the Varden, I will leave you. Encountering the Varden would be as dangerous for me as walking unarmed into Urû'baen with a fanfare of trumpets to announce my arrival."

"We won't have to part anytime soon," said Eragon. "It's a long way to Gil'ead." His voice cracked slightly, and he squinted at the sun to distract himself. "We should leave before the day grows any older."

"Are you strong enough to travel?" asked Murtagh, frowning.

"I have to do something or I'll go crazy," said Eragon brusquely. "Sparring, practicing magic, or sitting around twiddling my thumbs aren't good options right now, so I choose to ride."

They doused the fire, packed, and led the horses out of the cave. Eragon handed Cadoc's and Snowfire's reins to Murtagh, saying, "Go on, I'll be right down." Murtagh began the slow descent from the cave.

Eragon struggled up the sandstone, resting when his side made it impossible to breathe. When he reached the top, he found Saphira already there. They stood together before Brom's grave and paid their last respects. *I can't believe he's gone . . . forever.* As Eragon turned to depart, Saphira snaked out her long neck to touch the tomb with the tip of her nose. Her sides vibrated as a low humming filled the air.

The sandstone around her nose shimmered like gilded dew, turning clear with dancing silver highlights. Eragon watched in wonder as tendrils of white diamond twisted over the tomb's surface in a web of priceless filigree. Sparkling shadows were cast on the ground, reflecting splashes of brilliant colors that shifted dazzlingly as the sandstone continued to change. With a satisfied snort, Saphira stepped back and examined her handiwork.

The sculpted sandstone mausoleum of moments before had transformed into a sparkling gemstone vault—under which Brom's untouched face was visible. Eragon gazed with yearning at the old man, who seemed to be only sleeping. "What did you do?" he asked Saphira with awe.

I gave him the only gift I could. Now time will not ravage him. He can rest in peace for eternity.

Thank you. Eragon put a hand on her side, and they left together.

414

CAPTURE AT GIL'EAD

R iding was extremely painful for Eragon—
his broken ribs prevented them from going
faster than a walk, and it was impossible for
him to breathe deeply without a burst of agony.
Nevertheless, he refused to stop. Saphira flew
close by, her mind linked with his for solace and
strength.

Murtagh rode confidently beside Cadoc, flowing smoothly with his horse's movements. Eragon
watched the gray animal for a while. "You have a
beautiful horse. What's his name?"

"Tornac, after the man who taught me how to
fight." Murtagh patted the horse's side. "He was
given to me when he was just a foal. You'd be
hard pressed to find a more courageous and intelligent animal in all of Alagaësia, Saphira ex-
cepted, of course."

"He is a magnificent beast," said Eragon ad-
miringly.

Murtagh laughed. "Yes, but Snowfire is as close to his match as I've ever seen."

They covered only a short distance that day, yet Eragon was glad to be on the move again. It kept his mind off other, more morbid matters. They were riding through unsettled land. The road to Dras-Leona was several leagues to their left. They would skirt the city by a wide margin on the way to Gil'ead, which was almost as far to the north as Carvahall.

They sold Cadoc in a small village. As the horse was led away by his new owner, Eragon regretfully pocketed the few coins he had gained from the transaction. It was difficult to relinquish Cadoc after crossing half of Alagaësia—and outracing Urgals—on him.

The days rolled by unnoticed as their small group traveled in isolation. Eragon was pleased to find that he and Murtagh shared many of the same interests; they spent hours debating the finer points of archery and hunting.

There was one subject, however, they avoided discussing by unspoken consent: their pasts. Eragon did not explain how he had found Saphira, met Brom, or where he came from. Murtagh was likewise mute as to why the Empire was chasing him. It was a simple arrangement, but it worked.

Yet because of their proximity, it was inevitable that they learned about each other. Eragon was intrigued by Murtagh's familiarity with the power struggles and politics within the Empire. He seemed to know what every noble and courtier was doing and how it affected everyone else. Eragon listened carefully, suspicions whirling through his mind.

The first week went by without any sign of the Ra'zac, which allayed some of Eragon's fears. Even so, they still kept watches at night. Eragon had expected to encounter Urgals on the way to Gil'ead, but they found no trace of them. *I thought these remote places would be teeming with monsters,* he mused. *Still, I'm not one to complain if they've gone elsewhere.*

He dreamed of the woman no more. And though he tried to scry her, he saw only an empty cell. Whenever they passed a town or city, he checked to see if it had a jail. If it did, he would disguise himself and visit it, but she was not to be found. His disguises became increasingly elaborate as he saw notices featuring his name and description—and offering a substantial reward for his capture—posted in various towns.

Their travels north forced them toward the capital, Urû'baen. It was a heavily populated area, which made it difficult to escape notice. Soldiers patrolled the roads and guarded the bridges. It took them several tense, irritable days to skirt the capital.

Once they were safely past Urû'baen, they found themselves on the edge of a vast plain. It was the same one that Eragon had crossed after leaving Palancar Valley, except now he was on the opposite side. They kept to the perimeter of the plain and continued north, following the Ramr River.

Eragon's sixteenth birthday came and went during this time. At Carvahall a celebration would have been held for his entrance into manhood, but in the wilderness he did not even mention it to Murtagh.

At nearly six months of age, Saphira was much larger. Her wings were massive; every inch of them was needed to lift her muscular body and thick bones. The fangs that jutted from her jaw were nearly as thick around as Eragon's fist, their points as sharp as Zar'roc.

The day finally came when Eragon unwrapped his side for the last time. His ribs had healed completely, leaving him with only a small scar where the Ra'zac's boot had cut his side. As Saphira watched, he stretched slowly, then with increasing vigor when there was no pain. He flexed his muscles, pleased. In an earlier time he would have smiled, but after Brom's death, such expressions did not come easily.

He tugged his tunic on and walked back to the small fire they had made. Murtagh sat next to it, whittling a piece of wood. Eragon drew Zar'roc. Murtagh tensed, though his face remained calm. "Now that I am strong enough, would you like to spar?" asked Eragon.

Murtagh tossed the wood to the side. "With sharpened swords? We could kill each other."

"Here, give me your sword," said Eragon. Murtagh hesitated, then handed over his long hand-and-a-half sword. Eragon blocked the edges with magic, the way Brom had taught him. While Murtagh examined the blade, Eragon said, "I can undo that once we're finished."

Murtagh checked the balance of his sword. Satisfied, he said, "It will do." Eragon safed Zar'roc, settled into a crouch, then swung at Murtagh's shoulder. Their swords met in midair. Eragon disengaged with a flourish, thrust, and then riposted as Murtagh parried, dancing away.

He's fast! thought Eragon.

They struggled back and forth, trying to batter each other down. After a particularly intense series of blows, Murtagh started laughing. Not only was it impossible for either of them to gain an advantage, but they were so evenly matched that they tired at the same rate. Acknowledging with grins each other's skill, they fought on until their arms were leaden and sweat poured off their sides.

Finally Eragon called, "Enough, halt!" Murtagh stopped in mid-blow and sat down with a gasp.

Eragon staggered to the ground, his chest heaving. None of his fights with Brom had been this fierce.

As he gulped air, Murtagh exclaimed, "You're amazing! I've studied swordplay all my life, but never have I fought one like you. You could be the king's weapon master if you wanted to."

"You're just as good," observed Eragon, still panting. "The man who taught you, Tornac, could make a fortune with a fencing school. People would come from all parts of Alagaësia to learn from him."

"He's dead," said Murtagh shortly.

"I'm sorry."

Thus it became their custom to fight in the evening, which kept them lean and fit, like a pair of matched blades. With his return to health, Eragon also resumed practicing magic. Murtagh was curious about it and soon revealed that he knew a surprising amount about how it worked, though he lacked the precise details and could not use it himself. Whenever Eragon practiced speaking in the ancient language, Murtagh would listen quietly, occasionally asking what a word meant.

On the outskirts of Gil'ead they stopped the horses side by side. It had taken them nearly a month to reach it, during which time spring had finally nudged away the remnants of winter.

Eragon had felt himself changing during the trip, growing stronger and calmer. He still thought about Brom and spoke about him with Saphira, but for the most part he tried not to awaken painful memories.

From a distance they could see the city was a rough, barbaric place, filled with log houses and yapping dogs. There was a rambling stone fortress at its center. The air was hazy with blue smoke. The place seemed more like a temporary trading post than a permanent city. Five miles beyond it was the hazy outline of Isenstar Lake.

They decided to camp two miles from the city, for safety. While their dinner simmered, Murtagh said, "I'm not sure you should be the one to go into Gil'ead."

"Why? I can disguise myself well enough," said Eragon. "And Dormnad will want to see the gedwëy ignasia as proof that I really am a Rider."

"Perhaps," said Murtagh, "but the Empire wants you much more than me. If I'm captured, I could eventually escape. But if *you* are taken, they'll drag you to the king, where you'll be in for a slow death by torture—unless you join him. Plus, Gil'ead is one of the army's major staging points. Those aren't houses out there; they're barracks. Going in there would be like handing yourself to the king on a gilded platter."

Eragon asked Saphira for her opinion. She wrapped her tail around his legs and lay next to him. *You shouldn't have to ask me; he speaks sense. There are certain words I can give him that will convince Dormnad of his truthfulness. And Murtagh's right; if anyone is to risk capture it should be him, because he would live through it.*

He grimaced. *I don't like letting him put himself in danger for us.* "All right, you can go," he said reluctantly. "But if anything goes wrong, I'm coming after you."

Murtagh laughed. "That would be fit for a legend: how a lone Rider took on the king's army single-handedly." He chuckled again and stood. "Is there anything I should know before going?"

"Shouldn't we rest and wait until tomorrow?" asked Eragon cautiously.

"Why? The longer we stay here, the greater the chance that we'll be discovered. If this Dormnad can take you to the Varden, then he needs to be found as quickly as possible. Neither of us should remain near Gil'ead longer than a few days."

Again wisdom flies from his mouth, commented Saphira dryly. She told Eragon what should be said to Dormnad, and he relayed the information to Murtagh.

"Very well," said Murtagh, adjusting his sword. "Unless there's trouble, I'll be back within a couple of hours. Make sure there's some food left for me." With a wave of his hand, he jumped onto Tornac and rode away. Eragon sat by the fire, tapping Zar'roc's pommel apprehensively.

Hours passed, but Murtagh did not return. Eragon paced around the fire, Zar'roc in hand, while Saphira watched Gil'ead attentively. Only her eyes moved. Neither of them voiced their worries, though Eragon unobtrusively prepared to leave—in case a detachment of soldiers left the city and headed toward their camp.

Look, snapped Saphira.

Eragon swiveled toward Gil'ead, alert. He saw a distant horseman exit the city and ride furiously toward their camp. *I don't like this,* he said as he climbed onto Saphira. *Be ready to fly.*

I'm prepared for more than that.

As the rider approached, Eragon recognized Murtagh bent low over Tornac. No one seemed to be pursuing him, but he did not slow his reckless pace. He galloped into the camp and jumped to the ground, drawing his sword. "What's wrong?" asked Eragon.

Murtagh scowled. "Did anyone follow me from Gil'ead?"

"We didn't see anyone."

"Good. Then let me eat before I explain. I'm starving." He seized a bowl and began eating with gusto. After a few sloppy bites, he said through a full mouth, "Dormnad has agreed to meet us outside Gil'ead at sunrise tomorrow. If he's satisfied you really are a Rider and that it's not a trap, he'll take you to the Varden."

"Where are we supposed to meet him?" asked Eragon.

Murtagh pointed west. "On a small hill across the road."

"So what happened?"

Murtagh spooned more food into his bowl. "It's a rather simple thing, but all the more deadly because of it: I was seen in the street by someone who knows me. I did the only thing I could and ran away. It was too late, though; he recognized me."

It was unfortunate, but Eragon was unsure how bad it really was. "Since I don't know your friend, I have to ask: Will he tell anyone?"

Murtagh gave a strained laugh. "If you *had* met him, that wouldn't need answering. His mouth is loosely hinged and hangs open all the time, vomiting whatever happens to be in his mind. The question isn't *whether* he will tell people, but *whom* he will tell. If word of this reaches the wrong ears, we'll be in trouble."

"I doubt that soldiers will be sent to search for you in the dark," Eragon pointed out. "We can at least count on being safe until morning, and by then, if all goes well, we'll be leaving with Dormnad."

Murtagh shook his head. "No, only you will

accompany him. As I said before, I won't go to the Varden."

Eragon stared at him unhappily. He wanted Murtagh to stay. They had become friends during their travels, and he was loath to tear that apart. He started to protest, but Saphira hushed him and said gently, *Wait until tomorrow. Now is not the time.*

Very well, he said glumly. They talked until the stars were bright in the sky, then slept as Saphira took the first watch.

Eragon woke two hours before dawn, his palm tingling. Everything was still and quiet, but something sought his attention, like an itch in his mind. He buckled on Zar'roc and stood, careful not to make a sound. Saphira looked at him curiously, her large eyes bright. *What is it?* she asked.

425

I don't know, said Eragon. He saw nothing amiss.

Saphira sniffed the air curiously. She hissed a little and lifted her head. *I smell horses nearby, but they're not moving. They reek with an unfamiliar stench.*

Eragon crept to Murtagh and shook his shoulder. Murtagh woke with a start, yanked a dagger from under his blankets, then looked at Eragon quizzically. Eragon motioned for him to be silent, whispering, "There are horses close by."

Murtagh wordlessly drew his sword. They quietly stationed themselves on either side of Saphira, prepared for an attack. As they waited, the morning star rose in the east. A squirrel chattered.

Then an angry snarl from behind made Eragon spin around, sword held high. A broad Urgal stood at the edge of the camp, carrying a mattock with a nasty spike. *Where did he come from? We haven't seen their tracks anywhere!* thought Eragon. The Urgal roared and waved his weapon, but did not charge.

"Brisingr!" barked Eragon, stabbing out with magic. The Urgal's face contorted with terror as he exploded in a flash of blue light. Blood splattered Eragon, and a brown mass flew through the air. Behind him, Saphira bugled with alarm and reared. Eragon twisted around. While he had been occupied with the first Urgal, a group of them had run up from the side. *Of all the stupid tricks to fall for!*

Steel clashed loudly as Murtagh attacked the Urgals. Eragon tried to join him but was blocked by four of the monsters. The first one swung a sword at his shoulder. He ducked the blow and killed the Urgal with magic. He caught a second one in the throat with Zar'roc, wheeled wildly, and slashed a third through the heart. As he did, the fourth Urgal rushed at him, swinging a heavy club.

426

Eragon saw him coming and tried to lift his sword to block the club, but was a second too slow. As the club came down on his head, he screamed, "Fly, Saphira!" A burst of light filled his eyes and he lost consciousness.

Du Sundavar
Freohr

The first things Eragon noticed were that he was warm and dry, his cheek was pressed against rough fabric, and his hands were unbound. He stirred, but it was minutes before he was able to push himself upright and examine his surroundings.

He was sitting in a cell on a narrow, bumpy cot. A barred window was set high in the wall. The iron-bound door with a small window in its top half, barred like the one in the wall, was shut securely.

Dried blood cracked on Eragon's face when he moved. It took him a moment to remember that it was not his. His head hurt horribly—which was to be expected, considering the blow he had taken—and his mind was strangely fuzzy. He tried to use magic, but could not concentrate well enough to remember any of the ancient words. *They must have drugged me*, he finally decided.

With a groan he got up, missing the familiar weight of Zar'roc on his hip, and lurched to the window in the wall. He managed to see out of it by standing on his toes. It took a minute for his eyes to adjust to the bright light outside. The window was level with the ground. A street full of busy people ran past the side of his cell, beyond which were rows of identical log houses.

Feeling weak, Eragon slid to the floor and stared at it blankly. What he had seen outside disturbed him, but he was unsure why. Cursing his sluggish thinking, he leaned back his head and tried to clear his mind. A man entered the room and set a tray of food and a pitcher of water on the cot. *Wasn't that nice of him?* thought Eragon, smiling pleasantly. He took a couple of bites of the thin cabbage soup and stale bread, but was barely able to stomach it. *I wish he had brought me something better*, he complained, dropping the spoon.

He suddenly realized what was wrong. *I was captured by Urgals, not men! How did I end up here?* His befuddled brain grappled with the paradox unsuccessfully. With a mental shrug he filed the discovery away for a time when he would know what to do with it.

He sat on the cot and gazed into the distance. Hours later more food was brought in. *And I was just getting hungry,* he thought thickly. This time he was able to eat without feeling sick. When he finished, he decided it was time for a nap. After all, he was on a bed; what else was he going to do?

His mind drifted off; sleep began to envelop him. Then a gate clanged open somewhere, and the din of steel-shod boots marching on a stone floor filled the air. The noise grew louder and louder until it sounded like someone banging a pot inside Eragon's head. He grumbled to himself. *Can't they let me rest in peace?* Fuzzy curiosity slowly overcame his exhaustion, so he dragged himself to the door, blinking like an owl.

Through the window he saw a wide hallway nearly ten yards across. The opposing wall was lined with cells similar to his own. A column of soldiers marched through the hall, their swords drawn and ready. Every man was dressed in matching armor; their faces bore the same hard expression, and their feet came down on the floor with mechanical precision, never missing a beat. The sound was hypnotic. It was an impressive display of force.

Eragon watched the soldiers until he grew bored. Just then he noticed a break in the middle of the column. Carried between two burly men was an unconscious woman.

Her long midnight-black hair obscured her face, despite a leather strip bound around her head to hold the tresses back. She was dressed in dark leather pants and shirt. Wrapped around her slim waist was a shiny belt, from which hung an empty sheath on her right hip. Knee-high boots covered her calves and small feet.

Her head lolled to the side. Eragon gasped, feeling like he had been struck in the stomach. She was the woman from his dreams. Her sculpted face was as perfect as a painting. Her round chin, high cheekbones, and long eyelashes gave her an exotic look. The only mar in her beauty was a scrape along her jaw; nevertheless, she was the fairest woman he had ever seen.

Eragon's blood burned as he looked at her. Something awoke in him—something he had never felt before. It was like an obsession, except stronger, almost a fevered madness. Then the woman's hair shifted, revealing pointed ears. A chill crept over him. She was an elf.

The soldiers continued marching, taking her from his sight. Next strode a tall, proud man, a sable cape billowing behind him. His face was deathly white; his hair was red. Red like blood.

As he walked by Eragon's cell, the man turned his head and looked squarely at him with maroon eyes. His upper lip pulled back in a feral smile, revealing teeth filed to points. Eragon shrank back. He knew what the man was. *A Shade. So help me . . . a Shade*. The procession continued, and the Shade vanished from view.

Eragon sank to the floor, hugging himself.

Even in his bewildered state, he knew that the presence of a Shade meant that evil was loose in the land. Whenever they appeared, rivers of blood were sure to follow. *What is a Shade doing here? The soldiers should have killed him on sight!* Then his thoughts returned to the elf-woman, and he was grasped by strange emotions again.

I have to escape. But with his mind clouded, his determination quickly faded. He returned to the cot. By the time the hallway fell silent, he was fast asleep.

As soon as Eragon opened his eyes, he knew something was different. It was easier for him to think; he realized that he was in Gil'ead. *They made a mistake; the drug's wearing off!* Hopeful, he tried to contact Saphira and use magic, but both activities were still beyond his reach. A pit of worry twisted inside him as he wondered if she and Murtagh had managed to escape. He stretched his arms and looked out the window. The city was just awakening; the street was empty except for two beggars.

He reached for the water pitcher, ruminating about the elf and Shade. As he started to drink, he noticed that the water had a faint odor, as if it contained a few drops of rancid perfume. Grimacing, he set the pitcher down. *The drug must be in there and maybe in the food as well!* He remembered that when the Ra'zac had drugged him, it had taken hours to wear off. *If I can keep from drinking and eating for long enough, I should be able to use magic. Then I can rescue the elf. . . .* The thought made him smile. He sat in a corner, dreaming about how it could be done.

The portly jailer entered the cell an hour later with a tray of food. Eragon waited until he departed, then carried the tray to the window. The meal was composed only of bread, cheese, and an onion, but the smell made his stomach grumble hungrily. Resigning himself to a miserable day, he shoved the food out the window and onto the street, hoping that no one would notice.

Eragon devoted himself to overcoming the drug's effects. He had difficulty concentrating for any length of time, but as the day progressed, his mental acuity increased. He began to remember several of the ancient words, though nothing happened when he uttered them. He wanted to scream with frustration.

When lunch was delivered, he pushed it out the window after his breakfast. His hunger was distracting, but it was the lack of water that taxed him most. The back of his throat was parched. Thoughts of drinking cool water tortured him as each breath dried his mouth and throat a bit more. Even so, he forced himself to ignore the pitcher.

He was diverted from his discomfort by a commotion in the hall. A man argued in a loud voice,

"You can't go in there! The orders were clear: no one is to see him!"

"Really? Will you be the one to die stopping me, Captain?" cut in a smooth voice.

There was a subdued, "No . . . but the king—"

"*I* will handle the king," interrupted the second person. "Now, unlock the door."

After a pause, keys jangled outside Eragon's cell. He tried to adopt a languorous expression. *I have to act like I don't understand what's going on. I can't show surprise, no matter what this person says.*

The door opened. His breath caught as he looked into the Shade's face. It was like gazing at a death mask or a polished skull with skin pulled over it to give the appearance of life. "Greetings," said the Shade with a cold smile, showing his filed teeth. "I've waited a long time to meet you."

"Who—who're you?" asked Eragon, slurring his words.

"No one of consequence," answered the Shade, his maroon eyes alight with controlled menace. He sat with a flourish of his cloak. "My name does not matter to one in your position. It wouldn't mean a thing to you anyway. It's you that I'm interested in. Who are you?"

The question was posed innocently enough, but Eragon knew there had to be a catch or trap in it, though it eluded him. He pretended to struggle over the question for a while, then

434

slowly said, frowning, "I'm not sure. . . . M'name's Eragon, but that's not all I am, is it?"

The Shade's narrow lips stretched tautly over his mouth as he laughed sharply. "No, it isn't. You have an interesting mind, my young Rider." He leaned forward. The skin on his forehead was thin and translucent. "It seems I must be more direct. What is your name?"

"Era—"

"No! Not that one." The Shade cut him off with a wave of his hand. "Don't you have another one, one that you use only rarely?"

He wants my true name so he can control me! realized Eragon. *But I can't tell him. I don't even know it myself.* He thought quickly, trying to invent a deception that would conceal his ignorance. *What if I made up a name?* He hesitated—it could easily give him away—then raced to create a name that would withstand scrutiny. As he was about to utter it, he decided to take a chance and try to scare the Shade. He deftly switched a few letters, then nodded foolishly and said, "Brom told it to me once. It was . . ." The pause stretched for a few seconds, then his face brightened as he appeared to remember. "It was Du Sundavar Freohr." Which meant almost literally "death of the shadows."

A grim chill settled over the cell as the Shade sat motionless, eyes veiled. He seemed to be deep in thought, pondering what he had learned.

Eragon wondered if he had dared too much. He waited until the Shade stirred before asking ingenuously, "Why are you here?"

The Shade looked at him with contempt in his red eyes and smiled. "To gloat, of course. What use is a victory if one cannot enjoy it?" There was confidence in his voice, but he seemed uneasy, as if his plans had been disrupted. He stood suddenly. "I must attend to certain matters, but while I am gone you would do well to think on who you would rather serve: a Rider who betrayed your own order or a fellow man like me, though one skilled in arcane arts. When the time comes to choose, there will be no middle ground." He turned to leave, then glanced at Eragon's water pitcher and stopped, his face granite hard. "Captain!" he snapped.

A broad-shouldered man rushed into the cell, sword in hand. "What is it, my lord?" he asked, alarmed.

"Put that toy away," instructed the Shade. He turned to Eragon and said in a deadly quiet voice, "The boy hasn't been drinking his water. Why is that?"

"I talked with the jailer earlier. Every bowl and plate was scraped clean."

"Very well," said the Shade, mollified. "But make sure that he starts drinking again." He leaned toward the captain and murmured into his ear. Eragon caught the last few words, ". . . extra dose, just in case." The captain nodded. The Shade returned his attention to Eragon. "We will talk again tomorrow when I am not so pressed for time. You should know, I have an endless fascination for names. I will greatly enjoy discussing yours in *much* greater detail."

The way he said it gave Eragon a sinking feeling.

Once they left, he lay on the cot and closed his eyes. Brom's lessons proved their worth now; he relied on them to keep himself from panicking and to reassure himself. *Everything has been provided for me; I only have to take advantage of it.* His thoughts were interrupted by the sound of approaching soldiers.

Apprehensive, he went to the door and saw two soldiers dragging the elf down the hallway. When he could see her no more, Eragon slumped to the floor and tried to touch the magic again. Oaths flew from his lips when it eluded his grasp.

He looked out at the city and ground his teeth. It was only midafternoon. Taking a calming breath, he tried to wait patiently.

FIGHTING SHADOWS

438

It was dark in Eragon's cell when he sat up
with a start, electrified. The wrinkle had
shifted! He had felt the magic at the edge of
his consciousness for hours, but every time he
tried to use it, nothing happened. Eyes bright
with nervous energy, he clenched his hands and
said, "Nagz reisa!" With a flap, the cot's blanket
flew into the air and crumpled into a ball the size
of his fist. It landed on the floor with a soft
thump.

Exhilarated, Eragon stood. He was weak
from his enforced fast, but his excitement overcame his hunger. *Now for the real test.* He
reached out with his mind and felt the lock on
the door. Instead of trying to break or cut it, he
simply pushed its internal mechanism into the
unlocked position. With a click, the door
creaked inward.

When he had first used magic to kill the Urgals in Yazuac, it had consumed nearly all of his strength, but he had grown much stronger since then. What once would have exhausted him now only tired him slightly.

He cautiously stepped into the hall. *I have to find Zar'roc and the elf. She must be in one of these cells, but there isn't time to look in them all. As for Zar'roc, the Shade might have it with him.* He realized that his thinking was still muddled. *Why am I out here? I could escape right now if I went back into the cell and opened the window with magic. But then I wouldn't be able to rescue the elf. . . . Saphira, where are you? I need your help.* He silently berated himself for not contacting her sooner. That should have been the first thing he did after getting his power back.

Her reply came with surprising alacrity. *Eragon! I'm over Gil'ead. Don't do anything. Murtagh is on the way.*

What are— Footsteps interrupted him. He spun around, crouching as a squad of six soldiers marched into the hall. They halted abruptly, eyes flicking between Eragon and the open cell door. Blood drained from their faces. *Good, they know who I am. Maybe I can scare them off so we won't have to fight.*

"Charge!" yelled one of the soldiers, running forward. The rest of the men drew their blades and pounded down the hall.

It was madness to fight six men when he was unarmed and weak, but the thought of the elf kept him in place. He could not force himself to abandon her. Uncertain if the effort would leave him standing, he pulled on his power and raised his hand, the gedwëy ignasia glowing. Fear showed in the soldiers' eyes, but they were hardened warriors and did not slow. As Eragon opened his mouth to pronounce the fatal words, there was a low buzz, a flicker of motion. One of the men crashed to the floor with an arrow in his back. Two more were struck before anyone understood what was happening.

At the end of the hall, where the soldiers had entered, stood a ragged, bearded man with a bow. A crutch lay on the floor by his feet, apparently unneeded, for he stood tall and straight.

The three remaining soldiers turned to face this new threat. Eragon took advantage of the confusion. "Thrysta!" he shouted. One of the men clutched his chest and fell. Eragon staggered as the magic took its toll. Another soldier fell, pierced through the neck with an arrow. "Don't kill him!" called Eragon, seeing his rescuer take aim at the last soldier. The bearded man lowered his bow.

Eragon concentrated on the soldier before him. The man was breathing hard; the whites of his eyes showed. He seemed to understand that his life was being spared.

"You've seen what I can do," said Eragon harshly. "If you don't answer my questions, the rest of your life will be spent in utter misery and torment. Now where's my sword—its sheath and blade are red—and what cell is the elf in?"

The man clamped his mouth shut.

Eragon's palm glowed ominously as he reached for the magic. "That was the wrong answer," he snapped. "Do you know how much pain a grain of sand can cause you when it's embedded red hot in your stomach? Especially when it doesn't cool off for the next twenty years and slowly burns its way down to your toes! By the time it gets out of you, you'll be an old man." He paused for effect. "Unless you tell me what I want."

The soldier's eyes bulged, but he remained silent. Eragon scraped some dirt off the stone floor and observed dispassionately, "This is a bit more than a piece of sand, but be comforted; it'll burn through you faster. Still, it'll leave a bigger hole." At his word, the dirt shone cherry red, though it did not burn his hand.

"All right, just don't put that in me!" yelped the soldier. "The elf's in the last cell to the left! I don't know about your sword, but it's probably in the guardroom upstairs. All the weapons are there."

Eragon nodded, then murmured, "Slytha." The soldier's eyes rolled up in his head, and he collapsed limply.

441

"Did you kill him?"

Eragon looked at the stranger, who was now only a few paces away. He narrowed his eyes, trying to see past the beard. "Murtagh! Is that you?" he exclaimed.

"Yes," said Murtagh, briefly lifting the beard from his shaven face. "I don't want my face seen. Did you kill him?"

"No, he's only asleep. How did you get in?"

"There's no time to explain. We have to get up to the next floor before anyone finds us. There'll be an escape route for us in a few minutes. We don't want to miss it."

"Didn't you hear what I said?" asked Eragon, gesturing at the unconscious soldier. "There's an elf in the prison. I saw her! We have to rescue her. I need your help."

"An elf . . . !" Murtagh hurried down the hall, growling, "This is a mistake. We should flee while we have the chance." He stopped before the cell the soldier had indicated and produced a ring of keys from under his ragged cloak. "I took it from one of the guards," he explained.

Eragon motioned for the keys. Murtagh shrugged and handed them to him. Eragon found the right one and swung the door open. A single beam of moonlight slanted through the window, illuminating the elf's face with cool silver.

She faced him, tense and coiled, ready for whatever would happen next. She held her head high, with a queen's demeanor. Her eyes, dark green, almost black, and slightly angled like a cat's, lifted to Eragon's. Chills shot through him.

Their gaze held for a moment, then the elf trembled and collapsed soundlessly. Eragon barely caught her before she struck the floor. She was surprisingly light. The aroma of freshly crushed pine needles surrounded her.

Murtagh entered the cell. "She's beautiful!"

"But hurt."

"We can tend to her later. Are you strong enough to carry her?" Eragon shook his head. "Then I'll do it," said Murtagh as he slung the elf across his shoulders. "Now, upstairs!" He handed Eragon a dagger, then hurried back into the hall littered with soldiers' bodies.

With heavy footsteps Murtagh led Eragon to a stone-hewn staircase at the end of the hall. As they climbed it, Eragon asked, "How are we going to get out without being noticed?"

"We're not," grunted Murtagh.

That did not allay Eragon's fears. He listened anxiously for soldiers or anyone else who might be nearby, dreading what might happen if they met the Shade. At the head of the stairs was a banquet room filled with broad wooden tables. Shields lined the walls, and the wood ceiling was trussed with curved beams. Murtagh laid the elf on a table and looked at the ceiling worriedly. "Can you talk to Saphira for me?"

"Yes."

"Tell her to wait another five minutes."

There were shouts in the distance. Soldiers marched past the entrance to the banquet room. Eragon's mouth tightened with pent-up tension. "Whatever you're planning to do, I don't think we have much time."

"Just tell her, and stay out of sight," snapped Murtagh, running off.

As Eragon relayed the message, he was alarmed to hear men coming up the stairs. Fighting hunger and exhaustion, he dragged the elf off the table and hid her underneath it. He crouched next to her, holding his breath, tightly clenching the dagger.

444   Ten soldiers entered the room. They swept through it hurriedly, looking under only a couple of tables, and continued on their way. Eragon leaned against a table leg, sighing. The respite made him suddenly aware of his burning stomach and parched throat. A tankard and a plate of half-eaten food on the other side of the room caught his attention.

Eragon dashed from his hiding place, grabbed the food, then scurried back to the table. There was amber beer in the tankard, which he drank in two great gulps. Relief seeped through him as the cool liquid ran down his throat, soothing the irritated tissue. He suppressed a belch before ravenously tearing into a hunk of bread.

Murtagh returned carrying Zar'roc, a strange bow, and an elegant sword without a sheath. Murtagh gave Zar'roc to Eragon. "I found the other sword and bow in the guardroom. I've never seen weapons like them before, so I assumed they were the elf's."

"Let's find out," said Eragon through a mouthful of bread. The sword—slim and light with a curved crossguard, the ends of which narrowed into sharp points—fit the elf's sheath perfectly. There was no way to tell if the bow was hers, but it was shaped so gracefully he doubted it could be anyone else's. "What now?" he asked, cramming another bite of food into his mouth. "We can't stay here forever. Sooner or later the soldiers will find us."

"Now," said Murtagh, taking out his own bow and fitting an arrow to the string, "we wait. Like I said, our escape has been arranged."

"You don't understand; there's a Shade here! If he finds us, we're doomed."

"A Shade!" exclaimed Murtagh. "In that case, tell Saphira to come immediately. We were going to wait until the watch changed, but delaying even that long is too dangerous now." Eragon relayed the message succinctly, refraining from distracting Saphira with questions. "You messed up my plans by escaping yourself," groused Murtagh, watching the room's entrances for soldiers.

Eragon smiled. "In that case, perhaps I should

have waited. *Your* timing was perfect, though. I wouldn't have been able to even crawl if I had been forced to fight all those soldiers with magic."

"Glad to be of some use," remarked Murtagh. He stiffened as they heard men running nearby. "Let's just hope the Shade doesn't find us."

A cold chuckle filled the banquet room. "I'm afraid it's far too late for that."

Murtagh and Eragon spun around. The Shade stood alone at the end of the room. In his hand was a pale sword with a thin scratch on the blade. He unclasped the brooch that held his cape in place and let the garment fall to the floor. His body was like a runner's, thin and compact, but Eragon remembered Brom's warning and knew that the Shade's appearance was deceiving; he was many times stronger than a normal human.

"So, my young *Rider*, do you wish to test yourself against me?" sneered the Shade. "I shouldn't have trusted the captain when he said you ate all your food. I will not make that mistake again."

"I'll take care of him," said Murtagh quietly, putting down his bow and drawing his sword.

"No," said Eragon under his breath. "He wants me alive, not you. I can stall him for a short while, but then you'd better have a way out for us."

"Fine, go," said Murtagh. "You won't have to hold him off for long."

"I hope not," said Eragon grimly. He drew

Zar'roc and slowly advanced. The red blade glinted with light from torches on the wall.

The Shade's maroon eyes burned like coals. He laughed softly. "Do you really think to defeat me, Du Sundavar Freohr? What a pitiful name. I would have expected something more subtle from you, but I suppose that's all you're capable of."

Eragon refused to let himself be goaded. He stared at the Shade's face, waiting for a flicker of his eyes or twitch of his lip, anything that would betray his next move. *I can't use magic for fear of provoking him to do the same. He has to think that he can win without resorting to it—which he probably can.*

Before either of them moved, the ceiling boomed and shook. Dust billowed from it and turned the air gray while pieces of wood fell around them, shattering on the floor. From the roof came screams and the sound of clashing metal. Afraid of being brained by the falling timber, Eragon flicked his eyes upward. The Shade took advantage of his distraction and attacked.

Eragon barely managed to get Zar'roc up in time to block a slash at his ribs. Their blades met with a clang that jarred his teeth and numbed his arm. *Hellfire! He's strong!* He grasped Zar'roc with both hands and swung with all of his might at the Shade's head. The Shade blocked him with ease, whipping his sword through the air faster than Eragon had thought possible.

Terrible screeches sounded above them, like iron spikes being drawn across rock. Three long cracks split the ceiling. Shingles from the slate roof fell through the fissures. Eragon ignored them, even when one smashed into the floor next to him. Though he had trained with a master of the blade, Brom, and with Murtagh, who was also a deadly swordsman, he had never been this outclassed. The Shade was *playing* with him.

Eragon retreated toward Murtagh, arms trembling as he parried the Shade's blows. Each one seemed more powerful than the last. Eragon was no longer strong enough to call upon magic for help even if he had wanted to. Then, with a contemptuous flick of his wrist, the Shade knocked Zar'roc out of Eragon's hand. The force of the blow sent him to his knees, where he stayed, panting. The screeching was louder than ever. Whatever was happening, it was getting closer.

The Shade stared down at him haughtily. "A powerful piece you may be in the game that is being played, but I'm disappointed that this is your best. If the other Riders were this weak, they must have controlled the Empire only through sheer numbers."

Eragon looked up and shook his head. He had figured out Murtagh's plan. *Saphira, now would be a good time.* "No, you forget something."

"And what might that be?" asked the Shade mockingly.

There was a thunderous reverberation as a chunk of the ceiling was torn away to reveal the night sky. "The dragons!" roared Eragon over the noise, and threw himself out of the Shade's reach. The Shade snarled in rage, swinging his sword viciously. He missed and lunged. Surprise spread across his face as one of Murtagh's arrows sprouted from his shoulder.

The Shade laughed and snapped the arrow off with two fingers. "You'll have to do better than that if you want to stop me." The next arrow caught him between the eyes. The Shade howled with agony and writhed, covering his face. His skin turned gray. Mist formed in the air around him, obscuring his figure. There was a shattering cry; then the cloud vanished.

449

Where the Shade had been, nothing was left but his cape and a pile of clothes. "You killed him!" exclaimed Eragon. He knew of only two heroes of legend who had survived slaying a Shade.

"I'm not so sure," said Murtagh.

A man shouted, "That's it. He failed. Go in and get them!" Soldiers with nets and spears poured into the banquet room from both ends. Eragon and Murtagh backed up against the wall, dragging the elf with them. The men formed a menacing half-circle around them. Then Saphira stuck her head through the hole in the ceiling and roared. She gripped the edge of the opening with her powerful talons and ripped off another large section of the ceiling.

Three soldiers turned and ran, but the rest held their positions. With a resounding report, the center beam of the ceiling cracked and rained down heavy shingles. Confusion scattered the ranks as they tried to dodge the deadly barrage. Eragon and Murtagh pressed against the wall to avoid the falling debris. Saphira roared again, and the soldiers fled, some getting crushed on the way.

With a final titanic effort, Saphira tore off the rest of the ceiling before jumping into the banquet hall with her wings folded. Her weight splintered a table with a sharp crunch. Crying out with relief, Eragon threw his arms around her. She hummed contentedly. *I've missed you, little one.*

Same here. There's someone else with us. Can you carry three?

Of course, she said, kicking shingles and tables out of the way so she could take off. Murtagh and Eragon pulled the elf out of hiding. Saphira hissed in surprise as she saw her. *An elf!*

Yes, and the woman I saw in my dreams, said Eragon, picking up Zar'roc. He helped Murtagh secure the elf into the saddle, then they both climbed onto Saphira. *I heard fighting on the roof. Are there men up there?*

There were, but no more. Are you ready?

Yes.

Saphira leapt out of the banquet hall and onto the fortress's roof, where the bodies of watchmen lay scattered. "Look!" said Murtagh, pointing. A row of archers filed out of a tower on the other side of the roofless hall.

"Saphira, you have to take off. Now!" warned Eragon.

She unfurled her wings, ran toward the edge of the building, and propelled them over it with her powerful legs. The extra weight on her back made her drop alarmingly. As she struggled to gain altitude, Eragon heard the musical twang of bowstrings being released.

Arrows whizzed toward them in the dark. Saphira roared with pain as she was struck and quickly rolled to the left to avoid the next volley. More arrows perforated the sky, but the night protected them from the shafts' deadly bite. Distressed, Eragon bent over Saphira's neck. *Where are you hurt?*

My wings are pierced . . . one of the arrows didn't go all the way through. It's still there. Her breathing was labored and heavy.

How far can you take us?

Far enough. Eragon clutched the elf tightly as they skimmed over Gil'ead, then left the city behind and veered eastward, soaring upward through the night.

A Warrior
and a Healer

Saphira drifted down to a clearing, landed on the crest of a hill, and rested her out-stretched wings on the ground. Eragon could feel her shaking beneath him. They were only a half-league from Gil'ead.

Picketed in the clearing were Snowfire and Tornac, who snorted nervously at Saphira's arrival. Eragon slid to the ground and immediately turned to Saphira's injuries, while Murtagh readied the horses.

Unable to see well in the darkness, Eragon ran his hands blindly over Saphira's wings. He found three places where arrows had punctured the thin membrane, leaving bloody holes as thick around as his thumb. A small piece had also been torn out of the back edge of her left wing. She shivered when his fingers brushed the injuries. He tiredly healed the wounds with words from the ancient language. Then he went to the arrow that was embedded in one of the large muscles of her flying arm. The arrowhead poked through its underside. Warm blood dripped off it.

Eragon called Murtagh over and instructed, "Hold her wing down. I have to remove this arrow." He indicated where Murtagh should grip. *This will be painful*, he warned Saphira, *but it'll be over quickly. Try not to struggle—you'll hurt us.*

She extended her neck and grabbed a tall sapling between her curved teeth. With a yank of her head, she pulled the tree out of the ground and clamped it firmly in her jaws. *I'm ready.*

Okay, said Eragon. "Hold on," he whispered to Murtagh, then broke off the head of the arrow. Trying not to cause any more damage, he swiftly pulled the shaft out of Saphira. As it left her muscle, she threw back her head and whimpered past the tree in her mouth. Her wing jerked involuntarily, clipping Murtagh under the chin and knocking him to the ground.

With a growl, Saphira shook the tree, spraying them with dirt before tossing it away. After Eragon sealed the wound, he helped Murtagh up. "She caught me by surprise," admitted Murtagh, touching his scraped jaw.

I'm sorry.

"She didn't mean to hit you," assured Eragon. He checked on the unconscious elf. *You're going to have to carry her a bit longer*, he told Saphira.

453

We can't take her on the horses and ride fast enough. Flying should be easier for you now that the arrow is out.

Saphira dipped her head. *I will do it.*

Thank you, said Eragon. He hugged her fiercely. *What you did was incredible; I'll never forget it.*

Her eyes softened. *I will go now.* He backed away as she flew up in a flurry of air, the elf's hair streaming back. Seconds later they were gone. Eragon hurried to Snowfire, pulled himself into the saddle, and galloped away with Murtagh.

While they rode, Eragon tried to remember what he knew about elves. They had long lives—that fact was oft repeated—although he knew not how long. They spoke the ancient language, and many could use magic. After the Riders' fall, elves had retreated into seclusion. None of them had been seen in the Empire since. *So why is one here now? And how did the Empire manage to capture her? If she can use magic, she's probably drugged as I was.*

They traveled through the night, not stopping even when their flagging strength began to slow them. They continued onward despite burning eyes and clumsy movements. Behind them, lines of torch-bearing horsemen searched around Gil'ead for their trail.

After many bleary hours, dawn lightened the sky. By unspoken consent Eragon and Murtagh stopped the horses. "We have to make camp," said Eragon wearily. "I must sleep—whether they catch us or not."

"Agreed," said Murtagh, rubbing his eyes. "Have Saphira land. We'll meet her."

They followed Saphira's directions and found her drinking from a stream at the base of a small cliff, the elf still slouched on her back. Saphira greeted them with a soft bugle as Eragon dismounted.

Murtagh helped him remove the elf from Saphira's saddle and lower her to the ground. Then they sagged against the rock face, exhausted. Saphira examined the elf curiously. *I wonder why she hasn't woken. It's been hours since we left Gil'ead.*

Who knows what they did to her? said Eragon grimly.

Murtagh followed their gaze. "As far as I know, she's the first elf the king has captured. Ever since they went into hiding, he's been looking for them without success—until now. So he's either found their sanctuary, or she was captured by chance. I think it was chance. If he had found the elf haven, he would have declared war and sent his army after the elves. Since that hasn't happened, the question is, Were Galbatorix's men able to extract the elves' location before we rescued her?"

"We won't know until she regains consciousness. Tell me what happened after I was captured. How did I end up in Gil'ead?"

"The Urgals are working for the Empire," said Murtagh shortly, pushing back his hair. "And, it seems, the Shade as well. Saphira and I saw the Urgals give you to him—though I didn't know who it was at the time—and a group of soldiers. They were the ones who took you to Gil'ead."

It's true, said Saphira, curling up next to them.

Eragon's mind flashed back to the Urgals he had spoken with at Teirm and the "master" they had mentioned. *They meant the king! I insulted the most powerful man in Alagaësia!* he realized with dread. Then he remembered the horror of the slaughtered villagers in Yazuac. A sick, angry feeling welled in his stomach. *The Urgals were under Galbatorix's orders! Why would he commit such an atrocity on his own subjects?*

Because he is evil, stated Saphira flatly.

Glowering, Eragon exclaimed, "This will mean war! Once the people of the Empire learn of it, they will rebel and support the Varden."

Murtagh rested his chin in his hand. "Even if they heard of this outrage, few would make it to the Varden. With the Urgals under his command, the king has enough warriors to close the Empire's borders and remain in control, no matter how disruptive people are. With such a rule of terror, he will be able to shape the Empire however he wants. And though he is hated, people could be galvanized into joining him if they had a common enemy."

"Who would that be?" asked Eragon, confused.

"The elves and the Varden. With the right rumors they can be portrayed as the most despicable monsters in Alagaësia—fiends who are waiting to seize your land and wealth. The Empire could even say that the Urgals have been misunderstood all this time and that they are really friends and allies against such terrible enemies. I only wonder what the king promised them in return for their services."

"It wouldn't work," said Eragon, shaking his head. "No one could be deceived that easily about Galbatorix and the Urgals. Besides, why would he want to do that? He's already in power."

"But his authority is challenged by the Varden, with whom people sympathize. There's also Surda, which has defied him since it seceded from the Empire. Galbatorix is strong within the Empire, but his arm is weak outside of it. As for people seeing through his deceptions, they'll believe whatever he wants them to. It's happened before." Murtagh fell silent and gazed moodily into the distance.

His words troubled Eragon. Saphira touched him with her mind: *Where is Galbatorix sending the Urgals?*

What?

In both Carvahall and Teirm, you heard that Ur-

gals were leaving the area and migrating southeast, as if to brave the Hadarac Desert. *If the king truly does control them, why is he sending them in that direction? Maybe an Urgal army is being gathered for his private use or an Urgal city is being formed.*

Eragon shuddered at the thought. *I'm too tired to figure it out. Whatever Galbatorix's plans, they'll only cause us trouble. I just wish that we knew where the Varden are. That's where we should be going, but we're lost without Dormnad. It doesn't matter what we do; the Empire will find us.*

Don't give up, she said encouragingly, then added dryly, *though you're probably right.*

Thanks. He looked at Murtagh. "You risked your life to rescue me; I owe you for that. I couldn't have escaped on my own." It was more than that, though. There was a bond between them now, welded in the brotherhood of battle and tempered by the loyalty Murtagh had shown.

"I'm just glad I could help. It . . ." Murtagh faltered and rubbed his face. "My main worry now is how we're going to travel with so many men searching for us. Gil'ead's soldiers will be hunting us tomorrow; once they find the horses' tracks, they'll know you didn't fly away with Saphira."

Eragon glumly agreed. "How did you manage to get into the castle?"

Murtagh laughed softly. "By paying a steep bribe and crawling through a filthy scullery chute. But the plan wouldn't have worked without Saphira. She," he stopped and directed his words at her, "that is, you, are the only reason we escaped alive."

Eragon solemnly put a hand on her scaly neck. As she hummed contentedly, he gazed at the elf's face, captivated. Reluctantly, he dragged himself upright. "We should make a bed for her."

Murtagh got to his feet and stretched out a blanket for the elf. When they lifted her onto it, the cuff of her sleeve tore on a branch. Eragon began to pinch the fabric together, then gasped.

The elf's arm was mottled with a layer of bruises and cuts; some were half healed, while others were fresh and oozing. Eragon shook his head with anger and pulled the sleeve up higher. The injuries continued to her shoulder. With trembling fingers, he unlaced the back of her shirt, dreading what might be under it.

As the leather slipped off, Murtagh cursed. The elf's back was strong and muscled, but it was covered with scabs that made her skin look like dry, cracked mud. She had been whipped mercilessly and branded with hot irons in the shape of claws. Where her skin was still intact, it was purple and black from numerous beatings. On her left shoulder was a tattoo inscribed with indigo ink. It was the same symbol that had been on the sapphire of Brom's ring. Eragon silently swore an oath that he would kill whoever was responsible for torturing the elf.

"Can you heal this?" asked Murtagh.

"I—I don't know," said Eragon. He swallowed back sudden queasiness. "There's so much."

Eragon! said Saphira sharply. *This is an elf. She cannot be allowed to die. Tired or not, hungry or not, you must save her. I will meld my strength with yours, but you are the one who must wield the magic.*

Yes . . . you are right, he murmured, unable to tear his eyes from the elf. Determined, he pulled off his gloves and said to Murtagh, "This is going to take some time. Can you get me food? Also, boil rags for bandages; I can't heal all her wounds."

"We can't make a fire without being seen," objected Murtagh. "You'll have to use unwashed cloths, and the food will be cold." Eragon grimaced but acquiesced. As he gently laid a hand on the elf's spine, Saphira settled next to him, her glittering eyes fixed on the elf. He took a deep breath, then reached for the magic and started working.

He spoke the ancient words, "Waíse heill!" A burn shimmered under his palm, and new, unmarked skin flowed over it, joining together without a scar. He passed over bruises or other wounds that were not life-threatening—healing them all would consume the energy he needed for more serious injuries. As Eragon toiled, he marveled that the elf was still alive. She had been repeatedly tortured to the edge of death with a precision that chilled him.

Although he tried to preserve the elf's modesty, he could not help but notice that underneath the disfiguring marks, her body was exceptionally beautiful. He was exhausted and did not dwell upon it—though his ears turned red at times, and he fervently hoped that Saphira did not know what he was thinking.

He labored through dawn, pausing only at brief intervals to eat and drink, trying to replenish himself from his fast, the escape, and now healing the elf. Saphira remained by his side, lending her strength where she could. The sun was well into the sky when he finally stood, groaning as his cramped muscles stretched. His hands were gray and his eyes felt dry and gritty. He stumbled to the saddlebags and took a long drink from the wineskin. "Is it done?" asked Murtagh.

461

Eragon nodded, trembling. He did not trust himself to speak. The camp spun before him; he nearly fainted. *You did well,* said Saphira soothingly.

"Will she live?"

"I don't—don't know," he said in a ravaged voice. "Elves are strong, but even they cannot endure abuse like this with impunity. If I knew more about healing, I might be able to revive her, but . . ." He gestured helplessly. His hand was shaking so badly he spilled some of the wine. Another swig helped to steady him. "We'd better start riding again."

"No! You must sleep," protested Murtagh.

"I . . . can sleep in the saddle. But we can't afford to stay here, not with the soldiers closing on us."

Murtagh reluctantly gave in. "In that case I'll lead Snowfire while you rest." They resaddled the horses, strapped the elf onto Saphira, and departed the camp. Eragon ate while he rode, trying to replace his depleted energy before he leaned forward against Snowfire and closed his eyes.

WATER FROM SAND

When they stopped for the evening, Eragon felt no better and his temper had worsened. Most of the day had been spent on long detours to avoid detection by soldiers with hunting dogs. He dismounted Snowfire and asked Saphira, *How is she?*

I think no worse than before. She stirred slightly a few times, but that was all. Saphira crouched low to the ground to let him lift the elf out of the saddle. For a moment her soft form pressed against Eragon. Then he hurriedly put her down.

He and Murtagh made a small dinner. It was difficult for them to fight off the urge to sleep. When they had eaten, Murtagh said, "We can't keep up this pace; we aren't gaining any ground on the soldiers. Another day or two of this and they'll be sure to overtake us."

"What else can we do?" snapped Eragon. "If it

were just the two of us and you were willing to leave Tornac behind, Saphira could fly us out of here. But with the elf, too? Impossible."

Murtagh looked at him carefully. "If you want to go your own way, I won't stop you. I can't expect you and Saphira to stay and risk imprisonment."

"Don't insult me," Eragon muttered. "The only reason I'm free is because of you. I'm not going to abandon you to the Empire. Poor thanks that would be!"

Murtagh bowed his head. "Your words hearten me." He paused. "But they don't solve our problem."

"What can?" Eragon asked. He gestured at the elf. "I wish she could tell us where the elves are; perhaps we could seek sanctuary with them."

"Considering how they've protected themselves, I doubt she'd reveal their location. Even if she did, the others of her kind might not welcome us. Why would they want to shelter us anyway? The last Riders they had contact with were Galbatorix and the Forsworn. I doubt that left them with pleasant memories. And I don't even have the dubious honor of being a Rider like you. No, they would not want me at all."

They would accept us, said Saphira confidently as she shifted her wings to a more comfortable position.

Eragon shrugged. "Even if they would protect

us, we can't find them, and it's impossible to ask the elf until she regains consciousness. We must flee, but in which direction—north, south, east, or west?"

Murtagh laced his fingers together and pressed his thumbs against his temples. "I think the only thing we can do is leave the Empire. The few safe places within it are far from here. They would be difficult to reach without being caught or followed. . . . There's nothing for us to the north except the forest Du Weldenvarden—which we might be able to hide in, but I don't relish going back past Gil'ead. Only the Empire and the sea lie westward. To the south is Surda, where you might be able to find someone to direct you to the Varden. As for going east . . ." He shrugged. "To the east, the Hadarac Desert stands between us and whatever lands exist in that direction. The Varden are somewhere across it, but without directions it might take us years to find them."

We would be safe, though, remarked Saphira. *As long as we didn't encounter any Urgals.*

Eragon knitted his brow. A headache threatened to drown his thoughts in hot throbs. "It's too dangerous to go to Surda. We would have to traverse most of the Empire, avoiding every town and village. There are too many people between us and Surda to get there unnoticed."

Murtagh raised an eyebrow. "So you want to go across the desert?"

"I don't see any other options. Besides, that way we can leave the Empire before the Ra'zac get here. With their flying steeds, they'll probably arrive in Gil'ead in a couple of days, so we don't have much time."

"Even if we do reach the desert before they get here," said Murtagh, "they could still overtake us. It'll be hard to outdistance them at all."

Eragon rubbed Saphira's side, her scales rough under his fingers. "That's assuming they can follow our trail. To catch us, though, they'll have to leave the soldiers behind, which is to our advantage. If it comes to a fight, I think the three of us can defeat them . . . as long as we aren't ambushed the way Brom and I were."

466   "If we reach the other side of the Hadarac safely," said Murtagh slowly, "where will we go? Those lands are well outside of the Empire. There will be few cities, if any. And then there is the desert itself. What do you know of it?"

"Only that it's hot, dry, and full of sand," confessed Eragon.

"That about sums it up," replied Murtagh. "It's filled with poisonous and inedible plants, venomous snakes, scorpions, and a blistering sun. You saw the great plain on our way to Gil'ead?"

It was a rhetorical question, but Eragon answered anyway, "Yes, and once before."

"Then you are familiar with its immense range. It fills the heart of the Empire. Now imagine something two or three times its size, and you'll understand the vastness of the Hadarac Desert. That is what you're proposing to cross."

Eragon tried to envision a piece of land that gigantic but was unable to grasp the distances involved. He retrieved the map of Alagaësia from his saddlebags. The parchment smelled musty as he unrolled it on the ground. He inspected the plains and shook his head in amazement. "No wonder the Empire ends at the desert. Everything on the other side is too far away for Galbatorix to control."

Murtagh swept his hand over the right side of the parchment. "All the land beyond the desert, which is blank on this map, was under one rule when the Riders lived. If the king were to raise up new Riders under his command, it would allow him to expand the Empire to an unprecedented size. But that wasn't the point I was trying to make. The Hadarac Desert is so huge and contains so many dangers, the chances are slim that we can cross it unscathed. It is a desperate path to take."

"We *are* desperate," said Eragon firmly. He studied the map carefully. "If we rode through the belly of the desert, it would take well over a month, perhaps even two, to cross it. But if we angle southeast, toward the Beor Mountains, we could cut through much faster. Then we can either follow the Beor Mountains farther east into the wilderness or go west to Surda. If this map is accurate, the distance between here and the Beors is roughly equal to what we covered on our way to Gil'ead."

"But that took us nearly a month!"

Eragon shook his head impatiently. "Our ride to Gil'ead was slow on account of my injuries. If we press ourselves, it'll take only a fraction of that time to reach the Beor Mountains."

"Enough. You made your point," acknowledged Murtagh. "Before I consent, however, something must be solved. As I'm sure you noticed, I bought supplies for us and the horses while I was in Gil'ead. But how can we get enough water? The roving tribes who live in the Hadarac usually disguise their wells and oases so no one can steal their water. And carrying enough for more than a day is impractical. Just think about how much Saphira drinks! She and the horses consume more water at one time than we do in a week. Unless you can make it rain whenever we need, I don't see how we can go the direction you propose."

Eragon rocked back on his heels. Making rain was well beyond his power. He suspected that not even the strongest Rider could have done it. Moving that much air was like trying to lift a mountain. He needed a solution that would not drain all of his strength. *I wonder if it's possible to convert sand into water? That would solve our problem, but only if it doesn't take too much energy.*

"I have an idea," he said. "Let me experiment, then I'll give you an answer." Eragon strode out of the camp, with Saphira following closely.

What are you going to try? she asked.

"I don't know," he muttered. *Saphira, could you carry enough water for us?*

She shook her enormous head. *No, I wouldn't even be able to lift that much weight, let alone fly with it.*

Too bad. He knelt and picked up a stone with a cavity large enough for a mouthful of water. He pressed a clump of dirt into the hollow and studied it thoughtfully. Now came the hard part. Somehow he had to convert the dirt into water. *But what words should I use?* He puzzled over it for a moment, then picked two he hoped would work. The icy magic rushed through him as he breached the familiar barrier in his mind and commanded, "Deloi moi!"

469

Immediately the dirt began to absorb his strength at a prodigious rate. Eragon's mind flashed back to Brom's warning that certain tasks could consume all of his power and take his life. Panic blossomed in his chest. He tried to release the magic but could not. It was linked to him until the task was complete or he was dead. All he could do was remain motionless, growing weaker every moment.

Just as he became convinced that he would die kneeling there, the dirt shimmered and morphed into a thimbleful of water. Relieved, Eragon sat back, breathing hard. His heart pounded painfully and hunger gnawed at his innards.

What happened? asked Saphira.

Eragon shook his head, still in shock from the drain on his body's reserves. He was glad that he had not tried to transmute anything larger. *This . . . this won't work,* he said. *I don't even have the strength to give myself a drink.*

You should have been more careful, she chided. *Magic can yield unexpected results when the ancient words are combined in new ways.*

He glared at her. *I know that, but this was the only way I could test my idea. I wasn't going to wait until we were in the desert!* He reminded himself that she was only trying to help. *How did you turn Brom's grave into diamond without killing yourself? I can barely handle a bit of dirt, much less all that sandstone.*

I don't know how I did it, she stated calmly. *It just happened.*

Could you do it again, but this time make water?

Eragon, she said, looking him squarely in the face. *I've no more control over my abilities than a spider does. Things like that occur whether I will them or not. Brom told you that unusual events happen around dragons. He spoke truly. He gave no explanation for it, nor do I have one. Sometimes I can work changes just by feel, almost without thought. The rest of the time—like right now—I'm as powerless as Snowfire.*

You're never powerless, he said softly, putting a hand on her neck. For a long period they were both quiet. Eragon remembered the grave he had made and how Brom lay within it. He could still see the sandstone flowing over the old man's face. "At least we gave him a decent burial," he whispered.

He idly swirled a finger in the dirt, making twisting ridges. Two of the ridges formed a miniature valley, so he added mountains around it. With his fingernail he scratched a river down the valley, then deepened it because it seemed too shallow. He added a few more details until he found himself staring at a passable reproduction of Palancar Valley. Homesickness welled up within him, and he obliterated the valley with a swipe of his hand.

I don't want to talk about it, he muttered angrily, staving off Saphira's questions. He crossed his arms and glared at the ground. Almost against his will, his eyes flicked back to where he had gouged the earth. He straightened, surprised. Though the ground was dry, the furrow he had made was lined with moisture. Curious, he scraped away more dirt and found a damp layer a few inches under the surface. "Look at this!" he said excitedly.

Saphira lowered her nose to his discovery. *How does this help us? Water in the desert is sure to be buried so deeply we would have to dig for weeks to find it.*

Yes, said Eragon delightedly, *but as long as it's there, I can get it. Watch!* He deepened the hole, then mentally accessed the magic. Instead of changing the dirt into water, he simply summoned forth the moisture that was already in the earth. With a faint trickle, water rushed into the hole. He smiled and sipped from it. The liquid was cool and pure, perfect for drinking. *See! We can get all we need.*

Saphira sniffed the pool. *Here, yes. But in the desert? There may not be enough water in the ground for you to bring to the surface.*

It will work, Eragon assured her. *All I'm doing is lifting the water, an easy enough task. As long as it's done slowly, my strength will hold. Even if I have to draw the water from fifty paces down, it won't be a problem. Especially if you help me.*

Saphira looked at him dubiously. *Are you sure? Think carefully upon your answer, for it will mean our lives if you are wrong.*

Eragon hesitated, then said firmly, *I'm sure.*

Then go tell Murtagh. I will keep watch while you sleep.

But you've stayed up all night like us, he objected. *You should rest.*

I'll be fine—I'm stronger than you know, she said gently. Her scales rustled as she curled up with a watchful eye turned northward, toward their pursuers. Eragon hugged her, and she hummed deeply, sides vibrating. *Go.*

He lingered, then reluctantly returned to Murtagh, who asked, "Well? Is the desert open to us?"

"It is," acknowledged Eragon. He flopped onto his blankets and explained what he had learned. When he finished, Eragon turned to the elf. Her face was the last thing he saw before falling asleep.

THE RAMR RIVER

They forced themselves to rise early in the gray predawn hours. Eragon shivered in the cool air. "How are we going to transport the elf? She can't ride on Saphira's back much longer without getting sores from her scales. Saphira can't carry her in her claws—it tires her and makes landing dangerous. A sledge won't work; it would get battered to pieces while we ride, and I don't want the horses slowed by the weight of another person."

Murtagh considered the matter as he saddled Tornac. "If you were to ride Saphira, we could lash the elf onto Snowfire, but we'd have the same problem with sores."

I have a solution, said Saphira unexpectedly. *Why don't you tie the elf to my belly? I'll still be able to move freely, and she will be safer than anywhere else. The only danger will be if soldiers shoot arrows at me, but I can easily fly above those.*

None of them could come up with a better idea, so they quickly adopted hers. Eragon folded one of his blankets in half lengthwise, secured it around the elf's petite form, then took her to Saphira. Blankets and spare clothes were sacrificed to form ropes long enough to encircle Saphira's girth. With those ropes, the elf was tied back-first against Saphira's belly, her head between Saphira's front legs. Eragon looked critically at their handiwork. "I'm afraid your scales may rub through the ropes."

"We'll have to check them occasionally for fraying," commented Murtagh.

Shall we go now? Saphira asked, and Eragon repeated the question.

Murtagh's eyes sparked dangerously, a tight smile lifting his lips. He glanced back the way they had come, where smoke from soldiers' camps was clearly visible, and said, "I always did like races."

"And now we are in one for our lives!"

Murtagh swung into Tornac's saddle and trotted out of the camp. Eragon followed close behind on Snowfire. Saphira jumped into the air with the elf. She flew low to the ground to avoid being seen by the soldiers. In this fashion, the three of them made their way southeast toward the distant Hadarac Desert.

Eragon kept a quick eye out for pursuers as he rode. His mind repeatedly wandered back to the elf. *An elf!* He had actually seen one, and she was with them! He wondered what Roran would think of that. It struck him that if he ever returned to Carvahall, he would have a hard time convincing anyone that his adventures had actually occurred.

For the rest of the day, Eragon and Murtagh sped through the land, ignoring discomfort and fatigue. They drove the horses as hard as they could without killing them. Sometimes they dismounted and ran on foot to give Tornac and Snowfire a rest. Only twice did they stop—both times to let the horses eat and drink.

Though the soldiers of Gil'ead were far behind now, Eragon and Murtagh found themselves having to avoid new soldiers every time they passed a town or village. Somehow the alarm had been sent ahead of them. Twice they were nearly ambushed along the trail, escaping only because Saphira happened to smell the men ahead of them. After the second incident, they avoided the trail entirely.

Dusk softened the countryside as evening drew a black cloak across the sky. Through the night they traveled, relentlessly pacing out the miles. In the deepest hours of night, the ground rose beneath them to form low cactus-dotted hills.

Murtagh pointed forward. "There's a town, Bullridge, some leagues ahead that we must bypass. They're sure to have soldiers watching for us. We should try to slip past them now while it's dark."

After three hours they saw the straw-yellow lanterns of Bullridge. A web of soldiers patrolled between watch fires scattered around the town. Eragon and Murtagh muffled their sword sheaths and carefully dismounted. They led the horses in a wide detour around Bullridge, listening attentively to avoid stumbling on an encampment.

With the town behind them, Eragon relaxed slightly. Daybreak finally flooded the sky with a delicate blush and warmed the chilly night air. They halted on the crest of a hill to observe their surroundings. The Ramr River was to their left, but it was also five miles to their right. The river continued south for several leagues, then doubled back on itself in a narrow loop before curving west. They had covered over sixteen leagues in one day.

Eragon leaned against Snowfire's neck, happy with the distance they had gone. "Let's find a gully or hollow where we can sleep undisturbed." They stopped at a small stand of juniper trees and laid their blankets beneath them. Saphira waited patiently as they untied the elf from her belly.

"I'll take the first watch and wake you at midmorning," said Murtagh, setting his bare sword across his knees. Eragon mumbled his assent and pulled the blankets over his shoulders.

Nightfall found them worn and drowsy but determined to continue. As they prepared to leave, Saphira observed to Eragon, *This is the third night since we rescued you from Gil'ead, and the elf still hasn't woken. I'm worried. And,* she continued, *she has neither drunk nor eaten in that time. I know little of elves, but she is slender, and I doubt she can survive much longer without nourishment.*

"What's wrong?" asked Murtagh over Tornac's back.

"The elf," said Eragon, looking down at her. "Saphira is troubled that she hasn't woken or eaten; it disturbs me too. I healed her wounds, at least on the surface, but it doesn't seem to have done her any good."

"Maybe the Shade tampered with her mind," suggested Murtagh.

"Then we have to help her."

Murtagh knelt by the elf. He examined her intently, then shook his head and stood. "As far as I can tell, she's only sleeping. It seems as if I could wake her with a word or a touch, yet she slumbers on. Her coma might be something elves self-induce to escape the pain of injury, but if so, why doesn't she end it? There's no danger to her now."

"But does she know that?" asked Eragon quietly.

Murtagh put a hand on his shoulder. "This must wait. We have to leave now or risk losing our hard-won lead. You can tend to her later when we stop."

"One thing first," said Eragon. He soaked a rag, then squeezed the cloth so water dripped between the elf's sculpted lips. He did that several times and dabbed above her straight, angled eyebrows, feeling oddly protective.

They headed through the hills, avoiding the tops for fear of being spotted by sentries. Saphira stayed with them on the ground for the same reason. Despite her bulk, she was stealthy; only her tail could be heard scraping over the ground, like a thick blue snake.

Eventually the sky brightened in the east. The morning star Aiedail appeared as they reached the edge of a steep bank covered with mounds of brush. Water roared below as it tore over boulders and sluiced through branches.

"The Ramr!" said Eragon over the noise.

Murtagh nodded. "Yes! We have to find a place to ford safely."

That isn't necessary, said Saphira. *I can carry you across, no matter how wide the river is.*

Eragon looked up at her blue-gray form. *What about the horses? We can't leave them behind. They're too heavy for you to lift.*

As long as you're not on them and they don't

struggle too much, I'm sure that I can carry them. If I can dodge arrows with three people on my back, I can certainly fly a horse in a straight line over a river.

I believe you, but let's not attempt it unless we have to. It's too dangerous.

She clambered down the embankment. *We can't afford to squander time here.*

Eragon followed her, leading Snowfire. The bank came to an abrupt end at the Ramr, where the river ran dark and swift. White mist wafted up from the water, like blood steaming in winter. It was impossible to see the far side. Murtagh tossed a branch into the torrent and watched it race away, bobbing on the rough water.

"How deep do you think it is?" asked Eragon.

"I can't tell," said Murtagh, worry coloring his voice. "Can you see how far across it is with magic?"

"I don't think so, not without lighting up this place like a beacon."

With a gust of air, Saphira took off and soared over the Ramr. After a short time, she said, *I'm on the other bank. The river is over a half-mile wide. You couldn't have chosen a worse place to cross; the Ramr bends at this point and is at its widest.*

"A half-mile!" exclaimed Eragon. He told Murtagh about Saphira's offer to fly them.

"I'd rather not try it, for the horses' sake. Tornac isn't as accustomed to Saphira as Snowfire. He might panic and injure them both. Ask

Saphira to look for shallows where we can swim over safely. If there aren't any within a mile in either direction, then I suppose she can ferry us."

At Eragon's request, Saphira agreed to search for a ford. While she explored, they hunkered next to the horses and ate dry bread. It was not long before Saphira returned, her velvet wings whispering in the early dawn sky. *The water is both deep and strong, upstream as well as downstream.*

Once he was told, Murtagh said, "I'd better go over first, so I can watch the horses." He scrambled onto Saphira's saddle. "Be careful with Tornac. I've had him for many years. I don't want anything to happen to him." Then Saphira took off.

When she returned, the unconscious elf had been untied from her belly. Eragon led Tornac to Saphira, ignoring the horse's low whinnies. Saphira reared back on her haunches to grasp the horse around the belly with her forelegs. Eragon eyed her formidable claws and said, "Wait!" He repositioned Tornac's saddle blanket, strapping it to the horse's belly so it protected his soft underside, then gestured for Saphira to proceed.

Tornac snorted in fright and tried to bolt when Saphira's forelegs clamped around his sides, but she held him tightly. The horse rolled his eyes wildly, the whites rimming his dilated pupils. Eragon tried to gentle Tornac with his mind, but the horse's panic resisted his touch. Before Tornac could try to escape again, Saphira jumped skyward, her hind legs thrusting with such force that her claws gouged the rocks underneath. Her wings strained furiously, struggling to lift the enormous load. For a moment it seemed she would fall back to the ground. Then, with a lunge, she shot into the air. Tornac screamed in terror, kicking and tossing. It was a terrible sound, like screeching metal.

Eragon swore, wondering if anyone was close enough to hear. *You'd better hurry, Saphira.* He listened for soldiers as he waited, scanning the inky landscape for the telltale flash of torches. It soon met his eye in a line of horsemen sliding down a bluff almost a league away.

482

As Saphira landed, Eragon brought Snowfire to her. *Murtagh's silly animal is in hysterics. He had to tie Tornac down to prevent him from running away.* She gripped Snowfire and carried him off, ignoring the horse's trumpeted protestations. Eragon watched her go, feeling lonely in the night. The horsemen were only a mile away.

Finally Saphira came for him, and they were soon on firm ground once more, with the Ramr to their backs. Once the horses were calmed and the saddles readjusted, they resumed their flight toward the Beor Mountains. The air filled with the calls of birds waking to a new day.

Eragon dozed even when walking. He was barely aware that Murtagh was just as drowsy.

There were times when neither of them guided the horses, and it was only Saphira's vigilance that kept them on course.

Eventually the ground became soft and gave way under their feet, forcing them to halt. The sun was high overhead. The Ramr River was no more than a fuzzy line behind them.

They had reached the Hadarac Desert.

THE HADARAC
DESERT

A vast expanse of dunes spread to the horizon like ripples on an ocean. Bursts of wind twirled the reddish gold sand into the air. Scraggly trees grew on scattered patches of solid ground—ground any farmer would have declared unfit for crops. Rising in the distance was a line of purple crags. The imposing desolation was barren of any animals except for a bird gliding on the zephyrs.

"You're sure we'll find food for the horses out there?" queried Eragon, slurring his words. The hot, dry air stung his throat.

"See those?" asked Murtagh, indicating the crags. "Grass grows around them. It's short and tough, but the horses will find it sufficient."

"I hope you're right," said Eragon, squinting at the sun. "Before we continue, let's rest. My mind is slow as a snail, and I can barely move my legs."

They untied the elf from Saphira, ate, then lay in the shadow of a dune for a nap. As Eragon settled into the sand, Saphira coiled up next to him and spread her wings over them. *This is a wondrous place*, she said. *I could spend years here and not notice the passing time.*

Eragon closed his eyes. *It would be a nice place to fly*, he agreed drowsily.

Not only that, I feel as though I was made for this desert. It has the space I need, mountains where I could roost, and camouflaged prey that I could spend days hunting. And the warmth! Cold does not disturb me, but this heat makes me feel alive and full of energy. She craned her head toward the sky, stretching happily.

You like it that much? mumbled Eragon.

Yes.

Then when this is all done, perhaps we can return. . . . He drifted into slumber even as he spoke. Saphira was pleased and hummed gently while he and Murtagh rested.

It was the morning of the fourth day since leaving Gil'ead. They had already covered thirty-five leagues.

They slept just long enough to clear their minds and rest the horses. No soldiers could be seen to the rear, but that did not lull them into slowing their pace. They knew that the Empire would keep searching until they were far beyond the king's reach. Eragon said, "Couriers must have carried news of my escape to Galbatorix. He would have alerted the Ra'zac. They're sure to be on our trail by now. It'll take them a while to catch us even by flying, but we should be ready for them at all times."

And this time they will find I am not so easily bound with chains, said Saphira.

Murtagh scratched his chin. "I hope they won't be able to follow us past Bullridge. The Ramr was an effective way to lose pursuers; there's a good chance our tracks won't be found again."

"Something to hope for indeed," said Eragon as he checked the elf. Her condition was unchanged; she still did not react to his ministrations. "I place no faith in luck right now, though. The Ra'zac could be on our trail even as we speak."

At sunset they arrived at the crags they had viewed from afar that morning. The imposing stone bluffs towered over them, casting thin shadows. The surrounding area was free of dunes for a half mile. Heat assailed Eragon like a physical blow as he dismounted Snowfire onto the baked, cracked ground. The back of his neck and his face were sunburned; his skin was hot and feverish.

After picketing the horses where they could nibble the sparse grass, Murtagh started a small fire. "How far do you think we went?" Eragon asked, releasing the elf from Saphira.

"I don't know!" snapped Murtagh. His skin was red, his eyes bloodshot. He picked up a pot and muttered a curse. "We don't have enough water. And the horses have to drink."

Eragon was just as irritated by the heat and dryness, but he held his temper in check. "Bring the horses." Saphira dug a hole for him with her claws, then he closed his eyes, releasing the spell. Though the ground was parched, there was enough moisture for the plants to live on and enough for him to fill the hole several times over.

Murtagh refilled the waterskins as water pooled in the hole, then stood aside and let the horses drink. The thirsty animals quaffed gallons. Eragon was forced to draw the liquid from ever deeper in the earth to satisfy their desire. It taxed his strength to the limit. When the horses were finally sated, he said to Saphira, *If you need a drink, take it now*. Her head snaked around him and she took two long draughts, but no more.

Before letting the water flow back into the ground, Eragon gulped down as much as he could, then watched the last drops melt back into the dirt. Holding the water on the surface was harder than he had expected. *But at least it's within my abilities*, he reflected, remembering with some amusement how he had once struggled to lift even a pebble.

*　*　*

It was freezing when they rose the next day. The sand had a pink hue in the morning light, and the sky was hazy, concealing the horizon. Murtagh's mood had not improved with sleep, and Eragon found his own rapidly deteriorating. During breakfast, he asked, "Do you think it'll be long before we leave the desert?"

Murtagh glowered. "We're only crossing a small section of it, so I can't imagine that it'll take us more than two or three days."

"But look how far we've already come."

"All right, maybe it won't! All I care about right now is getting out of the Hadarac as quickly as possible. What we're doing is hard enough without having to pick sand from our eyes every few minutes."

They finished eating, then Eragon went to the elf. She lay as one dead—a corpse except for her measured breathing. "Where lies your injury?" whispered Eragon, brushing a strand of hair from her face. "How can you sleep like this and yet live?" The image of her, alert and poised in the prison cell, was still vivid in his mind. Troubled, he prepared the elf for travel, then saddled and mounted Snowfire.

As they left the camp, a line of dark smudges became visible on the horizon, indistinct in the hazy air. Murtagh thought they were distant hills.

488

Eragon was not convinced, but he could make out no details.

The elf's plight filled his thoughts. He was sure that something had to be done to help her or she would die, though he knew not what that might be. Saphira was just as concerned. They talked about it for hours, but neither of them knew enough about healing to solve the problem confronting them.

At midday they stopped for a brief rest. When they resumed their journey, Eragon noticed that the haze had thinned since morning, and the distant smudges had gained definition.

No longer were they indistinct purple-blue lumps, but rather broad, forest-covered mounds with clear outlines. The air above them was pale white, bleached of its usual hue—all color seemed to have been leached out of a horizontal band of sky that lay on top of the hills and extended to the horizon's edges.

He stared, puzzled, but the more he tried to make sense of it, the more confused he became. He blinked and shook his head, thinking that it must be some illusion of the desert air. Yet when he opened his eyes, the annoying incongruity was still there. Indeed, the whiteness blanketed half the sky before them. Sure that something was terribly wrong, he started to point this out to Murtagh and Saphira when he suddenly understood what he was seeing.

What they had taken to be hills were actually the bases of gigantic mountains, scores of miles wide. Except for the dense forest along their lower regions, the mountains were entirely covered with snow and ice. It was this that had deceived Eragon into thinking the sky white. He craned back his neck, searching for the peaks, but they were not visible. The mountains stretched up into the sky until they faded from sight. Narrow, jagged valleys with ridges that nearly touched split the mountains like deep gorges. It was like a ragged, toothy wall linking Alagaësia with the heavens.

There's no end to them! he thought, awestruck. Stories that mentioned the Beor Mountains always noted their size, but he had discounted such reports as fanciful embellishments. Now, however, he was forced to acknowledge their authenticity.

Sensing his wonder and surprise, Saphira followed his gaze with her own. Within a few seconds she recognized the mountains for what they were. *I feel like a hatchling again. Compared to them, even I feel small!*

We must be near the edge of the desert, said Eragon. *It's only taken two days and we can already see the far side and beyond!*

Saphira spiraled above the dunes. *Yes, but considering the size of those peaks, they could still be fifty leagues from here. It's hard to gauge distances against something so immense. Wouldn't they be a perfect hiding place for the elves or the Varden?*

You could hide more than the elves and Varden, he stated. *Entire nations could exist in secret there, hidden from the Empire. Imagine living with those behemoths looming over you!* He guided Snowfire to Murtagh and pointed, grinning.

"What?" grunted Murtagh, scanning the land.

"Look closely," urged Eragon.

Murtagh peered closely at the horizon. He shrugged. "What, I don't—" The words died in his mouth and gave way to slack-jawed wonder. Murtagh shook his head, muttering, "That's impossible!" He squinted so hard that the corners of his eyes crinkled. He shook his head again. "I knew the Beor Mountains were large, but not that monstrous size!"

"Let's hope the animals that live there aren't in proportion to the mountains," said Eragon lightly.

Murtagh smiled. "It will be good to find some shade and spend a few weeks in leisure. I've had enough of this forced march."

"I'm tired too," admitted Eragon, "but I don't want to stop until the elf is cured . . . or she dies."

"I don't see how continuing to travel will help her," said Murtagh gravely. "A bed will do her more good than hanging underneath Saphira all day."

Eragon shrugged. "Maybe . . . When we reach

the mountains, I could take her to Surda—it's not that far. There must be a healer there who can help her; we certainly can't."

Murtagh shaded his eyes with his hand and stared at the mountains. "We can talk about it later. For now our goal is to reach the Beors. There, at least, the Ra'zac will have trouble finding us, and we will be safe from the Empire."

As the day wore on, the Beor Mountains seemed to get no closer, though the landscape changed dramatically. The sand slowly transformed from loose grains of reddish hue to hard-packed, dusky-cream dirt. In place of dunes were ragged patches of plants and deep furrows in the ground where flooding had occurred. A cool breeze wafted through the air, bringing welcome refreshment. The horses sensed the change of climate and hurried forward eagerly.

When evening subdued the sun, the mountains' foothills were a mere league away. Herds of gazelles bounded through lush fields of waving grass. Eragon caught Saphira eyeing them hungrily. They camped by a stream, relieved to be out of the punishing Hadarac Desert.

A PATH REVEALED

Fatigued and haggard, but with triumphant smiles, they sat around the fire, congratulating each other. Saphira crowed jubilantly, which startled the horses. Eragon stared at the flames. He was proud that they had covered roughly sixty leagues in five days. It was an impressive feat, even for a rider able to change mounts regularly.

I am outside of the Empire. It was a strange thought. He had been born in the Empire, lived his entire life under Galbatorix's rule, lost his closest friends and family to the king's servants, and had nearly died several times within his domain. Now Eragon was free. No more would he and Saphira have to dodge soldiers, avoid towns, or hide who they were. It was a bittersweet realization, for the cost had been the loss of his entire world.

He looked at the stars in the gloaming sky. And though the thought of building a home in the safety of isolation appealed to him, he had witnessed too many wrongs committed in Galbatorix's name, from murder to slavery, to turn his back on the Empire. No longer was it just vengeance—for Brom's death as well as Garrow's—that drove him. As a Rider, it was his duty to assist those without strength to resist Galbatorix's oppression.

With a sigh he abandoned his deliberation and observed the elf stretched out by Saphira. The fire's orange light gave her face a warm cast. Smooth shadows flickered under her cheekbones. As he stared, an idea slowly came to him.

494   He could hear the thoughts of people and animals—and communicate with them in that manner if he chose to—but it was something he had done infrequently except with Saphira. He always remembered Brom's admonishment not to violate someone's mind unless absolutely necessary. Save for the one time he had tried to probe Murtagh's consciousness, he had refrained from doing so.

Now, however, he wondered if it were possible to contact the elf in her comatose state. *I might be able to learn from her memories why she remains like this. But if she recovers, would she forgive me for such an intrusion? . . . Whether she does or not, I must try. She's been in this condition for almost a week.* Without speaking of his intentions to

Murtagh or Saphira, he knelt by the elf and placed his palm on her brow.

Eragon closed his eyes and extended a tendril of thought, like a probing finger, toward the elf's mind. He found it without difficulty. It was not fuzzy and filled with pain as he had anticipated, but lucid and clear, like a note from a crystal bell. Suddenly an icy dagger drove into his mind. Pain exploded behind his eyes with splashes of color. He recoiled from the attack but found himself held in an iron grip, unable to retreat.

Eragon fought as hard as he could and used every defense he could think of. The dagger stabbed into his mind again. He frantically threw his own barriers before it, blunting the attack. The pain was less excruciating than the first time, but it jarred his concentration. The elf took the opportunity to ruthlessly crush his defenses.

A stifling blanket pressed down on Eragon from all directions, smothering his thoughts. The overpowering force slowly contracted, squeezing the life out of him bit by bit, though he held on, unwilling to give up.

The elf tightened her relentless grip even more, so as to extinguish him like a snuffed candle. He desperately cried in the ancient language, "Eka aí fricai un Shur'tugal!" I am a Rider and friend! The deadly embrace did not loosen its hold, but its constriction halted and surprise emanated from her.

Suspicion followed a second later, but he knew

she would believe him; he could not have lied in the ancient language. However, while he had said he was a friend, that did not mean he meant her no harm. For all she knew, Eragon believed himself to be her friend, making the statement true for him, though *she* might not consider him one. *The ancient language does have its limitations*, thought Eragon, hoping that the elf would be curious enough to risk freeing him.

She was. The pressure lifted, and the barriers around her mind hesitantly lowered. The elf warily let their thoughts touch, like two wild animals meeting for the first time. A cold shiver ran down Eragon's side. Her mind was alien. It felt vast and powerful, weighted with memories of uncounted years. Dark thoughts loomed out of sight and touch, artifacts of her race that made him cringe when they brushed his consciousness. Yet through all the sensations shimmered a melody of wild, haunting beauty that embodied her identity.

What is your name? she asked, speaking in the ancient language. Her voice was weary and filled with quiet despair.

Eragon. And yours? Her consciousness lured him closer, inviting him to submerge himself in the lyric strains of her blood. He resisted the summons with difficulty, though his heart ached to accept it. For the first time he understood the fey attraction of elves. They were creatures of magic, unbound by the mortal laws of the land—as different from humans as dragons were from animals.

. . . *Arya. Why have you contacted me in this manner? Am I still a captive of the Empire?*

No, you are free! said Eragon. Though he knew only scattered words in the ancient language, he managed to convey: *I was imprisoned in Gil'ead, like you, but I escaped and rescued you. In the five days since then, we've crossed the edge of the Hadarac Desert and are now camped by the Beor Mountains. You've not stirred nor said a word in all that time.*

Ah . . . so it was Gil'ead. She paused. *I know that my wounds were healed. At the time I did not understand why—preparation for some new torture, I was certain. Now I realize it was you.* Softly she added, *Even so, I have not risen, and you are puzzled.*

Yes.

During my captivity, a rare poison, the Skilna Bragh, was given to me, along with the drug to suppress my power. Every morning the antidote for the previous day's poison was administered to me, by force if I refused to take it. Without it I will die within a few hours. That is why I lie in this trance— it slows the Skilna Bragh's progress, though does not stop it. . . . I contemplated waking for the purpose of ending my life and denying Galbatorix, but I refrained from doing so out of hope that you might be an ally. . . . Her voice dwindled off weakly.

How long can you remain like this? asked Eragon.

For weeks, but I'm afraid I haven't that much time. This dormancy cannot restrain death forever . . . I can feel it in my veins even now. Unless I receive the antidote, I will succumb to the poison in three or four days.

Where can the antidote be found?

It exists in only two places outside of the Empire: with my own people and with the Varden. However, my home is beyond the reach of dragonback.

What about the Varden? We would have taken you straight to them, but we don't know where they are.

I will tell you—if you give me your word that you will never reveal their location to Galbatorix or to anyone who serves him. In addition you must swear that you have not deceived me in some manner and that you intend no harm to the elves, dwarves, Varden, or the race of dragons.

What Arya asked for would have been simple enough—if they had not been conversing in the ancient language. Eragon knew she wanted oaths more binding than life itself. Once made, they could never be broken. That weighed heavily on him as he gravely pledged his word in agreement.

It is understood. . . . A series of vertigo-inducing images suddenly flashed through his mind. He found himself riding along the Beor Mountain range, traveling eastward many leagues.

Eragon did his best to remember the route as craggy mountains and hills flashed past. He was heading south now, still following the mountains. Then everything wheeled abruptly, and he entered a narrow, winding valley. It snaked through the mountains to the base of a frothy waterfall that pounded into a deep lake.

The images stopped. *It is far,* said Arya, *but do not let the distance dissuade you. When you arrive at the lake Kósta-mérna at the end of the Beartooth River, take a rock, bang on the cliff next to the waterfall, and cry, Aí varden abr du Shur'-tugalar gata vanta. You will be admitted. You will be challenged, but do not falter no matter how perilous it seems.*

What should they give you for the poison? he asked.

Her voice quavered, but then she regained her strength. *Tell them—to give me Tunivor's Nectar. You must leave me now . . . I have expended too much energy already. Do not talk with me again unless there is no hope of reaching the Varden. If that is the case, there is information I must impart to you so the Varden will survive. Farewell, Eragon, rider of dragons . . . my life is in your hands.*

Arya withdrew from their contact. The unearthly strains that had echoed across their link were gone. Eragon took a shuddering breath and forced his eyes open. Murtagh and Saphira stood on either side of him, watching with concern.

"Are you all right?" asked Murtagh. "You've been kneeling here for almost fifteen minutes."

"I have?" asked Eragon, blinking.

Yes, and grimacing like a pained gargoyle, commented Saphira dryly.

Eragon stood, wincing as his cramped knees stretched. "I talked with Arya!" Murtagh frowned quizzically, as if to inquire if he had gone mad. Eragon explained, "The elf—that's her name."

And what is it that ails her? asked Saphira impatiently.

Eragon swiftly told them of his entire discussion. "How far away are the Varden?" asked Murtagh.

500 "I'm not exactly sure," confessed Eragon. "From what she showed me, I think it's even farther than from here to Gil'ead."

"And we're supposed to cover that in three or four days?" demanded Murtagh angrily. "It took us five *long* days to get here! What do you want to do, kill the horses? They're exhausted as it is."

"But if we do nothing, she'll die! If it's too much for the horses, Saphira can fly ahead with Arya and me; at least we would get to the Varden in time. You could catch up with us in a few days."

Murtagh grunted and crossed his arms. "Of course. Murtagh the pack animal. Murtagh the horse leader. I should have remembered that's all

I'm good for nowadays. Oh, and let's not forget, every soldier in the Empire is searching for me now because you couldn't defend yourself, and I had to go and *save* you. Yes, I suppose I'll just follow your instructions and bring up the horses in the rear like a good servant."

Eragon was bewildered by the sudden venom in Murtagh's voice. "What's wrong with you? I'm grateful for what you did. There's no reason to be angry with me! I didn't ask you to accompany me or to rescue me from Gil'ead. You chose that. I haven't forced you to do anything."

"Oh, not openly, no. What else could I do but help you with the Ra'zac? And then later, at Gil'ead, how could I have left with a clear conscience? The problem with you," said Murtagh, poking Eragon in the chest, "is that you're so totally helpless you force everyone to take care of you!"

The words stung Eragon's pride; he recognized a grain of truth in them. "Don't touch me," he growled.

Murtagh laughed, a harsh note in his voice. "Or what, you'll punch me? You couldn't hit a brick wall." He went to shove Eragon again, but Eragon grabbed his arm and struck him in the stomach.

"I said, don't touch me!"

Murtagh doubled over, swearing. Then he yelled and launched himself at Eragon. They fell in a tangle of arms and legs, pounding on each other. Eragon kicked at Murtagh's right hip, missed, and grazed the fire. Sparks and burning embers scattered through the air.

They scrabbled across the ground, trying to get leverage. Eragon managed to get his feet under Murtagh's chest and kicked mightily. Murtagh flew upside down over Eragon's head, landing flat on his back with a solid thump.

Murtagh's breath whooshed out. He rolled stiffly to his feet, then wheeled to face Eragon, panting heavily. They charged each other once more. Saphira's tail slapped between them, accompanied by a deafening roar. Eragon ignored her and tried to jump over her tail, but a taloned paw caught him in midair and flung him back to the ground.

Enough!

He futilely tried to push Saphira's muscled leg off his chest and saw that Murtagh was likewise pinned. Saphira roared again, snapping her jaws. She swung her head over Eragon and glared at him. *You of all people should know better! Fighting like starving dogs over a scrap of meat. What would Brom say?*

Eragon felt his cheeks burn and averted his eyes. He knew what Brom would have said. Saphira held them on the ground, letting them simmer, then said to Eragon pointedly, *Now, if you don't want to spend the night under my foot, you will politely ask Murtagh what is troubling him.* She snaked her head over to Murtagh and stared down at him with an impassive blue eye. *And tell him that I won't stand for insults from either of you.*

Won't you let us up? complained Eragon.

No.

Eragon reluctantly turned his head toward Murtagh, tasting blood in the side of his mouth. Murtagh avoided his eyes and looked up at the sky. "Well, is she going to get off us?"

"No, not unless we talk. . . . She wants me to ask you what's really the problem," said Eragon, embarrassed.

Saphira growled an affirmative and continued to stare at Murtagh. It was impossible for him to escape her piercing glare. Finally he shrugged, muttering something under his breath. Saphira's claws tightened on his chest, and her tail whistled through the air. Murtagh shot her an angry glance, then grudgingly said louder, "I told you before: I don't want to go to the Varden."

Eragon frowned. Was that all that was the matter? "Don't want to . . . or can't?"

Murtagh tried to shove Saphira's leg off him, then gave up with a curse. "Don't want to! They'll expect things from me that I can't deliver."

"Did you steal something from them?"

"I wish it were that simple."

Eragon rolled his eyes, exasperated. "Well,

503

what is it, then? Did you kill someone important or bed the wrong woman?"

"No, I was born," said Murtagh cryptically. He pushed at Saphira again. This time she released them both. They got to their feet under her watchful eye and brushed dirt from their backs.

"You're avoiding the question," Eragon said, dabbing his split lip.

"So what?" spat Murtagh as he stomped to the edge of the camp. After a minute he sighed. "It doesn't matter why I'm in this predicament, but I can tell you that the Varden wouldn't welcome me even if I came bearing the king's head. Oh, they might greet me nicely enough and let me into their councils, but trust me? Never. And if I were to arrive under less fortuitous circumstances, like the present ones, they'd likely clap me in irons."

"Won't you tell me what this is about?" asked Eragon. "I've done things I'm not proud of, too, so it's not as if I'm going to pass judgment."

Murtagh shook his head slowly, eyes glistening. "It isn't like that. I haven't *done* anything to deserve this treatment, though it would have been easier to atone for if I had. No . . . my only wrongdoing is existing in the first place." He stopped and took a shaky breath. "You see, my father—"

A sharp hiss from Saphira cut him off abruptly. *Look!*

They followed her gaze westward. Murtagh's face paled. "Demons above and below!"

A league or so away, parallel to the mountain range, was a column of figures marching east. The line of troops, hundreds strong, stretched for nearly a mile. Dust billowed from their heels. Their weapons glinted in the dying light. A standard-bearer rode before them in a black chariot, holding aloft a crimson banner.

"It's the Empire," said Eragon tiredly. "They've found us . . . somehow." Saphira poked her head over his shoulder and gazed at the column.

"Yes . . . but those are Urgals, not men," said Murtagh.

"How can you tell?"

Murtagh pointed at the standard. "That flag bears the personal symbol of an Urgal chieftain. He's a ruthless brute, given to violent fits and insanity."

"You've met him?"

Murtagh's eyes tightened. "Once, briefly. I still have scars from that encounter. These Urgals might not have been sent here for us, but I'm sure we've been seen by now and that they will follow us. Their chieftain isn't the sort to let a dragon escape his grasp, especially if he's heard about Gil'ead."

Eragon hurried to the fire and covered it with dirt. "We have to flee! You don't want to go to the Varden, but I have to take Arya to them be-

505

fore she dies. Here's a compromise: come with me until I reach the lake Kóstha-mérna, then go your own way." Murtagh hesitated. Eragon added quickly, "If you leave now, in sight of the column, Urgals will follow you. And then where will you be, facing them alone?"

"Very well," said Murtagh, tossing his saddle-bags over Tornac's flanks, "but when we near the Varden, I *will* leave."

Eragon burned to question Murtagh further, but not with Urgals so near. He gathered his belongings and saddled Snowfire. Saphira fanned her wings, took off in a rush, and circled above. She kept guard over Murtagh and Eragon as they left camp.

What direction shall I fly? she asked.

East, along the Beors.

Stilling her wings, Saphira rose on an updraft and teetered on the pillar of warm air, hovering in the sky over the horses. *I wonder why the Urgals are here. Maybe they were sent to attack the Varden.*

Then we should try to warn them, he said, guiding Snowfire past half-visible obstacles. As the night deepened, the Urgals faded into the gloom behind them.

A CLASH OF WILLS

When morning came, Eragon's cheek was raw from chafing against Snowfire's neck, and he was sore from his fight with Murtagh. They had alternated sleeping in their saddles throughout the night. It had allowed them to outdistance the Urgal troops, but neither of them knew if the lead could be retained. The horses were exhausted to the point of stopping, yet they still maintained a relentless pace. Whether it would be enough to escape depended on how rested the monsters were . . . and if Eragon and Murtagh's horses survived.

The Beor Mountains cast great shadows over the land, stealing the sun's warmth. To the north was the Hadarac Desert, a thin white band as bright as noonday snow.

I must eat, said Saphira. *Days have passed since I last hunted. Hunger claws my belly. If I start now,*

I might be able to catch enough of those bounding deer for a few mouthfuls.

Eragon smiled at her exaggeration. *Go if you must, but leave Arya here.*

I will be swift. He untied the elf from her belly and transferred her to Snowfire's saddle. Saphira soared away, disappearing in the direction of the mountains. Eragon ran beside the horses, close enough to Snowfire to keep Arya from falling. Neither he nor Murtagh intruded on the silence. Yesterday's fight no longer seemed as important because of the Urgals, but the bruises remained.

Saphira made her kills within the hour and notified Eragon of her success. Eragon was pleased that she would soon return. Her absence made him nervous.

They stopped at a pond to let the horses drink. Eragon idly plucked a stalk of grass, twirling it while he stared at the elf. He was startled from his reverie by the steely rasp of a sword being unsheathed. He instinctively grasped Zar'roc and spun around in search of the enemy. There was only Murtagh, his long sword held ready. He pointed at a hill ahead of them, where a tall, brown-cloaked man sat on a sorrel horse, mace in hand. Behind him was a group of twenty horsemen. No one moved. "Could they be Varden?" asked Murtagh.

Eragon surreptitiously strung his bow. "According to Arya, they're still scores of leagues away. This might be one of their patrols or raiding groups."

"Assuming they're not bandits." Murtagh swung onto Tornac and readied his own bow.

"Should we try to outrun them?" asked Eragon, draping a blanket over Arya. The horsemen must have seen her, but he hoped to conceal the fact that she was an elf.

"It wouldn't do any good," said Murtagh, shaking his head. "Tornac and Snowfire are fine war-horses, but they're tired, and they aren't sprinters. Look at the horses those men have; they're meant for running. They would catch us before we had gone a half-mile. Besides, they may have something important to say. You'd better tell Saphira to hurry back."

Eragon was already doing that. He explained the situation, then warned, *Don't show yourself unless it's necessary. We're not in the Empire, but I still don't want anyone to know about you.*

Never mind that, she replied. *Remember, magic can protect you where speed and luck fail.* He felt her take off and race toward them, skimming close to the ground.

The band of men watched them from the hill.

Eragon nervously gripped Zar'roc. The wire-wrapped hilt was secure under his glove. He said in a low voice, "If they threaten us, I can frighten them away with magic. If that doesn't work, there's Saphira. I wonder how they'd react to a Rider? So many stories have been told about their powers. . . . It might be enough to avoid a fight."

"Don't count on it," said Murtagh flatly. "If there's a fight, we'll just have to kill enough of them to convince them we're not worth the effort." His face was controlled and unemotional.

The man on the sorrel horse signaled with his mace, sending the horsemen cantering toward them. The men shook javelins over their heads, whooping loudly as they neared. Battered sheaths hung from their sides. Their weapons were rusty and stained. Four of them trained arrows on Eragon and Murtagh.

Their leader swirled the mace in the air, and his men responded with yells as they wildly encircled Eragon and Murtagh. Eragon's lips twitched. He almost loosed a blast of magic into their midst, then restrained himself. *We don't know what they want yet,* he reminded himself, containing his growing apprehension.

The moment Eragon and Murtagh were thoroughly surrounded, the leader reined in his horse, then crossed his arms and examined them critically. He raised his eyebrows. "Well, these are better than the usual dregs we find! At least we got healthy ones this time. And we didn't even have to shoot them. Grieg will be pleased." The men chuckled.

At his words, a sinking sensation filled Eragon's gut. A suspicion stirred in his mind. *Saphira* . . .

"Now as for you two," said the leader, speaking to Eragon and Murtagh, "if you would be so good as to drop your weapons, you'll avoid being turned into living quivers by my men." The archers grinned suggestively; the men laughed again.

Murtagh's only movement was to shift his sword. "Who are you and what do you want? We are free men traveling through this land. You have no right to stop us."

"Oh, I have every right," said the man contemptuously. "And as for my name, *slaves* do not address their masters in that manner, unless they want to be beaten."

Eragon cursed to himself. *Slavers!* He remembered vividly the people he had seen at auction in Dras-Leona. Rage boiled within him. He glared at the men around him with new hatred and disgust.

The lines deepened on the leader's face. "Throw down your swords and surrender!" The slavers tensed, staring at them with cold eyes as neither Eragon nor Murtagh lowered his weapon. Eragon's palm tingled. He heard a rustle behind him, then a loud curse. Startled, he spun around.

One of the slavers had pulled the blanket off Arya, revealing her face. He gaped in astonishment, then shouted, "Torkenbrand, this one's an elf!" The men stirred with surprise while the leader spurred his horse over to Snowfire. He looked down at Arya and whistled.

"Well, 'ow much is she worth?" someone asked.

Torkenbrand was quiet for a moment, then spread his hands and said, "At the very least? Fortunes upon fortunes. The Empire will pay a mountain of gold for her!"

The slavers yelled with excitement and pounded each other on the back. A roar filled Eragon's mind as Saphira banked sharply far overhead. *Attack now!* he cried. *But let them escape if they run.* She immediately folded her wings and plummeted downward. Eragon caught Murtagh's attention with a sharp signal. Murtagh took the cue. He smashed his elbow into a slaver's face, knocking the man out of his saddle, and jabbed his heels into Tornac.

With a toss of his mane, the war-horse jumped forward, twirled around, and reared. Murtagh brandished his sword as Tornac plunged back down, driving his forehooves into the back of the dismounted slaver. The man screamed.

Before the slavers could gather their senses, Eragon scrambled out of the commotion and raised his hands, invoking words in the ancient language. A globule of indigo fire struck the ground in the midst of the fray, bursting into a fountain of molten drops that dissipated like sun-warmed dew. A second later, Saphira dropped from the sky and landed next to him. She parted her jaws, displaying her massive fangs, and bellowed. "Behold!" cried Eragon over the furor, "I am a Rider!" He raised Zar'roc over his head, the red blade dazzling in the sunlight, then pointed it at the slavers. "Flee if you wish to live!"

The men shouted incoherently and scrambled over each other in their haste to escape. In the confusion, Torkenbrand was struck in the temple with a javelin. He tumbled to the ground, stunned. The men ignored their fallen leader and raced away in a ragged mass, casting fearful looks at Saphira.

Torkenbrand struggled to his knees. Blood ran from his temple, branching across his cheek with crimson tendrils. Murtagh dismounted and strode over to him, sword in hand. Torkenbrand weakly raised his arm as if to ward off a blow. Murtagh gazed at him coldly, then swung his blade at Torkenbrand's neck. "No!" shouted Eragon, but it was too late.

Torkenbrand's decapitated trunk crumpled to the ground in a puff of dirt. His head landed with a hard thump. Eragon rushed to Murtagh, his jaw working furiously. "Is your brain rotten?" he yelled, enraged. "Why did you kill him?"

Murtagh wiped his sword on the back of Torkenbrand's jerkin. The steel left a dark stain. "I don't see why you're so upset—"

"Upset!" exploded Eragon. "I'm well past that! Did it even occur to you that we could just leave him here and continue on our way? No! Instead you turn into an executioner and chop off his head. He was defenseless!"

Murtagh seemed perplexed by Eragon's wrath. "Well, we couldn't keep him around—he *was* dangerous. The others ran off . . . without a horse he wouldn't have made it far. I didn't want the Urgals to find him and learn about Arya. So I thought it would—"

"But to *kill* him?" interrupted Eragon. Saphira sniffed Torkenbrand's head curiously. She opened her mouth slightly, as if to snap it up, then appeared to decide better of it and prowled to Eragon's side.

"I'm only trying to stay alive," stated Murtagh. "No stranger's life is more important than my own."

"But you can't indulge in wanton violence. Where is your empathy?" growled Eragon, pointing at the head.

"Empathy? Empathy? What empathy can I afford my enemies? Shall I dither about whether to defend myself because it will cause someone pain? If that had been the case, I would have died years ago! You must be willing to protect yourself and what you cherish, no matter what the cost."

Eragon slammed Zar'roc back into its sheath, shaking his head savagely. "You can justify any atrocity with that reasoning."

"Do you think I enjoy this?" Murtagh shouted. "My life has been threatened from the day I was born! All of my waking hours have been spent avoiding danger in one form or another. And sleep never comes easily because I always worry if I'll live to see the dawn. If there ever was a time I felt secure, it must have been in my mother's womb, though I wasn't safe even there! You don't understand—if you lived with this *fear*, you would have learned the same lesson I did: *Do not take chances*." He gestured at Torkenbrand's body. "He was a risk that I removed. I refuse to repent, and I won't plague myself over what is done and past."

Eragon shoved his face into Murtagh's. "It was still the wrong thing to do." He lashed Arya to Saphira, then climbed onto Snowfire. "Let's go." Murtagh guided Tornac around Torkenbrand's prone form in the bloodstained dust.

They rode at a rate that Eragon would have thought impossible a week ago; leagues melted away before them as if wings were attached to their feet. They turned south, between two outstretched arms of the Beor Mountains. The arms were shaped like pincers about to close, the tips a day's travel apart. Yet the distance seemed less because of the mountains' size. It was as if they were in a valley made for giants.

When they stopped for the day, Eragon and Murtagh ate dinner in silence, refusing to look up from their food. Afterward, Eragon said tersely,

"I'll take the first watch." Murtagh nodded and lay on his blankets with his back to Eragon.

Do you want to talk? asked Saphira.

Not right now, murmured Eragon. *Give me some time to think; I'm . . . confused.*

She withdrew from his mind with a gentle touch and a whisper. *I love you, little one.*

And I you, he said. She curled into a ball next to him, lending him her warmth. He sat motionless in the dark, wrestling with his disquiet.

FLIGHT THROUGH
THE VALLEY

In the morning Saphira took off with both Eragon and Arya. Eragon wanted to get away from Murtagh for a time. He shivered, pulling his clothes tighter. It looked like it might snow. Saphira ascended lazily on an updraft and asked, *What are you thinking?*

Eragon contemplated the Beor Mountains, which towered above them even though Saphira flew far above the ground. *That was murder yesterday. I've no other word for it.*

Saphira banked to the left. *It was a hasty deed and ill considered, but Murtagh tried to do the right thing. The men who buy and sell other humans deserve every misfortune that befalls them. If we weren't committed to helping Arya, I would hunt down every slaver and tear them apart!*

Yes, said Eragon miserably, *but Torkenbrand was helpless. He couldn't shield himself or run. A moment* more and he probably would have surrendered. Murtagh didn't give him that chance. *If Torkenbrand had at least been able to fight, it wouldn't have been so bad.*

Eragon, even if Torkenbrand had fought, the results would have been the same. You know as well as I do that few can equal you or Murtagh with the blade. Torkenbrand would have still died, though you seem to think it would have been more just or honorable in a mismatched duel.

I don't know what's right! admitted Eragon, distressed. *There aren't any answers that make sense.*

Sometimes, said Saphira gently, *there are no answers. Learn what you can about Murtagh from this. Then forgive him. And if you can't forgive, at least forget, for he meant you no harm, however rash the act was. Your head is still attached, yes?*

Frowning, Eragon shifted in the saddle. He shook himself, like a horse trying to rid itself of a fly, and checked Murtagh's position over Saphira's shoulder. A patch of color farther back along their route caught his attention.

Camped by a streambed they had crossed late yesterday were the Urgals. Eragon's heartbeat quickened. How could the Urgals be on foot, yet still gain on them? Saphira saw the monsters as well and tilted her wings, brought them close to her body, and slipped into a steep dive, splitting the air. *I don't think they spotted us,* she said.

Eragon hoped not. He squinted against the

blast of air as she increased the angle of their dive. *Their chieftain must be driving them at a breakneck pace*, he said.

Yes—maybe they'll all die of exhaustion.

When they landed, Murtagh asked curtly, "What now?"

"The Urgals are overtaking us," said Eragon. He pointed back toward the column's camp.

"How far do we still have to go?" asked Murtagh, putting his hands against the sky and measuring the hours until sunset.

"Normally? . . . I would guess another five days. At the speed we've been traveling, only three. But unless we get there tomorrow, the Urgals will probably catch us, and Arya will certainly die."

"She might last another day."

"We can't count on it," objected Eragon. "The only way we can get to the Varden in time is if we don't stop for anything, least of all sleep. That's our only chance."

Murtagh laughed bitterly. "How can you expect to do that? We've already gone days without adequate sleep. Unless Riders are made of different stuff than us mortals, you're as tired as I am. We've covered a staggering distance, and the horses, in case you haven't noticed, are ready to drop. Another day of this might kill us all."

Eragon shrugged. "So be it. We don't have a choice."

Murtagh gazed at the mountains. "I could

519

leave and let you fly ahead with Saphira. . . . That would force the Urgals to divide their troops and would give you a better chance of reaching the Varden."

"It would be suicide," said Eragon, crossing his arms. "Somehow those Urgals are faster on foot than we are on horseback. They would run you down like a deer. The only way to evade them is to find sanctuary with the Varden." Despite his words, he was unsure if he wanted Murtagh to stay. *I like him*, Eragon confessed to himself, *but I'm no longer certain if that's a good thing.*

"I'll escape later," said Murtagh abruptly. "When we get to the Varden, I can disappear down a side valley and find my way to Surda, where I can hide without attracting too much attention."

"So you're staying?"

"Sleep or no sleep, I'll see you to the Varden," promised Murtagh.

With newfound determination, they struggled to distance themselves from the Urgals, yet their pursuers continued to creep nearer. At nightfall the monsters were a third closer than they had been that morning. As fatigue eroded his and Murtagh's strength, they slept in turns on the horses, while whoever was awake led the animals in the right direction.

Eragon relied heavily on Arya's memories to

guide them. Because of the alien nature of her mind, he sometimes made mistakes as to the route, costing them precious time. They gradually angled toward the foothills of the eastern arm of mountains, looking for the valley that would lead them to the Varden. Midnight arrived and passed without any sign of it.

When the sun returned, they were pleased to see that the Urgals were far behind. "This is the last day," said Eragon, yawning widely. "If we're not reasonably close to the Varden by noon, I'm going to fly ahead with Arya. You'll be free to go wherever you want then, but you'll have to take Snowfire with you. I won't be able to come back for him."

"That might not be necessary; we could still get there in time," said Murtagh. He rubbed the pommel of his sword.

Eragon shrugged. "We could." He went to Arya and put a hand on her forehead. It was damp and dangerously hot. Her eyes wandered uneasily beneath her eyelids, as if she suffered a nightmare. Eragon pressed a damp rag to her brow, wishing he could do more.

Late in the morning, after they circumnavigated an especially broad mountain, Eragon saw a narrow valley tucked against its far side. The valley was so restricted it could easily be overlooked.

The Beartooth River, which Arya had mentioned, flowed out of it and looped carelessly across the land. He smiled with relief; that was where they needed to go.

Looking back, Eragon was alarmed to see that the distance between them and the Urgals had shrunk to little more than a league. He pointed out the valley to Murtagh. "If we can slip in there without being seen, it might confuse them."

Murtagh looked skeptical. "It's worth a try. But they've followed us easily enough so far."

As they approached the valley, they passed under the knotted branches of the Beor Mountains' forest. The trees were tall, with creviced bark that was almost black, dull needles of the same color, and knobby roots that rose from the soil like bare knees. Cones littered the ground, each the size of a horse's head. Sable squirrels chattered from the treetops, and eyes gleamed from holes in the trunks. Green beards of tangled wolfsbane hung from the gnarled branches.

The forest gave Eragon an uneasy feeling; the hair on the back of his neck prickled. There was something hostile in the air, as if the trees resented their intrusion. *They are very old*, said Saphira, touching a trunk with her nose.

Yes, said Eragon, *but not friendly*. The forest grew denser the farther in they traveled. The lack of space forced Saphira to take off with Arya. Without a clear trail to follow, the tough underbrush slowed Eragon and Murtagh. The Beartooth River wound next to them, filling the air with the sound of gurgling water. A nearby peak obscured the sun, casting them into premature dusk.

At the valley's mouth, Eragon realized that although it looked like a slim gash between the peaks, the valley was really as wide as many of the Spine's vales. It was only the enormous size of the ridged and shadowy mountains that made it appear so confined. Waterfalls dotted its sheer sides. The sky was reduced to a thin strip winding overhead, mostly hidden by gray clouds. From the dank ground rose a clinging fog that chilled the air until their breath was visible. Wild strawberries crawled among a carpet of mosses and ferns, fighting for the meager sunlight. Sprouting on piles of rotting wood were red and yellow toadstools.

All was hushed and quiet, sounds dampened by the heavy air. Saphira landed by them in a nearby glade, the rush of her wings strangely muted. She took in the view with a swing of her head. *I just passed a flock of birds that were black and green with red markings on their wings. I've never seen birds like that before.*

Everything in these mountains seems unusual, replied Eragon. *Do you mind if I ride you awhile? I want to keep an eye on the Urgals.*

Of course.

523

He turned to Murtagh. "The Varden are hidden at the end of this valley. If we hurry, we might get there before nightfall."

Murtagh grunted, hands on his hips. "How am I going to get out of here? I don't see any valleys joining this one, and the Urgals are going to hem us in pretty soon. I need an escape route."

"Don't worry about it," said Eragon impatiently. "This is a long valley; there's sure to be an exit further in." He released Arya from Saphira and lifted the elf onto Snowfire. "Watch Arya—I'm going to fly with Saphira. We'll meet you up ahead." He scrambled onto Saphira's back and strapped himself onto her saddle.

"Be careful," Murtagh warned, his brow furrowed in thought, then clucked to the horses and hurried back into the forest.

As Saphira jumped toward the sky, Eragon said, *Do you think you could fly up to one of those peaks? We might be able to spot our destination, as well as a passage for Murtagh. I don't want to listen to him griping through the entire valley.*

We can try, agreed Saphira, *but it will get much colder.*

I'm dressed warmly.

Hold on, then! Saphira suddenly swooped straight up, throwing him back in the saddle. Her wings flapped strongly, driving their weight upward. The valley shrank to a green line below them. The Beartooth River shimmered like braided silver where light struck it.

They rose to the cloud layer, and icy moisture saturated the air. A formless gray blanket engulfed them, limiting their vision to an arm's length. Eragon hoped they would not collide with anything in the murk. He stuck out a hand experimentally, swinging it through the air. Water condensed on it and ran down his arm, soaking his sleeve.

A blurred gray mass fluttered past his head, and he glimpsed a dove, its wings pumping frantically. There was a white band around its leg. Saphira struck at the bird, tongue lashing out, jaws gaping. The dove squawked as Saphira's sharp teeth snapped together a hair's breadth behind its tail feathers. Then it darted away and disappeared into the haze, the frenzied thumping of its wings fading to silence.

When they breached the top of the clouds, Saphira's scales were covered with thousands of water droplets that reflected tiny rainbows and shimmered with the blue of her scales. Eragon shook himself, spraying water from his clothes, and shivered. He could no longer see the ground, only hills of clouds snaking between the mountains.

The trees on the mountains gave way to thick glaciers, blue and white under the sun. The glare from the snow forced Eragon to close his eyes. He tried to open them after a minute, but the light dazzled him. Irritated, he stared into the crook of his arm. *How can you stand it?* he asked Saphira.

My eyes are stronger than yours, she replied.

It was frigid. The water in Eragon's hair froze, giving him a shiny helmet. His shirt and pants were hard shells around his limbs. Saphira's scales became slick with ice; hoarfrost laced her wings. They had never flown this high before, yet the mountaintops were still miles above them.

Saphira's flapping gradually slowed, and her breathing became labored. Eragon gasped and panted; there didn't seem to be enough air. Fighting back panic, he clutched Saphira's neck spikes for support.

We . . . have to get out of here, he said. Red dots swam before his eyes. *I can't . . . breathe.* Saphira seemed not to hear him, so he repeated the message, louder this time. Again there was no response. *She can't hear me*, he realized. He swayed, finding it hard to think, then pounded on her side and shouted, "Take us down!"

The effort made him lightheaded. His vision faded into swirling darkness.

He regained consciousness as they emerged from the bottom of the clouds. His head was pounding. *What happened?* he asked, pushing himself upright and looking around with confusion.

You blacked out, answered Saphira.

He tried to run his fingers through his hair, but stopped when he felt icicles. *Yes, I know that, but why didn't you answer me?*

My brain was confused. Your words didn't make

*any sense. When you lost consciousness, I knew
something was wrong and descended. I didn't have to
sink far before I realized what had occurred.*

It's a good thing you didn't pass out as well, said
Eragon with a nervous laugh. Saphira only
swished her tail. He looked wistfully at where the
mountain peaks were now concealed by clouds.
*A pity we couldn't stand upon one of those sum-
mits. . . . Well, now we know: we can only fly out of
this valley the way we came in. Why did we run out
of air? How can we have it down here, but not up
above?*

*I don't know, but I'll never dare to fly so close to
the sun again. We should remember this experience.
The knowledge may be useful if we ever have to fight
another Rider.*

527

I hope that never happens, said Eragon. *Let's stay
down below for now. I've had enough adventure for
one day.*

They floated on the gentle air currents, drifting from one mountain to the next, until Eragon
saw that the Urgal column had reached the valley's mouth. *What drives them to such speed, and
how can they bear to sustain it?*

Now that we are closer to them, Saphira said, *I
can see that these Urgals are bigger than the ones
we've met before. They would stand chest and shoulders over a tall man. I don't know what land they
march from, but it must be a fierce place to produce
such brutes.*

Eragon glared at the ground below—he could

not see the detail that she did. *If they keep to this pace, they'll catch Murtagh before we find the Varden.*

Have hope. The forest may hamper their progress. . . . Would it be possible to stop them with magic?

Eragon shook his head. *Stop them . . . no. There are too many.* He thought of the thin layer of mist on the valley floor and grinned. *But I might be able to delay them a bit.* He closed his eyes, selected the words he needed, stared at the mist, and then commanded, "Gath un reisa du rakr!"

There was a disturbance below. From above, it looked as if the ground was flowing together like a great sluggish river. A leaden band of mist gathered in front of the Urgals and thickened into an intimidating wall, dark as a thunderhead. The Urgals hesitated before it, then continued forward like an unstoppable battering ram. The barrier swirled around them, concealing the lead ranks from view.

The drain on Eragon's strength was sudden and massive, making his heart flutter like a dying bird. He gasped, eyes rolling. He struggled to sever the magic's hold on him—to plug the breach through which his life streamed. With a savage growl he jerked away from the magic and broke contact. Tendrils of magic snapped through his mind like decapitated snakes, then reluctantly retreated from his consciousness, clutching at the dregs of his strength. The wall of mist dissipated, and the fog sluggishly collapsed across the ground like a tower of mud sliding apart. The Urgals had not been hindered at all.

Eragon lay limply on Saphira, panting. Only now did he remember Brom saying, "Magic is affected by distance, just like an arrow or a spear. If you try to lift or move something a mile away, it'll take more energy than if you were closer." *I won't forget that again*, he thought grimly.

You shouldn't have forgotten in the first place, Saphira inserted pointedly. *First the dirt at Gil'ead and now this. Weren't you paying attention to anything Brom told you? You'll kill yourself if you keep this up.*

I paid attention, he insisted, rubbing his chin. *It's just been a while, and I haven't had an opportunity to think back on it. I've never used magic at a distance, so how could I know it would be so difficult?*

She growled. *Next thing I know you'll be trying to bring corpses back to life. Don't forget what Brom said about that, too.*

I won't, he said impatiently. Saphira dipped toward the ground, searching for Murtagh and the horses. Eragon would have helped her, but he barely had the energy to sit up.

Saphira settled in a small field with a jolt, and Eragon was puzzled to see the horses stopped and Murtagh kneeling, examining the ground. When

Eragon did not dismount, Murtagh hurried over and inquired, "What's wrong?" He sounded angry, worried, and tired at the same time.

". . . I made a mistake," said Eragon truthfully. "The Urgals have entered the valley. I tried to confuse them, but I forgot one of the rules of magic, and it cost me a great deal."

Scowling, Murtagh jerked his thumb over his shoulder. "I just found some wolf tracks, but the footprints are as wide as both of my hands and an inch deep. There are animals around here that could be dangerous even to you, Saphira." He turned to her. "I know you can't enter the forest, but could you circle above me and the horses? That should keep these beasts away. Otherwise there may only be enough left of me to roast in a thimble."

"Humor, Murtagh?" asked Eragon, a quick smile coming to his face. His muscles trembled, making it hard for him to concentrate.

"Only on the gallows." Murtagh rubbed his eyes. "I can't believe that the same Urgals have been following us the whole time. They would have to be birds to catch up with us."

"Saphira said they're larger than any we've seen," remarked Eragon.

Murtagh cursed, clenching the pommel of his sword. "That explains it! Saphira, if you're right, then those are Kull, elite of the Urgals. I should have guessed that the chieftain had been put in charge of them. They don't ride because horses can't carry their weight—not one of them is under eight feet tall—and they can run for days without sleep and still be ready for battle. It can take five men to kill one. Kull never leave their caves except for war, so they must expect a great slaughter if they are out in such force."

"Can we stay ahead of them?"

"Who knows?" said Murtagh. "They're strong, determined, and large in numbers. It's possible that we may have to face them. If that happens, I only hope that the Varden have men posted nearby who'll help us. Despite our skill and Saphira, we can't hold off Kull."

Eragon swayed. "Could you get me some bread? I need to eat." Murtagh quickly brought him part of a loaf. It was old and hard, but Eragon chewed on it gratefully. Murtagh scanned the valley walls, worry in his eyes. Eragon knew he was searching for a way out. "There'll be one farther in."

"Of course," said Murtagh with forced optimism, then slapped his thigh. "We must go."

"How is Arya?" asked Eragon.

Murtagh shrugged. "The fever's worse. She's been tossing and turning. What do you expect? Her strength is failing. You should fly her to the Varden before the poison does any more damage."

"I won't leave you behind," insisted Eragon,

gaining strength with each bite. "Not with the Urgals so near."

Murtagh shrugged again. "As you wish. But I'm warning you, she won't live if you stay with me."

"Don't say that," insisted Eragon, pushing himself upright in Saphira's saddle. "Help me save her. We can still do it. Consider it a life for a life—atonement for Torkenbrand's death."

Murtagh's face darkened instantly. "It's not a debt owed. You—" He stopped as a horn echoed through the dark forest. "I'll have more to say to you later," he said shortly, stomping to the horses. He grabbed their reins and trotted away, shooting an angry glare at Eragon.

Eragon closed his eyes as Saphira took flight. He wished that he could lie on a soft bed and forget all their troubles. *Saphira,* he said at last, cupping his ears to warm them, *what if we did take Arya to the Varden? Once she was safe, we could fly back to Murtagh and help him out of here.*

The Varden wouldn't let you, said Saphira. *For all they know, you might be returning to inform the Urgals of their hiding place. We aren't arriving under the best conditions to gain their trust. They'll want to know why we've brought an entire company of Kull to their very gates.*

We'll just have to tell them the truth and hope they believe us, said Eragon.

And what will we do if the Kull attack Murtagh?

Fight them, of course! I won't let him and Arya be captured or killed, said Eragon indignantly.

There was a touch of sarcasm in her words. *How noble. Oh, we would fell many of the Urgals— you with magic and blade, whilst my weapons would be tooth and claw—but it would be futile in the end. They are too numerous. . . . We cannot defeat them, only be defeated.*

What, then? he demanded. *I'll not leave Arya or Murtagh to their mercy.*

Saphira waved her tail, the tip whistling loudly. *I'm not asking you to. However, if we attack first, we may gain the advantage.*

Have you gone crazy? They'll . . . Eragon's voice trailed off as he thought about it. *They won't be able to do a thing,* he concluded, surprised.

Exactly, said Saphira. *We can inflict lots of damage from a safe height.*

Let's drop rocks on them! proposed Eragon. *That should scatter them.*

If their skulls aren't thick enough to protect them. Saphira banked to the right and quickly descended to the Beartooth River. She grasped a mid-sized boulder with her strong talons while Eragon scooped up several fist-sized rocks. Laden with the stones, Saphira glided on silent wings until they were over the Urgal host. *Now!* she exclaimed, releasing the boulder. There were muffled cracks as the missiles plummeted through the forest top, smashing branches. A second later howls echoed through the valley.

Eragon smiled tightly as he heard the Urgals scramble for cover. *Let's find more ammunition,*

533

he suggested, bending low over Saphira. She growled in agreement and returned to the riverbed.

It was hard work, but they were able to hinder the Urgals' progress—though it was impossible to stop them altogether. The Urgals gained ground whenever Saphira went for stones. Despite that, their efforts allowed Murtagh to stay ahead of the advancing column.

The valley darkened as the hours slipped by. Without the sun to provide warmth, the sharp bite of frost crept into the air and the ground mist froze on the trees, coating them white. Night animals began to creep from their dens to peer from shadowed hideouts at the strangers trespassing on their land.

Eragon continued to examine the mountainsides, searching for the waterfall that would signify the end of their journey. He was painfully aware that every passing minute brought Arya closer to death. "Faster, faster," he muttered to himself, looking down at Murtagh. Before Saphira scooped up more rocks, he said, *Let's take a respite and check on Arya. The day is almost over, and I'm afraid her life is measured in hours, if not minutes.*

Arya's life is in Fate's hands now. You made your choice to stay with Murtagh; it's too late to change that, so stop agonizing over it. . . . You're making my scales itch. The best thing we can do right now is to keep bombarding the Urgals. Eragon knew she was right, yet her words did nothing to calm his anxiety. He resumed his search for the waterfall, but whatever lay before them was hidden by a thick mountain ridge.

True darkness began to fill the valley, settling over the trees and mountains like an inky cloud. Even with her keen hearing and delicate sense of smell, Saphira could no longer locate the Urgals through the dense forest. There was no moon to help them; it would be hours before it rose above the mountains.

Saphira made a long, gentle left turn and glided around the mountain ridge. Eragon vaguely sensed it pass by them, then squinted as he saw a faint white line ahead. *Could that be the waterfall?* he wondered.

He looked at the sky, which still held the afterglow of sunset. The mountains' dark silhouettes curved together and formed a rough bowl that closed off the valley. *The head of the valley isn't much farther!* he exclaimed, pointing at the mountains. *Do you think that the Varden know we're coming? Maybe they'll send men out to help us.*

I doubt they'll assist us until they know if we are friend or foe, Saphira said as she abruptly dropped toward the ground. *I'm returning to Murtagh—we should stay with him now. Since I can't find the Urgals, they could sneak up on him without us knowing.*

Eragon loosened Zar'roc in its sheath, wondering if he was strong enough to fight. Saphira landed to the left of the Beartooth River, then crouched expectantly. The waterfall rumbled in the distance. *He comes,* she said. Eragon strained his ears and caught the sound of pounding hooves. Murtagh ran out of the forest, driving the horses before him. He saw them but did not slow.

Eragon jumped off Saphira, stumbling a bit as he matched Murtagh's pace. Behind him Saphira went to the river so she could follow them without being hindered by the trees. Before Eragon could relay his news, Murtagh said, "I saw you dropping rocks with Saphira—ambitious. Have the Kull stopped or turned back?"

"They're still behind us, but we're almost to the head of the valley. How's Arya?"

"She hasn't died," Murtagh said harshly. His breath came in short bursts. His next words were deceptively calm, like those of a man concealing a terrible passion. "Is there a valley or gorge ahead that I can leave through?"

Apprehensive, Eragon tried to remember if he had seen any breaks in the mountains around them; he had not thought about Murtagh's dilemma for a while. "It's dark," he began evasively, dodging a low branch, "so I might have missed something, but . . . no."

Murtagh swore explosively and came to an abrupt stop, dragging on the horses' reins until they halted as well. "Are you saying that the only place I can go is to the Varden?"

"Yes, but keep running. The Urgals are almost upon us!"

"No!" said Murtagh angrily. He stabbed a finger at Eragon. "I warned you that I wouldn't go to the Varden, but you went ahead and trapped me between a hammer and an anvil! You're the one with the elf's memories. Why didn't you tell me this was a dead end?"

Eragon bristled at the barrage and retorted, "All I knew was where we had to go, not what lay in between. Don't blame me for choosing to come."

Murtagh's breath hissed between his teeth as he furiously spun away. All Eragon could see of him was a motionless, bowed figure. His own shoulders were tense, and a vein throbbed on the side of his neck. He put his hands on his hips, impatience rising.

Why have you stopped? asked Saphira, alarmed.

Don't distract me. "What's your quarrel with the Varden? It can't be so terrible that you must keep it hidden even now. Would you rather fight the Kull than reveal it? How many times will we go through this before you trust me?"

There was a long silence.

The Urgals! reminded Saphira urgently.

I know, said Eragon, pushing back his temper. *But we have to resolve this.*

Quickly, quickly.

"Murtagh," said Eragon earnestly, "unless you wish to die, we must go to the Varden. Don't let me walk into their arms without knowing how they will react to you. It's going to be dangerous enough without unnecessary surprises."

Finally Murtagh turned to Eragon. His breathing was hard and fast, like that of a cornered wolf. He paused, then said with a tortured voice, "You have a right to know. I . . . I am the son of Morzan, first and last of the Forsworn."

THE HORNS OF
A DILEMMA

Eragon was speechless. Disbelief roared through his mind as he tried to reject Murtagh's words. *The Forsworn never had any children, least of all Morzan. Morzan! The man who betrayed the Riders to Galbatorix and remained the king's favorite servant for the rest of his life. Could it be true?*

Saphira's own shock reached him a second later. She crashed through trees and brush as she barreled from the river to his side, fangs bared, tail raised threateningly. *Be ready for anything,* she warned. *He may be able to use magic.*

"You are his heir?" asked Eragon, surreptitiously reaching for Zar'roc. *What could he want with me? Is he really working for the king?*

"I didn't choose this!" cried Murtagh, anguish twisting his face. He ripped at his clothes with a desperate air, tearing off his tunic and shirt to bare his torso. "Look!" he pleaded, and turned his back to Eragon.

Unsure, Eragon leaned forward, straining his eyes in the darkness. There, against Murtagh's tanned and muscled skin, was a knotted white scar that stretched from his right shoulder to his left hip—a testament to some terrible agony.

"See that?" demanded Murtagh bitterly. He talked quickly now, as if relieved to have his secret finally revealed. "I was only three when I got it. During one of his many drunken rages, Morzan threw his sword at me as I ran by. My back was laid open by the very sword you now carry—the only thing I expected to receive as inheritance, until Brom stole it from my father's corpse. I was lucky, I suppose—there was a healer nearby who kept me from dying. You must understand, I don't love the Empire or the king. I have no allegiance to them, nor do I mean you harm!" His pleas were almost frantic.

Eragon uneasily lifted his hand from Zar'roc's pommel. "Then your father," he said in a faltering voice, "was killed by . . ."

"Yes, Brom," said Murtagh. He pulled his tunic back on with a detached air.

A horn rang out behind them, prompting Eragon to cry, "Come, run with me." Murtagh shook the horses' reins and forced them into a tired trot, eyes fixed straight ahead, while Arya bounced limply in Snowfire's saddle. Saphira stayed by Eragon's side, easily keeping pace with her long legs. *You could walk unhindered in the riverbed*, he said as she was forced to smash through a dense web of branches.

I'll not leave you with him.

Eragon was glad for her protection. *Morzan's son!* He said between strides, "Your tale is hard to believe. How do I know you aren't lying?"

"Why would I lie?"

"You could be—"

Murtagh interrupted him quickly. "I can't prove anything to you now. Keep your doubts until we reach the Varden. They'll recognize me quickly enough."

"I must know," pressed Eragon. "Do you serve the Empire?"

"No. And if I did, what would I accomplish by traveling with you? If I were trying to capture or kill you, I would have left you in prison." Murtagh stumbled as he jumped over a fallen log.

"You could be leading the Urgals to the Varden."

"Then," said Murtagh shortly, "why am I still with you? I know where the Varden are now. What reason could I have for delivering myself to them? If I were going to attack them, I'd turn around and join the Urgals."

"Maybe you're an assassin," stated Eragon flatly.

"Maybe. You can't really know, can you?"

541

Saphira? Eragon asked simply.

Her tail swished over his head. *If he wanted to harm you, he could have done it long ago.*

A branch whipped Eragon's neck, causing a line of blood to appear on his skin. The waterfall was growing louder. *I want you to watch Murtagh closely when we get to the Varden. He may do something foolish, and I don't want him killed by accident.*

I'll do my best, she said as she shouldered her way between two trees, scraping off slabs of bark. The horn sounded behind them again. Eragon glanced over his shoulder, expecting Urgals to rush out of the darkness. The waterfall throbbed dully ahead of them, drowning out the sounds of the night.

542   The forest ended, and Murtagh pulled the horses to a stop. They were on a pebble beach directly to the left of the mouth of the Beartooth River. The deep lake Kóstha-mérna filled the valley, blocking their way. The water gleamed with flickering starlight. The mountain walls restricted passage around Kóstha-mérna to a thin strip of shore on either side of the lake, both no more than a few steps wide. At the lake's far end, a broad sheet of water tumbled down a black cliff into boiling mounds of froth.

"Do we go to the falls?" asked Murtagh tightly.

"Yes." Eragon took the lead and picked his way along the lake's left side. The pebbles underfoot were damp and slime covered. There was barely enough room for Saphira between the sheer valley wall and the lake; she had to walk with two feet in the water.

They were halfway to the waterfall when Murtagh warned, "Urgals!"

Eragon whirled around, rocks spraying from under his heel. By the shore of Kóstha-mérna, where they had been only minutes before, hulking figures streamed out of the forest. The Urgals massed before the lake. One of them gestured at Saphira; guttural words drifted over the water. Immediately the horde split and started around both sides of the lake, leaving Eragon and Murtagh without an escape route. The narrow shore forced the bulky Kull to march single file.

"Run!" barked Murtagh, drawing his sword and slapping the horses on their flanks. Saphira took off without warning and wheeled back toward the Urgals.

"No!" cried Eragon, shouting with his mind, *Come back!* but she continued, heedless to his pleas. With an agonizing effort, he tore his gaze from her and plunged forward, wrenching Zar'roc from its sheath.

Saphira dived at the Urgals, bellowing fiercely. They tried to scatter but were trapped against the mountainside. She caught a Kull between her talons and carried the screaming creature aloft, tearing at him with her fangs. The silent body crashed into the lake a moment later, an arm and a leg missing.

The Kull continued around Kóstha-mérna

undeterred. With smoke streaming from her nostrils, Saphira dived at them again. She twisted and rolled as a cloud of black arrows shot toward her. Most of the darts glanced off her scaled sides, leaving no more than bruises, but she roared as the rest pierced her wings.

Eragon's arms twinged with sympathetic pain, and he had to restrain himself from rushing to her defense. Fear flooded his veins as he saw the line of Urgals closing in on them. He tried to run faster, but his muscles were too tired, the rocks too slippery.

Then, with a loud splash, Saphira plunged into Kóstha-mérna. She submerged completely, sending ripples across the lake. The Urgals nervously eyed the dark water lapping their feet. One growled something indecipherable and jabbed his spear at the lake.

The water exploded as Saphira's head shot out of the depths. Her jaws closed on the spear, breaking it like a twig as she tore it out of the Kull's hands with a vicious twist. Before she could seize the Urgal himself, his companions thrust at her with their spears, bloodying her nose.

Saphira jerked back and hissed angrily, beating the water with her tail. Keeping his spear pointed at her, the lead Kull tried to edge past, but halted when she snapped at his legs. The string of Urgals was forced to stop as she held him at bay. Meanwhile, the Kull on the other side of the lake still hurried toward the falls.

I've trapped them, she told Eragon tersely, *but hurry—I cannot hold them long*. Archers on the shore were already taking aim at her. Eragon concentrated on going faster, but a rock gave under his boot and he pitched forward. Murtagh's strong arm kept him on his feet, and clasping each other's forearms, they urged the horses forward with shouts.

They were almost to the waterfall. The noise was overwhelming, like an avalanche. A white wall of water gushed down the cliff, pounding the rocks below with a fury that sent mist spraying through the air to run down their faces. Four yards from the thunderous curtain, the beach widened, giving them room to maneuver.

Saphira roared as an Urgal spear grazed her haunch, then retreated underwater. With her withdrawal the Kull rushed forward with long strides. They were only a few hundred feet away. "What do we do now?" Murtagh demanded coldly.

"I don't know. Let me think!" cried Eragon, searching Arya's memories for her final instructions. He scanned the ground until he found a rock the size of an apple, grabbed it, then pounded on the cliff next to the falls, shouting, "Aí varden abr du Shur'tugalar gata vanta!"

Nothing happened.

He tried again, shouting louder than before, but only succeeded in bruising his hand. He turned in despair to Murtagh. "We're trap—" His words were cut off as Saphira leapt out of the lake, dousing them with icy water. She landed on the beach and crouched, ready to fight.

The horses backpedaled wildly, trying to bolt. Eragon reached out with his mind to steady them. *Behind you!* cried Saphira. He turned and glimpsed the lead Urgal running at him, heavy spear raised. Up close a Kull was as tall as a small giant, with legs and arms as thick as tree trunks.

Murtagh drew back his arm and threw his sword with incredible speed. The long weapon revolved once, then struck the Kull point first in the chest with a dull crunch. The huge Urgal toppled to the ground with a strangled gurgle. Before another Kull could attack, Murtagh dashed forward and yanked his sword out of the body.

Eragon raised his palm, shouting, "Jierda theirra kalfis!" Sharp cracks resounded off the cliff. Twenty of the charging Urgals fell into Kóstha-mérna, howling and clutching their legs where shards of bone protruded. Without breaking stride, the rest of the Urgals advanced over their fallen companions. Eragon struggled against his weariness, putting a hand on Saphira for support.

A flight of arrows, impossible to see in the

darkness, brushed past them and clattered against the cliff. Eragon and Murtagh ducked, covering their heads. With a small growl, Saphira jumped over them so that her armored sides shielded them and the horses. A chorus of clinks sounded as a second volley of arrows bounced off her scales.

"What now?" shouted Murtagh. There was still no opening in the cliff. "We can't stay here!"

Eragon heard Saphira snarl as an arrow caught the edge of her wing, tearing the thin membrane. He looked around wildly, trying to understand why Arya's instructions had not worked. "I don't know! This is where we're supposed to be!"

"Why don't you ask the elf to make sure?" demanded Murtagh. He dropped his sword, snatched his bow from Tornac's saddlebags, and with a swift motion loosed an arrow from between the spikes on Saphira's back. A moment later an Urgal toppled into the water.

"Now? She's barely alive! How's she going to find the energy to say anything?"

"I don't *know*," shouted Murtagh, "but you'd better think of *something* because we can't stave off an entire army!"

Eragon, growled Saphira urgently.

What!

We're on the wrong side of the lake! I've seen Arya's memories through you, and I just realized that this isn't the right place. She tucked her head against her breast as another flight of arrows sped toward them. Her tail flicked in pain as they struck her. *I can't keep this up! They're tearing me to pieces!*

Eragon slammed Zar'roc back into its sheath and exclaimed, "The Varden are on the other side of the lake. We have to go through the waterfall!" He noted with dread that the Urgals across Kósta-mérna were almost to the falls.

Murtagh's eyes shot toward the violent deluge blocking their way. "We'll never get the horses through there, even if we can hold our own footing."

"I'll convince them to follow us," snapped Eragon. "And Saphira can carry Arya." The Urgals' cries and bellows made Snowfire snort angrily. The elf lolled on his back, oblivious to the danger.

Murtagh shrugged. "It's better than being hacked to death." He swiftly cut Arya loose from Snowfire's saddle, and Eragon caught the elf as she slid to the ground.

I'm ready, said Saphira, rising into a half-crouch. The approaching Urgals hesitated, unsure of her intentions.

"Now!" cried Eragon. He and Murtagh heaved Arya onto Saphira, then secured her legs in the saddle's straps. The second they were finished, Saphira swept up her wings and soared over the lake. The Urgals behind her howled as they saw her escaping. Arrows clattered off her belly. The Kull on the other shore redoubled their pace so as to attain the waterfall before she landed.

Eragon reached out with his mind to force himself into the frightened thoughts of the horses. Using the ancient language, he told them that unless they swam through the waterfall, they would be killed and eaten by the Urgals. Though they did not understand everything he said, the meaning of his words was unmistakable.

Snowfire and Tornac tossed their heads, then dashed into the thundering downpour, whinnying as it struck their backs. They floundered, struggling to stay above water. Murtagh sheathed his sword and jumped after them; his head disappeared under a froth of bubbles before he bobbed up, sputtering. 549

The Urgals were right behind Eragon; he could hear their feet crunching on the gravel. With a fierce war cry he leapt after Murtagh, closing his eyes a second before the cold water pummeled him.

The tremendous weight of the waterfall slammed down on his shoulders with backbreaking force. The water's mindless roar filled his ears. He was driven to the bottom, where his knees gouged the rocky lakebed. He kicked off with all his strength and shot partway out of the water. Before he could take a gulp of air, the cascade rammed him back underwater.

All he could see was a white blur as foam billowed around him. He frantically tried to surface and relieve his burning lungs, but he only rose a few feet before the deluge halted his ascent. He panicked, thrashing his arms and legs, fighting the water. Weighed down by Zar'roc and his drenched clothes, he sank back to the lakebed, unable to speak the ancient words that could save him.

Suddenly a strong hand grasped the back of his tunic and dragged him through the water. His rescuer sliced through the lake with quick, short strokes; Eragon hoped it was Murtagh, not an Urgal. They surfaced and stumbled onto the pebble beach. Eragon was trembling violently; his entire body shivered in bursts.

Sounds of combat erupted to his right, and he whirled toward them, expecting an Urgal attack. The monsters on the opposite shore—where he had stood only moments before—fell beneath a withering hail of arrows from crevasses that pockmarked the cliff. Scores of Urgals already floated belly up in the water, riddled with shafts. The ones on Eragon's shore were similarly engaged. Neither group could retreat from their exposed positions, for rows of warriors had somehow appeared behind them, where the lake met the mountainsides. All that prevented the nearest Kull from rushing Eragon was the steady rain of arrows—the unseen archers seemed determined to keep the Urgals at bay.

A gruff voice next to Eragon said, "Akh Gûnteraz dorzada! What were they thinking? You would have drowned!" Eragon jerked with surprise. It was not Murtagh standing by him but a diminutive man no taller than his elbow.

The dwarf was busy wringing water out of his long braided beard. His chest was stocky, and he wore a chain-mail jacket cut off at the shoulders to reveal muscular arms. A war ax hung from a wide leather belt strapped around his waist. An iron-bound oxhide cap, bearing the symbol of a hammer surrounded by twelve stars, sat firmly on his head. Even with the cap, he barely topped four feet. He looked longingly at the fighting and said, "Barzûl, but I wish I could join them!"

A *dwarf!* Eragon drew Zar'roc and looked for 551 Saphira and Murtagh. Two twelve-foot-thick stone doors had opened in the cliff, revealing a broad tunnel nearly thirty feet tall that burrowed its way into the mysterious depths of the mountain. A line of flameless lamps filled the passageway with a pale sapphire light that spilled out onto the lake.

Saphira and Murtagh stood before the tunnel, surrounded by a grim mixture of men and dwarves. At Murtagh's elbow was a bald, beardless man dressed in purple and gold robes. He was taller than all the other humans—and he was holding a dagger to Murtagh's throat.

Eragon reached for his power, but the robed

man said in a sharp, dangerous voice, "Stop! If you use magic, I'll kill your lovely friend here, who was so kind as to mention you're a Rider. Don't think I won't know if you're drawing upon it. You can't hide anything from me." Eragon tried to speak, but the man snarled and pressed the dagger harder against Murtagh's throat. "None of that! If you say or do anything I don't tell you to, he will die. Now, everyone inside." He backed into the tunnel, pulling Murtagh with him and keeping his eyes on Eragon.

Saphira, what should I do? Eragon asked quickly as the men and dwarves followed Murtagh's captor, leading the horses along with them.

Go with them, she counseled, *and hope that we live.* She entered the tunnel herself, eliciting nervous glances from those around her. Reluctantly, Eragon followed her, aware that the warriors' eyes were upon him. His rescuer, the dwarf, walked alongside him with a hand on the haft of his war ax.

Utterly exhausted, Eragon staggered into the mountain. The stone doors swung shut behind them with only a whisper of sound. He looked back and saw a seamless wall where the opening had been. They were trapped inside. But were they any safer?

HUNTING FOR ANSWERS

"This way," snapped the bald man. He stepped back, keeping the dagger pressed under Murtagh's chin, then wheeled to the right, disappearing through an arched doorway. The warriors cautiously followed him, their attention centered on Eragon and Saphira. The horses were led into a different tunnel.

Dazed by the turn of events, Eragon started after Murtagh. He glanced at Saphira to confirm that Arya was still tied to her back. *She has to get the antidote!* he thought frantically, knowing that even then the Skilna Bragh was fulfilling its deadly purpose within her flesh.

He hurried through the arched doorway and down a narrow corridor after the bald man. The warriors kept their weapons pointed at him. They swept past a sculpture of a peculiar animal with thick quills. The corridor curved sharply to the left, then to the right. A door opened and they entered a bare room large enough for Saphira to move around with ease. There was a hollow boom as the door closed, followed by a loud scrape as a bolt was secured on the outside.

Eragon slowly examined his surroundings, Zar'roc tight in his hand. The walls, floor, and ceiling were made of polished white marble that reflected a ghost image of everyone, like a mirror of veined milk. One of the unusual lanterns hung in each corner. "There's an injured—" he began, but a sharp gesture from the bald man cut him off.

"Do not speak! It must wait until you have been tested." He shoved Murtagh over to one of the warriors, who pressed a sword against Murtagh's neck. The bald man clasped his hands together softly. "Remove your weapons and slide them to me." A dwarf unbuckled Murtagh's sword and dropped it on the floor with a clank.

Loath to be parted with Zar'roc, Eragon unfastened the sheath and set it and the blade on the floor. He placed his bow and quiver next to them, then pushed the pile toward the warriors. "Now step away from your dragon and slowly approach me," commanded the bald man.

Puzzled, Eragon moved forward. When they were a yard apart, the man said, "Stop there! Now remove the defenses from around your mind and prepare to let me inspect your thoughts and memories. If you try to hide anything from me, I will take what I want by force . . . which would drive you mad. If you don't submit, your companion will be killed."

"Why?" asked Eragon, aghast.

"To be sure you aren't in Galbatorix's service and to understand why hundreds of Urgals are banging on our front door," growled the bald man. His close-set eyes shifted from point to point with cunning speed. "No one may enter Farthen Dûr without being tested."

"There isn't time. We need a healer!" protested Eragon.

"Silence!" roared the man, pressing down his robe with thin fingers. "Until you are examined, your words are meaningless!"

"But she's dying!" retorted Eragon angrily, pointing at Arya. They were in a precarious position, but he would let nothing else happen until Arya was cared for.

"It will have to wait! No one will leave this room until we have discovered the truth of this matter. Unless you wish—"

The dwarf who had saved Eragon from the lake jumped forward. "Are you blind, Egraz Carn? Can't you see that's an elf on the dragon? We cannot keep her here if she's in danger. Ajihad and the king will have our heads if she's allowed to die!"

The man's eyes tightened with anger. After a moment he relaxed and said smoothly, "Of course, Orik, we wouldn't want that to happen." He snapped his fingers and pointed at Arya. "Remove her from the dragon." Two human warriors sheathed their swords and hesitantly approached Saphira, who watched them steadily. "Quickly, quickly!"

The men unstrapped Arya from the saddle and lowered the elf to the floor. One of the men inspected her face, then said sharply, "It's the dragon-egg courier, Arya!"

"What?" exclaimed the bald man. The dwarf Orik's eyes widened with astonishment. The bald man fixed his steely gaze on Eragon and said flatly, "You have much explaining to do."

Eragon returned the intense stare with all the determination he could muster. "She was poisoned with the Skilna Bragh while in prison. Only Tunivor's Nectar can save her now."

The bald man's face became inscrutable. He stood motionless, except for his lips, which twitched occasionally. "Very well. Take her to the healers, and tell them what she needs. Guard her until the ceremony is completed. I will have new orders for you by then." The warriors nodded curtly and carried Arya out of the room. Eragon watched them go, wishing that he could accompany her. His attention snapped back to the bald man as he said, "Enough of this, we have wasted too much time already. Prepare to be examined."

Eragon did not want this hairless threatening man inside his mind, laying bare his every thought and feeling, but he knew that resistance would be useless. The air was strained. Murtagh's gaze burned into his forehead. Finally he bowed his head. "I am ready."

"Good, then—"

He was interrupted as Orik said abruptly, "You'd better not harm him, Egraz Carn, else the king will have words for you."

The bald man looked at him irritably, then faced Eragon with a small smile. "Only if he resists." He bowed his head and chanted several inaudible words.

Eragon gasped with pain and shock as a mental probe clawed its way into his mind. His eyes rolled up into his head, and he automatically began throwing up barriers around his consciousness. The attack was incredibly powerful.

Don't do that! cried Saphira. Her thoughts joined his, filling him with strength. *You're putting Murtagh at risk!* Eragon faltered, gritted his teeth, then forced himself to remove his shielding, exposing himself to the ravening probe. Disappointment emanated from the bald man. His battering intensified. The force coming from his mind felt decayed and unwholesome; there was something profoundly wrong about it.

He wants me to fight him! cried Eragon as a fresh wave of pain racked him. A second later it subsided, only to be replaced by another. Saphira did her best to suppress it, but even she could not block it entirely.

Give him what he wants, she said quickly, *but protect everything else. I'll help you. His strength is no match for mine; I'm already shielding our words from him.*

Then why does it still hurt?

The pain comes from you.

Eragon winced as the probe dug in farther, hunting for information, like a nail being driven through his skull. The bald man roughly seized his childhood memories and began sifting through them. *He doesn't need those—get him out of there!* growled Eragon angrily.

I can't, not without endangering you, said Saphira. *I can conceal things from his view, but it must be done before he reaches them. Think quickly, and tell me what you want hidden!*

Eragon tried to concentrate through the pain. He raced through his memories, starting from when he had found Saphira's egg. He hid sections of his discussions with Brom, including all the ancient words he had been taught. Their travels through Palancar Valley, Yazuac, Daret, and Teirm he left mostly untouched. But he had Saphira conceal everything he remembered of Angela's fortunetelling and Solembum. He skipped from their burglary at Teirm, to Brom's death, to his imprisonment in Gil'ead, and lastly to Murtagh's revelation of his true identity.

Eragon wanted to hide that as well, but Saphira balked. *The Varden have a right to know who they shelter under their roof, especially if it's a son of the Forsworn!*

Just do it, he said tightly, fighting another wave of agony. *I won't be the one to unmask him, at least not to this man.*

It'll be discovered as soon as Murtagh is scanned, warned Saphira sharply.

Just do it.

With the most important information hidden, there was nothing else for Eragon to do but wait for the bald man to finish his inspection. It was like sitting still while his fingernails were extracted with rusty tongs. His entire body was rigid, jaw locked tightly. Heat radiated from his skin, and a line of sweat rolled down his neck. He was acutely aware of each second as the long minutes crept by.

The bald man wound through his experiences sluggishly, like a thorny vine pushing its way toward the sunlight. He paid keen attention to many things Eragon considered irrelevant, such as his mother, Selena, and seemed to linger on purpose so as to prolong the suffering. He spent a long time examining Eragon's recollections of the Ra'zac, and then later the Shade. It was not until his adventures had been exhaustively analyzed that the bald man began to withdraw from Eragon's mind.

The probe was extracted like a splinter being removed. Eragon shuddered, swayed, then fell toward the floor. Strong arms caught him at the last second, lowering him to the cool marble. He heard Orik exclaim from behind him, "You went too far! He wasn't strong enough for this."

"He'll live. That's all that is needed," answered the bald man curtly.

There was an angry grunt. "What did you find?"

Silence.

"Well, is he to be trusted or not?"

The words came reluctantly. "He . . . is not your enemy." There were audible sighs of relief throughout the room.

Eragon's eyes fluttered open. He gingerly pushed himself upright. "Easy now," said Orik, wrapping a thick arm around him and helping him to his feet. Eragon wove unsteadily, glaring at the bald man. A low growl rumbled in Saphira's throat.

The bald man ignored them. He turned to Murtagh, who was still being held at sword point. "It's your turn now."

Murtagh stiffened and shook his head. The sword cut his neck slightly. Blood dripped down his skin. "No."

"You will not be protected here if you refuse."

"Eragon has been declared trustworthy, so you cannot threaten to kill him to influence me. Since you can't do that, nothing you say or do will convince me to open my mind."

Sneering, the bald man cocked what would have been an eyebrow, if he had any. "What of your own life? I can still threaten that."

"It won't do any good," said Murtagh stonily and with such conviction that it was impossible to doubt his word.

The bald man's breath exploded angrily. "You don't have a choice!" He stepped forward and placed his palm on Murtagh's brow, clenching his hand to hold him in place. Murtagh stiffened, face growing as hard as iron, fists clenched, neck muscles bulging. He was obviously fighting the attack with all his strength. The bald man bared his teeth with fury and frustration at the resistance; his fingers dug mercilessly into Murtagh.

Eragon winced in sympathy, knowing the battle that raged between them. *Can't you help him?* he asked Saphira.

No, she said softly. *He will allow no one into his mind.*

Orik scowled darkly as he watched the combatants. "Ilf carnz orodûm," he muttered, then leapt forward and cried, "That is enough!" He grabbed the bald man's arm and tore him away from Murtagh with strength disproportional to his size.

The bald man stumbled back, then turned on

Orik furiously. "How dare you!" he shouted. "You questioned my leadership, opened the gates without permission, and now this! You've shown nothing but insolence and treachery. Do you think your king will protect you now?"

Orik bristled. "You would have let them die! If I had waited any longer, the Urgals would have killed them." He pointed at Murtagh, whose breath came in great heaves. "We don't have any right to torture him for information! Ajihad won't sanction it. Not after you've examined the Rider and found him free of fault. *And* they've brought us Arya."

"Would you allow him to enter unchallenged? Are you so great a fool as to put us all at risk?" demanded the bald man. His eyes were feral with loosely chained rage; he looked ready to tear the dwarf into pieces.

"Can he use magic?"

"That is—"

"Can he use magic?" roared Orik, his deep voice echoing in the room. The bald man's face suddenly grew expressionless. He clasped his hands behind his back.

"No."

"Then what do you fear? It's impossible for him to escape, and he can't work any devilry with all of us here, especially if your powers are as great as you say. But don't listen to me; ask Ajihad what he wants done."

The bald man stared at Orik for a moment, his face indecipherable, then looked at the ceiling and closed his eyes. A peculiar stiffness set into his shoulders while his lips moved soundlessly. An intense frown wrinkled the pale skin above his eyes, and his fingers clenched, as if they were throttling an invisible enemy. For several minutes he stood thus, wrapped in silent communication.

When his eyes opened, he ignored Orik and snapped at the warriors, "Leave, now!" As they filed through the doorway, he addressed Eragon coldly, "Because I was unable to complete my examination, you and . . . your friend will remain here for the night. He will be killed if he attempts to leave." With those words he turned on his heel and stalked out of the room, pale scalp gleaming in the lantern light.

"Thank you," whispered Eragon to Orik.

The dwarf grunted. "I'll make sure some food is brought." He muttered a string of words under his breath, then left, shaking his head. The bolt was secured once again on the outside of the door.

Eragon sat, feeling strangely dreamy from the day's excitement and their forced march. His eyelids were heavy. Saphira settled next to him. *We must be careful. It seems we have as many enemies here as we did in the Empire.* He nodded, too tired to talk.

Murtagh, eyes glazed and empty, leaned against the far wall and slid to the shiny floor. He held his sleeve against the cut on his neck to stop the bleeding. "Are you all right?" asked Eragon. Murtagh nodded jerkily. "Did he get anything from you?"

"No."

"How were you able to keep him out? He's so strong."

"I've . . . I've been well trained." There was a bitter note to his voice.

Silence enshrouded them. Eragon's gaze drifted to one of the lanterns hanging in a corner. His thoughts meandered until he abruptly said, "I didn't let them know who you are."

Murtagh looked relieved. He bowed his head. "Thank you for not betraying me."

"They didn't recognize you."

"No."

"And you still say that you are Morzan's son?"

"Yes," he sighed.

Eragon started to speak, but stopped when he felt hot liquid splash onto his hand. He looked down and was startled to see a drop of dark blood roll off his skin. It had fallen from Saphira's wing. *I forgot. You're injured!* he exclaimed, getting up with an effort. *I'd better heal you.*

Be careful. It's easy to make mistakes when you're this tired.

I know. Saphira unfolded one of her wings and

lowered it to the floor. Murtagh watched as Eragon ran his hands over the warm blue membrane, saying, "Waíse heill," whenever he found an arrow hole. Luckily, all the wounds were relatively easy to heal, even those on her nose.

Task completed, Eragon slumped against Saphira, breathing hard. He could feel her great heart beating with the steady throb of life. "I hope they bring food soon," said Murtagh.

Eragon shrugged; he was too exhausted to be hungry. He crossed his arms, missing Zar'roc's weight by his side. "Why are you here?"

"What?"

"If you really are Morzan's son, Galbatorix wouldn't let you wander around Alagaësia freely. How is it that you managed to find the Ra'zac by yourself? Why is it I've never heard of any of the Forsworn having children? And what are you doing here?" His voice rose to a near shout at the end.

Murtagh ran his hands over his face. "It's a long story."

"We're not going anywhere," rebutted Eragon.

"It's too late to talk."

"There probably won't be time for it tomorrow."

Murtagh wrapped his arms around his legs and rested his chin on his knees, rocking back and forth as he stared at the floor. "It's not a—" he said, then interrupted himself. "I don't want to stop . . . so make yourself comfortable. My story will take a while." Eragon shifted against Saphira's side and nodded. Saphira watched both of them intently.

Murtagh's first sentence was halting, but his voice gained strength and confidence as he spoke. "As far as I know . . . I am the only child of the Thirteen Servants, or the Forsworn as they're called. There may be others, for the Thirteen had the skill to hide whatever they wanted, but I doubt it, for reasons I'll explain later.

"My parents met in a small village—I never learned where—while my father was traveling on the king's business. Morzan showed my mother some small kindness, no doubt a ploy to gain her confidence, and when he left, she accompanied him. They traveled together for a time, and as is the nature of these things, she fell deeply in love with him. Morzan was delighted to discover this not only because it gave him numerous opportunities to torment her but also because he recognized the advantage of having a servant who wouldn't betray him.

"Thus, when Morzan returned to Galbatorix's court, my mother became the tool he relied upon most. He used her to carry his secret messages, and he taught her rudimentary magic, which helped her remain undiscovered and, on occasion, extract information from people. He did his best to protect her from the rest of the Thirteen—not out of any feelings for her, but because they would have used her against him, given the chance. . . . For three years things proceeded in this manner, until my mother became pregnant."

Murtagh paused for a moment, fingering a lock of his hair. He continued in a clipped tone, "My father was, if nothing else, a cunning man. He knew that the pregnancy put both him and my mother in danger, not to mention the baby—that is, me. So, in the dead of night, he spirited her away from the palace and took her to his castle. Once there, he laid down powerful spells that prevented anyone from entering his estate except for a few chosen servants. In this way the pregnancy was kept secret from everyone but Galbatorix.

"Galbatorix knew the intimate details of the Thirteen's lives: their plots, their fights—and most importantly—their thoughts. He enjoyed watching them battle each other and often helped one or the other for his own amusement. But for some reason he never revealed my existence.

"I was born in due time and given to a wet nurse so my mother could return to Morzan's side. She had no choice in the matter. Morzan allowed her to visit me every few months, but otherwise we were kept apart. Another three years passed like this, during which time he gave me the . . . scar on my back." Murtagh brooded a minute before continuing.

"I would have grown to manhood in this fashion if Morzan hadn't been summoned away to hunt for Saphira's egg. As soon as he departed, my mother, who had been left behind, vanished. No one knows where she went, or why. The king tried to hunt her down, but his men couldn't find her trail—no doubt because of Morzan's training.

"At the time of my birth, only five of the Thirteen were still alive. By the time Morzan left, that number had been reduced to three; when he finally faced Brom in Gil'ead, he was the only one remaining. The Forsworn died through various means: suicide, ambush, overuse of magic . . . but it was mostly the work of the Varden. I'm told that the king was in a terrible rage because of those losses.

"However, before word of Morzan's and the others' deaths reached us, my mother returned. Many months had passed since she had disappeared. Her health was poor, as if she had suffered a great illness, and she grew steadily worse. Within a fortnight, she died."

"What happened then?" prompted Eragon.

Murtagh shrugged. "I grew up. The king brought me to the palace and arranged for my upbringing. Aside from that, he left me alone."

"Then why did you leave?"

A hard laugh broke from Murtagh. "Escaped is more like it. At my last birthday, when I turned eighteen, the king summoned me to his quarters for a private dinner. The message surprised me because I had always distanced myself from the court and had rarely met him. We'd talked before, but always within earshot of eavesdropping nobles.

"I accepted the offer, of course, aware that it would be unwise to refuse. The meal was sumptuous, but throughout it his black eyes never left me. His gaze was disconcerting; it seemed that he was searching for something hidden in my face. I didn't know what to make of it and did my best to provide polite conversation, but he refused to talk, and I soon ceased my efforts.

"When the meal was finished, he finally began to speak. You've never heard his voice, so it's hard for me to make you understand what it was like. His words were entrancing, like a snake whispering gilded lies into my ears. A more convincing and frightening man I've never heard. He wove a vision: a fantasy of the Empire as he imagined it. There would be beautiful cities built across the country, filled with the greatest warriors, artisans, musicians, and philosophers. The Urgals would finally be eradicated. And the Empire would expand in every direction until it reached the four corners of Alagaësia. Peace and prosperity would flourish, but more wondrous yet, the Riders would be brought back to gently govern over Galbatorix's fiefdoms.

"Entranced, I listened to him for what must

have been hours. When he stopped, I eagerly asked how the Riders would be reinstated, for everyone knew there were no dragon eggs left. Galbatorix grew still then and stared at me thoughtfully. For a long time he was silent, but then he extended his hand and asked, 'Will you, O son of my friend, serve me as I labor to bring about this paradise?'

"Though I knew the history behind his and my father's rise to power, the dream he had painted for me was too compelling, too seductive to ignore. Ardor for this mission filled me, and I fervently pledged myself to him. Obviously pleased, Galbatorix gave me his blessing, then dismissed me, saying, 'I shall call upon you when the need arises.'

"Several months passed before he did. When the summons came, I felt all of my old excitement return. We met in private as before, but this time he was not pleasant or charming. The Varden had just destroyed three brigades in the south, and his wrath was out in full force. He charged me in a terrible voice to take a detachment of troops and destroy Cantos, where rebels were known to hide occasionally. When I asked what we should do with the people there and how we would know if they were guilty, he shouted, 'They're all traitors! Burn them at the stake and bury their ashes with dung!' He continued to rant, cursing his enemies and describing how he would scourge the land of everyone who bore him ill will.

"His tone was so different from what I had encountered before; it made me realize he didn't possess the mercy or foresight to gain the people's loyalty, and he ruled only through brute force guided by his own passions. It was at that moment I determined to escape him and Urû'baen forever.

"As soon as I was free of his presence, I and my faithful servant, Tornac, made ready for flight. We left that very night, but somehow Galbatorix anticipated my actions, for there were soldiers waiting for us outside the gates. Ah, my sword was bloody, flashing in the dim lantern glow. We defeated the men . . . but in the process Tornac was killed.

571

"Alone and filled with grief, I fled to an old friend who sheltered me in his estate. While I hid, I listened carefully to every rumor, trying to predict Galbatorix's actions and plan my future. During that time, talk reached me that the Ra'zac had been sent to capture or kill someone. Remembering the king's plans for the Riders, I decided to find and follow the Ra'zac, just in case they *did* discover a dragon. And that's how I found you. . . . I have no more secrets."

We still don't know if he's telling the truth, warned Saphira.

I know, said Eragon, *but why would he lie to us?*

He might be mad.

I doubt it. Eragon ran a finger over Saphira's hard scales, watching the light reflect off them. "So why don't you join the Varden? They'll distrust you for a time, but once you prove your loyalty they'll treat you with respect. And aren't they in a sense your allies? They strive to end the king's reign. Isn't that what you want?"

"Must I spell everything out for you?" demanded Murtagh. "I don't want Galbatorix to learn where I am, which is inevitable if people start saying that I've sided with his enemies, which I've never done. These," he paused, then said with distaste, "*rebels* are trying not only to overthrow the king but to destroy the Empire . . . and I don't want that to happen. It would sow mayhem and anarchy. The king is flawed, yes, but the system itself is sound. As for earning the Varden's respect: Ha! Once I am exposed, they'll treat me like a criminal or worse. Not only that, suspicion will fall upon you because we traveled together!"

He's right, said Saphira.

Eragon ignored her. "It isn't that bad," he said, trying to sound optimistic. Murtagh snorted derisively and looked away. "I'm sure that they won't be—" His words were cut short as the door opened a hand's breadth and two bowls were pushed through the space. A loaf of bread and a hunk of raw meat followed, then the door was shut again.

"Finally!" grumbled Murtagh, going to the food. He tossed the meat to Saphira, who snapped it out of the air and swallowed it whole. Then he tore the loaf in two, gave half to Eragon, picked up his bowl, and retreated to a corner.

They ate silently. Murtagh jabbed at his food. "I'm going to sleep," he announced, putting down his bowl without another word.

"Good night," said Eragon. He lay next to Saphira, his arms under his head. She curled her long neck around him, like a cat wrapping its tail around itself, and laid her head alongside his. One of her wings extended over him like a blue tent, enveloping him in darkness.

Good night, little one.

A small smile lifted Eragon's lips, but he was already asleep.

THE GLORY
OF TRONJHEIM

Eragon jolted upright as a growl sounded in his ear. Saphira was still asleep, her eyes wandering sightlessly under her eyelids, 574 and her upper lip trembled, as if she were going to snarl. He smiled, then jerked as she growled again.

She must be dreaming, he realized. He watched her for a minute, then carefully slid out from under her wing. He stood and stretched. The room was cool, but not unpleasantly so. Murtagh lay on his back in the far corner, his eyes closed.

As Eragon stepped around Saphira, Murtagh stirred. "Morning," he said quietly, sitting up.

"How long have you been awake?" asked Eragon in a hushed voice.

"Awhile. I'm surprised Saphira didn't wake you sooner."

"I was tired enough to sleep through a thunderstorm," said Eragon wryly. He sat by Murtagh and rested his head against the wall. "Do you know what time it is?"

"No. It's impossible to tell in here."

"Has anyone come to see us?"

"Not yet."

They sat together without moving or speaking. Eragon felt oddly bound to Murtagh. *I've been carrying his father's sword, which would have been his . . . his inheritance. We're alike in many ways, yet our outlook and upbringing are totally different.* He thought of Murtagh's scar and shivered. *What man could do that to a child?*

Saphira lifted her head and blinked to clear her eyes. She sniffed the air, then yawned expansively, her rough tongue curling at the tip. *Has anything happened?* Eragon shook his head. *I hope they give me more food than that snack last night. I'm hungry enough to eat a herd of cows.*

They'll feed you, he assured her.

They'd better. She positioned herself near the door and settled down to wait, tail flicking. Eragon closed his eyes, enjoying the rest. He dozed awhile, then got up and paced around. Bored, he examined one of the lanterns. It was made of a single piece of teardrop-shaped glass, about twice the size of a lemon, and filled with soft blue light that neither wavered nor flickered. Four slim metal ribs wrapped smoothly around the glass, meeting at the top to form a small hook and again at the bottom where they melded together into three graceful legs. The whole piece was quite attractive.

Eragon's inspection was interrupted by voices outside the room. The door opened, and a dozen warriors marched inside. The first man gulped when he saw Saphira. They were followed by Orik and the bald man, who declared, "You have been summoned to Ajihad, leader of the Varden. If you must eat, do so while we march." Eragon and Murtagh stood together, watching him warily.

"Where are our horses? And can I have my sword and bow back?" asked Eragon.

The bald man looked at him with disdain. "Your weapons will be returned to you when Ajihad sees fit, not before. As for your horses, they await you in the tunnel. Now come!"

As he turned to leave, Eragon asked quickly, "How is Arya?"

The bald man hesitated. "I do not know. The healers are still with her." He exited the room, accompanied by Orik.

One of the warriors motioned. "You go first." Eragon went through the doorway, followed by Saphira and Murtagh. They returned through the corridor they had traversed the night before, passing the statue of the quilled animal. When they reached the huge tunnel through which they had first entered the mountain, the bald man was waiting with Orik, who held Tornac's and Snowfire's reins.

"You will ride single file down the center of the tunnel," instructed the bald man. "If you attempt to go anywhere else, you will be stopped." When Eragon started to climb onto Saphira, the bald man shouted, "No! Ride your horse until I tell you otherwise."

Eragon shrugged and took Snowfire's reins. He swung into the saddle, guided Snowfire in front of Saphira, and told her, *Stay close in case I need your help.*

Of course, she said.

Murtagh mounted Tornac behind Saphira. The bald man examined their small line, then gestured at the warriors, who divided in half to surround them, giving Saphira as wide a berth as possible. Orik and the bald man went to the head of the procession.

After looking them over once more, the bald man clapped twice and started walking forward. Eragon tapped Snowfire lightly on his flanks. The entire group headed toward the heart of the mountain. Echoes filled the tunnel as the horses' hooves struck the hard floor, the sounds amplified in the deserted passageway. Doors and gates occasionally disturbed the smooth walls, but they were always closed.

Eragon marveled at the sheer size of the tunnel, which had been mined with incredible skill—the walls, floor, and ceiling were crafted with flawless precision. The angles at the bases of the walls were perfectly square, and as far as he could tell, the tunnel itself did not vary from its course by even an inch.

As they proceeded, Eragon's anticipation about meeting Ajihad increased. The leader of the Varden was a shadowy figure to the people within the Empire. He had risen to power nearly twenty years ago and since then had waged a fierce war against King Galbatorix. No one knew where he came from or even what he looked like. It was rumored that he was a master strategist, a brutal fighter. With such a reputation, Eragon worried about how they would be received. Still, knowing that Brom had trusted the Varden enough to serve them helped to allay his fears.

Seeing Orik again had brought forth new questions in his mind. The tunnel was obviously dwarf work—no one else could mine with such skill—but were the dwarves part of the Varden, or were they merely sheltering them? And who was the king that Orik had mentioned? Was it Ajihad? Eragon understood now that the Varden had been able to escape discovery by hiding underground, but what about the elves? Where were they?

For nearly an hour the bald man led them through the tunnel, never straying nor turning.

We've probably already gone a league, Eragon realized. *Maybe they're taking us all the way through the mountain!* At last a soft white glow became visible ahead of them. He strained his eyes, trying to discern its source, but it was still too far away to make out any details. The glow increased in strength as they neared it.

Now he could see thick marble pillars laced with rubies and amethysts standing in rows along the walls. Scores of lanterns hung between the pillars, suffusing the air with liquid brilliance. Gold tracery gleamed from the pillars' bases like molten thread. Arching over the ceiling were carved raven heads, their beaks open in midscreech. At the end of the hallway rested two colossal black doors, accented by shimmering silver lines that depicted a seven-pointed crown that spanned both sides.

The bald man stopped and raised a hand. He turned to Eragon. "You will ride upon your dragon now. Do not attempt to fly away. There will be people watching, so remember who and what you are."

Eragon dismounted Snowfire, and then clambered onto Saphira's back. *I think they want to show us off*, she said as he settled into the saddle.

We'll see. I wish I had Zar'roc, he replied, tightening the straps around his legs.

It might be better that you aren't wearing Morzan's sword when the Varden first see you.

True. "I'm ready," Eragon said, squaring his shoulders.

"Good," said the bald man. He and Orik retreated to either side of Saphira, staying far enough back so she was clearly in the lead. "Now walk to the doors, and once they open, follow the path. Go slowly."

Ready? asked Eragon.

Of course. Saphira approached the doors at a measured pace. Her scales sparkled in the light, sending glints of color dancing over the pillars. Eragon took a deep breath to steady his nerves.

Without warning, the doors swung outward on hidden joints. As the rift widened between them, rays of sunlight streamed into the tunnel, 580 falling on Saphira and Eragon. Temporarily blinded, Eragon blinked and squinted. When his eyes adjusted to the light, he gasped.

They were inside a massive volcanic crater. Its walls narrowed to a small ragged opening so high above that Eragon could not judge the distance—it might have been more than a dozen miles. A soft beam of light fell through the aperture, illuminating the crater's center, though it left the rest of the cavernous expanse in hushed twilight.

The crater's far side, hazy blue in the distance, looked to be nearly ten miles away. Giant icicles hundreds of feet thick and thousands of feet long hung leagues above them like glistening daggers. Eragon knew from his experience in the valley that no one, not even Saphira, could reach those lofty points. Farther down the crater's inner walls, dark mats of moss and lichen covered the rock.

He lowered his gaze and saw a wide cobblestone path extending from the doors' threshold. The path ran straight to the center of the crater, where it ended at the base of a snowy-white mountain that glittered like an uncut gem with thousands of colored lights. It was less than a tenth of the height of the crater that loomed over and around it, but its diminutive appearance was deceiving, for it was slightly higher than a mile.

Long as it was, the tunnel had only taken them through one side of the crater wall. As Eragon stared, he heard Orik say deeply, "Look well, human, for no Rider has set eyes upon this for nigh over a hundred years. The airy peak under which we stand is Farthen Dûr—discovered thousands of years ago by the father of our race, Korgan, while he tunneled for gold. And in the center stands our greatest achievement: Tronjheim, the city-mountain built from the purest marble." The doors grated to a halt.

A city!

Then Eragon saw the crowd. He had been so engrossed by the sights that he had failed to notice a dense sea of people clustered around the tunnel's entrance. They lined the cobblestone pathway—dwarves and humans packed together like trees in a thicket. There were hundreds . . . thousands of them. Every eye, every face was focused on Eragon. And every one of them was silent.

Eragon gripped the base of one of Saphira's neck spikes. He saw children in dirty smocks, hardy men with scarred knuckles, women in homespun dresses, and stout, weathered dwarves who fingered their beards. All of them bore the same taut expression—that of an injured animal when a predator is nearby and escape is impossible.

A bead of sweat rolled down Eragon's face, but he dared not move to wipe it away. *What should I do?* he asked frantically.

Smile, raise your hand, anything! replied Saphira sharply.

Eragon tried to force out a smile, but his lips only twitched. Gathering his courage, he pushed a hand into the air, jerking it in a little wave. When nothing happened, he flushed with embarrassment, lowered his arm, and ducked his head.

A single cheer broke the silence. Someone clapped loudly. For a brief second the crowd hesitated, then a wild roar swept through it, and a wave of sound crashed over Eragon.

"Very good," said the bald man from behind him. "Now start walking."

Relieved, Eragon sat straighter and playfully asked Saphira, *Shall we go?* She arched her neck and stepped forward. As they passed the first row of people, she glanced to each side and exhaled a puff of smoke. The crowd quieted and shrank back, then resumed cheering, their enthusiasm only intensified.

Show-off, chided Eragon. Saphira flicked her tail and ignored him. He stared curiously at the jostling crowd as she proceeded along the path. Dwarves greatly outnumbered humans . . . and many of them glared at him resentfully. Some even turned their backs and walked away with stony faces.

The humans were hard, tough people. All the men had daggers or knives at their waists; many were armed for war. The women carried themselves proudly, but they seemed to conceal a deep-abiding weariness. The few children and babies stared at Eragon with large eyes. He felt certain that these people had experienced much hardship and that they would do whatever was necessary to defend themselves.

The Varden had found the perfect hiding place. Farthen Dûr's walls were too high for a dragon to fly over, and no army could break through the entranceway, even if it managed to find the hidden doors.

The crowd followed close behind them, giving Saphira plenty of room. Gradually the people quieted, though their attention remained on Eragon. He looked back and saw Murtagh riding stiffly, his face pale.

They neared the city-mountain, and Eragon saw that the white marble of Tronjheim was highly polished and shaped into flowing contours, as if it had been poured into place. It was dotted with countless round windows framed by elaborate carvings. A colored lantern hung in each window, casting a soft glow on the surrounding rock. No turrets or smokestacks were visible. Directly ahead, two thirty-foot-high gold griffins guarded a massive timber gate—recessed twenty yards into the base of Tronjheim—which was shadowed by thick trusses that supported an arched vault far overhead.

When they reached Tronjheim's base, Saphira paused to see if the bald man had any instructions. When none were forthcoming, she continued to the gate. The walls were lined with fluted pillars of bloodred jasper. Between the pillars hulked statues of outlandish creatures, captured forever by the sculptor's chisel.

The heavy gate rumbled open before them as hidden chains slowly raised the mammoth beams. A four-story-high passageway extended straight toward the center of Tronjheim. The top three levels were pierced by rows of archways that revealed gray tunnels curving off into the distance. Clumps of people filled the arches, eagerly watching Eragon and Saphira. On ground level, however, the archways were barred by stout doors. Rich tapestries hung between the different levels, embroidered with heroic figures and tumultuous battle scenes.

A cheer rang in their ears as Saphira stepped into the hall and paraded down it. Eragon raised his hand, eliciting another roar from the throng, though many of the dwarves did not join the welcoming shout.

The mile-long hall ended in an arch flanked by black onyx pillars. Yellow zircons three times the size of a man capped the dark columns, coruscating piercing gold beams along the hall. Saphira stepped through the opening, then stopped and craned back her neck, humming deeply in her chest.

They were in a circular room, perhaps a thousand feet across, that reached up to Tronjheim's peak a mile overhead, narrowing as it rose. The walls were lined with arches—one row for each level of the city-mountain—and the floor was made of polished carnelian, upon which was etched a hammer girdled by twelve silver pentacles, like on Orik's helm.

The room was a nexus for four hallways—including the one they had just exited—that divided Tronjheim into quarters. The halls were identical except for the one opposite Eragon. To the right and left of that hall were tall arches that opened to descending stairs, which mirrored each other as they curved underground.

The ceiling was capped by a dawn-red star sapphire of monstrous size. The jewel was twenty yards across and nearly as thick. Its face had been carved to resemble a rose in full bloom, and so skilled was the craftsmanship, the flower almost seemed to be real. A wide belt of lanterns wrapped around the edge of the sapphire, which cast striated bands of blushing light over everything below. The flashing rays of the star within the gem made it appear as if a giant eye gazed down at them.

Eragon could only gape with wonder. Nothing had prepared him for this. It seemed impossible that Tronjheim had been built by mortal beings. The city-mountain shamed everything he had seen in the Empire. He doubted if even Urû'baen could match the wealth and grandeur displayed here. Tronjheim was a stunning monument to the dwarves' power and perseverance.

The bald man walked in front of Saphira and said, "You must go on foot from here." There was scattered booing from the crowd as he spoke. A dwarf took Tornac and Snowfire away. Eragon dismounted Saphira but stayed by her side as the bald man led them across the carnelian floor to the right-hand hallway.

They followed it for several hundred feet, then entered a smaller corridor. Their guards remained despite the cramped space. After four sharp turns, they came to a massive cedar door, stained black with age. The bald man pulled it open and conducted everyone but the guards inside.

AJIHAD

E ragon entered an elegant, two-story study
paneled with rows of cedar bookshelves. A
wrought-iron staircase wound up to a small
588 balcony with two chairs and a reading table.
White lanterns hung along the walls and ceiling
so a book could be read anywhere in the room.
The stone floor was covered by an intricate oval
rug. At the far end of the room, a man stood behind a large walnut desk.

His skin gleamed the color of oiled ebony. The
dome of his head was shaved bare, but a closely
trimmed black beard covered his chin and upper
lip. Strong features shadowed his face, and grave,
intelligent eyes lurked under his brow. His shoulders were broad and powerful, emphasized by a
tapered red vest embroidered with gold thread
and clasped over a rich purple shirt. He bore
himself with great dignity, exuding an intense,
commanding air.

When he spoke, his voice was strong, confident: "Welcome to Tronjheim, Eragon and Saphira. I am Ajihad. Please, seat yourselves."

Eragon slipped into an armchair next to Murtagh, while Saphira settled protectively behind them. Ajihad raised his hand and snapped his fingers. A man stepped out from behind the staircase. He was identical to the bald man beside him. Eragon stared at the two of them with surprise, and Murtagh stiffened. "Your confusion is understandable; they are twin brothers," said Ajihad with a small smile. "I would tell you their names, but they have none."

Saphira hissed with distaste. Ajihad watched her for a moment, then sat in a high-backed chair behind the desk. The Twins retreated under the stairs and stood impassively beside each other. Ajihad pressed his fingers together as he stared at Eragon and Murtagh. He studied them for a long time with an unwavering gaze.

Eragon squirmed, uncomfortable. After what seemed like several minutes, Ajihad lowered his hands and beckoned to the Twins. One of them hurried to his side. Ajihad whispered in his ear. The bald man suddenly paled and shook his head vigorously. Ajihad frowned, then nodded as if something had been confirmed.

He looked at Murtagh. "You have placed me in a difficult position by refusing to be examined. You have been allowed into Farthen Dûr because the Twins have assured me that they can control

589

you and because of your actions on behalf of Eragon and Arya. I understand that there may be things you wish to keep hidden in your mind, but as long as you do, we cannot trust you."

"You wouldn't trust me anyway," said Murtagh defiantly.

Ajihad's face darkened as Murtagh spoke, and his eyes flashed dangerously. "Though it's been twenty and three years since it last broke upon my ear . . . I know that voice." He stood ominously, chest swelling. The Twins looked alarmed and put their heads together, whispering frantically. "It came from another man, one more beast than human. Get up."

Murtagh warily complied, his eyes darting between the Twins and Ajihad. "Remove your shirt," ordered Ajihad. With a shrug, Murtagh pulled off his tunic. "Now turn around." As he pivoted to the side, light fell upon the scar on his back.

"Murtagh," breathed Ajihad. A grunt of surprise came from Orik. Without warning, Ajihad turned on the Twins and thundered, "Did you know of this?"

The Twins bowed their heads. "We discovered his name in Eragon's mind, but we did not suspect that this *boy* was the son of one as powerful as Morzan. It never occurred—"

"And you didn't tell me?" demanded Ajihad. He raised a hand, forestalling their explanation. "We will discuss it later." He faced Murtagh again. "First I must untangle this muddle. Do you still refuse to be probed?"

"Yes," said Murtagh sharply, slipping back into his tunic. "I won't let anyone inside my head."

Ajihad leaned on his desk. "There will be unpleasant consequences if you don't. Unless the Twins can certify that you aren't a threat, we cannot give you credence, despite, and perhaps because of, the assistance you have given Eragon. Without that verification, the people here, dwarf and human alike, will tear you apart if they learn of your presence. I'll be forced to keep you confined at all times—as much for your protection as for ours. It will only get worse once the dwarf king, Hrothgar, demands custody of you. Don't force yourself into that situation when it can easily be avoided."

Murtagh shook his head stubbornly. "No . . . even if I were to submit, I would still be treated like a leper and an outcast. All I wish is to leave. If you let me do that peacefully, I'll never reveal your location to the Empire."

"What will happen if you are captured and brought before Galbatorix?" demanded Ajihad. "He will extract every secret from your mind, no matter how strong you may be. Even if you could resist him, how can we trust that you won't rejoin him in the future? I cannot take that chance."

"Will you hold me prisoner forever?" demanded Murtagh, straightening.

"No," said Ajihad, "only until you let yourself

be examined. If you are found trustworthy, the Twins will remove all knowledge of Farthen Dûr's location from your mind before you leave. We won't risk someone with those memories falling into Galbatorix's hands. What is it to be, Murtagh? Decide quickly or else the path will be chosen for you."

Just give in, Eragon pleaded silently, concerned for Murtagh's safety. *It's not worth the fight.*

Finally Murtagh spoke, the words slow and distinct. "My mind is the one sanctuary that has not been stolen from me. Men have tried to breach it before, but I've learned to defend it vigorously, for I am only safe with my innermost thoughts. You have asked for the one thing I cannot give, least of all to those two." He gestured at the Twins. "Do with me what you will, but know this: death will take me before I'll expose myself to their probing."

Admiration glinted in Ajihad's eyes. "I'm not surprised by your choice, though I had hoped otherwise. . . . Guards!" The cedar door slammed open as warriors rushed in, weapons ready. Ajihad pointed at Murtagh and commanded, "Take him to a windowless room and bar the door securely. Post six men by the entrance and allow no one inside until I come to see him. Do not speak to him, either."

The warriors surrounded Murtagh, watching him suspiciously. As they left the study, Eragon caught Murtagh's attention and mouthed, "I'm sorry." Murtagh shrugged, then stared forward resolutely. He vanished into the hallway with the men. The sound of their feet faded into silence.

Ajihad said abruptly, "I want everyone out of this room but Eragon and Saphira. Now!"

Bowing, the Twins departed, but Orik said, "Sir, the king will want to know of Murtagh. And there is still the matter of my insubordination. . . ."

Ajihad frowned, then waved his hand. "I will tell Hrothgar myself. As for your actions . . . wait outside until I call for you. And don't let the Twins get away. I'm not done with them, either."

"Very well," said Orik, inclining his head. He closed the door with a solid thump.

After a long silence, Ajihad sat with a tired sigh. He ran a hand over his face and stared at the ceiling. Eragon waited impatiently for him to speak. When nothing was forthcoming, he blurted, "Is Arya all right?"

Ajihad looked down at him and said gravely, "No . . . but the healers tell me she will recover. They worked on her all through the night. The poison took a dreadful toll on her. She wouldn't have lived if not for you. For that you have the Varden's deepest thanks."

Eragon's shoulders slumped with relief. For the first time he felt that their flight from Gil'ead had been worth the effort. "So, what now?" he asked.

"I need you to tell me how you found Saphira and everything that's happened since," said Ajihad, forming a steeple with his fingers. "Some of it I know from the message Brom sent us, other parts from the Twins. But I want to hear it from you, especially the details concerning Brom's death."

Eragon was reluctant to share his experiences with a stranger, but Ajihad was patient. *Go on,* urged Saphira gently. Eragon shifted, then began his story. It was awkward at first but grew easier as he proceeded. Saphira helped him to remember things clearly with occasional comments. Ajihad listened intently the entire time.

Eragon talked for hours, often pausing between his words. He told Ajihad of Teirm, though he kept Angela's fortunetelling to himself, and how he and Brom had found the Ra'zac. He even related his dreams of Arya. When he came to Gil'ead and mentioned the Shade, Ajihad's face hardened, and he leaned back with veiled eyes.

When his narrative was complete, Eragon fell silent, brooding on all that had occurred. Ajihad stood, clasped his hands behind his back, and absently studied one of the bookshelves. After a time he returned to the desk.

"Brom's death is a terrible loss. He was a close friend of mine and a powerful ally of the Varden. He saved us from destruction many times through his bravery and intelligence. Even now, when he is gone, he's provided us with the one thing that can ensure our success—you."

"But what can you expect me to accomplish?" asked Eragon.

"I will explain it in full," said Ajihad, "but there are more urgent matters to be dealt with first. The news of the Urgals' alliance with the Empire is extremely serious. If Galbatorix is gathering an Urgal army to destroy us, the Varden will be hard pressed to survive, even though many of us are protected here in Farthen Dûr. That a Rider, even one as evil as Galbatorix, would consider a pact with such monsters is indeed proof of madness. I shudder to think of what he promised them in return for their fickle loyalty. And then there is the Shade. Can you describe him?"

Eragon nodded. "He was tall, thin, and very pale, with red eyes and hair. He was dressed all in black."

"What of his sword—did you see it?" asked Ajihad intensely. "Did it have a long scratch on the blade?"

"Yes," said Eragon, surprised. "How did you know?"

"Because I put it there while trying to cut out his heart," said Ajihad with a grim smile. "His name is Durza—one of the most vicious and cunning fiends to ever stalk this land. He is the perfect servant for Galbatorix and a dangerous enemy for us. You say that you killed him. How was it done?"

Eragon remembered it vividly. "Murtagh shot him twice. The first arrow caught him in the shoulder; the second one struck him between the eyes."

"I was afraid of that," said Ajihad, frowning. "You didn't kill him. Shades can only be destroyed by a thrust through the heart. Anything short of that will cause them to vanish and then reappear elsewhere in spirit form. It's an unpleasant process, but Durza will survive and return stronger than ever."

A moody silence settled over them like a foreboding thunderhead. Then Ajihad stated, "You are an enigma, Eragon, a quandary that no one knows how to solve. Everyone knows what the Varden want—or the Urgals, or even Galbatorix—but no one knows what *you* want. And that makes you dangerous, especially to Galbatorix. He fears you because he doesn't know what you will do next."

"Do the Varden fear me?" asked Eragon quietly.

"No," said Ajihad carefully. "We are hopeful. But if that hope proves false, then yes, we will be afraid." Eragon looked down. "You must understand the unusual nature of your position. There are factions who want you to serve their interests and no one else's. The moment you entered Farthen Dûr, their influence and power began tugging on you."

"Including yours?" asked Eragon.

Ajihad chuckled, though his eyes were sharp. "Including mine. There are certain things you should know: first is how Saphira's egg happened to appear in the Spine. Did Brom ever tell you what was done with her egg after he brought it here?"

"No," said Eragon, glancing at Saphira. She blinked and flicked her tongue at him.

Ajihad tapped his desk before beginning. "When Brom first brought the egg to the Varden, everyone was deeply interested in its fate. We had thought the dragons were exterminated. The dwarves were solely concerned with making sure that the future Rider would be an ally—though some of them were opposed to having a new Rider at all—while the elves and Varden had a more personal stake in the matter. The reason was simple enough: throughout history all the Riders have been either elven or human, with the majority being elven. There has never been a dwarf Rider.

"Because of Galbatorix's betrayals, the elves were reluctant to let any of the Varden handle the egg for fear that the dragon inside would hatch for a human with similar instabilities. It was a challenging situation, as both sides wanted the Rider for their own. The dwarves only aggravated the problem by arguing obstinately with both the elves and us whenever they had the chance. Tensions escalated, and before long, threats were made that were later regretted. It was then that Brom suggested a compromise that allowed all sides to save face.

"He proposed that the egg be ferried between the Varden and the elves every year. At each place children would parade past it, and then the bearers of the egg would wait to see if the dragon would hatch. If it didn't, they would leave and return to the other group. But if the dragon *did* hatch, the new Rider's training would be undertaken immediately. For the first year or so he or she would be instructed here, by Brom. Then the Rider would be taken to the elves, who would finish the education.

"The elves reluctantly accepted this plan . . . with the stipulation that if Brom were to die before the dragon hatched, they would be free to train the new Rider without interference. The agreement was slanted in their favor—we both knew that the dragon would likely choose an elf—but it provided a desperately needed semblance of equality."

Ajihad paused, his rich eyes somber. Shadows bit into his face under his cheekbones, making them jut out. "It was hoped that this new Rider would bring our two races closer together. We waited for well over a decade, but the egg never hatched. The matter passed from our minds, and we rarely thought about it except to lament the egg's inactivity.

"Then last year we suffered a terrible loss. Arya and the egg disappeared on her return from Tronjheim to the elven city Osilon. The elves were the first to discover she was missing. They found her steed and guards slain in Du Welden-varden and a group of slaughtered Urgals nearby. But neither Arya nor the egg was there. When this news reached me, I feared that Urgals had both of them and would soon learn the location of Farthen Dûr and the elves' capital, Ellesméra, where their queen, Islanzadí, lives. Now I understand they were working for the Empire, which is far worse.

"We won't know exactly what occurred during that attack until Arya wakes, but I have deduced a few details from what you've said." Ajihad's vest rustled as he leaned his elbows on the desk. "The attack must have been swift and decisive, else Arya would have escaped. Without any warning, and deprived of a place to hide, she could have done only one thing—used magic to transport the egg elsewhere."

"She can use magic?" asked Eragon. Arya had mentioned that she had been given a drug to suppress her power; he wanted to confirm that she meant magic. He wondered if she could teach him more words of the ancient language.

"It was one of the reasons why she was chosen

to guard the egg. Anyway, Arya couldn't have returned it to us—she was too far away—and the elves' realm is warded by arcane barriers that prevent anything from entering their borders through magical means. She must have thought of Brom and, in desperation, sent the egg toward Carvahall. Without time to prepare, I'm not surprised she missed by the margin she did. The Twins tell me it is an imprecise art."

"Why was she closer to Palancar Valley than the Varden?" asked Eragon. "Where do the elves really live? Where is this . . . Ellesméra?"

Ajihad's keen gaze bored into Eragon as he considered the question. "I don't tell you this lightly, for the elves guard the knowledge jealously. But you should know, and I do this as a display of trust. Their cities lie far to the north, in the deepest reaches of the endless forest Du Weldenvarden. Not since the Riders' time has anyone, dwarf or human, been elf-friend enough to walk in their leafy halls. I do not even know how to find Ellesméra. As for Osilon . . . based on where Arya disappeared, I suspect it is near Du Weldenvarden's western edge, toward Carvahall. You must have many other questions, but bear with me and keep them until I have finished."

He gathered his memories, then spoke at a quickened pace. "When Arya disappeared, the elves withdrew their support from the Varden.

Queen Islanzadí was especially enraged and refused any further contact with us. As a result, even though I received Brom's message, the elves are still ignorant of you and Saphira. . . . Without their supplies to sustain my troops, we have fared badly these past months in skirmishes with the Empire.

"With Arya's return and your arrival, I expect the queen's hostility will abate. The fact that you rescued Arya will greatly help our case with her. Your training, however, is going to present a problem for both Varden and elves. Brom obviously had a chance to teach you, but we need to know how thorough he was. For that reason, you'll have to be tested to determine the extent of your abilities. Also, the elves will expect you to finish your training with them, though I'm not sure if there's time for that."

"Why not?" asked Eragon.

"For several reasons. Chief among them, the tidings you brought about the Urgals," said Ajihad, his eyes straying to Saphira. "You see, Eragon, the Varden are in an extremely delicate position. On one hand, we have to comply with the elves' wishes if we want to keep them as allies. At the same time, we cannot anger the dwarves if we wish to lodge in Tronjheim."

"Aren't the dwarves part of the Varden?" asked Eragon.

Ajihad hesitated. "In a sense, yes. They allow

us to live here and provide assistance in our struggle against the Empire, but they are loyal only to their king. I have no power over them except for what Hrothgar gives me, and even he often has trouble with the dwarf clans. The thirteen clans are subservient to Hrothgar, but each clan chief wields enormous power; they choose the new dwarf king when the old one dies. Hrothgar is sympathetic to our cause, but many of the chiefs aren't. He can't afford to anger them unnecessarily or he'll lose the support of his people, so his actions on our behalf have been severely circumscribed."

"These clan chiefs," said Eragon, "are they against me as well?"

"Even more so, I'm afraid," said Ajihad wearily. "There has long been enmity between dwarves and dragons—before the elves came and made peace, dragons made a regular habit of eating the dwarves' flocks and stealing their gold—and the dwarves are slow to forget past wrongs. Indeed, they never fully accepted the Riders or allowed them to police their kingdom. Galbatorix's rise to power has only served to convince many of them that it would be better never to deal with Riders or dragons ever again." He directed his last words at Saphira.

Eragon said slowly, "Why doesn't Galbatorix know where Farthen Dûr and Ellesméra are? Surely he was told of them when he was instructed by the Riders."

"Told of them, yes—shown where they are, no. It's one thing to know that Farthen Dûr lies within these mountains, quite another to find it. Galbatorix hadn't been taken to either place before his dragon was killed. After that, of course, the Riders didn't trust him. He tried to force the information out of several Riders during his rebellion, but they chose to die rather than reveal it to him. As for the dwarves, he's never managed to capture one alive, though it's only a matter of time."

"Then why doesn't he just take an army and march through Du Weldenvarden until he finds Ellesméra?" asked Eragon.

"Because the elves still have enough power to resist him," said Ajihad. "He doesn't dare test his strength against theirs, at least not yet. But his cursed sorcery grows stronger each year. With another Rider at his side, he would be unstoppable. He keeps trying to get one of his two eggs to hatch, but so far he's been unsuccessful."

Eragon was puzzled. "How can his power be increasing? The strength of his body limits his abilities—it can't build itself up forever."

"We don't know," said Ajihad, shrugging his broad shoulders, "and neither do the elves. We can only hope that someday he will be destroyed by one of his own spells." He reached inside his vest and somberly pulled out a battered piece of parchment. "Do you know what this is?" he asked, placing it on the desk.

603

Eragon bent forward and examined it. Lines of black script, written in an alien language, were inked across the page. Large sections of the writing had been destroyed by blots of blood. One edge of the parchment was charred. He shook his head. "No, I don't."

"It was taken from the leader of the Urgal host we destroyed last night. It cost us twelve men to do so—they sacrificed themselves so that you might escape safely. The writing is the king's invention, a script he uses to communicate with his servants. It took me a while, but I was able to devise its meaning, at least where it's legible. It reads:

> . . . gatekeeper at Ithrö Zhâda is to let this bearer and his minions pass. They are to be bunked with the others of their kind and by . . . but only if the two factions refrain from fighting. Command will be given under Tarok, under Gashz, under Durza, under Ushnark the Mighty.

"Ushnark is Galbatorix. It means 'father' in the Urgal tongue, an affectation that pleases him.

> Find what they are suitable for and . . . The footmen and . . . are to be kept separate. No weapons are to be distributed until . . . for marching.

"Nothing else can be read past there, except for a few vague words," said Ajihad.

"Where's Ithrö Zhâda? I've never heard of it."

"Nor have I," confirmed Ajihad, "which makes me suspect that Galbatorix has renamed an existing place for his own purposes. After deciphering this, I asked myself what hundreds of Urgals were doing by the Beor Mountains where you first saw them and where they were going. The parchment mentions 'others of their kind,' so I assume there are even more Urgals at their destination. There's only one reason for the king to gather such a force—to forge a bastard army of humans and monsters to destroy us.

"For now, there is nothing to do but wait and watch. Without further information we cannot find this Ithrö Zhâda. Still, Farthen Dûr has not yet been discovered, so there is hope. The only Urgals to have seen it died last night."

"How did you know we were coming?" asked Eragon. "One of the Twins was waiting for us, and there was an ambush in place for the Kull." He was aware of Saphira listening intently. Though she kept her own counsel, he knew she would have things to say later.

"We have sentinels placed at the entrance of the valley you traveled through—on either side of the Beartooth River. They sent a dove to warn us," explained Ajihad.

Eragon wondered if it was the same bird

Saphira had tried to eat. "When the egg and Arya disappeared, did you tell Brom? He said that he hadn't heard anything from the Varden."

"We tried to alert him," said Ajihad, "but I suspect our men were intercepted and killed by the Empire. Why else would the Ra'zac have gone to Carvahall? After that, Brom was traveling with you, and it was impossible to get word to him. I was relieved when he contacted me via messenger from Teirm. It didn't surprise me that he went to Jeod; they were old friends. And Jeod could easily send us a message because he smuggles supplies to us through Surda.

"All of this has raised serious questions. How did the Empire know where to ambush Arya and, later, our messengers to Carvahall? How has Galbatorix learned which merchants help the Varden? Jeod's business has been virtually destroyed since you left him, as have those of other merchants who support us. Every time one of their ships sets sail, it disappears. The dwarves cannot give us everything we need, so the Varden are in desperate need of supplies. I'm afraid that we have a traitor, or traitors, in our midst, despite our efforts to examine people's minds for deceit."

Eragon sank deep in thought, pondering what he had learned. Ajihad waited calmly for him to speak, undisturbed by the silence. For the first time since finding Saphira's egg, Eragon felt that he understood what was going on around him. At last he knew where Saphira came from and what might lie in his future. "What do you want from me?" he asked.

"How do you mean?"

"I mean, what is expected of me in Tronjheim? You and the elves have plans for me, but what if I don't like them?" A hard note crept into his voice. "I'll fight when needed, revel when there's occasion, mourn when there is grief, and die if my time comes . . . but I won't let anyone use me against my will." He paused to let the words sink in. "The Riders of old were arbiters of justice above and beyond the leaders of their time. I don't claim that position—I doubt people would accept such oversight when they've been free of it all their lives, especially from one as young as me. But I *do* have power, and I will wield it as I see fit. What I want to know is how *you* plan to use me. Then I will decide whether to agree to it."

Ajihad looked at him wryly. "If you were anyone else and were before another leader, you would likely have been killed for that insolent speech. What makes you think I will expose my plans just because you demand it?" Eragon flushed but did not lower his gaze. "Still, you are right. Your position gives you the privilege to say such things. You cannot escape the politics of your situation—you *will* be influenced, one way or another. I don't want to see you become a pawn of any one group or purpose any more than

607

you do. You must retain your freedom, for in it lies your true power: the ability to make choices independent of any leader or king. My own authority over you will be limited, but I believe it's for the best. The difficulty lies in making sure that those with power include you in their deliberations.

"Also, despite your protests, the people here have certain expectations of you. They are going to bring you their problems, no matter how petty, and demand that you solve them." Ajihad leaned forward, his voice deadly serious. "There will be cases where someone's future will rest in your hands . . . with a word you can send them careening into happiness or misery. Young women will seek your opinion on whom they should marry—many will pursue you as a husband—and old men will ask which of their children should receive an inheritance. You *must* be kind and wise with them all, for they put their trust in you. Don't speak flippantly or without thought, because your words will have impact far beyond what you intend."

Ajihad leaned back, his eyes hooded. "The burden of leadership is being responsible for the well-being of the people in your charge. I have dealt with it from the day I was chosen to head the Varden, and now you must as well. Be careful. I won't tolerate injustice under my command. Don't worry about your youth and inexperience; they will pass soon enough."

Eragon was uncomfortable with the idea of

people asking him for advice. "But you still haven't said what I'm to do here."

"For now, nothing. You covered over a hundred and thirty leagues in eight days, a feat to be proud of. I'm sure that you'll appreciate rest. When you've recovered, we will test your competency in arms and magic. After that—well, I will explain your options, and then you'll have to decide your course."

"And what about Murtagh?" asked Eragon bitingly.

Ajihad's face darkened. He reached beneath his desk and lifted up Zar'roc. The sword's polished sheath gleamed in the light. Ajihad slid his hand over it, lingering on the etched sigil. "He will stay here until he allows the Twins into his mind."

609

"You can't imprison him," argued Eragon. "He's committed no crime!"

"We can't give him his freedom without being sure that he won't turn against us. Innocent or not, he's potentially as dangerous to us as his father was," said Ajihad with a hint of sadness.

Eragon realized that Ajihad would not be convinced otherwise, and his concern *was* valid. "How were you able to recognize his voice?"

"I met his father once," said Ajihad shortly. He tapped Zar'roc's hilt. "I wish Brom had told me he had taken Morzan's sword. I suggest that you don't carry it within Farthen Dûr. Many here remember Morzan's time with hate, especially the dwarves."

"I'll remember that," promised Eragon.

Ajihad handed Zar'roc to him. "That reminds me, I have Brom's ring, which he sent as confirmation of his identity. I was keeping it for when he returned to Tronjheim. Now that he's dead, I suppose it belongs to you, and I think he would have wanted you to have it." He opened a desk drawer and took the ring from it.

Eragon accepted it with reverence. The symbol cut into the face of the sapphire was identical to the tattoo on Arya's shoulder. He fit the ring onto his index finger, admiring how it caught the light. "I . . . I am honored," he said.

Ajihad nodded gravely, then pushed back his chair and stood. He faced Saphira and spoke to her, his voice swelling in power. "Do not think that I have forgotten you, O mighty dragon. I have said these things as much for your benefit as for Eragon's. It is even more important that you know them, for to you falls the task of guarding him in these dangerous times. Do not underestimate your might nor falter at his side, because without you he will surely fail."

Saphira lowered her head until their eyes were level and stared at him through slitted black pupils. They examined each other silently, neither of them blinking. Ajihad was the first to move. He lowered his eyes and said softly, "It is indeed a privilege to meet you."

He'll do, said Saphira respectfully. She swung her head to face Eragon. *Tell him that I am impressed both with Tronjheim and with him. The Empire is right to fear him. Let him know, however, that if he had decided to kill you, I would have destroyed Tronjheim and torn him apart with my teeth.*

Eragon hesitated, surprised by the venom in her voice, then relayed the message. Ajihad looked at her seriously. "I would expect nothing less from one so noble—but I doubt you could have gotten past the Twins."

Saphira snorted with derision. *Bah!*

Knowing what she meant, Eragon said, "Then they must be much stronger than they appear. I think they would be sorely dismayed if they ever faced a dragon's wrath. The two of them might be able to defeat me, but never Saphira. You should know, a Rider's dragon strengthens his magic beyond what a normal magician might have. Brom was always weaker than me because of that. I think that in the absence of Riders, the Twins have overestimated their power."

Ajihad looked troubled. "Brom was considered one of our strongest spell weavers. Only the elves surpassed him. If what you say is true, we will have to reconsider a great many things." He bowed to Saphira. "As it is, I am glad it wasn't necessary to harm either of you." Saphira dipped her head in return.

Ajihad straightened with a lordly air and called, "Orik!" The dwarf hurried into the room

611

and stood before the desk, crossing his arms. Ajihad frowned at him, irritated. "You've caused me a great deal of trouble, Orik. I've had to listen to one of the Twins complain all morning about your insubordination. They won't let it rest until you are punished. Unfortunately they're right. It's a serious matter that cannot be ignored. An accounting is due."

Orik's eyes flicked toward Eragon, but his face betrayed no emotion. He spoke quickly in rough tones. "The Kull were almost around Kósthamérna. They were shooting arrows at the dragon, Eragon, and Murtagh, but the Twins did nothing to stop it. Like . . . sheilven, they refused to open the gates even though we could see Eragon shouting the opening phrase on the other side of the waterfall. And they refused to take action when Eragon did not rise from the water. Perhaps I did wrong, but I couldn't let a Rider die."

"I wasn't strong enough to get out of the water myself," offered Eragon. "I would have drowned if he hadn't pulled me out."

Ajihad glanced at him, then asked Orik seriously, "And later, why did you oppose them?"

Orik raised his chin defiantly. "It wasn't right for them to force their way into Murtagh's mind. But I wouldn't have stopped them if I'd known who he was."

"No, you did the right thing, though it would be simpler if you hadn't. It isn't our place to force our way into people's minds, no matter who they are." Ajihad fingered his dense beard. "Your actions were honorable, but you did defy a direct order from your commander. The penalty for that has always been death." Orik's back stiffened.

"You can't kill him for that! He was only helping me," cried Eragon.

"It isn't your place to interfere," said Ajihad sternly. "Orik broke the law and must suffer the consequences." Eragon started to argue again, but Ajihad stopped him with a raised hand. "But you are right. The sentence will be mitigated because of the circumstances. As of now, Orik, you are removed from active service and forbidden to engage in any military activities under my command. Do you understand?"

613

Orik's face darkened, but then he only looked confused. He nodded sharply. "Yes."

"Furthermore, in the absence of your regular duties, I appoint you Eragon and Saphira's guide for the duration of their stay. You are to make sure they receive every comfort and amenity we have to offer. Saphira will stay above Isidar Mithrim. Eragon may have quarters wherever he wants. When he recovers from his trip, take him to the training fields. They're expecting him," said Ajihad, a twinkle of amusement in his eye.

Orik bowed low. "I understand."

"Very well, you all may go. Send in the Twins as you leave."

Eragon bowed and began to leave, then asked, "Where can I find Arya? I would like to see her."

"No one is allowed to visit her. You will have to wait until she comes to you." Ajihad looked down at his desk in a clear dismissal.

BLESS THE CHILD, ARGETLAM

Eragon stretched in the hall; he was stiff from sitting so long. Behind him, the Twins entered Ajihad's study and closed the door. Eragon looked at Orik. "I'm sorry that you're in trouble because of me," he apologized.

"Don't bother yourself," grunted Orik, tugging on his beard. "Ajihad gave me what I wanted."

Even Saphira was startled by the statement. "What do you mean?" said Eragon. "You can't train or fight, and you're stuck guarding me. How can that be what you wanted?"

The dwarf eyed him quietly. "Ajihad is a good leader. He understands how to keep the law yet remain just. I have been punished by his command, but I'm also one of Hrothgar's subjects. Under his rule, I'm still free to do what I wish."

Eragon realized it would be unwise to forget Orik's dual loyalty and the split nature of power within Tronjheim. "Ajihad just placed you in a powerful position, didn't he?"

Orik chuckled deeply. "That he did, and in such a way the Twins can't complain about it. This'll irritate them for sure. Ajihad's a tricky one, he is. Come, lad, I'm sure you're hungry. And we have to get your dragon settled in."

Saphira hissed. Eragon said, "Her name is Saphira."

Orik made a small bow to her. "My apologies, I'll be sure to remember that." He took an orange lamp from the wall and led them down the hallway.

"Can others in Farthen Dûr use magic?" asked Eragon, struggling to keep up with the dwarf's brisk pace. He cradled Zar'roc carefully, concealing the symbol on the sheath with his arm.

"Few enough," said Orik with a swift shrug under his mail. "And the ones we have can't do much more than heal bruises. They've all had to tend to Arya because of the strength needed to heal her."

"Except for the Twins."

"Oeí," grumbled Orik. "She wouldn't want their help anyway; their arts are not for healing. Their talents lie in scheming and plotting for power—to everyone else's detriment. Deynor, Ajihad's predecessor, allowed them to join the Varden because he needed their support . . . you can't oppose the Empire without spellcasters who can hold their own on the field of battle. They're a nasty pair, but they do have their uses."

They entered one of the four main tunnels that divided Tronjheim. Clusters of dwarves and humans strolled through it, voices echoing loudly off the polished floor. The conversations stopped abruptly as they saw Saphira; scores of eyes fixed on her. Orik ignored the spectators and turned left, heading toward one of Tronjheim's distant gates. "Where are we going?" asked Eragon.

"Out of these halls so Saphira can fly to the dragonhold above Isidar Mithrim, the Star Rose. The dragonhold doesn't have a roof—Tronjheim's peak is open to the sky, like that of Farthen Dûr—so she, that is, you, Saphira, will be able to glide straight down into the hold. It is where the Riders used to stay when they visited Tronjheim."

"Won't it be cold and damp without a roof?" asked Eragon.

"Nay." Orik shook his head. "Farthen Dûr protects us from the elements. Neither rain nor snow intrude here. Besides, the hold's walls are lined with marble caves for dragons. They provide all the shelter necessary. All you need fear are the icicles; when they fall they've been known to cleave a horse in two."

I will be fine, assured Saphira. *A marble cave is safer than any of the other places we've stayed.*

Perhaps . . . Do you think Murtagh will be all right?

Ajihad strikes me as an honorable man. Unless Murtagh tries to escape, I doubt he will be harmed.

Eragon crossed his arms, unwilling to talk further. He was dazed by the change in circumstances from the day before. Their mad race from Gil'ead was finally over, but his body expected to continue running and riding. "Where are our horses?"

"In the stables by the gate. We can visit them before leaving Tronjheim."

They exited Tronjheim through the same gate they had entered. The gold griffins gleamed with colored highlights garnered from scores of lanterns. The sun had moved during Eragon's talk with Ajihad—light no longer entered Farthen Dûr through the crater opening. Without those moted rays, the inside of the hollow mountain was velvety black. The only illumination came from Tronjheim, which sparkled brilliantly in the gloom. The city-mountain's radiance was enough to brighten the ground hundreds of feet away.

Orik pointed at Tronjheim's white pinnacle. "Fresh meat and pure mountain water await you up there," he told Saphira. "You may stay in any of the caves. Once you make your choice, bedding will be laid down in it and then no one will disturb you."

"I thought we were going to go together. I don't want to be separated," protested Eragon.

Orik turned to him. "Rider Eragon, I will do everything to accommodate you, but it would be best if Saphira waits in the dragonhold while you eat. The tunnels to the banquet halls aren't large enough for her to accompany us."

"Why can't you just bring me food in the hold?"

"Because," said Orik with a guarded expression, "the food is prepared down here, and it is a long way to the top. If you wish, a servant could be sent up to the hold with a meal for you. It will take some time, but you could eat with Saphira then."

He actually means it, Eragon thought, aston- 619 ished that they would do so much for him. But the way Orik said it made him wonder if the dwarf was testing him somehow.

I'm weary, said Saphira. *And this dragonhold sounds to my liking. Go, have your meal, then come to me. It will be soothing to rest together without fear of wild animals or soldiers. We have suffered the hardships of the trail too long.*

Eragon looked at her thoughtfully, then said to Orik, "I'll eat down here." The dwarf smiled, seeming satisfied. Eragon unstrapped Saphira's saddle so she could lie down without discomfort. *Would you take Zar'roc with you?*

Yes, she said, gathering up the sword and saddle with her claws. *But keep your bow. We must trust these people, though not to the point of foolishness.*

I know, he said, disquieted.

With an explosive leap Saphira swept off the ground and into the still air. The steady whoosh of her wings was the only sound in the darkness. As she disappeared over the rim of Tronjheim's peak, Orik let out a long breath. "Ah boy, you have been blessed indeed. I find a sudden longing in my heart for open skies and soaring cliffs and the thrill of hunting like a hawk. Still, my feet are better on the ground—preferably under it."

He clapped his hands loudly. "I neglect my duties as host. I know you've not dined since that pitiful dinner the Twins saw fit to give you, so come, let's find the cooks and beg meat and bread from them!"

Eragon followed the dwarf back into Tronjheim and through a labyrinth of corridors until they came to a long room filled with rows of stone tables only high enough for dwarves. Fires blazed in soapstone ovens behind a long counter.

Orik spoke words in an unfamiliar language to a stout ruddy-faced dwarf, who promptly handed them stone platters piled with steaming mushrooms and fish. Then Orik took Eragon up several flights of stairs and into a small alcove carved out of Tronjheim's outer wall, where they sat cross-legged. Eragon wordlessly reached for his food.

When their platters were empty, Orik sighed with contentment and pulled out a long-stemmed pipe. He lit it, saying, "A worthy repast, though it needed a good draught of mead to wash it down properly."

Eragon surveyed the ground below. "Do you farm in Farthen Dûr?"

"No, there's only enough sunlight for moss, mushrooms, and mold. Tronjheim cannot survive without supplies from the surrounding valleys, which is one reason why many of us choose to live elsewhere in the Beor Mountains."

"Then there are other dwarf cities?"

"Not as many as we would like. And Tronjheim is the greatest of them." Leaning on an elbow, Orik took a deep pull on his pipe. "You have only seen the lower levels, so it hasn't been apparent, but most of Tronjheim is deserted. The farther up you go, the emptier it gets. Entire floors have remained untouched for centuries. Most dwarves prefer to dwell under Tronjheim and Farthen Dûr in the caverns and passageways that riddle the rock. Through the centuries we have tunneled extensively under the Beor Mountains. It is possible to walk from one end of the mountain range to the other without ever setting foot on the surface."

"It seems like a waste to have all that unused space in Tronjheim," commented Eragon.

Orik nodded. "Some have argued for abandoning this place because of its drain on our resources, but Tronjheim does perform one invaluable task."

"What's that?"

"In times of misfortune it can house our entire nation. There have been only three instances in our history when we have been forced to that extreme, but each time it has saved us from certain and utter destruction. That is why we always keep it garrisoned, ready for use."

"I've never seen anything as magnificent," admitted Eragon.

Orik smiled around his pipe. "I'm glad you find it so. It took generations to build Tronjheim— and our lives are much longer than those of men. Unfortunately, because of the cursed Empire, few outsiders are allowed to see its glory."

"How many Varden are here?"

"Dwarves or humans?"

"Humans—I want to know how many have fled the Empire."

Orik exhaled a long puff of smoke that coiled lazily around his head. "There are about four thousand of your kin here. But that's a poor indicator of what you want to know. Only people who wish to fight come here. The rest of them are under King Orrin's protection in Surda."

So few? thought Eragon with a sinking feeling. The royal army alone numbered nearly sixteen thousand when it was fully marshaled, not counting the Urgals. "Why doesn't Orrin fight the Empire himself?" he asked.

"If he were to show open hostility," said Orik, "Galbatorix would crush him. As it is, Galbatorix withholds that destruction because he considers Surda a minor threat, which is a mistake. It's through Orrin's assistance that the Varden have most of their weapons and supplies. Without him, there would be no resisting the Empire.

"Don't despair over the number of humans in Tronjheim. There are many dwarves here—many more than you have seen—and all will fight when the time comes. Orrin has also promised us troops for when we battle Galbatorix. The elves pledged their help as well."

Eragon absently touched Saphira's mind and found her busy eating a bloody haunch with gusto. He noticed once more the hammer and stars engraved on Orik's helm. "What does that mean? I saw it on the floor in Tronjheim."

Orik lifted the iron-bound cap off his head and brushed a rough finger over the engraving. "It is the symbol of my clan. We are the Ingeitum, metalworkers and master smiths. The hammer and stars are inlaid into Tronjheim's floor because it was the personal crest of Korgan, our founder. One clan to rule, with twelve surrounding. King Hrothgar is Dûrgrimst Ingeitum as well and has brought my house much glory, much honor."

623

When they returned the platters to the cook, they passed a dwarf in the hall. He stopped before Eragon, bowed, and said respectfully, "Argetlam."

The dwarf left Eragon fumbling for an answer, flushed with unease, yet also strangely pleased with the gesture. No one had bowed to him before. "What did he say?" he asked, leaning closer to Orik.

Orik shrugged, embarrassed. "It's an elven word that was used to refer to the Riders. It means 'silver hand.'" Eragon glanced at his gloved hand, thinking of the gedwëy ignasia that whitened his palm. "Do you wish to return to Saphira?"

"Is there somewhere I could bathe first? I haven't been able to wash off the grime of the road for a long time. Also, my shirt is bloodstained and torn, and it stinks. I'd like to replace it, but I don't have any money to buy a new one. Is there a way I could work for one?"

"Do you seek to insult Hrothgar's hospitality, Eragon?" demanded Orik. "As long as you are in Tronjheim, you won't have to buy a thing. You'll pay for it in other ways—Ajihad and Hrothgar will see to that. Come. I'll show you where to wash, then fetch you a shirt."

He took Eragon down a long staircase until they were well below Tronjheim. The corridors were tunnels now—which cramped Eragon because they were only five feet high—and all the lanterns were red. "So the light doesn't blind you when you leave or enter a dark cavern," explained Orik.

They entered a bare room with a small door on the far side. Orik pointed. "The pools are through there, along with brushes and soap. Leave your clothes here. I'll have new ones waiting when you get out."

Eragon thanked him and started to undress. It felt oppressive being alone underground, especially with the low rock ceiling. He stripped quickly and, cold, hurried through the door, into total darkness. He inched forward until his foot touched warm water, then eased himself into it.

The pool was mildly salty, but soothing and calm. For a moment he was afraid of drifting away from the door, into deeper water, but as he waded forward, he discovered the water reached only to his waist. He groped over a slippery wall until he found the soap and brushes, then scrubbed himself. Afterward he floated with his eyes closed, enjoying the warmth.

When he emerged, dripping, into the lighted room, he found a towel, a fine linen shirt, and a pair of breeches. The clothes fit him reasonably well. Satisfied, he went out into the tunnel.

Orik was waiting for him, pipe in hand. They climbed the stairs back up into Tronjheim, then exited the city-mountain. Eragon gazed at Tronjheim's peak and called Saphira with his mind. As she flew down from the dragonhold, he asked, "How do you communicate with people at the top of Tronjheim?"

Orik chuckled. "That's a problem we solved long ago. You didn't notice, but behind the open arches that line each level is a single, unbroken staircase that spirals around the wall of Tronjheim's central chamber. The stairs climb all the way to the dragonhold above Isidar Mithrim. We call it Vol Turin, The Endless Staircase. Running up or down it isn't swift enough for an emergency, nor convenient enough for casual use. Instead, we use flashing lanterns to convey messages. There is another way too, though it is seldom used. When Vol Turin was constructed, a polished trough was cut next to it. The trough acts as a giant slide as high as a mountain."

Eragon's lips twitched with a smile. "Is it dangerous?"

"Do not think of trying it. The slide was built for dwarves and is too narrow for a man. If you slipped out of it, you could be thrown onto the stairs and against the arches, perhaps even into empty space."

Saphira landed a spear's throw away, her scales rustling dryly. As she greeted Eragon, humans and dwarves trickled out of Tronjheim, gathering around her with murmurs of interest. Eragon regarded the growing crowd uneasily. "You'd better go," said Orik, pushing him forward. "Meet me by this gate tomorrow morning. I'll be waiting."

Eragon balked. "How will I know when it's morning?"

"I'll have someone wake you. Now go!" Without further protest, Eragon slipped through the jostling group that surrounded Saphira and jumped onto her back.

Before she could take off, an old woman stepped forward and grasped Eragon's foot with a fierce grip. He tried to pull away, but her hand was like an iron talon around his ankle—he could not break her tenacious hold. The burning gray eyes she fixed on him were surrounded by a lifetime's worth of wrinkles—the skin was folded in long creases down her sunken cheeks. A tattered bundle rested in the crook of her left arm.

Frightened, Eragon asked, "What do you want?"

The woman tilted her arm, and a cloth fell from the bundle, revealing a baby's face. Hoarse and desperate, she said, "The child has no parents—there is no one to care for her but me, and I am weak. Bless her with your power, Argetlam. Bless her for luck!"

Eragon looked to Orik for help, but the dwarf only watched with a guarded expression. The small crowd fell silent, waiting for his response. The woman's eyes were still fastened on him. "Bless her, Argetlam, bless her," she insisted.

627

Eragon had never blessed anyone. It was not something done lightly in Alagaësia, as a blessing could easily go awry and prove to be more curse than boon—especially if it was spoken with ill intent or lack of conviction. *Do I dare take that responsibility?* he wondered.

"Bless her, Argetlam, bless her."

Suddenly decided, he searched for a phrase or expression to use. Nothing came to mind until, inspired, he thought of the ancient language. This would be a true blessing, spoken with words of power, by one of power.

He bent down and tugged the glove off his right hand. Laying his palm on the babe's brow, he intoned, "Atra guliä un ilian tauthr ono un atra ono waíse skölir fra rauthr." The words left him unexpectedly weak, as if he had used magic. He slowly pulled the glove back on and said to the woman, "That is all I can do for her. If any words have the power to forestall tragedy, it will be those."

"Thank you, Argetlam," she whispered, bowing slightly. She started to cover the baby again, but Saphira snorted and twisted until her head loomed over the child. The woman grew rigid; her breath caught in her chest. Saphira lowered her snout and brushed the baby between the eyes with the tip of her nose, then smoothly lifted away.

A gasp ran through the crowd, for on the

child's forehead, where Saphira had touched her, was a star-shaped patch of skin as white and silvery as Eragon's gedwëy ignasia. The woman stared at Saphira with a feverish gaze, wordless thanks in her eyes.

Immediately Saphira took flight, battering the awestruck spectators with the wind from her powerful wing strokes. As the ground dwindled away, Eragon took a deep breath and hugged her neck tightly. *What did you do?* he asked softly.

I gave her hope. And you gave her a future.

Loneliness suddenly flowered within Eragon, despite Saphira's presence. Their surroundings were so foreign—it struck him for the first time exactly how far he was from home. A destroyed home, but still where his heart lay. *What have I become, Saphira?* he asked. *I'm only in the first year of manhood, yet I've consulted with the leader of the Varden, am pursued by Galbatorix, and have traveled with Morzan's son—and now blessings are sought from me! What wisdom can I give people that they haven't already learned? What feats can I achieve that an army couldn't do better? It's insanity! I should be back in Carvahall with Roran.*

Saphira took a long time to answer, but her words were gentle when they came. *A hatchling, that is what you are. A hatchling struggling into the world. I may be younger than you in years, but I am ancient in my thoughts. Do not worry about these things. Find peace in where and what you are. People often know what must be done. All you need do is show them the way—that is wisdom. As for feats, no army could have given the blessing you did.*

But it was nothing, he protested. A trifle.

Nay, it wasn't. What you saw was the beginning of another story, another legend. Do you think that child will ever be content to be a tavern keeper or a farmer when her brow is dragon-marked and your words hang over her? You underestimate our power and that of fate.

Eragon bowed his head. *It's overwhelming. I feel as if I am living in an illusion, a dream where all things are possible. Amazing things do happen, I know, but always to someone else, always in some far-off place and time. But I found your egg, was tutored by a Rider, and dueled a Shade—those can't be the actions of the farm boy I am, or was. Something is changing me.*

It is your wyrd that shapes you, said Saphira. *Every age needs an icon—perhaps that lot has fallen to you. Farm boys are not named for the first Rider without cause. Your namesake was the beginning, and now you are the continuation. Or the end.*

Ach, said Eragon, shaking his head. *It's like speaking in riddles. . . . But if all is foreordained, do our choices mean anything? Or must we just learn to accept our fate?*

Saphira said firmly, *Eragon, I chose you from within my egg. You have been given a chance most would die for. Are you unhappy with that? Clear your mind of such thoughts. They cannot be answered and will make you no happier.*

True, he said glumly. *All the same, they continue to bounce around within my skull.*

Things have been . . . unsettled . . . ever since Brom died. It has made me uneasy, acknowledged Saphira, which surprised him because she rarely seemed perturbed. They were above Tronjheim now. Eragon looked down through the opening in its peak and saw the floor of the dragonhold: Isidar Mithrim, the great star sapphire. He knew that beneath it was nothing but Tronjheim's great central chamber. Saphira descended to the dragonhold on silent wings. She slipped over its rim and dropped to Isidar Mithrim, landing with the sharp clack of claws.

631

Won't you scratch it? asked Eragon.

I think not. It's no ordinary gem. Eragon slid off her back and slowly turned in a circle, absorbing the unusual sight. They were in a round roofless room sixty feet high and sixty feet across. The walls were lined with the dark openings of caves, which differed in size from grottoes no larger than a man to a gaping cavern larger than a house. Shiny rungs were set into the marble walls so that people could reach the highest caves. An enormous archway led out of the dragonhold.

Eragon examined the great gem under his feet and impulsively lay down on it. He pressed his cheek against the cool sapphire, trying to see through it. Distorted lines and wavering spots of color glimmered through the stone, but its thickness made it impossible to discern anything clearly on the floor of the chamber a mile below them.

Will I have to sleep apart from you?

Saphira shook her enormous head. *No, there is a bed for you in my cave. Come see.* She turned and, without opening her wings, jumped twenty feet into the air, landing in a medium-sized cave. He clambered up after her.

The cave was dark brown on the inside and deeper than he had expected. The roughly chiseled walls gave the impression of a natural formation. Near the far wall was a thick cushion large enough for Saphira to curl up on. Beside it was a bed built into the side of the wall. The cave was lit by a single red lantern equipped with a shutter so its glow could be muted.

I like this, said Eragon. *It feels safe.*

Yes. Saphira curled up on the cushion, watching him. With a sigh he sank onto the mattress, weariness seeping through him.

Saphira, you haven't said much while we've been here. What do you think of Tronjheim and Ajihad?

We shall see. . . . It seems, Eragon, that we are embroiled in a new type of warfare here. Swords and claws are useless, but words and alliances may have the same effect. The Twins dislike us—we should be on our guard for any duplicities they might attempt.

Not many of the dwarves trust us. The elves didn't want a human Rider, so there will be opposition from them as well. The best thing we can do is identify those in power and befriend them. And quickly, too.

Do you think it's possible to remain independent of the different leaders?

She shuffled her wings into a more comfortable position. *Ajihad supports our freedom, but we may be unable to survive without pledging our loyalty to one group or another. We'll soon know either way.*

Mandrake Root
and Newt's
Tongue

The blankets were bunched underneath Eragon when he woke, but he was still warm. Saphira was asleep on her cushion, her breath coming in steady gusts.

For the first time since entering Farthen Dûr, Eragon felt secure and hopeful. He was warm and fed and had been able to sleep as long as he liked. Tension unknotted inside him—tension that had been accumulating since Brom's death and, even before, since leaving Palancar Valley.

I don't have to be afraid anymore. But what about Murtagh? No matter the Varden's hospitality, Eragon could not accept it in good conscience, knowing that—intentionally or not—he had led Murtagh to his imprisonment. Somehow the situation had to be resolved.

His gaze roamed the cave's rough ceiling as he thought of Arya. Chiding himself for daydreaming, he tilted his head and looked out at the drag-onhold. A large cat sat on the edge of the cave, licking a paw. It glanced at him, and he saw a flash of slanted red eyes.

Solembum? he asked incredulously.

Obviously. The werecat shook his rough mane and yawned languorously, displaying his long fangs. He stretched, then jumped out of the cave, landing with a solid thump on Isidar Mithrim, twenty feet below. *Coming?*

Eragon looked at Saphira. She was awake now, watching him motionlessly. *Go. I will be fine,* she murmured. Solembum was waiting for him under the arch that led to the rest of Tronjheim.

The moment Eragon's feet touched Isidar Mithrim, the werecat turned with a flick of his paws and disappeared through the arch. Eragon chased after him, rubbing the sleep from his face. He stepped through the archway and found himself standing at the top of Vol Turin, The Endless Staircase. There was nowhere else to go, so he descended to the next level.

He stood in an open arcade that curved gently to the left and encircled Tronjheim's central chamber. Between the slender columns support-ing the arches, Eragon could see Isidar Mithrim sparkling brilliantly above him, as well as the city-mountain's distant base. The circumference of the central chamber increased with each suc-cessive level. The staircase cut through the arcade's floor to an identical level below and descended through scores of arcades until it disappeared in the distance. The sliding trough ran along the outside curve of the stairs. At the top of Vol Turin was a pile of leather squares to slide on. To Eragon's right, a dusty corridor led to that level's rooms and apartments. Solembum padded down the hall, flipping his tail.

Wait, said Eragon.

He tried to catch up with Solembum, but glimpsed him only fleetingly in the abandoned passageways. Then, as Eragon rounded a corner, he saw the werecat stop before a door and yowl. Seemingly of its own accord, the door slid inward. Solembum slipped inside, then the door shut. Eragon halted in front of it, perplexed. He raised his hand to knock, but before he did, the door opened once more, and warm light spilled out. After a moment's indecision he stepped inside.

He entered an earthy two-room suite, lavishly decorated with carved wood and clinging plants. The air was warm, fresh, and humid. Bright lanterns hung on the walls and from the low ceiling. Piles of intriguing items cluttered the floor, obscuring the corners. A large four-poster bed, curtained by even more plants, was in the far room.

In the center of the main room, on a plush leather chair, sat the fortuneteller and witch, Angela. She smiled brightly.

"What are you doing here?" blurted Eragon.

Angela folded her hands in her lap. "Well, why don't you sit on the floor and I'll tell you? I'd offer you a chair, but I'm sitting on the only one." Questions buzzed through Eragon's mind as he settled between two flasks of acrid bubbling green potions.

"So!" exclaimed Angela, leaning forward. "You *are* a Rider. I suspected as much, but I didn't know for certain until yesterday. I'm sure Solembum knew, but he never told me. I should have figured it out the moment you mentioned Brom. Saphira . . . I like the name—fitting for a dragon."

"Brom's dead," said Eragon abruptly. "The Ra'zac killed him."

Angela was taken aback. She twirled a lock of her dense curls. "I'm sorry. I truly am," she said softly.

Eragon smiled bitterly. "But not surprised, are you? You foretold his death, after all."

"I didn't know whose death it would be," she said, shaking her head. "But no . . . I'm not surprised. I met Brom once or twice. He didn't care for my 'frivolous' attitude toward magic. It irritated him."

Eragon frowned. "In Teirm you laughed at his fate and said that it was something of a joke. Why?"

Angela's face tightened momentarily. "In retrospect, it was in rather bad taste, but I didn't know what would befall him. How do I put this? . . . Brom was cursed in a way. It was his wyrd to fail at all of his tasks except one, although through no fault of his own. He was chosen as a Rider, but his dragon was killed. He loved a woman, but it was his affection that was her undoing. And he was chosen, I assume, to guard and train you, but in the end he failed at that as well. The only thing he succeeded at was killing Morzan, and a better deed he couldn't have done."

"Brom never mentioned a woman to me," retorted Eragon.

Angela shrugged carelessly. "I heard it from one who couldn't have lied. But enough of this talk! Life goes on, and we should not trouble the dead with our worries." She scooped a pile of reeds from the floor and deftly started plaiting them together, closing the subject to discussion.

Eragon hesitated, then gave in. "All right. So why are you in Tronjheim instead of Teirm?"

"Ah, at last an interesting question," said Angela. "After hearing Brom's name again during your visit, I sensed a return of the past in Alagaësia. People were whispering that the Empire was hunting a Rider. I knew then that the Varden's dragon egg must have hatched, so I closed my shop and set out to learn more."

"You knew about the egg?"

"Of course I did. I'm not an idiot. I've been

around much longer than you would believe. Very little happens that I don't know about." She paused and concentrated on her weaving. "Anyway, I knew I had to get to the Varden as fast as possible. I've been here for nearly a month now, though I really don't care for this place—it's far too musty for my taste. And everyone in Farthen Dûr is *so* serious and noble. They're probably all doomed to tragic deaths anyway." She gave a long sigh, a mocking expression on her face. "And the dwarves are just a superstitious bunch of ninnies content to hammer rocks all their lives. The only redeeming aspect of this place is all the mushrooms and fungi that grow inside Farthen Dûr."

"Then why stay?" asked Eragon, smiling.

"Because I like to be wherever important events are occurring," said Angela, cocking her head. "Besides, if I had stayed in Teirm, Solembum would have left without me, and I enjoy his company. But tell me, what adventures have befallen you since last we talked?"

For the next hour, Eragon summarized his experiences of the last two and a half months. Angela listened quietly, but when he mentioned Murtagh's name she sputtered, "Murtagh!"

Eragon nodded. "He told me who he is. But let me finish my story before you make any judgments." He continued with his tale. When it was complete, Angela leaned back in her chair thoughtfully, her reeds forgotten. Without warning, Solembum jumped out of a hiding place and landed in her lap. He curled up, eyeing Eragon haughtily.

Angela petted the werecat. "Fascinating. Galbatorix allied with the Urgals, and Murtagh finally out in the open. . . . I'd warn you to be careful with Murtagh, but you're obviously aware of the danger."

"Murtagh has been a steadfast friend and an unwavering ally," said Eragon firmly.

"All the same, be careful." Angela paused, then said distastefully, "And then there's the matter of this Shade, Durza. I think he's the greatest threat to the Varden right now, aside from Galbatorix. I *loathe* Shades—they practice the most unholy magic, after necromancy. I'd like to dig his heart out with a dull hairpin and feed it to a pig!"

Eragon was startled by her sudden vehemence. "I don't understand. Brom told me that Shades were sorcerers who used spirits to accomplish their will, but why does that make them so evil?"

Angela shook her head. "It doesn't. Ordinary sorcerers are just that, ordinary—neither better nor worse than the rest of us. They use their magical strength to control spirits and the spirits' powers. Shades, however, relinquish that control in their search for greater power and allow their bodies to be controlled *by* spirits. Unfortunately, only the evilest spirits seek to possess humans, and once ensconced they never leave. Such possession can happen by accident if a sorcerer summons a spirit stronger than himself. The problem is, once a Shade is created, it's terribly difficult to kill. As I'm sure you know, only two people, Laetrí the Elf and Irnstad the Rider, ever survived that feat."

"I've heard the stories." Eragon gestured at the room. "Why are you living so high up in Tronjheim? Isn't it inconvenient being this isolated? And how did you get all this stuff up here?"

Angela threw back her head and laughed wryly. "Truthfully? I'm in hiding. When I first came to Tronjheim, I had a few days of peace—until one of the guards who let me into Farthen Dûr blabbed about who I was. Then all the magic users here, though they *barely* rate the term, pestered me to join their secret group. Especially those drajl Twins who control it. Finally, I threatened to turn the lot of them into toads, excuse me, frogs, but when that didn't deter them, I sneaked up here in the middle of the night. It was less work than you might imagine, especially for one with my skills."

"Did you have to let the Twins into your mind before you were allowed into Farthen Dûr?" asked Eragon. "I was forced to let them sift through my memories."

A cold gleam leapt into Angela's eye. "The

Twins wouldn't dare probe me, for fear of what I might do to them. Oh, they'd love to, but they know the effort would leave them broken and gibbering nonsense. I've been coming here long before the Varden began examining people's minds . . . and they're not about to start on me now."

She peered into the other room and said, "Well! This has been an enlightening talk, but I'm afraid you have to go now. My brew of mandrake root and newt's tongue is about to boil, and it needs attending. Do come back again when you have the time. And *please* don't tell anyone that I'm here. I'd hate to have to move again. It would make me very . . . *irritated*. And you don't want to see me irritated!"

"I'll keep your secret," assured Eragon, getting up.

Solembum jumped off Angela's lap as she stood. "Good!" she exclaimed.

Eragon said farewell and left the room. Solembum guided him back to the dragonhold, then dismissed him with a twitch of his tail before sauntering away.

HALL OF THE
MOUNTAIN KING

A dwarf was waiting for Eragon in the dragonhold. After bowing and muttering, "Argetlam," the dwarf said with a thick accent,
"Good. Awake. Knurla Orik waits for you." He
bowed again and scurried away. Saphira jumped
out of her cave, landing next to Eragon. Zar'roc
was in her claws.

What's that for? he asked, frowning.

She tilted her head. *Wear it. You are a Rider
and should bear a Rider's sword. Zar'roc may have a
bloody history, but that should not shape your actions. Forge a new history for it, and carry it with
pride.*

Are you sure? Remember Ajihad's counsel.

Saphira snorted, and a puff of smoke rose from
her nostrils. *Wear it, Eragon. If you wish to remain
above the forces here, do not let anyone's disapproval
dictate your actions.*

As you wish, he said reluctantly, buckling on the sword. He clambered onto her back, and Saphira flew out of Tronjheim. There was enough light in Farthen Dûr now that the hazy mass of the crater walls—five miles away in each direction—was visible. While they spiraled down to the city-mountain's base, Eragon told Saphira about his meeting with Angela.

As soon as they landed by one of Tronjheim's gates, Orik ran to Saphira's side. "My king, Hrothgar, wishes to see both of you. Dismount quickly. We must hurry."

Eragon trotted after the dwarf into Tronjheim. Saphira easily kept pace beside them. Ignoring stares from people within the soaring corridor, Eragon asked, "Where will we meet Hrothgar?"

Without slowing, Orik said, "In the throne room beneath the city. It will be a private audience as an act of otho—of 'faith.' You do not have to address him in any special manner, but speak to him respectfully. Hrothgar is quick to anger, but he is wise and sees keenly into the minds of men, so think carefully before you speak."

Once they entered Tronjheim's central chamber, Orik led the way to one of the two descending stairways that flanked the opposite hall. They started down the right-hand staircase, which gently curved inward until it faced the direction they had come from. The other stairway merged with theirs to form a broad cascade of dimly lit steps that ended, after a hundred feet, before two granite doors. A seven-pointed crown was carved across both doors.

Seven dwarves stood guard on each side of the portal. They held burnished mattocks and wore gem-encrusted belts. As Eragon, Orik, and Saphira approached, the dwarves pounded the floor with the mattocks' hafts. A deep boom rolled back up the stairs. The doors swung inward.

A dark hall lay before them, a good bowshot long. The throne room was a natural cave; the walls were lined with stalagmites and stalactites, each thicker than a man. Sparsely hung lanterns cast a moody light. The brown floor was smooth and polished. At the far end of the hall was a black throne with a motionless figure upon it.

Orik bowed. "The king awaits you." Eragon put his hand on Saphira's side, and the two of them continued forward. The doors closed behind them, leaving them alone in the dim throne room with the king.

Their footsteps echoed through the hall as they advanced toward the throne. In the recesses between the stalagmites and stalactites rested large statues. Each sculpture depicted a dwarf king crowned and sitting on a throne; their sightless eyes gazed sternly into the distance, their

645

lined faces set in fierce expressions. A name was chiseled in runes beneath each set of feet.

Eragon and Saphira strode solemnly between the two rows of long-dead monarchs. They passed more than forty statues, then only dark and empty alcoves awaiting future kings. They stopped before Hrothgar at the end of the hall.

The dwarf king himself sat like a statue upon a raised throne carved from a single piéce of black marble. It was blocky, unadorned, and cut with unyielding precision. Strength emanated from the throne, strength that harked back to ancient times when dwarves had ruled in Alagaësia without opposition from elves or humans. A gold helm lined with rubies and diamonds rested on Hrothgar's head in place of a crown. His visage was grim, weathered, and hewn of many years' experience. Beneath a craggy brow glinted deep-set eyes, flinty and piercing. Over his powerful chest rippled a shirt of mail. His white beard was tucked under his belt, and in his lap he held a mighty war hammer with the symbol of Orik's clan embossed on its head.

Eragon bowed awkwardly and knelt. Saphira remained upright. The king stirred, as if awakening from a long sleep, and rumbled, "Rise, Rider, you need not pay tribute to me."

Straightening, Eragon met Hrothgar's impenetrable eyes. The king inspected him with a hard gaze, then said gutturally, "Âz knurl demn lanok.

'Beware, the rock changes'—an old dictum of ours. . . . And nowadays the rock changes very fast indeed." He fingered the war hammer. "I could not meet with you earlier, as Ajihad did, because I was forced to deal with my enemies within the clans. They demanded that I deny you sanctuary and expel you from Farthen Dûr. It has taken much work on my part to convince them otherwise."

"Thank you," said Eragon. "I didn't anticipate how much strife my arrival would cause."

The king accepted his thanks, then lifted a gnarled hand and pointed. "See there, Rider Eragon, where my predecessors sit upon their graven thrones. One and forty there are, with I the forty-second. When I pass from this world into the care of the gods, my hírna will be added to their ranks. The first statue is the likeness of my ancestor Korgan, who forged this mace, Volund. For eight millennia—since the dawn of our race—dwarves have ruled under Farthen Dûr. We are the bones of the land, older than both the fair elves and the savage dragons." Saphira shifted slightly.

Hrothgar leaned forward, his voice gravelly and deep. "I am old, human—even by our reckoning—old enough to have seen the Riders in all their fleeting glory, old enough to have spoken with their last leader, Vrael, who paid tribute to me within these very walls. Few are still alive who can claim that much. I remember the Riders and how they meddled in our affairs. I also remember the peace they kept that made it possible to walk unharmed from Tronjheim to Narda.

"And now you stand before me—a lost tradition revived. Tell me, and speak truly in this, why have you come to Farthen Dûr? I know of the events that made you flee the Empire, but what is your intent now?"

"For now, Saphira and I merely want to recuperate in Tronjheim," Eragon replied. "We are not here to cause trouble, only to find sanctuary from the dangers we've faced for many months. Ajihad may send us to the elves, but until he does, we have no wish to leave."

"Then was it only the desire for safety that drove you?" asked Hrothgar. "Do you just seek to live here and forget your troubles with the Empire?"

Eragon shook his head, his pride rejecting that statement. "If Ajihad told you of my past, you should know that I have grievances enough to fight the Empire until it is nothing but scattered ashes. More than that, though . . . I want to aid those who cannot escape Galbatorix, including my cousin. I have the strength to help, so I must."

The king seemed satisfied by his answer. He turned to Saphira and asked, "Dragon, what think you in this matter? For what reason have you come?"

Saphira lifted the edge of her lip to growl. *Tell him that I thirst for the blood of our enemies and eagerly await the day when we ride to battle against Galbatorix. I've no love or mercy for traitors and egg breakers like that false king. He held me for over a century and, even now, still has two of my brethren, whom I would free if possible. And tell Hrothgar I think you ready for this task.*

Eragon grimaced at her words, but dutifully relayed them. The corner of Hrothgar's mouth lifted in a hint of grim amusement, deepening his wrinkles. "I see that dragons have not changed with the centuries." He rapped the throne with a knuckle. "Do you know why this seat was quarried so flat and angular? So that no one would sit comfortably on it. I have not, and will relinquish it without regret when my time comes. What is there to remind you of your obligations, Eragon? If the Empire falls, will you take Galbatorix's place and claim his kingship?"

"I don't seek to wear the crown or rule," said Eragon, troubled. "Being a Rider is responsibility enough. No, I would not take the throne in Urû'baen . . . not unless there was no one else willing or competent enough to take it."

Hrothgar warned gravely, "Certainly you would be a kinder king than Galbatorix, but no race should have a leader who does not age or leave the throne. The time of the Riders has passed, Eragon. They will never rise again—not even if Galbatorix's other eggs were to hatch."

A shadow crossed his face as he gazed at Eragon's side. "I see that you carry an enemy's sword; I was told of this, and that you travel with a son of the Forsworn. It does not please me to see this weapon." He extended a hand. "I would like to examine it."

Eragon drew Zar'roc and presented it to the king, hilt first. Hrothgar grasped the sword and ran a practiced eye over the red blade. The edge caught the lantern light, reflecting it sharply. The dwarf king tested the point with his palm, then said, "A masterfully forged blade. Elves rarely choose to make swords—they prefer bows and spears—but when they do, the results are unmatched. This is an ill-fated blade; I am not glad to see it within my realm. But carry it if you will; perhaps its luck has changed." He returned Zar'roc, and Eragon sheathed it. "Has my nephew proved helpful during your time here?"

"Who?"

Hrothgar raised a tangled eyebrow. "Orik, my youngest sister's son. He's been serving under Ajihad to show my support for the Varden. It seems that he has been returned to my command, however. I was gratified to hear that you defended him with your words."

Eragon understood that this was another sign

of otho, of "faith," on Hrothgar's part. "I couldn't ask for a better guide."

"That is good," said the king, clearly pleased. "Unfortunately, I cannot speak with you much longer. My advisors wait for me, as there are matters I must deal with. I will say this, though: If you wish the support of the dwarves within my realm, you must first prove yourself to them. We have long memories and do not rush to hasty decisions. Words will decide nothing, only deeds."

"I will keep that in mind," said Eragon, bowing again.

Hrothgar nodded regally. "You may go, then."

Eragon turned with Saphira, and they proceeded out of the hall of the mountain king. Orik was waiting for them on the other side of the stone doors, an anxious expression on his face. He fell in with them as they climbed back up to Tronjheim's main chamber. "Did all go well? Were you received favorably?"

"I think so. But your king is cautious," said Eragon.

"That is how he has survived this long."

I would not want Hrothgar angry at us, observed Saphira.

Eragon glanced at her. *No, I wouldn't either. I'm not sure what he thought of you—he seems to disapprove of dragons, though he didn't say it outright.*

That seemed to amuse Saphira. *In that he is wise, especially since he's barely knee-high to me.*

In Tronjheim's center, under the sparkling Isidar Mithrim, Orik said, "Your blessing yesterday has stirred up the Varden like an overturned beehive. The child Saphira touched has been hailed as a future hero. She and her guardian have been quartered in the finest rooms. Everyone is talking about your 'miracle.' All the human mothers seem intent on finding you and getting the same for their children."

Alarmed, Eragon furtively looked around. "What should we do?"

"Aside from taking back your actions?" asked Orik dryly. "Stay out of sight as much as possible. Everyone will be kept out of the dragonhold, so you won't be disturbed there."

Eragon did not want to return to the dragonhold yet. It was early in the day, and he wanted to explore Tronjheim with Saphira. Now that they were out of the Empire, there was no reason for them to be apart. But he wanted to avoid attention, which would be impossible with her at his side. *Saphira, what do you want to do?*

She nosed him, scales brushing his arm. *I'll return to the dragonhold. There's someone there I want to meet. Wander around as long as you like.*

All right, he said, *but who do you want to meet?* Saphira only winked a large eye at him before padding down one of Tronjheim's four main tunnels.

Eragon explained to Orik where she was going, then said, "I'd like some breakfast. And then I'd like to see more of Tronjheim; it's such an incredible place. I don't want to go to the training grounds until tomorrow, as I'm still not fully recovered."

Orik nodded, his beard bobbing on his chest. "In that case, would you like to visit Tronjheim's library? It's quite old and contains many scrolls of great value. You might find it interesting to read a history of Alagaësia that hasn't been tainted by Galbatorix's hand."

With a pang, Eragon remembered how Brom had taught him to read. He wondered if he still had the skill. A long time had passed since he had seen any written words. "Yes, let's do that."

"Very well."

After they ate, Orik guided Eragon through myriad corridors to their destination. When they reached the library's carved arch, Eragon stepped through it reverently.

The room reminded him of a forest. Rows of graceful colonnades branched up to the dark, ribbed ceiling five stories above. Between the pillars, black-marble bookcases stood back to back. Racks of scrolls covered the walls, interspersed with narrow walkways reached by three twisting staircases. Placed at regular intervals around the walls were pairs of facing stone benches. Between them were small tables whose bases flowed seamlessly into the floor.

Countless books and scrolls were stored in the room. "This is the true legacy of our race," said Orik. "Here reside the writings of our greatest kings and scholars, from antiquity to the present. Also recorded are the songs and stories composed by our artisans. This library may be our most precious possession. It isn't all our work, though—there are human writings here as well. Yours is a short-lived—but prolific—race. We have little or nothing of the elves'. They guard their secrets jealously."

"How long may I stay?" asked Eragon, moving toward the shelves.

"As long as you want. Come to me if you have any questions."

Eragon browsed through the volumes with delight, reaching eagerly for those with interesting titles or covers. Surprisingly, dwarves used the same runes to write as humans. He was somewhat disheartened by how hard reading was after months of neglect. He skipped from book to book, slowly working his way deep into the vast library. Eventually he became immersed in a translation of poems by Dóndar, the tenth dwarf king.

As he scanned the graceful lines, unfamiliar footsteps approached from behind the bookcase.

The sound startled him, but he berated himself for being silly—he could not be the only person in the library. Even so, he quietly replaced the book and slipped away, senses alert for danger. He had been ambushed too many times to ignore such feelings. He heard the footsteps again; only now there were two sets of them. Apprehensive, he darted across an opening, trying to remember exactly where Orik was sitting. He sidestepped around a corner and started as he found himself face to face with the Twins.

The Twins stood together, their shoulders meeting, a blank expression on their smooth faces. Their black snake eyes bored into him. Their hands, hidden within the folds of their purple robes, twitched slightly. They both bowed, but the movement was insolent and derisive.

"We have been searching for you," one said. His voice was uncomfortably like the Ra'zac's.

Eragon suppressed a shiver. "What for?" He reached out with his mind and contacted Saphira. She immediately joined thoughts with him.

"Ever since you met with Ajihad, we have wanted to . . . apologize for our actions." The words were mocking, but not in a way Eragon could challenge. "We have come to pay homage to you." Eragon flushed angrily as they bowed again.

Careful! warned Saphira.

He pushed back his rising temper. He could not afford to be riled by this confrontation. An idea came to him, and he said with a small smile, "Nay, it is I who pay homage to you. Without your approval I never could have gained entrance to Farthen Dûr." He bowed to them in turn, making the movement as insulting as he could.

There was a flicker of irritation in the Twins' eyes, but they smiled and said, "We are honored that one so . . . important . . . as yourself thinks so highly of us. We are in your debt for your kind words."

Now it was Eragon's turn to be irritated. "I will remember that when I'm in need."

Saphira intruded sharply in his thoughts. *You're overdoing it. Don't say anything you'll regret. They will remember every word they can use against you.*

This is difficult enough without you making comments! he snapped. She subsided with an exasperated grumble.

The Twins moved closer, the hems of their robes brushing softly over the floor. Their voices became more pleasant. "We have searched for you for another reason as well, Rider. The few magic users who live in Tronjheim have formed a group. We call ourselves Du Vrangr Gata, or the—"

"The Wandering Path, I know," interrupted

Eragon, remembering what Angela had said about it.

"Your knowledge of the ancient language is impressive," said a Twin smoothly. "As we were saying, Du Vrangr Gata has heard of your mighty feats, and we have come to extend an invitation of membership. We would be honored to have one of your stature as a member. And I suspect that we might be able to assist you as well."

"How?"

The other Twin said, "The two of us have garnered much experience in magical matters. We could guide you . . . show you spells we've discovered and teach you words of power. Nothing would gladden us more than if we could assist, in some small way, your path to glory. No repayment would be necessary, though if you saw fit to share some scraps of your own knowledge, we would be satisfied."

Eragon's face hardened as he realized what they were asking for. "Do you think I'm a half-wit?" he demanded harshly. "I won't apprentice myself to you so you can learn the words Brom taught me! It must have angered you when you couldn't steal them from my mind."

The Twins abruptly dropped their facade of smiles. "We are not to be trifled with, boy! We are the ones who will test your abilities with magic. And that could be *most* unpleasant. Remember, it only takes one misconceived spell to kill someone. You may be a Rider, but the two of us are still stronger than you."

Eragon kept his face expressionless, even as his stomach knotted painfully. "I will consider your offer, but it may—"

"Then we will expect your answer tomorrow. Make sure that it is the right one." They smiled coldly and stalked deeper into the library.

Eragon scowled. *I'm not going to join Du Vrangr Gata, no matter what they do.*

You should talk to Angela, said Saphira. *She's dealt with the Twins before. Perhaps she could be there when they test you. That might prevent them from harming you.*

That's a good idea. Eragon wound through the bookcases until he found Orik sitting on a bench, busily polishing his war ax. "I'd like to return to the dragonhold."

The dwarf slid the haft of the ax through a leather loop at his belt, then escorted Eragon to the gate where Saphira waited. People had already gathered around her. Ignoring them, Eragon scrambled onto Saphira's back, and they escaped to the sky.

This problem must be resolved quickly. You cannot let the Twins intimidate you, Saphira said as she landed on Isidar Mithrim.

I know. But I hope we can avoid angering them. They could be dangerous enemies. He dismounted quickly, keeping a hand on Zar'roc.

So can you. Do you want them as allies?

He shook his head. *Not really . . . I'll tell them tomorrow that I won't join Du Vrangr Gata.*

Eragon left Saphira in her cave and wandered out of the dragonhold. He wanted to see Angela, but he didn't remember how to find her hiding place, and Solembum was not there to guide him. He roamed the deserted corridors, hoping to meet Angela by chance.

When he grew tired of staring at empty rooms and endless gray walls, he retraced his footsteps to the hold. As he neared it, he heard someone speaking within the room. He halted and listened, but the clear voice fell silent. *Saphira? Who's in there?*

A female . . . She has an air of command. I'll distract her while you come in. Eragon loosened Zar'roc in its sheath. *Orik said that intruders would be kept out of the dragonhold, so who could this be?* He steadied his nerves, then stepped into the hold, his hand on the sword.

A young woman stood in the center of the room, looking curiously at Saphira, who had stuck her head out of the cave. The woman appeared to be about seventeen years old. The star sapphire cast a rosy light on her, accentuating skin the same deep shade as Ajihad's. Her velvet dress was wine red and elegantly cut. A jeweled dagger, worn with use, hung from her waist in a tooled leather sheath.

659

Eragon crossed his arms, waiting for the woman to notice him. She continued to look at Saphira, then curtsied and asked sweetly, "Please, could you tell me where Rider Eragon is?" Saphira's eyes sparkled with amusement.

With a small smile, Eragon said, "I am here."

The woman whirled to face him, hand flying to her dagger. Her face was striking, with almond-shaped eyes, wide lips, and round cheekbones. She relaxed and curtsied again. "I am Nasuada," she said.

Eragon inclined his head. "You obviously know who I am, but what do you want?"

Nasuada smiled charmingly. "My father, Ajihad, sent me here with a message. Would you like to hear it?"

The Varden's leader had not struck Eragon as one inclined to marriage and fatherhood. He wondered who Nasuada's mother was—she must have been an uncommon woman to have attracted Ajihad's eye. "Yes, I would."

Nasuada tossed her hair back and recited: "He is pleased that you are doing well, but he cautions you against actions like your benediction yesterday. They create more problems than they solve. Also, he urges you to proceed with the testing as soon as possible—he needs to know how capable you are before he communicates with the elves."

"Did you climb all the way up here just to tell

me that?" Eragon asked, thinking of Vol Turin's length.

Nasuada shook her head. "I used the pulley system that transports goods to the upper levels. We could have sent the message with signals, but I decided to bring it myself and meet you in person."

"Would you like to sit down?" asked Eragon. He motioned toward Saphira's cave.

Nasuada laughed lightly. "No, I am expected elsewhere. You should also know, my father decreed that you may visit Murtagh, if you wish." A somber expression disturbed her previously smooth features. "I met Murtagh earlier. . . . He's anxious to speak with you. He seemed lonely; you should visit him." She gave Eragon directions to Murtagh's cell.

Eragon thanked her for the news, then asked, "What about Arya? Is she better? Can I see her? Orik wasn't able to tell me much."

She smiled mischievously. "Arya is recovering swiftly, as all elves do. No one is allowed to see her except my father, Hrothgar, and the healers. They have spent much time with her, learning all that occurred during her imprisonment." She swept her eyes over Saphira. "I must go now. Is there anything you would have me convey to Ajihad on your behalf?"

"No, except a desire to visit Arya. And give him my thanks for the hospitality he's shown us."

"I will take your words directly to him.

Farewell, Rider Eragon. I hope we shall soon meet again." She curtsied and exited the dragonhold, head held high.

If she really came all the way up Tronjheim just to meet me—pulleys or no pulleys—there was more to this meeting than idle chatter, remarked Eragon.

Aye, said Saphira, withdrawing her head into the cave. Eragon climbed up to her and was surprised to see Solembum curled up in the hollow at the base of her neck. The werecat was purring deeply, his black-tipped tail flicking back and forth. The two of them looked at Eragon impudently, as if to ask, "What?"

Eragon shook his head, laughing helplessly. *Saphira, is Solembum who you wanted to meet?*

They both blinked at him and answered, *Yes.*

Just wondering, he said, mirth still bubbling inside him. It made sense that they would befriend each other—their personalities were similar, and they were both creatures of magic. He sighed, releasing some of the day's tension as he unbuckled Zar'roc. *Solembum, do you know where Angela is? I couldn't find her, and I need her advice.*

Solembum kneaded his paws against Saphira's scaled back. *She is somewhere in Tronjheim.*

When will she return?

Soon.

How soon? he asked impatiently. *I need to talk to her today.*

Not that soon.

The werecat refused to say more, despite Eragon's persistent questions. He gave up and nestled against Saphira. Solembum's purring was a low thrum above his head. *I have to visit Murtagh tomorrow*, he thought, fingering Brom's ring.

ARYA'S TEST

On the morning of their third day in Tronjheim, Eragon rolled out of bed refreshed
and energized. He belted Zar'roc to his
waist and slung his bow and half-full quiver
across his back. After a leisurely flight inside Farthen Dûr with Saphira, he met Orik by one of
Tronjheim's four main gates. Eragon asked him
about Nasuada.

"An unusual girl," answered Orik, glancing
disapprovingly at Zar'roc. "She's totally devoted
to her father and spends all her time helping him.
I think she does more for Ajihad than he
knows—there have been times when she's ma-
neuvered his enemies without ever revealing her
part in it."

"Who is her mother?"

"That I don't know. Ajihad was alone when he
brought Nasuada to Farthen Dûr as a newborn

child. He's never said where he and Nasuada came from."

So she too grew up without knowing her mother. He shook off the thought. "I'm restless. It'll be good to use my muscles. Where should I go for this 'testing' of Ajihad's?"

Orik pointed out into Farthen Dûr. "The training field is half a mile from Tronjheim, though you can't see it from here because it's behind the city-mountain. It's a large area where both dwarves and humans practice."

I'm coming as well, stated Saphira.

Eragon told Orik, and the dwarf tugged on his beard. "That might not be a good idea. There are many people at the training field; you will be sure to attract attention."

Saphira growled loudly. *I will come!* And that settled the matter.

The unruly clatter of fighting reached them from the field: the loud clang of steel clashing on steel, the solid thump of arrows striking padded targets, the rattle and crack of wooden staves, and the shouts of men in mock battle. The noise was confusing, yet each group had a unique rhythm and pattern.

The bulk of the training ground was occupied by a crooked block of foot soldiers struggling with shields and poleaxes nearly as tall as themselves. They drilled as a group in formations.

Practicing beside them were hundreds of individual warriors outfitted with swords, maces, spears, staves, flails, shields of all shapes and sizes, and even, Eragon saw, someone with a pitchfork. Nearly all the fighters wore armor, usually chain mail and a helmet; plate armor was not as common. There were as many dwarves as humans, though the two kept mainly to themselves. Behind the sparring warriors, a broad line of archers fired steadily at gray sackcloth dummies.

Before Eragon had time to wonder what he was supposed to do, a bearded man, his head and blocky shoulders covered by a mail coif, strode over to them. The rest of him was protected by a rough oxhide suit that still had hair on it. A huge sword—almost as long as Eragon—hung across his broad back. He ran a quick eye over Saphira and Eragon, as if evaluating how dangerous they were, then said gruffly, "Knurla Orik. You've been gone too long. There's nobody left for me to spar with."

Orik smiled. "Oeí, that's because you bruise everyone from head to toe with your monster sword."

"Everyone except you," he corrected.

"That's because I'm faster than a giant like you."

The man looked at Eragon again. "I'm Fredric. I've been told to find out what you can do. How strong are you?"

"Strong enough," answered Eragon. "I have to be in order to fight with magic."

Fredric shook his head; the coif clinked like a bag of coins. "Magic has no place in what we do here. Unless you've served in an army, I doubt any fights you've been in lasted more than a few minutes. What we're concerned about is how you'll be able to hold up in a battle that may drag on for hours, or even weeks if it's a siege. Do you know how to use any weapons besides that sword and bow?"

Eragon thought about it. "Only my fists."

"Good answer!" laughed Fredric. "Well, we'll start you off with the bow and see how you do. Then once some space has cleared up on the field, we'll try—" He broke off suddenly and stared past Eragon, scowling angrily.

The Twins stalked toward them, their bald heads pale against their purple robes. Orik muttered something in his own language as he slipped his war ax out of his belt. "I told you two to stay away from the training area," said Fredric, stepping forward threateningly. The Twins seemed frail before his bulk.

They looked at him arrogantly. "We were ordered by Ajihad to test Eragon's proficiency with magic—*before* you exhaust him banging on pieces of metal."

Fredric glowered. "Why can't someone else test him?"

"No one else is powerful enough," sniffed the

Twins. Saphira rumbled deeply and glared at them. A line of smoke trickled from her nostrils, but they ignored her. "Come with us," they ordered, and strode to an empty corner of the field.

Shrugging, Eragon followed with Saphira. Behind him he heard Fredric say to Orik, "We have to stop them from going too far."

"I know," answered Orik in a low voice, "but I can't interfere again. Hrothgar made it clear he won't be able to protect me the next time it happens."

Eragon forced back his growing apprehension. The Twins might know more techniques and words. . . . Still, he remembered what Brom had told him: Riders were stronger in magic than ordinary men. But would that be enough to resist the combined power of the Twins?

Don't worry so much; I will help you, said Saphira. *There are two of us as well.*

He touched her gently on the leg, relieved by her words. The Twins looked at Eragon and asked, "And how do you answer us, Eragon?"

Overlooking the puzzled expressions of his companions, he said flatly, "No."

Sharp lines appeared at the corners of the Twins' mouths. They turned so they faced Eragon obliquely and, bending at the waists, drew a large pentagram on the ground. They stepped in the middle of it, then said harshly, "We begin now. You will attempt to complete the tasks we assign you . . . that is all."

One of the Twins reached into his robe, produced a polished rock the size of Eragon's fist, and set it on the ground. "Lift it to eye level."

That's easy enough, commented Eragon to Saphira. "Stenr reisa!" The rock wobbled, then smoothly rose from the ground. Before it went more than a foot, an unexpected resistance halted it in midair. A smile touched the Twins' lips. Eragon stared at them, enraged—they were trying to make him fail! If he became exhausted now, it would be impossible to complete the harder tasks. Obviously they were confident that their combined strength could easily wear him down.

But I'm not alone either, snarled Eragon to himself. *Saphira, now!* Her mind melded with his, and the rock jerked through the air to stop, quivering, at eye level. The Twins' eyes narrowed cruelly.

"Very . . . good," they hissed. Fredric looked unnerved by the display of magic. "Now move the stone in a circle." Again Eragon struggled against their efforts to stop him, and again—to their obvious anger—he prevailed. The exercises quickly increased in complexity and difficulty until Eragon was forced to think carefully about which words to use. And each time, the Twins fought him bitterly, though the strain never showed on their faces.

It was only with Saphira's support that Eragon was able to hold his ground. In a break between two of the tasks, he asked her, *Why do they con-*

tinue this testing? Our abilities were clear enough from what they saw in my mind. She cocked her head thoughtfully. *You know what?* he said grimly as comprehension came to him. *They're using this as an opportunity to figure out what ancient words I know and perhaps learn new ones themselves.*

Speak softly then, so that they cannot hear you, and use the simplest words possible.

From then on, Eragon used only a handful of basic words to complete the tasks. But finding ways to make them perform in the same manner as a long sentence or phrase stretched his ingenuity to the limit. He was rewarded by the frustration that contorted the Twins' faces as he foiled them again and again. No matter what they tried, they could not get him to use any more words in the ancient language.

More than an hour passed, but the Twins showed no sign of stopping. Eragon was hot and thirsty, but refrained from asking for a reprieve—he would continue as long as they did. There were many tests: manipulating water, casting fire, scrying, juggling rocks, hardening leather, freezing items, controlling the flight of an arrow, and healing scratches. He wondered how long it would take for the Twins to run out of ideas.

Finally the Twins raised their hands and said, "There is only one thing left to do. It is simple enough—any *competent* user of magic should find this easy." One of them removed a silver ring from his finger and smugly handed it to Eragon. "Summon the essence of silver."

Eragon stared at the ring in confusion. What was he supposed to do? The essence of silver, what was that? And how was it to be summoned? Saphira had no idea, and the Twins were not going to help. He had never learned silver's name in the ancient language, though he knew it had to be part of *argetlam*. In desperation he combined the only word that might work, *ethgrí*, or "invoke," with *arget*.

Drawing himself upright, he gathered together what power he had left and parted his lips to deliver the invocation. Suddenly a clear, vibrant voice split the air.

"Stop!"

The word rushed over Eragon like cool water— the voice was strangely familiar, like a half-remembered melody. The back of his neck tingled. He slowly turned toward its source.

A lone figure stood behind them: Arya. A leather strip encircled her brow, restraining her voluminous black hair, which tumbled behind her shoulders in a lustrous cascade. Her slender sword was at her hip, her bow on her back. Plain black leather clothed her shapely frame, poor raiment for one so fair. She was taller than most men, and her stance was perfectly balanced and relaxed. An unmarked face reflected none of the horrific abuse she had endured.

Arya's blazing emerald eyes were fixed on the Twins, who had turned pale with fright. She approached on silent footsteps and said in soft, menacing tones, "Shame! Shame to ask of him what only a master can do. Shame that you should use such methods. Shame that you told Ajihad you didn't know Eragon's abilities. He is competent. Now leave!" Arya frowned dangerously, her slanted eyebrows meeting like lightning bolts in a sharp V, and pointed at the ring in Eragon's hand. "Arget!" she exclaimed thunderously.

The silver shimmered, and a ghostly image of the ring materialized next to it. The two were identical except that the apparition seemed purer and glowed white-hot. At the sight of it, the Twins spun on their heels and fled, robes flapping wildly. The insubstantial ring vanished from Eragon's hand, leaving the circlet of silver behind. Orik and Fredric were on their feet, eyeing Arya warily. Saphira crouched, ready for action.

The elf surveyed them all. Her angled eyes paused on Eragon. Then she turned and strode toward the heart of the training field. The warriors ceased their sparring and looked at her with wonder. Within a few moments the entire field fell silent in awe of her presence.

Eragon was inexorably dragged forward by his own fascination. Saphira spoke, but he was oblivious to her comments. A large circle formed around Arya. Looking only at Eragon, she proclaimed, "I claim the right of trial by arms. Draw your sword."

She means to duel me!

But not, I think, to harm you, replied Saphira slowly. She nudged him with her nose. *Go and acquit yourself well. I will watch.*

Eragon reluctantly stepped forward. He did not want to do this when he was exhausted from magic use and when there were so many people watching. Besides, Arya could be in no shape for sparring. It had only been two days since she had received Tunivor's Nectar. *I will soften my blows so I don't hurt her*, he decided.

They faced each other across the circle of warriors. Arya drew her sword with her left hand. The weapon was thinner than Eragon's, but just as long and sharp. He slid Zar'roc out of its polished sheath and held the red blade point-down by his side. For a long moment they stood motionless, elf and human watching each other. It flashed through Eragon's mind that this was how many of his fights with Brom had started.

He moved forward cautiously. With a blur of motion Arya jumped at him, slashing at his ribs. Eragon reflexively parried the attack, and their swords met in a shower of sparks. Zar'roc was batted aside as if it were no more than a fly. The elf did not take advantage of the opening, however, but spun to her right, hair whipping through the air, and struck at his other side. He barely stopped the blow and backpedaled frantically, stunned by her ferocity and speed.

Belatedly, Eragon remembered Brom's warning that even the weakest elf could easily overpower a human. He had about as much chance of defeating Arya as he did Durza. She attacked again, swinging at his head. He ducked under the razor-sharp edge. But then why was she . . . *toying* with him? For a few long seconds he was too busy warding her off to think about it, then he realized, *She wants to know how proficient I am.*

Understanding that, he began the most complicated series of attacks he knew. He flowed from one pose to another, recklessly combining and modifying them in every possible way. But no matter how inventive he was, Arya's sword always stopped his. She matched his actions with effortless grace.

Engaged in a fiery dance, their bodies were linked and separated by the flashing blades. At times they nearly touched, taut skin only a hair's breadth away, but then momentum would whirl them apart, and they would withdraw for a second, only to join again. Their sinuous forms wove together like twisting ropes of windblown smoke.

Eragon could never remember how long they fought. It was timeless, filled with nothing but action and reaction. Zar'roc grew leaden in his hand; his arm burned ferociously with each stroke. At last, as he lunged forward, Arya nimbly sidestepped, sweeping the point of her sword up to his jawbone with supernatural speed.

Eragon froze as the icy metal touched his skin. His muscles trembled from the exertion. Dimly he heard Saphira bugle and the warriors cheering raucously around them. Arya lowered her sword and sheathed it. "You have passed," she said quietly amid the noise.

Dazed, he slowly straightened. Fredric was beside him now, thumping his back enthusiastically. "That was incredible swordsmanship! I even learned some new moves from watching the two of you. And the elf—stunning!"

But I lost, he protested silently. Orik praised his performance with a broad smile, but all Eragon noticed was Arya, standing alone and silent. She motioned slightly with a finger, no more than a twitch, toward a knoll about a mile from the practice field, then turned and walked away. The crowd melted before her. A hush fell over the men and dwarves as she passed.

Eragon turned to Orik. "I have to go. I'll return to the dragonhold soon." With a swift jab, Eragon sheathed Zar'roc and pulled himself onto Saphira. She took off over the training field, which turned into a sea of faces as everyone looked at her.

As they soared toward the knoll, Eragon saw Arya running below them with clean, easy strides.

Saphira commented, *You find her form pleasing, do you not?*

Yes, he admitted, blushing.

Her face does have more character than that of most humans, she sniffed. *But it's long, like a horse's, and overall she's rather shapeless.*

Eragon looked at Saphira with amazement. *You're jealous, aren't you!*

Impossible. I never get jealous, she said, offended.

You are now, admit it! he laughed.

She snapped her jaws together loudly. *I am not!* He smiled and shook his head, but let her denial stand. She landed heavily on the knoll, jostling him roughly. He jumped down without remarking on it.

676

Arya was close behind them. Her fleet stride carried her faster than any runner Eragon had seen. When she reached the top of the knoll, her breathing was smooth and regular. Suddenly tongue-tied, Eragon dropped his gaze. She strode past him and said to Saphira, "Skulblaka, eka celöbra ono un mulabra ono un onr Shur'tugal né haina. Atra nosu waisé fricaya."

Eragon did not recognize most of the words, but Saphira obviously understood the message. She shuffled her wings and surveyed Arya curiously. Then she nodded, humming deeply. Arya smiled. "I am glad that you recovered," Eragon said. "We didn't know if you would live or not."

"That is why I came here today," said Arya, facing him. Her rich voice was accented and exotic. She spoke clearly, with a hint of trill, as if she were about to sing. "I owe you a debt that must be repaid. You saved my life. That can never be forgotten."

"It—it was nothing," said Eragon, fumbling with the words and knowing they were not true, even as he spoke them. Embarrassed, he changed the subject. "How did you come to be in Gil'ead?"

Pain shadowed Arya's face. She looked away into the distance. "Let us walk." They descended from the knoll and meandered toward Farthen Dûr. Eragon respected Arya's silence as they walked. Saphira padded quietly beside them. Finally Arya lifted her head and said with the grace of her kind, "Ajihad told me you were present when Saphira's egg appeared."

"Yes." For the first time, Eragon thought about the energy it must have taken to transport the egg over the dozens of leagues that separated Du Weldenvarden from the Spine. To even attempt such a feat was courting disaster, if not death.

Her next words were heavy. "Then know this: at the moment you first beheld it, I was captured by Durza." Her voice filled with bitterness and grief. "It was he who led the Urgals that ambushed and slew my companions, Fäolin and Glenwing. Somehow he knew where to wait for us—we had no warning. I was drugged and transported to Gil'ead. There, Durza was charged by Galbatorix to learn where I had sent the egg and all I knew of Ellesméra."

She stared ahead icily, jaw clenched. "He tried for months without success. His methods were . . . harsh. When torture failed, he ordered his soldiers to use me as they would. Fortunately, I still had the strength to nudge their minds and make them incapable. At last Galbatorix ordered that I was to be brought to Urû'baen. Dread filled me when I learned this, as I was weary in both mind and body and had no strength to resist him. If it were not for you, I would have stood before Galbatorix in a week's time."

Eragon shuddered inwardly. It was amazing what she had survived. The memory of her injuries was still vivid in his mind. Softly, he asked, "Why do you tell me all this?"

"So that you know what I was saved from. Do not presume I can ignore your deed."

Humbled, he bowed his head. "What will you do now—return to Ellesméra?"

"No, not yet. There is much that must be done here. I cannot abandon the Varden—Ajihad needs my help. I've seen you tested in both arms and magic today. Brom taught you well. You are ready to proceed in your training."

"You mean for me to go to Ellesméra?"

"Yes."

Eragon felt a flash of irritation. Did he and Saphira have no say in the matter? "When?"

"That is yet to be decided, but not for some weeks."

At least they gave us that much time, thought Eragon. Saphira mentioned something to him, and he in turn asked Arya, "What did the Twins want me to do?"

Arya's sculpted lip curled with disgust. "Something not even they can accomplish. It is possible to speak the name of an object in the ancient language and summon its true form. It takes years of work and great discipline, but the reward is complete control over the object. That is why one's true name is always kept hidden, for if it were known by any with evil in their hearts, they could dominate you utterly."

"It's strange," said Eragon after a moment, "but before I was captured at Gil'ead, I had visions of you in my dreams. It was like scrying— and I was able to scry you later—but it was always during my sleep."

Arya pursed her lips pensively. "There were times I felt as if another presence was watching me, but I was often confused and feverish. I've never heard of anyone, either in lore or legend, being able to scry in their sleep."

"I don't understand it myself," said Eragon, looking at his hands. He twirled Brom's ring around his finger. "What does the tattoo on your shoulder mean? I didn't mean to see it, but when I was healing your wounds . . . it couldn't be helped. It's just like the symbol on this ring."

"You have a ring with the yawë on it?" she asked sharply.

"Yes. It was Brom's. See?"

He held out the ring. Arya examined the sapphire, then said, "This is a token given only to the most valued elf-friends—so valued, in fact, it has not been used in centuries. Or so I thought. I never knew that Queen Islanzadí thought so highly of Brom."

"I shouldn't wear it, then," said Eragon, afraid that he had been presumptuous.

"No, keep it. It will give you protection if you meet my people by chance, and it may help you gain favor with the queen. Tell no one of my tattoo. It should not be revealed."

"Very well."

He enjoyed talking with Arya and wished their conversation could have lasted longer. When they parted, he wandered through Farthen Dûr, conversing with Saphira. Despite his prodding, she refused to tell him what Arya had said to her. Eventually his thoughts turned to Murtagh and then to Nasuada's advice. *I'll get something to eat, then go see him,* he decided. *Will you wait for me so I can return to the dragonhold with you?*

I will wait—go, said Saphira.

With a grateful smile, Eragon dashed to Tronjheim, ate in an obscure corner of a kitchen, then followed Nasuada's instructions until he reached a small gray door guarded by a man and a dwarf. When he requested entrance, the dwarf banged on the door three times, then unbolted it. "Just holler when you want to leave," said the man with a friendly smile.

The cell was warm and well lit, with a washbasin in one corner and a writing desk—equipped with quills and ink—in another. The ceiling was extensively carved with lacquered figures; the floor was covered with a plush rug. Murtagh lay on a stout bed, reading a scroll. He looked up in surprise and exclaimed cheerily, "Eragon! I'd hoped you would come!"

"How did . . . I mean I thought—"

"You thought I was stuck in some rat hole chewing on hardtack," said Murtagh, rolling upright with a grin. "Actually, I expected the same thing, but Ajihad lets me have all this as long as I don't cause trouble. And they bring me huge meals, as well as anything I want from the library. If I'm not careful, I'll turn into a fat scholar."

Eragon laughed, and with a wondering smile seated himself next to Murtagh. "But aren't you angry? You're still a prisoner."

"Oh, I was at first," said Murtagh with a shrug. "But the more I thought about it, the more I came to realize that this is really the best place for me. Even if Ajihad gave me my freedom, I would stay in my room most of the time anyway."

"But why?"

"You know well enough. No one would be at ease around me, knowing my true identity, and there would always be people who wouldn't limit themselves to harsh looks or words. But enough of that, I'm eager to know what's new. Come, tell me."

Eragon recounted the events of the past two days, including his encounter with the Twins in the library. When he finished, Murtagh leaned back reflectively. "I suspect," he said, "that Arya is more important than either of us thought. Consider what you've learned: she is a master of the sword, powerful in magic, and, most significantly, was chosen to guard Saphira's egg. She cannot be ordinary, even among the elves."

Eragon agreed.

Murtagh stared at the ceiling. "You know, I find this imprisonment oddly peaceful. For once in my life I don't have to be afraid. I know I ought to be . . . yet something about this place puts me at ease. A good night's sleep helps, too."

"I know what you mean," said Eragon wryly. He moved to a softer place on the bed. "Nasuada said that she visited you. Did she say anything interesting?"

Murtagh's gaze shifted into the distance, and

he shook his head. "No, she only wanted to meet me. Doesn't she look like a princess? And the way she carries herself! When she first entered through that doorway, I thought she was one of the great ladies of Galbatorix's court. I've seen earls and counts who had wives that, compared to her, were more fitted for life as a hog than of nobility."

Eragon listened to his praise with growing apprehension. *It may mean nothing,* he reminded himself. *You're leaping to conclusions.* Yet the foreboding would not leave him. Trying to shake off the feeling, he asked, "How long are you going to remain imprisoned, Murtagh? You can't hide forever."

Murtagh shrugged carelessly, but there was weight behind his words. "For now I'm content to stay and rest. There's no reason for me to seek shelter elsewhere nor submit myself to the Twins' examination. No doubt I'll tire of this eventually, but for now . . . I am content."

THE SHADOWS
LENGTHEN

S aphira woke Eragon with a sharp rap of her snout, bruising him with her hard jaw. "Ouch!" he exclaimed, sitting upright. The cave was dark except for a faint glow emanating from the shuttered lantern. Outside in the dragonhold, Isidar Mithrim glittered with a thousand different colors, illuminated by its girdle of lanterns.

An agitated dwarf stood in the entrance to the cave, wringing his hands. "You must come, Argetlam! Great trouble—Ajihad summons you. There is no time!"

"What's wrong?" asked Eragon.

The dwarf only shook his head, beard wagging. "Go, you must! Carkna brâgha! Now!"

Eragon belted on Zar'roc, grabbed his bow and arrows, then strapped the saddle onto Saphira. *So much for a good night's sleep,* she groused, crouching low to the floor so he could clamber onto her back. He yawned loudly as Saphira launched herself from the cave.

Orik was waiting for them with a grim expression when they landed at Tronjheim's gates. "Come, the others are waiting." He led them through Tronjheim to Ajihad's study. On the way, Eragon plied him with questions, but Orik would only say, "I don't know enough myself— wait until you hear Ajihad."

The large study door was opened by a pair of burly guards. Ajihad stood behind his desk, bleakly inspecting a map. Arya and a man with wiry arms were there as well. Ajihad looked up. "Good, you're here, Eragon. Meet Jörmundur, my second in command."

They acknowledged each other, then turned their attention to Ajihad. "I roused the five of you because we are all in grave danger. About half an hour ago a dwarf ran out of an abandoned tunnel under Tronjheim. He was bleeding and nearly incoherent, but he had enough sense left to tell the dwarves what was pursuing him: an army of Urgals, maybe a day's march from here."

Shocked silence filled the study. Then Jörmundur swore explosively and began asking questions at the same time Orik did. Arya remained silent. Ajihad raised his hands. "Quiet! There is more. The Urgals aren't approaching *over* land, but *under* it. They're in the tunnels . . . we're going to be attacked from below."

Eragon raised his voice in the din that followed. "Why didn't the dwarves know about this sooner? How did the Urgals find the tunnels?"

"We're lucky to know about it this early!" bellowed Orik. Everyone stopped talking to hear him. "There are hundreds of tunnels throughout the Beor Mountains, uninhabited since the day they were mined. The only dwarves who go in them are eccentrics who don't want contact with anyone. We could have just as easily received no warning at all."

Ajihad pointed at the map, and Eragon moved closer. The map depicted the southern half of Alagaësia, but unlike Eragon's, it showed the entire Beor Mountain range in detail. Ajihad's finger was on the section of the Beor Mountains that touched Surda's eastern border. "This," he said, "is where the dwarf claimed to have come from."

"Orthíad!" exclaimed Orik. At Jörmundur's puzzled inquiry, he explained, "It's an ancient dwelling of ours that was deserted when Tronjheim was completed. During its time it was the greatest of our cities. But no one's lived there for centuries."

"And it's old enough for some of the tunnels to have collapsed," said Ajihad. "That's how we surmise it was discovered from the surface. I suspect that Orthíad is now being called Ithrö Zhâda. That's where the Urgal column that was chasing Eragon and Saphira was supposed to go, and I'm sure it's where the Urgals have been migrating all year. From Ithrö Zhâda they can travel anywhere they want in the Beor Mountains. They have the power to destroy both the Varden and the dwarves."

Jörmundur bent over the map, eyeing it carefully. "Do you know how many Urgals there are? Are Galbatorix's troops with them? We can't plan a defense without knowing how large their army is."

Ajihad replied unhappily, "We're unsure about both those things, yet our survival rests on that last question. If Galbatorix has augmented the Urgals' ranks with his own men, we don't stand a chance. But if he hasn't—because he still doesn't want his alliance with the Urgals revealed, or for some other reason—it's possible we can win. Neither Orrin nor the elves can help us at this late hour. Even so, I sent runners to both of them with news of our plight. At the very least they won't be caught by surprise if we fall."

He drew a hand across his coal-black brow. "I've already talked with Hrothgar, and we've decided on a course of action. Our only hope is to contain the Urgals in three of the larger tunnels and channel them into Farthen Dûr so they don't swarm inside Tronjheim like locusts.

"I need you, Eragon and Arya, to help the dwarves collapse extraneous tunnels. The job is too big for normal means. Two groups of dwarves are already working on it: one outside Tronjheim, the other beneath it. Eragon, you're to work with the group outside. Arya, you'll be with the one underground; Orik will guide you to them."

"Why not collapse all the tunnels instead of leaving the large ones untouched?" asked Eragon.

"Because," said Orik, "that would force the Urgals to clear away the rubble, and they might decide to go in a direction we don't want them to. Plus, if we cut ourselves off, they could attack other dwarf cities—which we wouldn't be able to assist in time."

"There's also another reason," said Ajihad. "Hrothgar warned me that Tronjheim sits on such a dense network of tunnels that if too many are weakened, sections of the city will sink into the ground under their own weight. We can't risk that."

Jörmundur listened intently, then asked, "So there won't be any fighting inside Tronjheim? You said the Urgals would be channeled outside the city, into Farthen Dûr."

Ajihad responded quickly, "That's right. We can't defend Tronjheim's entire perimeter—it's too big for our forces—so we're going to seal all the passageways and gates leading into it. That will force the Urgals out onto the flats surrounding Tronjheim, where there's plenty of maneuvering room for our armies. Since the Urgals have access to the tunnels, we cannot risk an extended battle. As long as they are here, we will be in constant danger of them quarrying up through Tronjheim's floor. If that happens, we'll be trapped, attacked from both the outside and inside. We have to prevent the Urgals from taking Tronjheim. If they secure it, it's doubtful we will have the strength to roust them."

"And what of our families?" asked Jörmundur. "I won't see my wife and son murdered by Urgals."

The lines deepened on Ajihad's face. "All the women and children are being evacuated into the surrounding valleys. If we are defeated, they have guides who will take them to Surda. That's all I can do, under the circumstances."

Jörmundur struggled to hide his relief. "Sir, is Nasuada going as well?"

"She is not pleased, but yes." All eyes were on Ajihad as he squared his shoulders and announced, "The Urgals will arrive in a matter of hours. We know their numbers are great, but we *must* hold Farthen Dûr. Failure will mean the dwarves' downfall, death to the Varden—and eventual defeat for Surda and the elves. This is one battle we cannot lose. Now go and complete your tasks! Jörmundur, ready the men to fight."

They left the study and scattered: Jörmundur to the barracks, Orik and Arya to the stairs leading

689

underground, and Eragon and Saphira down one of Tronjheim's four main halls. Despite the early hour, the city-mountain swarmed like an anthill. People were running, shouting messages, and carrying bundles of belongings.

Eragon had fought and killed before, but the battle that awaited them sent stabs of fear into his chest. He had never had a chance to anticipate a fight. Now that he did, it filled him with dread. He was confident when facing only a few opponents—he knew he could easily defeat three or four Urgals with Zar'roc and magic—but in a large conflict, anything could happen.

They exited Tronjheim and looked for the dwarves they were supposed to help. Without the sun or moon, the inside of Farthen Dûr was dark as lampblack, punctuated by glittering lanterns bobbing jerkily in the crater. *Perhaps they're on the far side of Tronjheim*, suggested Saphira. Eragon agreed and swung onto her back.

They glided around Tronjheim until a clump of lanterns came into sight. Saphira angled toward them, then with no more than a whisper landed beside a group of startled dwarves who were busy digging with pickaxes. Eragon quickly explained why he was there. A sharp-nosed dwarf told him, "There's a tunnel about four yards directly underneath us. Any help you could give us would be appreciated."

"If you clear the area over the tunnel, I'll see

what I can do." The sharp-nosed dwarf looked doubtful, but ordered the diggers off the site.

Breathing slowly, Eragon prepared to use magic. It might be possible to actually move all the dirt off the tunnel, but he needed to conserve his strength for later. Instead, he would try to collapse the tunnel by applying force to weak sections of its ceiling.

"Thrysta deloi," he whispered and sent tentacles of power into the soil. Almost immediately they encountered rock. He ignored it and reached farther down until he felt the hollow emptiness of the tunnel. Then he began searching for flaws in the rock. Every time he found one, he pushed on it, elongating and widening it. It was strenuous work, but no more than it would have been to split the stone by hand. He made no visible progress—a fact that was not lost on the impatient dwarves.

Eragon persevered. Before long he was rewarded by a resounding crack that could be heard clearly on the surface. There was a persistent screech, then the ground slid inward like water draining from a tub, leaving a gaping hole seven yards across.

As the delighted dwarves walled off the tunnel with rubble, the sharp-nosed dwarf led Eragon to the next tunnel. This one was much more difficult to collapse, but he managed to duplicate the feat. Over the next few hours, he collapsed over a

691

half-dozen tunnels throughout Farthen Dûr, with Saphira's help.

Light crept into the small patch of sky above them as he worked. It was not enough to see by, but it bolstered Eragon's confidence. He turned away from the crumpled ruins of the latest tunnel and surveyed the land with interest.

A mass exodus of women and children, along with the Varden's elders, streamed out of Tronjheim. Everyone carried loads of provisions, clothes, and belongings. A small group of warriors, predominantly boys and old men, accompanied them.

Most of the activity, however, was at the base of Tronjheim, where the Varden and dwarves were assembling their army, which was divided into three battalions. Each section bore the Varden's standard: a white dragon holding a rose above a sword pointing downward on a purple field.

The men were silent, ironfisted. Their hair flowed loosely from under their helmets. Many warriors had only a sword and a shield, but there were several ranks of spear- and pikemen. In the rear of the battalions, archers tested their bowstrings.

The dwarves were garbed in heavy battle gear. Burnished steel hauberks hung to their knees, and thick roundshields, stamped with the crests of their clan, rested on their left arms. Short swords were sheathed at their waists, while in their right hands they carried mattocks or war axes. Their legs were covered with extra-fine mail. They wore iron caps and brass-studded boots.

A small figure detached itself from the far battalion and hurried toward Eragon and Saphira. It was Orik, clad like the other dwarves. "Ajihad wants you to join the army," he said. "There are no more tunnels to cave in. Food is waiting for both of you."

Eragon and Saphira accompanied Orik to a tent, where they found bread and water for Eragon and a pile of dried meat for Saphira. They ate it without complaint; it was better than going hungry.

693

When they finished, Orik told them to wait and disappeared into the battalion's ranks. He returned, leading a line of dwarves burdened with tall piles of plate armor. Orik lifted a section of it and handed it to Eragon.

"What is this?" asked Eragon, fingering the polished metal. The armor was intricately wrought with engraving and gold filigree. It was an inch thick in places and very heavy. No man could fight under that much weight. And there were far too many pieces for one person.

"A gift from Hrothgar," said Orik, looking pleased with himself. "It has lain so long among our other treasures that it was almost forgotten. It was forged in another age, before the fall of the Riders."

"But what's it *for?*" asked Eragon.

"Why, it's dragon armor, of course! You don't think that dragons went into battle unprotected? Complete sets are rare because they took so long to make and because dragons were always growing. Still, Saphira isn't too big yet, so this should fit her reasonably well."

Dragon armor! As Saphira nosed one of the pieces, Eragon asked, *What do you think?*

Let's try it on, she said, a fierce gleam in her eye.

After a good deal of struggling, Eragon and Orik stepped back to admire the result. Saphira's entire neck—except for the spikes along its ridge—was covered with triangular scales of overlapping armor. Her belly and chest were protected by the heaviest plates, while the lightest ones were on her tail. Her legs and back were completely encased. Her wings were left bare. A single molded plate lay on top of her head, leaving her lower jaw free to bite and snap.

Saphira arched her neck experimentally, and the armor flexed smoothly with her. *This will slow me down, but it'll help stop the arrows. How do I look?*

Very intimidating, replied Eragon truthfully. That pleased her.

Orik picked up the remaining items from the

ground. "I brought you armor as well, though it took much searching to find your size. We rarely forge arms for men or elves. I don't know who this was made for, but it has never been used and should serve you well."

Over Eragon's head went a stiff shirt of leather-backed mail that fell to his knees like a skirt. It rested heavily on his shoulders and clinked when he moved. He belted Zar'roc over it, which helped keep the mail from swinging. On his head went a leather cap, then a mail coif, and finally a gold-and-silver helm. Bracers were strapped to his forearms, and greaves to his lower legs. For his hands there were mail-backed gloves. Last, Orik handed him a broad shield emblazoned with an oak tree.

695

Knowing that what he and Saphira had been given was worth several fortunes, Eragon bowed and said, "Thank you for these gifts. Hrothgar's presents are greatly appreciated."

"Don't give thanks now," said Orik with a chuckle. "Wait until the armor saves your life."

The warriors around them began marching away. The three battalions were repositioning themselves in different parts of Farthen Dûr. Unsure of what they should do, Eragon looked at Orik, who shrugged and said, "I suppose we should accompany them." They trailed behind a battalion as it headed toward the crater wall. Eragon asked about the Urgals, but Orik only knew that scouts had been posted underground in the tunnels and that nothing had been seen or heard yet.

The battalion halted at one of the collapsed tunnels. The dwarves had piled the rubble so that anyone inside the tunnel could easily climb out. *This must be one of the places they're going to force the Urgals to surface*, Saphira pointed out.

Hundreds of lanterns were fixed atop poles and stuck into the ground. They provided a great pool of light that glowed like an evening sun. Fires blazed along the rim of the tunnel's roof, huge cauldrons of pitch heating over them. Eragon looked away, fighting back revulsion. It was a terrible way to kill anyone, even an Urgal.

696 Rows of sharpened saplings were being pounded into the ground to provide a thorny barrier between the battalion and the tunnel. Eragon saw an opportunity to help and joined a group of men digging trenches between the saplings. Saphira assisted as well, scooping out the dirt with her giant claws. While they labored, Orik left to supervise the construction of a barricade to shield the archers. Eragon drank gratefully from the wineskin whenever it was passed around. After the trenches were finished and filled with pointed stakes, Saphira and Eragon rested.

Orik returned to find them seated together. He wiped his brow. "All the men and dwarves are on the battlefield. Tronjheim has been sealed off. Hrothgar has taken charge of the battalion to our left. Ajihad leads the one ahead of us."

"Who commands this one?"

"Jörmundur." Orik sat with a grunt and placed his war ax on the ground.

Saphira nudged Eragon. *Look.* His hand tightened on Zar'roc as he saw Murtagh, helmed, carrying a dwarven shield and his hand-and-a-half sword, approaching with Tornac.

Orik cursed and leapt to his feet, but Murtagh said quickly, "It's all right; Ajihad released me."

"Why would he do that?" demanded Orik.

Murtagh smiled wryly. "He said this was an opportunity to prove my good intentions. Apparently, he doesn't think I would be able to do much damage even if I did turn on the Varden."

Eragon nodded in welcome, relaxing his grip. Murtagh was an excellent and merciless fighter— exactly whom Eragon wanted by his side during battle.

"How do we know you're not lying?" asked Orik.

"Because I say so," announced a firm voice. Ajihad strode into their midst, armed for battle with a breastplate and an ivory-handled sword. He put a strong hand on Eragon's shoulder and drew him away where the others could not hear. He cast an eye over Eragon's armor. "Good, Orik outfitted you."

"Yes . . . has anything been seen in the tunnels?"

"Nothing." Ajihad leaned on his sword. "One of the Twins is staying in Tronjheim. He's going to watch the battle from the dragonhold and relay information through his brother to me. I know you can speak with your mind. I need you to tell the Twins anything, *anything*, unusual that you see while fighting. Also, I'll relay orders to you through them. Do you understand?"

The thought of being linked to the Twins filled Eragon with loathing, but he knew it was necessary. "I do."

Ajihad paused. "You're not a foot soldier or horseman, nor any other type of warrior I'm used to commanding. Battle may prove differently, but I think you and Saphira will be safer on the ground. In the air, you'll be a choice target for Urgal archers. Will you fight from Saphira's back?"

Eragon had never been in combat on horseback, much less on Saphira. "I'm not sure what we'll do. When I'm on Saphira, I'm up too high to fight all but a Kull."

"There will be plenty of Kúll, I'm afraid," said Ajihad. He straightened, pulling his sword out of the ground. "The only advice I can give you is to avoid unnecessary risks. The Varden cannot afford to lose you." With that, he turned and left.

Eragon returned to Orik and Murtagh and hunkered next to Saphira, leaning his shield against his knees. The four of them waited in silence like the hundreds of warriors around them. Light from Farthen Dûr's opening waned as the sun crept below the crater rim.

Eragon turned to scan the encampment and froze, heart jolting. About thirty feet away sat Arya with her bow in her lap. Though he knew it was unreasonable, he had hoped she might accompany the other women out of Farthen Dûr. Concerned, he hastened to her. "You will fight?"

"I do what I must," Arya said calmly.

"But it's too dangerous!"

Her face darkened. "Do not pamper me, human. Elves train both their men and women to fight. I am not one of your helpless females to run away whenever there is danger. I was given the task of protecting Saphira's egg . . . which I failed. My breoal is dishonored and would be further shamed if I did not guard you and Saphira on this field. You forget that I am stronger with magic than any here, including you. If the Shade comes, who can defeat him but me? And who else has the right?"

Eragon stared at her helplessly, knowing she was right and hating the fact. "Then stay safe." Out of desperation, he added in the ancient language, "Wiol pömnuria ilian." For my happiness.

Arya turned her gaze away uneasily, the fringe of her hair obscuring her face. She ran a hand along her polished bow, then murmured, "It is my wyrd to be here. The debt must be paid."

He abruptly retreated to Saphira. Murtagh looked at him curiously. "What did she say?"

"Nothing."

Wrapped in their own thoughts, the defenders sank into a brooding silence as the hours crawled by. Farthen Dûr's crater again grew black, except for the sanguine lantern glow and the fires heating the pitch. Eragon alternated between myopically examining the links of his mail and spying on Arya. Orik repeatedly ran a whetstone over the blade of his ax, periodically eyeing the edge between strokes; the rasp of metal on stone was irritating. Murtagh just stared into the distance.

Occasionally, messengers ran through the encampment, causing the warriors to surge to their feet. But it always proved to be a false alarm. The men and dwarves became strained; angry voices were often heard. The worst part about Farthen Dûr was the lack of wind—the air was dead, motionless. Even when it grew warm and stifling and filled with smoke, there was no reprieve.

As the night dragged on, the battlefield stilled, silent as death. Muscles stiffened from the waiting. Eragon stared blankly into the darkness with heavy eyelids. He shook himself to alertness and tried to focus through his stupor.

Finally Orik said, "It's late. We should sleep. If anything happens, the others will wake us."

Murtagh grumbled, but Eragon was too tired to complain. He curled up against Saphira, using his shield as a pillow. As his eyes closed, he saw that Arya was still awake, watching over them.

His dreams were confused and disturbing, full of horned beasts and unseen menaces. Over and over he heard a deep voice ask, "Are you ready?" But he never had an answer. Plagued by such visions, his sleep was shallow and uneasy until something touched his arm. He woke with a start.

BATTLE UNDER
FARTHEN DÛR

It has begun," Arya said with a sorrowful expression. The troops in the encampment stood alertly with their weapons drawn. Orik swung his ax to make sure he had enough room. Arya nocked an arrow and held it ready to shoot.

"A scout ran out of a tunnel a few minutes ago," said Murtagh to Eragon. "The Urgals are coming."

Together they watched the dark mouth of the tunnel through the ranks of men and sharpened stakes. A minute dragged by, then another . . . and another. Without taking his eyes from the tunnel, Eragon hoisted himself into Saphira's saddle, Zar'roc in his hand, a comfortable weight. Murtagh mounted Tornac beside him. Then a man cried, "I hear them!"

The warriors stiffened; grips tightened on

weapons. No one moved . . . no one breathed. Somewhere a horse nickered.

Harsh Urgal shouts shattered the air as dark shapes boiled upward in the tunnel's opening. At a command, the cauldrons of pitch were tilted on their sides, pouring the scalding liquid into the tunnel's hungry throat. The monsters howled in pain, arms flailing. A torch was thrown onto the bubbling pitch, and an orange pillar of greasy flames roared up in the opening, engulfing the Urgals in an inferno. Sickened, Eragon looked across Farthen Dûr at the other two battalions and saw similar fires by each. He sheathed Zar'roc and strung his bow.

More Urgals soon tamped the pitch down and clambered out of the tunnels over their burned brethren. They clumped together, presenting a solid wall to the men and dwarves. Behind the palisade Orik had helped build, the first row of archers pulled on their bows and fired. Eragon and Arya added their arrows to the deadly swarm and watched the shafts eat through the Urgals' ranks.

The Urgal line wavered, threatening to break, but they covered themselves with their shields and weathered the attack. Again the archers fired, but the Urgals continued to stream onto the surface at a ferocious rate.

Eragon was dismayed by their numbers. They were supposed to kill every single one? It seemed a madman's task. His only encouragement was that he saw none of Galbatorix's troops with the Urgals. Not yet, at least.

The opposing army formed a solid mass of bodies that seemed to stretch endlessly. Tattered and sullen standards were raised in the monsters' midst. Baleful notes echoed through Farthen Dûr as war horns sounded. The entire group of Urgals charged with savage war cries.

They dashed against the rows of stakes, covering them with slick blood and limp corpses as the ranks at the vanguard were crushed against the posts. A cloud of black arrows flew over the barrier at the crouched defenders. Eragon ducked behind his shield, and Saphira covered her head. Arrows rattled harmlessly against her armor.

Momentarily foiled by the pickets, the Urgal horde milled with confusion. The Varden bunched together, waiting for the next attack. After a pause, the war cries were raised again as the Urgals surged forward. The assault was bitter. Its momentum carried the Urgals through the stakes, where a line of pikemen jabbed frantically at their ranks, trying to repel them. The pikemen held briefly, but the ominous tide of Urgals could not be halted, and they were overwhelmed.

The first lines of defense breached, the main bodies of the two forces collided for the first time. A deafening roar burst from the men and dwarves as they rushed into the conflict. Saphira bellowed and leapt toward the fight, diving into a whirlwind of noise and blurred action.

With her jaws and talons, Saphira tore through an Urgal. Her teeth were as lethal as any sword, her tail a giant mace. From her back, Eragon parried a hammer blow from an Urgal chief, protecting her vulnerable wings. Zar'roc's crimson blade seemed to gleam with delight as blood spurted along its length.

From the corner of his eye, Eragon saw Orik hewing Urgal necks with mighty blows of his ax. Beside the dwarf was Murtagh on Tornac, his face disfigured by a vicious snarl as he swung his sword angrily, cutting through every defense. Then Saphira spun around, and Eragon saw Arya leap past the lifeless body of an opponent.

An Urgal bowled over a wounded dwarf and hacked at Saphira's front right leg. His sword skated off her armor with a burst of sparks. Eragon smote him on the head, but Zar'roc stuck in the monster's horns and was yanked from his grasp. With a curse he dived off Saphira and tackled the Urgal, smashing his face with the shield. He jerked Zar'roc out of the horns, then dodged as another Urgal charged him.

Saphira, I need you! he shouted, but the battle's tide had separated them. Suddenly a Kull jumped at him, club raised for a blow. Unable to lift his shield in time, Eragon uttered, "Jierda!" The Kull's head snapped back with a sharp report as his neck broke. Four more Urgals succumbed to Zar'roc's thirsty bite, then Murtagh rode up beside Eragon, driving the press of Urgals backward.

"Come on!" he shouted, and reached down from Tornac, pulling Eragon onto the horse. They rushed toward Saphira, who was embroiled in a mass of enemies. Twelve spear-wielding Urgals encircled her, needling her with their lances. They had already managed to prick both of her wings. Her blood splattered the ground. Every time she rushed at one of the Urgals, they bunched together and jabbed at her eyes, forcing her to retreat. She tried to sweep the spears away with her talons, but the Urgals jumped back and evaded her.

The sight of Saphira's blood enraged Eragon. He swung off Tornac with a wild cry and stabbed the nearest Urgal through the chest, withholding nothing in his frenzied attempt to help Saphira. His attack provided the distraction she needed to break free. With a kick, she sent an Urgal flying, then barreled to him. Eragon grabbed one of her neck spikes and pulled himself back into her saddle. Murtagh raised his hand, then charged into another knot of Urgals.

By unspoken consent, Saphira took flight and rose above the struggling armies, seeking a respite from the madness. Eragon's breath trembled. His muscles were clenched, ready to ward off the next attack. Every fiber of his being thrilled with energy, making him feel more alive than ever before.

Saphira circled long enough for them to recover their strength, then descended toward the Urgals, skimming the ground to avoid detection. She approached the monsters from behind, where their archers were gathered.

Before the Urgals realized what was happening, Eragon lopped off the heads of two archers, and Saphira disemboweled three others. She took off again as alarms sounded, quickly soaring out of bow range.

They repeated the tactic on a different flank of the army. Saphira's stealth and speed, combined with the dim lighting, made it nearly impossible for the Urgals to predict where she would strike next. Eragon used his bow whenever Saphira was in the air, but he quickly ran out of arrows. Soon the only thing left in his quiver was magic, which he wanted to keep in reserve until it was desperately needed.

Saphira's flights over the combatants gave Eragon a unique understanding of how the battle was progressing. There were three separate fights raging in Farthen Dûr, one by each open tunnel. The Urgals were disadvantaged by the dispersal of their forces and their inability to get all of their army out of the tunnels at once. Even so, the Varden and dwarves could not keep the monsters from advancing and were slowly being driven back toward Tronjheim. The defenders seemed insignificant against the mass of Urgals, whose numbers continued to increase as they poured out of the tunnels.

The Urgals had organized themselves around several standards, each representing a clan, but it was unclear who commanded them overall. The clans paid no attention to each other, as if they were receiving orders from elsewhere. Eragon wished he knew who was in charge so he and Saphira could kill him.

Remembering Ajihad's orders, he began relaying information to the Twins. They were interested by what he had to say about the Urgals' apparent lack of a leader and questioned him closely. The exchange was smooth, if brief. The Twins told him, *You're ordered to assist Hrothgar; the fight goes badly for him.*

Understood, Eragon responded.

Saphira swiftly flew to the besieged dwarves, swooping low over Hrothgar. Arrayed in golden armor, the dwarf king stood at the fore of a small knot of his kin, wielding Volund, the hammer of his ancestors. His white beard caught the lantern light as he looked up at Saphira. Admiration glinted in his eyes.

Saphira landed beside the dwarves and faced the oncoming Urgals. Even the bravest Kull quailed before her ferocity, allowing the dwarves to surge forward. Eragon tried to keep Saphira safe. Her left flank was protected by the dwarves, but to her front and right raged a sea of enemies. He showed no mercy on those and took every advantage he could, using magic whenever Zar'roc could not serve him. A spear bounced off his shield, denting it and leaving him with a bruised shoulder. Shaking off the pain, he cleaved open an Urgal's skull, mixing brains with metal and bone.

He was in awe of Hrothgar—who, though he was ancient by both the standards of men and dwarves, was still undiminished on the battlefield. No Urgal, Kull or not, could stand before the dwarf king and his guards and live. Every time Volund struck, it sounded the gong of death for another enemy. After a spear downed one of his warriors, Hrothgar grabbed the spear himself and, with astounding strength, hurled it completely through its owner twenty yards away. Such heroism emboldened Eragon to ever greater risks, seeking to hold his own with the mighty king.

Eragon lunged at a giant Kull nearly out of reach and almost fell from Saphira's saddle. Before he could recover, the Kull darted past Saphira's defenses and swung his sword. The brunt of the blow caught Eragon on the side of his helm, throwing him backward and making his vision flicker and his ears ring thunderously.

Stunned, he tried to pull himself upright, but the Kull had already prepared for another blow. As the Kull's arm descended, a slim steel blade suddenly sprouted from his chest. Howling, the monster toppled to the side. In his place stood Angela.

The witch wore a long red cape over outlandish flanged armor enameled black and green. She bore a strange two-handed weapon—a long wooden shaft with a sword blade attached to each end. Angela winked at Eragon mischievously, then dashed away, spinning her staff-sword like a dervish. Close behind her was Solembum in the form of a young shaggy-haired boy. He held a small black dagger, sharp teeth bared in a feral snarl.

Still dazed from his battering, Eragon managed to straighten himself in the saddle. Saphira jumped into the air and wheeled high above, letting him recuperate. He scanned Farthen Dûr's plains and saw, to his dismay, that all three battles were going badly. Neither Ajihad, Jörmundur, nor Hrothgar could stop the Urgals. There were simply too many.

Eragon wondered how many Urgals he could kill at once with magic. He knew his limits fairly well. If he were to kill enough to make a difference . . . it would probably be suicide. That might be what it took to win.

The fighting continued for one endless hour

after another. The Varden and dwarves were exhausted, but the Urgals remained fresh with reinforcements.

It was a nightmare for Eragon. Though he and Saphira fought their hardest, there was always another Urgal to take the place of the one just killed. His whole body hurt—especially his head. Every time he used magic he lost a little more energy. Saphira was in better condition, though her wings were punctured with small wounds.

As he parried a blow, the Twins contacted him urgently. *There are loud noises under Tronjheim. It sounds like Urgals are trying to dig into the city! We need you and Arya to collapse any tunnels they're excavating.*

Eragon dispatched his opponent with a sword thrust. *We'll be right there.* He looked for Arya and saw her engaged with a knot of struggling Urgals. Saphira quickly forged a path to the elf, leaving a pile of crumpled bodies in her wake. Eragon extended his hand and said, "Get on!"

Arya jumped onto Saphira's back without hesitation. She wrapped her right arm around Eragon's waist, wielding her bloodstained sword with the other. As Saphira crouched to take off, an Urgal ran at her, howling, then lifted an ax and smashed her in the chest.

Saphira roared with pain and lurched forward, feet leaving the ground. Her wings snapped open, straining to keep them from crashing as she veered wildly to one side, right wingtip scraping the ground. Below them, the Urgal pulled back his arm to throw the ax. But Arya raised her palm, shouting, and an emerald ball of energy shot from her hand, killing the Urgal. With a colossal heave of her shoulders, Saphira righted herself, barely making it over the heads of the warriors. She pulled away from the battlefield with powerful wing strokes and rasping breath.

Are you all right? asked Eragon, concerned. He could not see where she had been struck.

I'll live, she said grimly, *but the front of my armor has been crushed together. It hurts my chest, and I'm having trouble moving.*

712   *Can you get us to the dragonhold?*

. . . We'll see.

Eragon explained Saphira's condition to Arya. "I'll stay and help Saphira when we land," she offered. "Once she is free of the armor, I will join you."

"Thank you," he said. The flight was laborious for Saphira; she glided whenever she could. When they reached the dragonhold, she dropped heavily to Isidar Mithrim, where the Twins were supposed to be watching the battle, but it was empty. Eragon jumped to the floor and winced as he saw the damage the Urgal had done. Four of the metal plates on Saphira's chest had been hammered together, restricting her ability to bend and breathe. "Stay well," he said, putting a hand on her side, then ran out the archway.

He stopped and swore. He was at the top of Vol Turin, The Endless Staircase. Because of his worry for Saphira, he had not considered how he would get to Tronjheim's base—where the Urgals were breaking in. There was no time to climb down. He looked at the narrow trough to the right of the stairs, then grabbed one of the leather pads and threw himself down on it.

The stone slide was smooth as lacquered wood. With the leather underneath him, he accelerated almost instantly to a frightening speed, the walls blurring and the curve of the slide pressing him high against the wall. Eragon lay completely flat so he would go faster. The air rushed past his helm, making it vibrate like a weather vane in a gale. The trough was too confined for him, and he was perilously close to flying out, but as long as he kept his arms and legs still, he was safe.

It was a swift descent, but it still took him nearly ten minutes to reach the bottom. The slide leveled out at the end and sent him skidding halfway across the huge carnelian floor.

When he finally came to a stop, he was too dizzy to walk. His first attempt to stand made him nauseated, so he curled up, head in his hands, and waited for things to stop spinning. When he felt better, he stood and warily looked around.

713

The great chamber was completely deserted, the silence unsettling. Rosy light filtered down from Isidar Mithrim. He faltered—Where was he supposed to go?—and cast out his mind for the Twins. Nothing. He froze as loud knocking echoed through Tronjheim.

An explosion split the air. A long slab of the chamber floor buckled and blew thirty feet up. Needles of rocks flew outward as it crashed down. Eragon stumbled back, stunned, groping for Zar'roc. The twisted shapes of Urgals clambered out of the hole in the floor.

Eragon hesitated. Should he flee? Or should he stay and try to close the tunnel? Even if he managed to seal it before the Urgals attacked him,

what if Tronjheim was already breached elsewhere? He could not find all the places in time to prevent the city-mountain from being captured. *But if I run to one of Tronjheim's gates and blast it open, the Varden could retake Tronjheim without having to siege it.* Before he could decide, a tall man garbed entirely in black armor emerged from the tunnel and looked directly at him.

It was Durza.

The Shade carried his pale blade marked with the scratch from Ajihad. A black roundshield with a crimson ensign rested on his arm. His dark helmet was richly decorated, like a general's, and a long snakeskin cloak billowed around him. Madness burned in his maroon eyes, the madness of one who enjoys power and finds himself in the position to use it.

Eragon knew he was neither fast enough nor strong enough to escape the fiend before him. He immediately warned Saphira, though he knew it was impossible for her to rescue him. He dropped into a crouch and quickly reviewed what Brom had told him about fighting another magic user. It was not encouraging. And Ajihad had said that Shades could only be destroyed by a thrust through the heart.

Durza gazed at him contemptuously and said, "Kaz jtierl trazhid! Otrag bagh." The Urgals eyed Eragon suspiciously and formed a circle around the perimeter of the room. Durza slowly approached Eragon with a triumphant expression. "So, my young Rider, we meet again. You were foolish to escape from me in Gil'ead. It will only make things worse for you in the end."

"You'll never capture me alive," growled Eragon.

"Is that so?" asked the Shade, raising an eyebrow. The light from the star sapphire gave his skin a ghastly tint. "I don't see your 'friend' Murtagh around to help you. You can't stop me now. No one can!"

Fear touched Eragon. *How does he know about Murtagh?* Putting all the derision he could into his voice, he jeered, "How did you like being shot?"

Durza's face tightened momentarily. "I will be repaid in blood for that. Now tell me where your dragon is hiding."

"Never."

The Shade's countenance darkened. "Then I will force it from you!" His sword whistled through the air. The moment Eragon caught the blade on his shield, a mental probe spiked deep into his thoughts. Fighting to protect his consciousness, he shoved Durza back and attacked with his own mind.

Eragon battered with all his strength against the iron-hard defenses surrounding Durza's mind, but to no avail. He swung Zar'roc, trying to catch Durza off guard. The Shade knocked the blow aside effortlessly, then stabbed in return with lightning speed.

The point of the sword caught Eragon in the ribs, piercing his mail and driving out his breath. The mail slipped, though, and the blade missed his side by the width of a wire. The distraction was all Durza needed to break into Eragon's mind and begin taking control.

"No!" cried Eragon, throwing himself at the Shade. His face contorted as he grappled with Durza, yanking on his sword arm. Durza tried to cut Eragon's hand, but it was protected by the mail-backed glove, which sent the blade glancing downward. As Eragon kicked his leg, Durza snarled and swept his black shield around, knocking him to the floor. Eragon tasted blood in his mouth; his neck throbbed. Ignoring his injuries, he rolled over and hurled his shield at Durza. Despite the Shade's superior speed, the heavy shield clipped him on the hip. As Durza stumbled, Eragon caught him on the upper arm with Zar'roc. A line of blood traced down the Shade's arm.

Eragon thrust at the Shade with his mind and drove through Durza's weakened defenses. A flood of images suddenly engulfed him, rushing through his consciousness—

Durza as a young boy living as a nomad with his parents on the empty plains. The tribe abandoned them and called his father "oathbreaker." Only it was not Durza then, but Carsaib—the name his mother crooned while combing his hair. . . .

The Shade reeled wildly, face twisted in pain. Eragon tried to control the torrent of memories, but the force of them was overwhelming.

Standing on a hill over the graves of his parents, weeping that the men had not killed him as well. Then turning and stumbling blindly away, into the desert. . . .

Durza faced Eragon. Terrible hatred flowed from his maroon eyes. Eragon was on one knee—almost standing—struggling to seal his mind.

*How the old man looked when he first saw Car-
saib lying near death on a sand dune. The days it had
taken Carsaib to recover and the fear he felt upon discovering that his rescuer was a sorcerer. How he had
pleaded to be taught the control of spirits. How Haeg
had finally agreed. Called him "Desert Rat.". . .*

Eragon was standing now. Durza charged . . .
sword raised . . . shield ignored in his fury.

*The days spent training under the scorching sun,
always alert for the lizards they caught for food. How
his power slowly grew, giving him pride and confidence. The weeks spent nursing his sick master after
a failed spell. His joy when Haeg recovered . . .*

718

There was not enough time to react . . . not
enough time. . . .

*The bandits who attacked during the night, killing
Haeg. The rage Carsaib had felt and the spirits he
had summoned for vengeance. But the spirits were
stronger than he expected. They turned on him, pos-
sessing mind and body. He had screamed. He was—
I AM DURZA!*

The sword smote heavily across Eragon's
back, cutting through both mail and skin. He
screamed as pain blasted through him, forcing
him to his knees. Agony bowed his body in half

and obliterated all thought. He swayed, barely conscious, hot blood running down the small of his back. Durza said something he could not hear.

In anguish, Eragon raised his eyes to the heavens, tears streaming down his cheeks. Everything had failed. The Varden and dwarves were destroyed. He was defeated. Saphira would give herself up for his sake—she had done it before—and Arya would be recaptured or killed. Why had it ended like this? What justice could this be? All was for nothing.

As he looked at Isidar Mithrim far above his tortured frame, a flash of light erupted in his eyes, blinding him. A second later, the chamber rang with a deafening report. Then his eyes cleared, and he gaped with disbelief.

The star sapphire had shattered. An expanding torus of huge dagger-like pieces plummeted toward the distant floor—the shimmering shards near the walls. In the center of the chamber, hurtling downward headfirst, was Saphira. Her jaws were open and from between them erupted a great tongue of flame, bright yellow and tinged with blue. On her back was Arya: hair billowing wildly, arm uplifted, palm glowing with a nimbus of green magic.

Time seemed to slow as Eragon saw Durza tilt his head toward the ceiling. First shock, then anger contorted the Shade's face. Sneering defiantly, he raised his hand and pointed at Saphira, a word forming on his lips.

A hidden reserve of strength suddenly welled up inside Eragon, dredged from the deepest part of his being. His fingers curled around the hilt of his sword. He plunged through the barrier in his mind and took hold of the magic. All his pain and rage focused on one word:

"Brisingr!"

Zar'roc blazed with bloody light, heatless flames running along it . . .

He lunged forward . . .

And stabbed Durza in the heart.

Durza looked down with shock at the blade protruding from his breast. His mouth was open, but instead of words, an unearthly howl burst from him. His sword dropped from nerveless fingers. He grasped Zar'roc as if to pull it out, but it was lodged firmly in him.

Then Durza's skin turned transparent. Under it was neither flesh nor bone, but swirling patterns of darkness. He shrieked even louder as the darkness pulsated, splitting his skin. With one last cry, Durza was rent from head to toe, releasing the darkness, which separated into three entities who flew through Tronjheim's walls and out of Farthen Dûr. The Shade was gone.

Bereft of strength, Eragon fell back with arms outstretched. Above him, Saphira and Arya had nearly reached the floor—it looked as if they were going to smash into it with the deadly remains of Isidar Mithrim. As his sight faded, Saphira, Arya, the myriad fragments—all seemed to stop falling and hang motionless in the air.

THE MOURNING
SAGE

Snatches of the Shade's memories continued to flash through Eragon. A whirlwind of dark events and emotions overwhelmed him, making it impossible to think. Submerged in the maelstrom, he knew neither who nor where he was. He was too weak to cleanse himself of the alien presence that clouded his mind. Violent, cruel images from the Shade's past exploded behind his eyes until his spirit cried out in anguish at the bloody sights.

A pile of bodies rose before him . . . innocents slaughtered by the Shade's orders. He saw still more corpses—whole villages of them—taken from life by the sorcerer's hand or word. There was no escape from the carnage that surrounded him. He wavered like a candle flame, unable to withstand the tide of evil. He prayed for someone to lift him out of the nightmare, but there was no one to guide him. If only he could remember what he was supposed to be: boy or man, villain or hero, Shade or Rider; all was jumbled together in a meaningless frenzy. He was lost, completely and utterly, in the roiling mass.

Suddenly a cluster of his own memories burst through the dismal cloud left by the Shade's malevolent mind. All the events since he had found Saphira's egg came to him in the cold light of revelation. His accomplishments and failures were displayed equally. He had lost much that was dear to him, yet fate had given him rare and great gifts; for the first time, he was proud of simply who he was. As if in response to his brief self-confidence, the Shade's smothering blackness assaulted him anew. His identity trailed into the void as uncertainty and fear consumed his perceptions. Who was he to think he could challenge the powers of Alagaësia and live?

He fought against the Shade's sinister thoughts, weakly at first, then more strongly. He whispered words of the ancient language and found they gave him enough strength to withstand the shadow blurring his mind. Though his defenses faltered dangerously, he slowly began to draw his shattered consciousness into a small bright shell around his core. Outside his mind he was aware of a pain so great it threatened to blot out his very life, but something—or someone— seemed to keep it at bay.

He was still too weak to clear his mind completely, but he was lucid enough to examine his experiences since Carvahall. Where would he go now . . . and who would show him the way? Without Brom, there was no one to guide or teach him.

Come to me.

He recoiled at the touch of another consciousness—one so vast and powerful it was like a mountain looming over him. This was who was blocking the pain, he realized. Like Arya's mind, music ran through this one: deep amber-gold chords that throbbed with magisterial melancholy.

Finally, he dared ask, Who . . . who are you?

One who would help. *With a flicker of an unspoken thought, the Shade's influence was brushed aside like an unwanted cobweb. Freed from the oppressive weight, Eragon let his mind expand until he touched a barrier beyond which he could not pass.* I have protected you as best I can, but you are so far away I can do no more than shield your sanity from the pain.

Again: Who are you to do this?

There was a low rumble. I am Osthato Chetowä, the Mourning Sage. And Togira Ikonoka, the Cripple Who Is Whole. Come to me, Eragon, for I have answers to all you ask. You will not be safe until you find me.

But how can I find you if I don't know where you are? *he asked, despairing.*

Trust Arya and go with her to Ellesméra—I will be there. I have waited many seasons, so do not delay or it may soon be too late. . . . You are greater than you know, Eragon. Think of what you have done and rejoice, for you have rid the land of a great evil. You have wrought a deed no one else could. Many are in your debt.

The stranger was right; what he had accomplished

*was worthy of honor, of recognition. No matter what
his trials might be in the future, he was no longer just
a pawn in the game of power. He had transcended
that and was something else, something more. He
had become what Ajihad wanted: an authority independent of any king or leader.*

He sensed approval as he reached that conclusion.
You are learning, *said the Mourning Sage, drawing
nearer. A vision passed from him to Eragon: a burst
of color blossomed in his mind, resolving into a
stooped figure dressed in white, standing on a sun-
drenched stone cliff.* It is time for you to rest,
Eragon. When you wake, do not speak of me to
anyone, *said the figure kindly, face obscured by a silver nimbus.* Remember, you must go to the elves.
Now, sleep. . . . *He raised a hand, as if in benedic-*
tion, and peace crept through Eragon.

*His last thought was that Brom would have been
proud of him.*

"Wake," commanded the voice. "Awake, Eragon,
for you have slept far too long." He stirred unwillingly, loath to listen. The warmth that surrounded him was too comfortable to leave. The
voice sounded again. "Rise, Argetlam! You are
needed!"

He reluctantly forced his eyes open and found
himself on a long bed, swathed in soft blankets.
Angela sat in a chair beside him, staring at his
face intently. "How do you feel?" she asked.

Disoriented and confused, he let his eyes roam

over the small room. "I . . . I don't know," he said, his mouth dry and sore.

"Then don't move. You should conserve your strength," said Angela, running a hand through her curly hair. Eragon saw that she still wore her flanged armor. Why was that? A fit of coughing made him dizzy, lightheaded, and ache all over. His feverish limbs felt heavy. Angela lifted a gilt horn from the floor and held it to his lips. "Here, drink."

Cool mead ran down his throat, refreshing him. Warmth bloomed in his stomach and rose to his cheeks. He coughed again, which worsened his throbbing head. *How did I get here? There was a battle . . . we were losing . . . then Durza and . . .* "Saphira!" he exclaimed, sitting upright. He sagged back as his head swam and clenched his eyes, feeling sick. "What about Saphira? Is she all right? The Urgals were winning . . . she was falling. And Arya!"

"They lived," assured Angela, "and have been waiting for you to wake. Do you wish to see them?" He nodded feebly. Angela got up and threw open the door. Arya and Murtagh filed inside. Saphira snaked her head into the room after them, her body too big to fit through the doorway. Her chest vibrated as she hummed deeply, eyes sparkling.

Smiling, Eragon touched her thoughts with relief and gratitude. *It is good to see you well, little one,* she said tenderly.

And you too, but how—?

The others want to explain it, so I will let them.

You breathed fire! I saw you!

Yes, she said with pride.

He smiled weakly, still confused, then looked at Arya and Murtagh. Both of them were bandaged: Arya on her arm, Murtagh around his head. Murtagh grinned widely. "About time you were up. We've been sitting in the hall for hours."

"What . . . what happened?" asked Eragon.

Arya looked sad. But Murtagh crowed, "We won! It was incredible! When the Shade's spirits—if that's what they were—flew across Farthen Dûr, the Urgals ceased fighting to watch them go. It was as though they were released from a spell then, because their clans suddenly turned and attacked each other. Their entire army disintegrated within minutes. We routed them after that!"

"They're all dead?" asked Eragon.

Murtagh shook his head. "No, many of them escaped into the tunnels. The Varden and dwarves are busy ferreting them out right now, but it's going to take a while. I was helping until an Urgal banged me on the head and I was sent back here."

"They aren't going to lock you up again?"

His face grew sober. "No one really cares about that right now. A lot of Varden and dwarves were killed; the survivors are busy trying to recover from the battle. But at least you have cause to be happy. You're a hero! Everyone's talking about how you killed Durza. If it hadn't been for you, we would have lost."

Eragon was troubled by his words but pushed them away for later consideration. "Where were the Twins? They weren't where they were supposed to be—I couldn't contact them. I needed their help."

Murtagh shrugged. "I was told they bravely fought off a group of Urgals that broke into Tronjheim somewhere else. They were probably too busy to talk with you."

That seemed wrong for some reason, but Eragon could not decide why. He turned to Arya. Her large bright eyes had been fixed upon him the entire time. "How come you didn't crash? You and Saphira were . . ." His voice trailed off.

She said slowly, "When you warned Saphira of Durza, I was still trying to remove her damaged armor. By the time it was off, it was too late to slide down Vol Turin—you would have been captured before I reached the bottom. Besides, Durza would have killed you before letting me rescue you." Regret entered her voice, "So I did the one thing I could to distract him: I broke the star sapphire."

And I carried her down, added Saphira.

Eragon struggled to understand as another

bout of lightheadedness made him close his eyes. "But why didn't any of the pieces hit you or me?"

"I didn't allow them to. When we were almost to the floor, I held them motionless in the air, then slowly lowered them to the floor—else they would have shattered into a thousand pieces and killed you," stated Arya simply. Her words betrayed the power within her.

Angela added sourly, "Yes, and it almost killed you as well. It's taken all of my skill to keep the two of you alive."

A twinge of unease shot through Eragon, matching the intensity of his throbbing head. *My back* . . . But he felt no bandages there. "How long have I been here?" he asked with trepidation.

"Only a day and a half," answered Angela. "You're lucky I was around, otherwise it would've taken you weeks to heal—if you had even lived." Alarmed, Eragon pushed the blankets off his torso and twisted around to feel his back. Angela caught his wrist with her small hand, worry reflected in her eyes. "Eragon . . . you have to understand, my power is not like yours or Arya's. It depends on the use of herbs and potions. There are limits to what I can do, especially with such a large—"

He yanked his hand out of her grip and reached back, fingers groping. The skin on his back was smooth and warm, flawless. Hard muscles flexed under his fingertips as he moved. He slid his hand toward the base of his neck and unexpectedly felt a hard bump about a half-inch wide. He followed it down his back with growing horror. Durza's blow had left him with a huge, ropy scar, stretching from his right shoulder to the opposite hip.

Pity showed on Arya's face as she murmured, "You have paid a terrible price for your deed, Eragon Shadeslayer."

Murtagh laughed harshly. "Yes. Now you're just like me."

Dismay filled Eragon, and he closed his eyes. He was disfigured. Then he remembered something from when he was unconscious . . . a figure in white who had helped him. A cripple who was whole—Togira Ikonoka. He had said, *Think of what you have done and rejoice, for you have rid the land of a great evil. You have wrought a deed no one else could. Many are in your debt. . . .*

Come to me Eragon, for I have answers to all you ask.

A measure of peace and satisfaction consoled Eragon.

I will come.

END OF BOOK ONE

THE STORY WILL
CONTINUE IN
ELDEST,
BOOK TWO OF
INHERITANCE

Pronunciation

Ajihad—AH-zhi-hod

Alagaësia—al-uh-GAY-zee-uh

Arya—AR-ee-uh

Carvahall—CAR-vuh-hall

Dras-Leona—DRAHS-lee-OH-nuh

Du Weldenvarden—doo WELL-den-VAR-den

Ellesméra—el-uhs-MEER-uh

Eragon—EHR-uh-gahn

Farthen Dûr—FAR-then DURE (*dure* rhymes with *lure*)

Galbatorix—gal-buh-TOR-icks

Gil'ead—GILL-ee-id

Islanzadí—iss-lan-ZAH-dee

Jeod—JODE (rhymes with *load*)

Murtagh—MUR-tag (*mur* rhymes with *purr*)

Nasuada—nah-soo-AH-duh

Ra'zac—RAA-zack

Saphira—suh-FEAR-uh

Shruikan—SHREW-kin

Sílthrim—SEAL-thrim (*síl* is a hard sound to transcribe; it's made by flicking the tip of the tongue off the roof of the mouth.)

Teirm—TEERM

Tronjheim—TRONJ-heem

Urû'baen—OO-roo-bane

Vrael—VRAIL

Yazuac—YA-zoo-ack

Zar'roc—ZAR-rock

THE ANCIENT LANGUAGE

Note: As Eragon is not yet a master of the ancient language, his words and remarks were *not* translated literally, so as to save readers from his atrocious grammar. Quotations from other characters, however, have been left untouched.

Aí varden abr du Shur'tugalar gata vanta.—A warden of the Riders lacks passage.

Aiedail—the morning star

arget—silver

Argetlam—Silver Hand

Atra guliä un ilian tauthr ono un atra ono waíse skölir fra rauthr.—Let luck and happiness follow you and may you be shielded from misfortune.

breoal—family; house

brisingr—fire

Deloi moi!—Earth, change!

delois—a green-leafed plant with purple flowers

Domia abr Wyrda—*Dominance of Fate* (book)

dras—city

draumr kópa—dream stare

Du grind huildr!—Hold the gate!

"Du Silbena Datia"—"The Sighing Mists" (a poem song)

Du Sundavar Freohr—Death of the Shadows

Du Vrangr Gata—The Wandering Path

Du Weldenvarden—The Guarding Forest

Edoc'sil—Unconquerable

eitha—go; leave

Eka aí fricai un Shur'tugal!—I am a Rider and friend!

ethgrí—invoke

Fethrblaka, eka weohnata néiat haina ono. Blaka eom iet lam.—Bird, I will not harm you. Flap to my hand.

735

garjzla—light

Gath un reisa du rakr!—Unite and raise the mist!

gedwëy ignasia—shining palm

Gëuloth du knífr!—Dull the knife!

Helgrind—The Gates of Death

iet—my (informal)

Istalrí boetk!—Broad fire!

jierda—break; hit

Jierda theirra kalfis!—Break their calves!

Manin! Wyrda! Hügin!—Memory! Fate! Thought!

Moi stenr!—Stone, change!

Nagz reisa!—Blanket, rise!

Osthato Chetowä—the Mourning Sage

pömnuria—my (formal)

Ristvak'baen—Place of Sorrow (*baen*—used here and in Urû'baen, the capital of the Empire—is always pronounced *bane* and is an expression of great sadness/grief)

seithr—witch

Shur'tugal—Dragon Rider

Skulblaka, eka celöbra ono un mulabra ono un onr Shur'tugal né haina. Atra nosu waíse fricaya.—Dragon, I honor you and mean you and your Rider no harm. Let us be friends.

slytha—sleep

Stenr reisa!—Raise stone!

thrysta—thrust; compress

Thrysta deloi.—Compress the earth.

Thverr stenr un atra eka hórna!—Traverse stone and let me hear!

Togira Ikonoka—the Cripple Who Is Whole

tuatha du orothrim—tempering the fool's wisdom (level in Riders' training)

Varden—the Warders

vöndr—a thin, straight stick

Waíse heill!—Be healed!

Wiol pömnuria ilian.—For my happiness.

wyrda—fate

yawë—a bond of trust

THE DWARF LANGUAGE

Akh Gûnteraz dorzada!—For Guntéra's
adoration!

Âz knurl demn lanok.—Beware, the rock
changes.

barzûl—a curse; ill fate

Carkna brâgha!—Great danger!

dûrgrimst—clan (literally, our hall/home)

Egraz Carn—Bald One

Farthen Dûr—Our Father

hírna—likeness; statue

Ilf carnz orodûm.—It is one's obligation/fate.

Ingeitum—metalworkers; smiths

Isidar Mithrim—Star Sapphire

knurl—stone; rock

knurla—dwarf (literally, one of stone)

Kóstha-mérna—Foot Pool (a lake)

oeí—yes; affirmative

otho—faith

sheilven—cowards

Tronjheim—Helm of Giants

Vol Turin—The Endless Staircase

THE URGAL LANGUAGE

738 drajl—spawn of maggots

Ithrö Zhâda (Orthíad)—Rebel Doom

Kaz jtierl trazhid! Otrag bagh.—Do not attack!
   Circle him.

ushnark—father

ACKNOWLEDGMENTS

I created *Eragon*, but its success is the result of the enthusiastic efforts of friends, family, fans, librarians, teachers, students, school administrators, distributors, booksellers, and many more. I wish I could mention by name all the people who have helped, but the list is very, very long. You know who you are, and I thank you!

Eragon was first published in early 2002 by my parents' publishing company, Paolini International LLC. They had already released three books, so it was only natural to do the same with *Eragon*. We knew *Eragon* would appeal to a wide range of readers; our challenge was to spread the word about it.

During 2002 and the beginning of 2003, I traveled throughout the United States doing over 130 book signings and presentations in schools, bookstores, and libraries. My mother and

I arranged all the events. At first I had only one or two appearances per month, but as we became more efficient at scheduling, our homemade book tour expanded to the point where I was on the road almost continuously.

I met thousands of wonderful people, many of whom became loyal fans and friends. One of those fans is Michelle Frey, now my editor at Knopf Books for Young Readers, who approached me with an offer to acquire *Eragon*. Needless to say, I was delighted that Knopf was interested in my book.

Thus, there are two groups of people who deserve thanks. The first assisted with the production of the Paolini International LLC edition of *Eragon*, while the second is responsible for the Knopf edition.

Here are the brave souls who helped bring *Eragon* into existence:

The original gang: my mother for her thoughtful red pen and wonderful help with commas, colons, semicolons, and other assorted beasties; my father for his smashing editing job, all the time he spent hammering my vague, wayward thoughts into line, formatting the book and designing the cover, and listening to so many presentations; Grandma Shirley for helping me create a satisfactory beginning and ending; my sister for her plot advice, her good humor at being portrayed as an herbalist in *Eragon*, and her long hours Photoshopping Saphira's eye on the cover; Kathy Tyers for giving me the means to do a brutal—and much-needed—rewrite of the first three chapters; John Taliaferro for his advice and wonderful review; a fan named Tornado—Eugene Walker—who caught a number of copy-editing errors; and Donna Overall for her love of the story, editing and formatting advice, and keen eye for all things concerning ellipses, em dashes, widows, orphans, kerning, and run-on sentences. If there's a real-life Dragon Rider, she's one—selflessly coming to the rescue of writers lost in the Swamp of Commas. And I thank my family for supporting me wholeheartedly . . . and for reading this saga more times than any sane person should have to.

The new gang: a big thank-you to Carl Hiaasen's stepson, Ryan, who enjoyed *Eragon* so much that Carl referred it to his editor at Knopf. If not for them, millions of people would have never read *Eragon*, and my life and that of my family would be completely different. Thank you both. Michelle Frey, who not only loved the story enough to take a chance on an epic fantasy written by a teenager but also managed to streamline *Eragon*'s pacing through her insightful editing; my agent, Simon Lipskar, who helped find the best home for *Eragon*; Chip Gibson and Beverly

Horowitz for the wonderful offer; Lawrence Levy for his good humor and legal advice; Judith Haut, publicity whiz of the first degree; Daisy Kline for the awe-inspiring marketing campaign; Isabel Warren-Lynch, who designed the lovely book jacket, interior, and map; John Jude Palencar, who painted the jacket art (I actually named Palancar Valley for him long before he ever worked on *Eragon*); Artie Bennett, the doyen of copyediting and the only man alive who understood the difference between *to scry it* and *to scry on it*; and the entire team at Knopf who have made this adventure possible.

Lastly, a very special thanks to my characters, who bravely face the dangers I force them to confront, and without whom I wouldn't have a story.

May your swords stay sharp!

Christopher Paolini

742

A SPECIAL PREVIEW OF

ELDEST,

BOOK TWO OF INHERITANCE

A TWIN DISASTER

he songs of the dead are the lamentations of the
living.

So thought Eragon as he stepped over a
twisted and hacked Urgal, listening to the keening of women who removed loved ones from the
blood-muddied ground of Farthen Dûr. Behind
him Saphira delicately skirted the corpse, her
glittering blue scales the only color in the gloom
that filled the hollow mountain.

It was three days since the Varden and
dwarves had fought the Urgals for possession of
Tronjheim, the mile-high, conical city nestled in
the center of Farthen Dûr, but the battlefield was
still strewn with carnage. The sheer number of
bodies had stymied their attempts to bury the

dead. In the distance, a mountainous fire glowed sullenly by Farthen Dûr's wall where the Urgals were being burned. No burial or honored resting place for them.

Since waking to find his wound healed by Angela, Eragon had tried three times to assist in the recovery effort. On each occasion he had been racked by terrible pains that seemed to explode from his spine. The healers gave him various potions to drink. Arya and Angela said that he was perfectly sound. Nevertheless, he hurt. Nor could Saphira help, only share his pain as it rebounded across their mental link.

Eragon ran a hand over his face and looked up at the stars showing through Farthen Dûr's distant top, which were smudged with sooty smoke from the pyre. *Three days.* Three days since he had killed Durza; three days since people began calling him Shadeslayer; three days since the remnants of the sorcerer's consciousness had ravaged his mind and he had been saved by the mysterious Togira Ikonoka, the Cripple Who Is Whole. He had told no one about that vision but Saphira. Fighting Durza and the dark spirits that controlled him had transformed Eragon; although for better or for worse he was still unsure. He felt fragile, as if a sudden shock would shatter his reconstructed body and consciousness.

And now he had come to the site of the combat, driven by a morbid desire to see its aftermath. Upon arriving, he found nothing but the uncomfortable presence of death and decay, not the glory that heroic songs had led him to expect.

Before his uncle, Garrow, was slain by the Ra'zac months earlier, the brutality that Eragon had witnessed between the humans, dwarves, and Urgals would have destroyed him. Now it numbed him. He had realized, with Saphira's help, that the only way to stay rational amid such pain was to *do* things. Beyond that, he no longer believed that life possessed inherent meaning— not after seeing men torn apart by the Kull, a race of giant Urgals, and the ground a bed of thrashing limbs and the dirt so wet with blood it soaked through the soles of his boots. If any honor existed in war, he concluded, it was in fighting to protect others from harm.

He bent and plucked a tooth, a molar, from the dirt. Bouncing it on his palm, he and Saphira slowly made a circuit through the trampled plain. They stopped at its edge when they noticed Jörmundur—Ajihad's second in command in the Varden—hurrying toward them from Tronjheim. When he came near, Jörmundur bowed, a gesture Eragon knew he would never have made just days before.

"I'm glad I found you in time, Eragon." He clutched a parchment note in one hand. "Ajihad is returning, and he wants you to be there when he arrives. The others are already waiting for him by Tronjheim's west gate. We'll have to hurry to get there in time."

Eragon nodded and headed toward the gate, keeping a hand on Saphira. Ajihad had been gone most of the three days, hunting down Urgals who had managed to escape into the dwarf tunnels that honeycombed the stone beneath the Beor Mountains. The one time Eragon had seen him between expeditions, Ajihad was in a rage over discovering that his daughter, Nasuada, had disobeyed his orders to leave with the other women and children before the battle. Instead, she had secretly fought among the Varden's archers.

Murtagh and the Twins had accompanied Ajihad: the Twins because it was dangerous work and the Varden's leader needed the protection of their magical skills, and Murtagh because he was eager to continue proving that he bore the Varden no ill will. It surprised Eragon how much people's attitudes toward Murtagh had changed, considering that Murtagh's father was the Dragon Rider Morzan, who had betrayed the Riders to Galbatorix. Even though Murtagh despised his father and was loyal to Eragon, the Varden had not trusted him. But now, no one was willing to waste energy on a petty hate when so much work remained. Eragon missed talking with Murtagh and looked forward to discussing all that had happened, once he returned.

As Eragon and Saphira rounded Tronjheim, a

small group became visible in the pool of lantern light before the timber gate. Among them were Orik—the dwarf shifting impatiently on his stout legs—and Arya. The white bandage around her upper arm gleamed in the darkness, reflecting a faint highlight onto the bottom of her hair. Eragon felt a strange thrill, as he always did when he saw the elf. She looked at him and Saphira, green eyes flashing, then continued watching for Ajihad.

By breaking Isidar Mithrim—the great star sapphire that was sixty feet across and carved in the shape of a rose—Arya had allowed Eragon to kill Durza and so win the battle. Still, the dwarves were furious with her for destroying their most prized treasure. They refused to move the sapphire's remains, leaving them in a massive circle inside Tronjheim's central chamber. Eragon had walked through the splintered wreckage and shared the dwarves' sorrow for all the lost beauty.

He and Saphira stopped by Orik and looked out at the empty land that surrounded Tronjheim, extending to Farthen Dûr's base five miles away in each direction. "Where will Ajihad come from?" asked Eragon.

Orik pointed at a cluster of lanterns staked around a large tunnel opening a couple of miles away. "He should be here soon."

Eragon waited patiently with the others, answering comments directed at him but preferring to speak with Saphira in the peace of his mind. The quiet that filled Farthen Dûr suited him.

Half an hour passed before motion flickered in the distant tunnel. A group of ten men climbed out onto the ground, then turned and helped up as many dwarves. One of the men—Eragon assumed it was Ajihad—raised a hand, and the warriors assembled behind him in two straight lines. At a signal, the formation marched proudly toward Tronjheim.

Before they went more than five yards, the tunnel behind them swarmed with a flurry of activity as more figures jumped out. Eragon squinted, unable to see clearly from so far away.

Those are Urgals! exclaimed Saphira, her body tensing like a drawn bowstring.

Eragon did not question her. "Urgals!" he cried, and leaped onto Saphira, berating himself for leaving his sword, Zar'roc, in his room. No one had expected an attack now that the Urgal army had been driven away.

His wound twinged as Saphira lifted her azure wings, then drove them down and jumped forward, gaining speed and altitude each second. Below them, Arya ran toward the tunnel, nearly keeping apace with Saphira. Orik trailed her with several men, while Jörmundur sprinted back toward the barracks.

Eragon was forced to watch helplessly as the Urgals fell on the rear of Ajihad's warriors; he could not work magic over such a distance. The monsters had the advantage of surprise and quickly cut down four men, forcing the rest of the warriors, men and dwarves alike, to cluster around Ajihad in an attempt to protect him. Swords and axes clashed as the groups pressed together. Light flashed from one of the Twins, and an Urgal fell, clutching the stump of his severed arm.

For a minute, it seemed the defenders would be able to resist the Urgals, but then a swirl of motion disturbed the air, like a faint band of mist wrapping itself around the combatants. When it cleared, only four warriors were standing: Ajihad, the Twins, and Murtagh. The Urgals converged on them, blocking Eragon's view as he stared with rising horror and fear.

No! No! No!

Before Saphira could reach the fight, the knot of Urgals streamed back to the tunnel and scrambled underground, leaving only prone forms behind.

The moment Saphira touched down, Eragon vaulted off, then faltered, overcome by grief and anger. *I can't do this.* It reminded him too much of when he had returned to the farm to find his uncle Garrow dying. Fighting back his dread with every step, he began to search for survivors.

The site was eerily similar to the battlefield he had inspected earlier, except that here the blood was fresh.

In the center of the massacre lay Ajihad, his breastplate rent with numerous gashes, surrounded by five Urgals he had slain. His breath still came in ragged gasps. Eragon knelt by him and lowered his face so his tears would not land on the leader's ruined chest. No one could heal such wounds. Running up to them, Arya paused and stopped, her face transformed with sorrow when she saw that Ajihad could not be saved.

"Eragon." The name slipped from Ajihad's lips—no more than a whisper.

"Yes, I am here."

"Listen to me, Eragon. . . . I have one last command for you." Eragon leaned closer to catch the dying man's words. "You must promise me something: promise that you . . . won't let the Varden fall into chaos. They are the only hope for resisting the Empire. . . . They must be kept strong. You must promise me."

"I promise."

"Then peace be with you, Eragon Shadeslayer. . . ." With his last breath, Ajihad closed his eyes, setting his noble face in repose, and died.

Eragon bowed his head. He had trouble breathing past the lump in his throat, which was so hard it hurt. Arya blessed Ajihad in a ripple of the ancient language, then said in her musical voice, "Alas, his death will cause much strife. He is right, you must do all you can to avert a struggle for power. I will assist where possible."

Unwilling to speak, Eragon gazed at the rest of the bodies. He would have given anything to be elsewhere. Saphira nosed one of the Urgals and said, *This should not have happened. It is an evil doing, and all the worse for coming when we should be safe and victorious.* She examined another body, then swung her head around. *Where are the Twins and Murtagh? They're not among the dead.*

Eragon scanned the corpses. *You're right!* Elation surged within him as he hurried to the tunnel's mouth. There pools of thickening blood filled the hollows in the worn marble steps like a series of black mirrors, glossy and oval, as if several torn bodies had been dragged down them. *The Urgals must have taken them! But why? They don't keep prisoners or hostages.* Despair instantly returned. *It doesn't matter. We can't pursue them without reinforcements; you wouldn't even fit through the opening.*

They may still be alive. Would you abandon them?

What do you expect me to do? The dwarf tunnels are an endless maze! I would only get lost. And I couldn't catch Urgals on foot, though Arya might be able to.

Then ask her to.

Arya! Eragon hesitated, torn between his desire for action and his loathing to put her in danger. Still, if any one person in the Varden could handle the Urgals, it was she. With a groan, he explained what they had found.

Arya's slanted eyebrows met in a frown. "It makes no sense."

"Will you pursue them?"

She stared at him for a heavy moment. "Wiol ono." For you. Then she bounded forward, sword flashing in her hand as she dove into the earth's belly.

Burning with frustration, Eragon settled cross-legged by Ajihad, keeping watch over the body. He could barely assimilate the fact that Ajihad was dead and Murtagh missing. *Murtagh.* Son of one of the Forsworn—the thirteen Riders who had helped Galbatorix destroy their order and anoint himself king of Alagaësia—and Eragon's friend. At times Eragon had wished Murtagh gone, but now that he had been forcibly removed, the loss left an unexpected void. He sat motionless as Orik approached with the men.

When Orik saw Ajihad, he stamped his feet and swore in Dwarvish, swinging his ax into the body of an Urgal. The men only stood in shock. Rubbing a pinch of dirt between his callused hands, the dwarf growled, "Ah, now a hornet's nest has broken; we'll have no peace among the Varden after this. *Barzûln*, but this makes things complicated. Were you in time to hear his last words?"

Eragon glanced at Saphira. "They must wait for the right person before I'll repeat them."

"I see. And where'd be Arya?"

Eragon pointed.

Orik swore again, then shook his head and sat on his heels.

Jörmundur soon arrived with twelve ranks of six warriors each. He motioned for them to wait outside the radius of bodies while he proceeded onward alone. He bent and touched Ajihad on the shoulder. "How can fate be this cruel, my old friend? I would have been here sooner if not for the size of this cursed mountain, and then you might have been saved. Instead, we are wounded at the height of our triumph."

Eragon softly told him about Arya and the disappearance of the Twins and Murtagh.

"She should not have gone," said Jörmundur, straightening, "but we can do naught about it now. Guards will be posted here, but it will be at least an hour before dwarf guides can be found for another expedition into the tunnels."

"I'd be willing to lead it," offered Orik.

Jörmundur looked back at Tronjheim, his gaze distant. "No, Hrothgar will need you now; someone else will have to go. I'm sorry, Eragon, but everyone important *must* stay here until Ajihad's successor is chosen. Arya will have to fend for herself. . . . We could not overtake her anyway."

Eragon nodded, accepting the inevitable.

Jörmundur swept his gaze around before saying so all could hear, "Ajihad has died a warrior's death! Look, he slew five Urgals where a lesser man might have been overwhelmed by one. We will give him every honor and hope his spirit pleases the gods. Bear him and our companions back to Tronjheim on your shields . . . and do not be ashamed to let your tears be seen, for this is a day of sorrow that all will remember. May we soon have the privilege of sheathing our blades in the monsters who have slain our leader!"

As one, the warriors knelt, baring their heads in homage to Ajihad. Then they stood and reverently lifted him on their shields so he lay between their shoulders. Already many of the Varden wept, tears flowing into beards, yet they did not disgrace their duty and allow Ajihad to fall. With solemn steps, they marched back to Tronjheim, Saphira and Eragon in the middle of the procession.

ERAGON

is also available in an unabridged audio edition
from Listening Library:

ISBN 978-1-4000-9068-6 (CD)
$39.95 U.S. / $54.95 Can.

ISBN 978-0-8072-1964-5 (Digital Download)
$19.95 U.S. / $19.95 Can.